Morgan was not in the mood for confessions.

"You heard everything he said, and you can come, easily enough, to your own conclusions."

"And you think it is as easy as that?" Barbara asked, her voice caught between surprise and impatience.

Morgan's lean features were impassive. "What don't you understand about the activities of a man named Jack Carter?"

Barbara put her hands on her hips. "Well, I know for one thing that he has turned up in North Point, Maryland, calling himself Morgan Harris."

Morgan Harris smiled perfunctorily and complimented her. "I did not think you lacked for understanding."

This remark was not calculated to improve Barbara's mood. "You either rate my intelligence too high," she snapped, "to think I have pieced together the whole, or you rate it too low to think you can get away with explaining nothing . . . !"

Dear Reader,

Welcome to another great month of Harlequin Historicals. These four selections are guaranteed to add spice to your summer reading list.

Garters and Spurs, from popular author DeLoras Scott, is the tale of Fargo Tanner and his search for the man who killed his brother. But when clues lead him to lovely Sara Carter, Fargo finds himself doubting his intentions.

In the last installment of the TEXAS series, Ruth Langan tells the story of *Texas Hero* Thad Conway, an ex-gunslinger who just wants to run his own ranch—alone. But prim schoolmarm Caroline Adams is determined to change his mind.

When impoverished Sir Giles of Rathborne hatches a scheme to enrich his coffers in *The Cygnet* by Marianne Willman, he turns a young bandit into a missing heiress and falls under her spell.

As a secondary character in *Sweet Seduction,* the first book in the NORTH POINT series, Barbara Johnson was a woman of exceptional courage and depth. Now, in *Sweet Sensations,* author Julie Tetel gives Barbara her own story in which she enters into a bargain with a mysterious drifter in order to keep her family safe.

July also marks the release of our Western short-story collection—*Untamed—Maverick Hearts* with stories by Heather Graham Pozzessere, Joan Johnston and Patricia Potter. Whether you like reading on the beach or by the pool, Harlequin Historicals offers four great books each month to be enjoyed all year round!

Sincerely,

Tracy Farrell
Senior Editor

Sweet Sensations

JULIE TETEL

Harlequin Books

TORONTO • NEW YORK • LONDON
AMSTERDAM • PARIS • SYDNEY • HAMBURG
STOCKHOLM • ATHENS • TOKYO • MILAN
MADRID • WARSAW • BUDAPEST • AUCKLAND

Harlequin Historicals first edition July 1993

ISBN 0-373-28782-8

SWEET SENSATIONS

Books by Julie Tetel

Harlequin Historicals

Sweet Suspicions #128
Sweet Seduction #167
Sweet Sensations #182

JULIE TETEL

has always loved both history and romance, making it easy for her to love reading and writing historical romances. She is from a suburb of Chicago and currently lives in Durham, North Carolina. She has two sons, two careers, at least two points of view, and one husband.

All sweet sensations, all ennobling thoughts,
All adoration of the God in nature,
All lovely and all honourable things,
Whatever makes this mortal spirit feel
The joy and greatness of its future being?

—Samuel Taylor Coleridge
Fears in Solitude

Chapter One

North Point, Maryland
The Johnson Farm
November 1815

She believed that she could never love anything as purely or as fiercely as she loved her baby daughter.

She cradled her in her arms, holding on to her just a moment longer, watching her little eyelids droop and close with sleepy satisfaction. Sighing softly with her own contentment, the woman rose from the rocking chair and drew the baby away from the breast where she had been nursing. Then she bundled her into the cradle, which was set up near enough to the large stone hearth to take advantage of the heat, but far enough away to be safe from stray sparks.

She gazed down lovingly at her daughter before rearranging her heavy breasts comfortably within the folds of her nursing chemise and rebuttoning her bodice. She adjusted the shawl that lay across her shoulders, smoothed down her skirts and moved toward the trestle table at the other side of the room, intending to prepare her supper now that the baby was fed.

There came a knock at the door.

She was expecting no one, and she rarely had visitors. She felt a prick of anxiety and hesitated, wondering if she should open the door. Then she shook her head. Silently chiding herself—*Foolish Barbara!*—she dismissed her anxiety as a remnant from the time, more than a year before, when red-coats had swarmed the area and threatened to capture Baltimore. She reasoned that the person at the door was one of her neighbors calling with news or a favor to ask. Most likely it was old Ben Skinner, or Michael Gorsuch, or even Jacob Shaw.

She took the several steps to the front door and opened it to reveal a figure, standing in the shadows of her porch, whose height and rugged outline did not belong to any man of her acquaintance. Her mild anxiety returned, but it was too late to close the door against him. The gloom of a late-November day looked darkly in at her.

She heard a warm, gravelly voice inquire from the shadows, "Mrs. Johnson?"

"Yes," she replied, coolly, as if it were no business of his. "I am Mrs. Johnson."

The man stepped forward, out of the shadows and into the oblong of light framed by the angle of the half-open door. He doffed his hat, and she saw a deeply chiseled face, all masculine planes and angles. She looked up and into midnight-blue eyes.

He held his hat calmly in both hands. He wore no gloves. "I was told that you recently lost a tenant couple," he said, "and might need an extra pair of hands on your farm this winter."

She swallowed once and considered the statement. "Who told you that?"

He gestured vaguely in the direction of the road that led to Long Log Lane. "A man at the meetinghouse—Ben Skinner, I think, was his name—told me about you this afternoon when I asked if there was work in the area. He said that Jacob Shaw had recently been looking for extra hands, as well, and I went there first. I've just come now from Shaw's spread, where he told me that he had hired all the new men he needed this past week. So I've come to you."

Barbara Johnson was reassured that the man was telling the truth. She also knew now that he was not from the Baltimore area; if he were, he would know that the large tobacco farmers in this corner of the world called their "spreads" plantations. She ran her eye over his form. He had a look of lean strength about him that the bulk of his shabby overcoat did not disguise. Her eyes came back to his face. It looked as lean and strong as his body. He looked hungry, too.

When she did not immediately reply, he continued, "The men at the meetinghouse asked me all the questions you are asking yourself now, and they were satisfied with my answers before giving me your name." A faint gleam lit his remarkable blue eyes. "Jacob Shaw repeated the process before he would tell me how to get here from his spread." He paused. "The men in the area know I'm here, and I know you're a widow."

She liked the way he said that last bit, straight and matter-of-fact. He looked down at the wedding band she still wore. He was not playing games. He was not trying to importune a woman who lived alone. He was here for work, pure and simple.

And she had work to give. She stepped out onto the porch, pulling the door mostly closed behind her so that no cold drafts would get into the house and possibly chill the baby. She kept one hand on the door latch and, with the other, pulled her shawl around her. She could see her breath.

"We'd have to bargain for terms," she said.

"Of course," he said easily. "I can put you in a better bargaining position from the outset by telling you that I don't reckon to work here a long time, but only plan to stay through the winter. Since it's temporary work I'm looking for, it should cost you cheaper."

"You'd work only through the winter?"

Half his face was in deep shadow. "Only through the winter."

Again, she liked the way he said that, flat. He did not feel compelled to tell her his life story. He did not explain why he had appeared on her doorstep now, as winter approached, or why he would be on his way come spring. He was simply here now, and she could take him or leave him.

She knew he must be hoping that she would take him, but he was not going to beg or bully or sweet-talk her.

"It goes without saying that I would help with the early planting," he added.

She hesitated a fraction of a second longer. She was feeling the cold now, and she came to a decision. She pushed the door open behind her. With a minimal kind of welcoming nod to him, she said, "All right, then. Let's come inside to bargain for our terms. We can do it over supper."

In the renewed light spilling out onto the porch, she thought his features might have shown a trace of relief. Then again, they might not have. Perhaps the faint picking up of the corners of his mouth was in response to the offer of dinner, or simply the idea of the warmth inside.

"Yes, ma'am," he said evenly, "but if we're going to be a while, I'll want to stable my horse."

She peered around him into the darkness of the nearly dead day. She had not heard him approach, it was true, so she had thought he must have come on foot. Then she saw the horse, a great rawboned beast that looked as hungry as his master. She could just discern the faint outline of a bed-roll lashed to its rump. The horse shifted its legs in the cold and whinnied, as if on cue.

She pointed to the shed on the other side of the rutted drive, across from the house. "There's a stable, more or less, over there, where I put my horse and buggy when I don't have time to get to the barn, which is down the drive a ways."

As the man descended the porch steps to go to his horse, she said, "The straw in the shed is fresh enough, I think. I put a full bucket of water in there yesterday, as well, and most of it is probably still there. Help yourself."

With another "Yes, ma'am," he unhitched the reins from the post by the bottom step and walked his horse in the direction she had indicated.

Barbara went inside, briskly rubbing her upper arms to warm them. She automatically glanced at the baby—still slumbering peacefully—and smiled unconsciously. She could not resist going to the cot and adjusting the little blanket, though it did not need adjusting.

She straightened from the loving task and went to the opposite corner of the sitting room, which served as the kitchen. She fetched the extra bowl, plate, spoon, napkin and mug and set them across from her place at the table. She reached for a blue glazed-earthenware pitcher on an open shelf and went to fill it from a jug of cider she had cooling in the trap off the back door. As she put out a loaf of bread and a knife, she mused that this would be the first time she had had a man to dinner since Jonas's death. On an afterthought, she lit two candles and placed them on one side of the table. She paused to wonder at the oddity of her asking the man in to dinner, then remembered his hungry look. Since she was unused to generous impulses, she decided that she must have realized that if she was going to pay her new hired hand an honest day's wage, he would have to be in a condition to earn it.

Presently the sound of his boots could be heard on the porch, and then his perfunctory knock at the door, followed by his entrance. He shut the door behind him precisely, making sure the latch caught, and tested for a sound fit with the length of his body. He had brought in his musket, which he stood upright beside the door, the butt on the floor, the barrel resting in the groove formed by the wall and the door. He shed his coat, looked above his musket to the row of pegs there and hung his coat next to Barbara's. He placed his black leather hat over the coat. He seemed to fill the room with his presence.

Seeing him now in the full light of the fire, Barbara Johnson noticed that his hair was so black that it had blue highlights, and that he wore it pulled back in a queue. She took in the details of his dress. He was wearing well-worn boots, old buckskin breeches stained in interesting places, a black leather vest, a white cotton shirt that looked incongruously clean, a navy blue jacket far past its prime, and several days' worth of dark stubble. He was not a handsome man by conventional standards, although she found that the fit of his irregular features had a compelling appeal. He was not a young man, either. She imagined that he was past his mid-thirties. He struck her as a quiet man. No, not quiet. Intense.

Polite, too, she noted after a moment, when he did not move from the door. He was waiting for her invitation.

"Come," she said, gesturing to his place at the table. "Sit."

He sat down on the bench opposite her. She took his bowl, along with hers, and crossed to the hearth, where a cast-iron pot hung from a hook. She ladled out the stew and gave him a portion that was double the size of hers. While she set the bowls on the table, he cut the bread. She returned to the hearth and, using two dish pads, handled a crockery bowl that had been warming on the brick shelf built into one side of the fireplace. She set the steaming bowl on the table, thrust a serving spoon into it and moved it toward him.

"Okra and tomatoes," she said. Then, with a glance at the bowls: "Rabbit stew, and to drink we have cider." So saying, she poured out two mugfuls, then shook out her napkin, folded her hands before her on the table and said a few words of thanks.

He repeated her "Amen" and shook out his own napkin.

She picked up her spoon, then lowered it again when a thought struck her. "I'm sorry that I forgot to offer a washing-up before supper." She raised her eyes to him.

He shook his head minimally and held up his clean hands. "I got first crack at the water in the bucket that's in the shed."

"That water must have been freezing," she said, a tiny frown between her brows. She was feeling out of practice with hospitality.

"It'll freeze tonight, no doubt" was all he said.

Which brought her to her first point of information. "For sleeping quarters, you can have the house that the couple occupied." She picked up her spoon to eat. "It's located at the end of the drive behind the barn and faces the west field. It's not big, only one room, but the chimney works, and you can keep it as warm as you like."

Following her lead, he picked up his spoon. "Do you charge rent on it?" he asked. "Or does the house figure as part of the terms we're to bargain for?"

She had not anticipated the question. "I consider that the house comes with the job."

He took a sip of cider. "Bargaining leverage, then."

"Are you suggesting that you are considering an alternative form of accommodation?" she asked, raising her brows. "Such as camping out the entire winter?"

"I might. It depends on the terms."

She was mildly surprised. "Are you meaning to drive a hard bargain?"

He smiled, rather charmingly. "No. Just trying to recoup from having played most of my cards when I told you I would come cheap as a temporary worker."

"Then why did you tell me that, so early on?"

"To get in the door," he answered. When he saw her expression, he added, "As a figure of speech, ma'am." He lowered his eyes and concentrated on eating his stew.

He's reassuring me, she thought.

She liked him for the tact he showed in lowering his disconcerting blue gaze. She liked him for the way he was letting her know again that he would not presume on her position as a woman alone. She imagined that he could be a dangerous man, if the occasion demanded it, but his words and the way he held his body, relaxed yet contained, carried no threat to her.

"But how do I know that you won't try the ploy twice," she asked dryly, "since it worked the first time?"

His black lashes swept up, and a gleam of humor lit the depths of his eyes as they focused on her. He clearly caught her meaning, but it seemed he was a cautious man. "Ma'am?" he asked politely.

"By tipping your hand so early on," she said, "and pointing it out to me now, you might suppose I could be

disarmed into paying you higher wages than I might have
initially—without the tip of the hand.''

"I might," he acknowledged, "but I won't suppose it.
And I always play dollar for dollar." He gestured with a
spoon full of rabbit stew. "It's a good meal you've given me
for the privilege of bargaining for my wages, so after supper I'll cut you some wood in payment."

She was low on wood, and chopping it was her least favorite chore. She said, immediately, "Done."

"And I'll stack it—" He broke off when he glanced over
at the very small pile of wood next to the hearth. It was not,
however, the relative lack of wood that caught his attention. He looked back at her curiously. "Is that a baby in the
cradle?"

She smiled. "Yes, I have a daughter. Her name is Sarah."

He glanced back at the cradle. He seemed quite amazed.
"How old is she?"

"Five months."

"Your only child?"

"Yes."

He drew a deep breath and looked at the cradle again.
When he looked back at the woman, he studiously avoided
looking at her full breasts, which he had already duly noticed. So she was a nursing mother. Nodding slowly, he said,
"It can't have been easy for you these past months."

Barbara smiled again—or, rather, her smile remained.
"Sarah's been no trouble. I've enjoyed having her. Oh, I
was a little tired at first," she conceded, "but my neighbors
were kindly and helpful. With winter coming, it may be
more difficult, since I'll be reluctant to take her around with
me during my outdoor chores all the time. That is why, in
large part, I'm needing a new man to help me...." Her voice
trailed off, and her smile became a little wry. "Well, now
I've tipped *my* hand to you, sir."

"You'd be needing a man around here even without your
daughter," he said graciously.

"True," she said, "but it's a question of the urgency of
the need."

"Let's bargain, then," he said in his straightforward manner. "What is the work you expect from me?"

She outlined chores that he would have expected of the owner, or foreman, of a medium-size farm in winter, with four extra field hands helping. What he had not expected was the impression he got that he would be taking these duties over from her, and not her dead husband. While they ate, he made the usual inquiries into the state of the various ongoing farm duties—the winter care of the animals, the maintenance of the fences and the outbuildings, the working of the soil, the storing of the grains—and discovered that she was surprisingly caught up.

"It seems you've done a lot as a widowed mother," he commented at one point in the discussion.

"I was well used to all of those chores before Sarah came," she answered.

He picked up the loaf of bread and the knife. Rather more from interest in the job than from curiosity, he asked, "How long has Mr. Johnson been dead, ma'am?"

After a moment, she said, "Four years."

He did not make the mistake of looking over at the cradle. The knife did not even hesitate as it sliced through the bread. He offered her the top slice, which she took, then put the loaf down. "All right, then. This is what I recommend you pay me per month," he said, and named his figure. "With the field house for my accommodations."

She did not take his first offer. They haggled, almost amicably, until they arrived at a figure they could both live with. She imagined that he had bothered with the process only to maintain a certain pretense. She had the strange fancy that he would have taken almost any amount, for she sensed that what he wanted most was a place to stay for several months—a refuge, perhaps—and he had found it here. The money was, somehow, secondary.

When they were done with their negotiations, he pushed his bench slightly back from the table, wiped his hands on the napkin on his lap and placed the square of cloth by his empty bowl. He reached his hand across the table and said,

"It's a respectable deal you've given me, Mrs. Johnson, and you might be wanting to know that my name is Morgan Harris."

Her smile dazzled him. It was the first fully unconstrained expression he had seen from her, and it illuminated her face. He had thought her an unusually good-looking woman the moment he laid eyes on her. With the smile, she radiated a beauty without equal, her hair a fairy-tale blond and her eyes the color of an enchanted lake. No one had told him that the widow Johnson was so young and desirable. As he thought back on the inquisition he had endured from the men at the meetinghouse, he realized that he should have guessed then that Mrs. Johnson was someone special.

Barbara's smile was produced by both embarrassment and a turn of rare humor. She thought, I *am* out of practice, not to have even wondered what the man's name was! She accepted his handshake across the table and said, "It's a pleasure to meet you, Mr. Harris, and you must think me foolish not to have asked you earlier."

"No, I think you're a woman who looks after business first, as is proper," he said, not holding her hand a moment longer than was necessary.

She pushed her bench back. "To make up for my lapse of manners, let me offer you a cup of coffee," she said, still smiling with a remaining trace of self-deprecatory humor. "To give you strength for chopping the wood, that is."

He nodded his acceptance of her offer and, at a gesture from her, rose from the table and walked over to the sitting area of the room while she cleared the table. Before sitting down again, he took a poker from the hearth and teased the fire. He rearranged the burning logs and added a new one. He gazed down a moment at the perfect baby cuddled so blissfully in her blankets, thinking that mother and daughter were quite a pair. He felt a fleeting curiosity concerning this baby's presence in the world.

She called over to him, "How do you take your coffee, Mr. Harris?"

He replied, "Black, please."

He chose to sit on the little brown settee against the wall opposite the hearth, and relaxed, as best he could, on its hard cushions. He stretched an arm across the top, leaned his head back and unfolded his legs before him. He had ridden far this day, and under some strain, and this was the first time he had been at his ease since before the dawn. It was the first time he had been at his ease in four days, in fact.

He observed, impassively, the sparse furnishings and Spartan orderliness of the main room. He glanced at the two doors on either side of the fireplace, evidently leading to the only two other rooms of the little house. He noted, with interest, the three stringed instruments—two guitars and a banjo—hanging on the wall adjacent to the fireplace. They were the only bit of decoration to relieve the harsh practicality of the room. A small loom stood in one corner, a weaving filling a third of its frame, the warp strung with hunter green, the weft with ocean blue. A spinning wheel stood in the other corner, empty.

Then he narrowed his eyes and contemplated the fire, aware on some level of the pleasant sounds of Mrs. Johnson's domestic movements coming from across the room. He felt good—as good as a man in his precarious position could feel.

She came to him with the cup of coffee. He realized that he must have had some look in his eyes when he glanced up at her, for, when their eyes made contact, she almost backed away from him, as if from a fire. He straightened slightly on the settee and looked down at the cup she held out to him. He took it from her, being careful not to touch her, and murmured his thanks.

She sat down opposite him in the rocking chair, next to the baby's cradle.

She was calm enough when she asked him to describe to her some of his previous jobs, so he imagined that he had covered whatever it was in his eyes that might have frightened her. He answered her directly and truthfully.

At one point, she asked, "And where are you from, Mr. Harris?"

He opened his mouth to answer with his standard reply to that question, but just then a scuffling of boots was heard on the front porch, followed by an imperious rapping at the door.

She looked at him, utterly surprised, with a question on her face.

"No, ma'am," he said, answering her question. "I've had no one following me so closely." He glanced over at the door and noticed that, if it was opened, the caller would have a direct view of him on the settee.

At the insistent knocking, Barbara rose, a little nervously, and put her cup on the mantelshelf.

Morgan rose, as well. He thought he had done a good job of shaking the one or two men he guessed were on his tail. Nevertheless, as a precaution, he put his cup on the kitchen table and went to stand, out of the way, on the other side of the door.

Barbara drew a breath and opened the door. Nothing could have exceeded her astonishment when she saw who stood there.

Chapter Two

"Lieutenant Richards," she breathed, hardly believing her eyes.

"Mrs. Johnson," the man replied, cool as you please. "I give you good evening."

The sound of his voice, his British accent, convinced her of the reality of his presence and his identity. She did not return his greeting. Instead, she said the first thing that came to mind: "This is not a pleasant surprise."

Unruffled by her rudeness, the lieutenant said, "I did not imagine it would be."

"Then why did you come?" she demanded, not opening the door further than two feet.

"To visit with you, to catch up on your news since last I saw you," he said.

She had no good memories of the man, no good associations. She did not like him; she did not like the fact that he was here; and she most certainly did not like being surprised by his visit. She had never imagined that she would see him again, and the sight of him caused the unaccustomed anxiety she had been feeling all evening long to blossom into fear—a fear as strong as her love for her child. She quelled the fear in order to save her wits and devise a way to get rid of this man as quickly as possible.

"I have no news," she stated.

"Then you will hardly object to sharing your lack of news with me."

"I strongly object to sharing my lack of news with you, and I strongly object to wasting any more of my time with you. You redcoats were run out of the country last year and invited never to return. Your manners are at fault, Lieutenant Richards, and I will thank you to leave me."

She began to close the door in his face, but he managed to get his foot in the door before she could latch it. With a strong arm, he pushed the door back. She held him off, and they settled for a stalemate in that the door was once again open two feet.

Lieutenant Richards was keeping the door open with just enough strength to counter hers. It seemed he was not prepared to force an undignified entry—at least not yet. "But you see, Mrs. Johnson, I insist on speaking with you, since I do not come for myself."

Barbara was leaning the whole of her weight into the door. She nearly sneered. "You come to avenge the dead, perhaps?"

"Avenge, no," the lieutenant said smoothly, "but I do come, in a manner of speaking, on behalf of the dead."

This statement piqued Barbara's curiosity. "You come on behalf of the dead?"

"On behalf of a woman who wants to meet you."

"A woman?" Barbara echoed. "A woman who is dead?"

"It is not the woman who is dead," the lieutenant replied, "but her husband."

An eerie dread settled in her stomach. "Who is she?" Barbara asked.

"Mrs. Robert Ross," came the answer.

"Where is she?"

"In Baltimore."

The dread became real fear and leapt up from Barbara's stomach to clutch at her throat. She began to push harder against the door to keep the man out. At just that fateful moment, however, little Sarah awoke and began to cry, in sweet baby sounds, distracting Barbara and electrifying the man on the opposite side of the door.

"You have a baby, Mrs. Johnson!" the lieutenant exclaimed softly, his tone half reproachful, half wondering.

The next moment, Barbara's strength gave way, and Lieutenant Richards had enough of an opening to step into the sitting room. It was only then that Barbara saw the hulking shadows of two other men on the porch who had accompanied Lieutenant Richards on this mission. It was evident that the lieutenant could have entered her house at any moment he chose, notwithstanding her attempts to bar him.

"How kind of you to invite me in," the lieutenant said, with a remarkable lack of irony.

Acknowledging defeat and accepting the inevitable, Barbara favored him with a withering look and went to pick up Sarah, whose whimpers pulled her more strongly than any fear or loathing. She needed to hold Sarah to her and never let her go.

"Men," Richards said over his shoulder to the two thugs on the porch. His brief nod indicated that they, too, should enter the house, and they slid in to stand by the settee. Only when the lieutenant closed the door, squeezing out the cold, did he become aware of Morgan Harris, who was standing there, regarding him with a kind of calm curiosity.

The lieutenant looked from the large man with the blue eyes to Mrs. Johnson, who had lifted her baby up and into her arms, then back to the man. He cocked his head questioningly and calculated rapidly.

Barbara saw his look, and a finger of true inspiration touched her brow, making her feel momentarily light and giddy. She had the perfect explanation for all the vexing, fearful questions Lieutenant Richards could ask her. Her plan was bold and brilliant and obvious.

She said, in a kind of leading tone, "Surprised, Lieutenant Richards?" She walked forward from the cradle, holding her baby, and came right up to the lieutenant. "I'd like to introduce you to my husband," she said. She kept the lieutenant's eyes pinned on her with her own forceful gaze while she let Morgan Harris absorb the impact of her statement. "Lieutenant Richards," she said slowly, "Morgan Harris." Only then did she turn to Morgan Harris. She was relieved to find that his face betrayed neither consternation nor confusion. "Morgan, dear," she continued, "this is Lieutenant Richards, of the British army, who was stationed at North Point last year."

Morgan Harris did not extend his hand. He did not move or even immediately respond. He continued to regard the newcomer a moment longer, then flicked his eyes over to the two men by the settee. He assessed them at some length. Then he said, low, his deep voice gravelly, "You heard my wife. You're not wanted here."

Barbara felt a spurt of melting relief. Lieutenant Richards looked disconcerted at seeing a man in the house, and his manner changed slightly, becoming more ingratiating. "But I have not yet heard her news—and she has so much, it seems."

Morgan had only the barest sense of what was happening, but he was nothing if not adaptable. His eyes never wavered from the lieutenant's face. He said, baldly, "The fact remains that she doesn't want to talk to you." He followed the comment by glancing deliberately over at the musket standing upright against the door jamb.

Lieutenant Richards responded by shedding his greatcoat to expose nonmilitary dress that must have been formal and fashionable by London standards and was certainly at great variance with the setting of Barbara Johnson's sitting room. A pearled pistol could be seen against his elegantly tailored coat, its barrel thrust into the waist of his pantaloons. The two men at the settee took the hint and drew back the folds of their greatcoats, without removing them, to display similarly placed weapons.

"Nevertheless, and begging your indulgence," the lieutenant said, in something of the grand manner, "I have a desire to speak with Mrs. John—your wife. I've come a long way, on behalf of a widow, as I've said, whose husband was known to your wife, and I would like the benefit of a few minutes of her time."

Considering the silent yet powerful language spoken by the three pistols, Morgan said, succinctly, "Persuasive." Turning to his new employer, he said, "Nevertheless, I will leave the decision to her."

Barbara shifted the baby on her hip and held the now-cooing bundle close to her breast. She saw the benefit of switching tactics. With the safety of Morgan Harris's presence, she might as well meet with the lieutenant, since he had come so far and would not give up easily.

"Five minutes of my time, more or less, with Lieutenant Richards," she said to her new hired hand, "will not overly disturb our privacy. Do you have any objections, Morgan?"

"Not if you do not, my love," he answered evenly.

She held his glance for a brief, electric moment before she looked away, embarrassed by his use of the endearment. "Well, then," she said, sending him a meaningful look, "we might invite Lieutenant Richards to join us in a cup of coffee." She turned to the lieutenant. "Coffee, sir?"

Richards bowed and accepted the offer. "With a spot of cream, please, if you have it available."

Having received her unspoken message, Morgan accompanied Barbara across the room to the kitchen area, where, with practiced ease, she got down another coffee cup with her free hand while balancing the baby with her other. She motioned to Morgan to grind some more beans. Under her lashes, she glanced at the lieutenant, who was standing not more than ten feet away.

While the lieutenant exchanged some words with his two thugs, Barbara leaned forward and asked swiftly, in a whisper, "What do you think?"

He replied, "I think you would do well to get a dog."

She blinked in response to the irrelevance of the remark and looked straight into his remarkable blue eyes.

"A dog would alert you, in future, to the approach of a visitor," he explained in barely audible tones, "and give you time to devise a story that would involve the least risk to yourself." In a normal voice, he said, "I'll fetch the coffee-pot."

Morgan crossed to the hearth, where the tin pot stood on its trivet over some glowing coals. Barbara went to the trap at the back door for the cream, all the while shielding the contented baby from any drafts. She turned over his remark about the dog and realized, incredulous, that Morgan Harris had lent a kind of whimsy to a situation he recognized as dangerous to her—in more ways than one. They met again at the table, where Barbara prepared the lieutenant's cup.

When it was ready, she crossed the room, feeling like an accused criminal walking to the witness stand. Despite Morgan Harris's easy acceptance of her plan, she felt an apprehension bordering on anxiety at the reason for the lieutenant's visit, for she had an uncanny foreknowledge of why he was here. She handed the cup of hot coffee to the lieutenant, who was standing by the settee, waiting for her.

Only when Barbara had settled herself in the rocker did the lieutenant sit down. Morgan Harris took up a position behind the rocker, and the two brutes stood sentry on either side of the door.

"I've come all this long way to tell you a story," the lieutenant began. "It's a story about Mrs. Ross. You don't know Mrs. Ross, do you, Mrs. John—"

At that moment, Morgan interrupted by dropping light, inquiring fingers onto Barbara's shoulder. "Before the lieutenant goes too far into his story, my love," he said, "do you wish for your own cup again?"

She willed herself not to react in a startled manner to Morgan's touch. She looked up at him with what she hoped was a convincingly adoring look. She shook her head slightly. "No, thank you," she said, and the brief eye contact with him soothed her anxious heart.

Morgan nodded and glanced over at the lieutenant. "Excuse the interruption, sir," he said calmly. "You may proceed."

Although Lieutenant Richards had watched this affecting byplay through skeptical eyes, the diversion had served its purpose, and his voice was a shade less confident when he began again. "As I was saying, I've come to tell you a story about Mrs. Ross. My story begins one morning five months ago, when Mrs. Ross awoke from a dream. An odd dream it was, and so strong that she was convinced that it would change her life."

Barbara was listening with an expression that she hoped was both polite and impassive. "A dream?" she said, with the merest hint of amusement.

"Yes. It was a dream that she was having a child. Her husband's child. Her dead husband's child," the lieutenant said, with sly emphasis. "It was curious, of course, because her husband had been dead nine months, and she had not been with him for several months before he was killed."

Barbara felt her heart twist uncomfortably, but she kept her face immobile and her eyes distant, though they remained on the lieutenant's face all the while. She felt the blood draining from her face, and could do nothing to stop it.

"And so?"

"And so Mrs. Ross became quite convinced that her husband had left a child of his in this world."

"He may have left many, for all I know," Barbara said indifferently.

"Mrs. Ross was not blessed with children in the twenty years of her marriage," the lieutenant replied. "Her husband had no other known children."

The strange fear returned to claw at Barbara's throat. She began to rock gently in her chair. Under other circumstances, she would have put little Sarah back in her cradle. At the moment, however, she had no intention of letting her go.

"I am very sorry for Mrs. Ross, to be sure," Barbara said, with conventional sympathy.

"Yes, it was always a sorrow for Mrs. Ross to be childless," the lieutenant told her. "Until she had this dream."

Barbara frowned. "But why should the dream ease her sorrow?"

The lieutenant looked pointedly at the bundle in Barbara's arms. "Because it gave her hope that there was a child."

Her fear receded. If the lieutenant was indeed telling the truth—that he had crossed the ocean with Mrs. Ross because of a *dream* she had had—then she had no grounds for real worry. And yet . . .

"Women have dreams of childbirth all the time, I should think," she said matter-of-factly. "Perhaps her dream was the result of the passing of nine sad months of grieving for her dead husband. Or perhaps she has a history of such dreams, if she has been barren all these years."

"Mrs. Ross assured me that she never had such a dream before," the lieutenant replied.

Barbara returned the lieutenant's pointed look with one of her own. "I do not understand why you are telling me this, Lieutenant."

"Perhaps, before we continue, Mrs.—" the lieutenant glanced up at the man who was standing behind Barbara's chair "—Harris, you might prefer our discussion to be private."

"Not at all, Lieutenant," she said firmly.

The lieutenant coughed into his fist. "But what we have to discuss is, perhaps, of a personal nature, and involves the time before you were married."

"I have no secrets from my husband," she said, without so much as a blink. She looked over at the two brutes who were guarding either side of the door. "And if we were to be truly private, you would have to ask your two traveling companions to adjourn to the porch."

Since Lieutenant Richards had no intention of doing that, he favored Barbara with a you-asked-for-it look and said directly, "Mrs. Ross is looking for her child."

"Her husband's child—at best," Barbara countered. "According to her own dream, the baby could not have been hers."

"Ah, but that is where interpretation of these delicate matters enters," the lieutenant said, with the curve of a confident smile. "When she told me her dream and described the mother of her husband's child as having blond hair and blue eyes—like Mrs. Ross herself, or, perhaps, like you, Mrs. Harris—well, I remembered that Mrs. Ross's husband came here, to Maryland, a year ago this past August. I remembered that he died here a month later, in September. I remembered that he had known you, rather intimately, before his death, and I began to wonder..."

After a pause, she asked, "About what?" Her voice was a little breathless, but it was steady.

"Oh, about interpreting dreams and interpreting laws," the lieutenant said carelessly. "I began to wonder about questions of paternity, and financial arrangements, and custody." He paused, significantly. "Things like that."

He had issued her a threat, a vague threat that was all the more threatening for its vagueness. She felt her fear and anxiety return. She tried to push them away, but they would not budge. They clamped, like iron bands, upon her heart. She felt the blood return to her cheeks.

"You have come to the wrong house," she said, with a betraying touch of emotion.

The lieutenant saw his opening and pushed his way in. He asked, abruptly, "How old is your baby?"

Barbara steeled herself. "Three months," she lied.

Richards eyed the white blanket. He was no judge of babies. "Did your baby come late, perhaps?"

Barbara was impervious to the insult. "No, she came just on time," she replied, as calmly as she could. She knew that there was nothing Lieutenant Richards could do—for the moment—to disprove her statement. "We've been married a year." Here she looked up again at Morgan and attempted a loving smile at him.

Morgan returned the look. "Yes, we are to celebrate our first anniversary this week."

"This week, is it?" the lieutenant prodded. "The last time I saw Mrs. John—your wife—she was a widow."

"And now you find her remarried," Morgan affirmed. "One year, as of this week."

The lieutenant's eyes narrowed, and he played a tricky card. "For a husband, you've been mighty cool about what your wife and I have been discussing."

Morgan was more than equal to the gibe. "She's kept no secrets from me, as she's said, and a good husband knows when to let his wife take care of her own business." The moment seemed to call for something dramatic, for he had seen a trace of panic and an appeal for help in Mrs. Johnson's eyes when she had looked up at him. He reached down and gently pulled the baby away from her mother's arms and into his. He was willing to risk the infant squealing and squirming, rejecting his touch and scent. "And the one you should be addressing, sir, is the baby's father. If I'm certain Sarah is mine," he said, recalling the child's name, "then the matter is closed."

"Sarah?" the lieutenant repeated, in a strange tone. The look on his face was one of wonder and disbelief.

The moment was electric.

"Yes, Sarah," Barbara managed, feeling a bolt of true fear pass through her.

The lieutenant was eyeing the baby in Morgan Harris's arms. His face continued to register awe. "Sarah is Mrs. Ross's name," he said, "and the name of the baby in her dream."

"It is also my mother's name," Barbara lied again, but this time she choked over the words and had to clear her throat.

"A common enough name," Morgan said, aware that the baby's acceptance of his touch had gone unnoticed in the strange tension in the atmosphere, "and an interesting coincidence that proves nothing, as I have said, when I claim to be the father."

"That claim may be contested," the lieutenant pointed out.

"You're on shaky ground, man," Morgan Harris said, with enough heat in his deep voice to make his meaning felt, "on a number of issues."

Wordlessly, almost mechanically, Barbara lifted her hands to take the baby, and Morgan willingly surrendered the daughter to the mother. Barbara took her, feeling stunned and fearful, and remembering how she had woken up, alone, on the day her contractions had started and had thought, out of the blue, *I am going to name the baby Sarah!*

The lieutenant met Morgan Harris's eye. "What do you mean by that?" he demanded.

Morgan Harris strolled over to the lieutenant and looked down at him. The lieutenant was forced to rise from the settee and meet him at eye level. Morgan said, pleasantly, "I see that there are two men by the door. One of the men is standing in front of my musket. The three of you are armed. You spoke earlier of interpretations. If you interpret what I just said as a threat you wish to challenge, I can't hope to persuade you otherwise." He paused, then continued, "You also spoke earlier about financial considerations. I hope, for your trouble, that Mrs. Ross is paying you handsomely for this visit."

The lieutenant's eyes blazed. "Mrs. Ross is a very rich woman," he said angrily. It was a bullying move.

Morgan shook his head, unimpressed. He deftly turned the tone of the encounter from confrontation to negotiation. "So what do you want from us? Or, rather, what does the rich Mrs. Ross want? She's come a long way on the strength of her dream. Would it satisfy her to see the baby?"

Since Lieutenant Richards had not expected to find a man in Mrs. Johnson's house, and had only half expected to find a baby, he did not immediately know how to answer that. As for Mrs. Ross, he knew that nothing less than boarding the ship for the return voyage to England with her husband's child in her possession would satisfy her.

Barbara wanted to cry out, *No, she can't see her! To see her is to fall in love with her! To fall in love with her is to want her as you've never wanted anything before!*

The lieutenant replied, "Perhaps that would be enough."

"And then you would leave us in peace?" Morgan pressed.

"That will depend on Mrs. Ross's wishes."

"And ours," Morgan said. He was hardly afraid of a rich Englishwoman, as he had more fearsome demons pursuing him. "I heard you say that Mrs. Ross is in Baltimore. Bring her here tomorrow, and let's have done with this fantasy. Her evidently strong sensibilities might ease up once she's met the child's father."

Lieutenant Ross rapidly reviewed this offer. It had been his plan to invite Mrs. Johnson to come with him to Baltimore on the morrow to see Mrs. Ross, but of course that had been before he knew that Mrs. Johnson had remarried.

Or had she?

The lieutenant had his doubts.

And whose baby was she holding?

The mysterious Mrs. Johnson was beginning to intrigue him as she had intrigued Mrs. Ross's late husband. The situation was interesting enough, the stakes were high enough, and his position was strong enough, for him to put the various questions to the test.

"Yes, Mrs. Ross might be encouraged to come here tomorrow," the lieutenant replied. "I will propose it to her when I see her in the morning. Although Baltimore is not far, the hour is late, and the sun is long gone. For tonight, then, I think I will avail myself of your continuing hospitality." When he saw the look on the beautiful young mother's face, he asked, smoothly, "You have some reason to deny me a night's lodging, Mrs. Harris?" Then he glanced to the lean, rugged man at her side. "Mr. Harris?"

Chapter Three

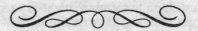

Morgan Harris had to think fast. He looked at the thugs by the door. "It's not an inn we run here, to lodge three men, and you're not invited guests."

The lieutenant glanced back at his brutes. "You deny us your hospitality?"

Morgan shook his head. "No, I deny only your assumption that it should come free of charge."

The lieutenant's brows rose. With obvious condescension, he said, "I'll offer you five pounds for the night."

Morgan countered swiftly, "Make it five pounds a person—Mrs. Ross being so rich—and we have a deal."

The lieutenant did not immediately respond.

"Well, now," Morgan said softly, after a brief silence, "we're not obliged to let Mrs. Ross see the baby at all, and then you'll have come all this way for nothing."

"You're quite the bargainer," the lieutenant remarked, his condescension even more pronounced.

Morgan nodded, as if at a compliment. "And we'll take the equivalent of fifteen pounds in dollars. Half up front." When the lieutenant did not immediately respond, Morgan said flatly, "For my wife's trouble. I don't believe in inconveniencing people to no purpose and to no profit."

It was an insult, and the lieutenant read it as such. He mustered an answering insult. "In my year's absence, I had forgotten rough-and-ready American manners."

"Which is why I had to remind you," Morgan replied easily.

The lieutenant slowly put his hand in his pocket, dug deep, and withdrew several weighty coins. He handed these over to Morgan, who accepted them and put them in his breeches pocket.

The lieutenant looked at Barbara. "Was this, then, the nature of the surprise I read on your face when I announced my intention to spend the night in your home?" he asked. "My rather shocking assumption that you would simply offer me a roof?"

Although she was hardly pleased that Morgan Harris was making money from the occasion, the brief negotiations had given Barbara time to recover her wits. She was in an awkward, even dangerous position—in more ways than one, as Morgan Harris had pointed out—and she needed steady nerves to see her through. Now was not the moment to expose any weaknesses in her story.

She remembered with a fine hatred the British assumption of hospitality during the weeks of their invasion of Maryland the year before. "Of course," she said. "What else could I have been surprised about?"

"The sleeping arrangements, for instance," the lieutenant said, watching her closely.

"There's little surprise on that score," she said. Then she deflected his implication by explaining, "My house is not large, and I have only one spare room, with a daybed which you may have. I'm afraid that your two traveling companions will have to avail themselves of the floor in the sitting room." She turned to Morgan Harris, so that her back was to the three men. She looked into his eyes and said calmly, "You'll be wanting to chop extra wood tonight, while I prepare everything for our guests. However, before you go outside, could I ask you to move Sarah's cradle into our bedroom?"

She went to her bedroom door, which was ajar, and opened it for him, as if he could not easily have shouldered his way through the doorway. The purpose of her gesture was, of course, to indicate to him which of the doors on either side of the fireplace was the one to her bedroom, so that he would not have to show his ignorance. With the three men watching her, she told Morgan Harris to put the cradle at the end of the bed, then thanked him as he brushed past her on his way out of the room again.

While Morgan crossed the room to get his overcoat down from the peg by the front door, Barbara moved in the direction of the back door, throwing him a glance over her shoulder, hoping that he would take the hint and follow her. He did.

To the three guests, she said, "I suppose that you have some things to collect from outside. If you're wanting to bed your horses down for the night, there's a shed on the other side of the drive by the house."

To Morgan Harris, she whispered, as she opened the back door for him, "Look left and you'll find the wood for chopping on the other side of the well."

The air was cold and clear. The moon, a disk of hard silver, was high overhead, shedding bright light on everything below. Morgan nodded his understanding, and she closed the door behind him, leaving it unlatched so that he could reenter with an armload of wood. She turned to the center of the room again, and her gaze clashed with the lieutenant's.

He had sent his men outside to attend to their duties. He said to his lovely, reluctant hostess, "I confess that I am surprised by all the changes in your life since I last saw you."

Barbara did not like being alone with the lieutenant, but she derived reassurance from the faint, rhythmic sounds of Morgan Harris chopping wood outside. She confined herself to saying, merely, "Fourteen months is a long time, and life does not stand still." Then, swiftly: "Let me put the baby down, and I will prepare your room."

With that, she disappeared into her bedroom and stood in the relative dark for a moment, shaking with fear and clutching at her precious baby. She drew several long breaths, to steady herself. Although she hated the thought of Sarah being out of her sight even for one minute with the lieutenant in her house, she knew she would have to put the baby down in order to prepare the spare room. She walked over to the bedroom windows and, before drawing the winter curtains against the chilly panes, paused for a frozen moment to watch Morgan Harris at his labors. It was strange to see a man standing there, bathed in moonlight. She could almost see the ghostly presence of her dead husband, Jonas, standing next to him.

She turned away from the window and prepared Sarah for bed. That task done, she put the happy baby in her cradle. It took great willpower. She went to the inside corner of the room, where the bedroom's small fireplace piggybacked on the masonry of the hearth in the sitting room. She stirred the embers of the fire she had built in the late afternoon to warm the room for Sarah. Then she went to her dresser and pulled some fresh sheets and a blanket out of the bottom drawer.

She carried these out of her bedroom and into the sitting room, where the lieutenant was waiting. She explained the design of the little house. "The chimney is built centrally, so that each of the two bedrooms has a corner fireplace. Since it's going to be very cold tonight and I have not used the spare room yet this winter, I'll make a small fire in your room to chase out the initial chill." She bade him follow her into the spare room, indicating that he should take a candle from the table.

The room was tiny, with space only for a single bed and a night table, upon which the lieutenant placed the candle. In silence, he accepted from her hands the pillow and comforter that had been stored atop the unmade bed and watched her snap out the bed linens, fit them and smooth out the blanket. Then she took the pillow and comforter from him and plumped them atop the other covers.

"There, sir," she said, turning to him, when her task was done. She looked around the little room. "It will be a fine night's lodging for you once I tend to the fire." She nodded toward the corner made by the intersection of the two inside walls, indicating the little fireplace, identical to the one in her bedroom.

She heard the sounds of the return into the sitting room of the lieutenant's two men.

"A most interesting night's lodging," the lieutenant said.

The look on her enemy's face in the soft, eerie candle-light was so knowing that Barbara was relieved to escape the room and to encounter Morgan at the moment he was reen-tering the house through the back door, his arms laden with wood. The lieutenant followed her back into the sitting room, where he conferred with his men and sorted through the belongings they had brought in.

"Bring some wood into the spare room," she said to Morgan, "and help me establish a small fire for the lieuten-ant before we tend to the embers in our bedroom." Her heart skipped a beat when she realized that she had almost slipped and said "my bedroom."

Morgan stacked all but three logs by the hearth and then followed Barbara into the spare room, where they quickly got a welcoming little blaze going in the fireplace. They did not dare any private conversation. When they returned to the sitting room, it was to confront the three men, all in a line, staring at them.

The lieutenant stepped forward. "We're curious to know why it is, Mr. Harris, that there's a bedroll on the back of your horse. Do you not live here?"

Since Morgan had stabled his horse with the intention of merely eating supper here, he had naturally not brought in his gear. He draped his arm possessively over Barbara's shoulder and drew her to him, thereby inadvertently help-ing to restrain her immediate impulse to run into her bed-room and grab her baby. He said, "I've been away from home for three days on a hunt and was more interested to get inside—for obvious reasons—than to unpack my horse. Call it the enthusiasm of a newlywed man." He shrugged. "I hardly need the bedroll tonight, anyway."

"Where's the game you shot?" the lieutenant wanted to know.

"Sold," Morgan replied levelly. "We've enough game locally for our own consumption."

The lieutenant regarded the couple, who were standing together so intimately, and was almost persuaded to believe their story. There was no reason to doubt it, in fact, except some sense that told him that all was not as it seemed.

"And, for that matter," Morgan continued, the deep rumble of his voice vibrating through Barbara's body as she stood against him, "we were interrupted in the midst of a rather, ah, satisfying homecoming when you three came calling."

With his free hand, he took Barbara's chin and lifted it so that she would look into his eyes. She succeeded in playing along with his story by sending him a sultry look that far exceeded his expectations and sent desire coursing through him.

He looked away from her and then back at the men, his midnight-blue eyes glittering. He said, roughly, "Well, now, you've got what you need, and I've got what I need. Good night, men."

Still holding her, he turned her toward her bedroom. When they arrived at the threshold, the lieutenant called out to his back, "And the guitars, those are yours, Mr. Harris?"

Morgan looked back over his shoulder and saw the lieutenant regarding the stringed instruments hanging on the wall. "Who else's would they be?" he returned.

"You'll play for us now, Mr. Harris?" the lieutenant asked. "A little entertainment before retiring?"

Morgan shook his head. "We keep country hours, and it's late for a man who's been up since before dawn. In any case, my sense of entertainment goes in another direction just now," he said, his meaning obvious. He nodded toward the instruments. "Bring Mrs. Ross tomorrow, and I'll entertain her with American music and song for as long as she likes." He said again, by way of dismissal, "Good night, then, men."

With her back to his front, he gently propelled his temporary wife to the door to their temporary bedroom.

At the threshold, she glanced up at him. "Morgan?"

"Yes, my love?"

"Do we need to worry about properly banking the fire in the sitting room?"

Morgan surveyed the men, who were still standing there in the sitting room, watching them wordlessly. "They're big boys and know about fires," he replied.

"And the doors," she added. "They'll need to bar both the front and back doors."

"They'll see to the doors, as well," Morgan said, with a nod to the men. Then he closed the bedroom door with his boot, and it shut behind them with a definitive click.

Suddenly they were alone in her bedroom, which was warm and dimly lit by the live coals of the fireplace. His arm was still around her, and he moved his hand from her shoulder to her mouth so that she would not cry out. When he clamped down her her other hand with his free one, her heart lurched painfully in fear.

He bent to whisper into her ear, "Don't be afraid. This is for you." He emphasized his statement with a gesture of the hand that held hers.

She had just barely become aware that he was handing her the coins he had received from Lieutenant Richards when he continued, low, into her ear, "I'm sorry I covered your mouth, but I did not want you speaking to me at a moment when we were supposed to be locked in a passionate embrace."

She nodded her understanding, and he lowered his hand from her mouth and released her fingers. Her heart returned to its accustomed place. They did not move away from one another, but stood together and listened, briefly, to the sounds coming from the other side of the door. They heard the movements and muffled comments of the men as they prepared to retire for the night.

He whispered, "There's no choice but for me to spend the night in this room. I'll take the armchair by the windows."

In the glow from the fireplace, she could see the earnest set of his features. She nodded and whispered back, standing on tiptoe to reach his ear, "Maybe you should bring the chair closer to the fire."

He shook his head. "I couldn't move it without making noises that might be suspicious. We'll have to leave things as they are. Now, there's a question I still need to ask you. A crucial question."

She raised her brows, inviting the demand.

She could just discern the gleam of humor in the depths of his eyes when he sounded out the words, "What is your name?"

She bit her lower lip to keep from laughing. In swallowing her nervous laugh, she brushed her breasts against his chest. She hardly noticed it, but he did, acutely.

"Barbara," she breathed.

"All right, then, Barbara." He moved away from her. "I didn't think 'my love' could serve me on every occasion." He thought it a good idea just then to put some distance between them.

She, too, was happy to move away from his unsettling nearness. She went quietly to her dresser, where she took the coins he had handed her and slipped them into the top drawer. At the time Morgan had taken the money from the lieutenant, she had doubted his motives. She realized now that, upon recognizing that the lieutenant was determined to stay the night, her new hired hand had decided not to waste an opportunity to bring her some much-needed cash.

She hesitated before opening the second drawer of her dresser, which held her flannel night shift. She cast a glance over her shoulder and saw him standing on the other side of the bed with his back to her, staring down at the chair that was to be his for the night. He stood there immobile, and it occurred to her that he was giving her a chance to undress. She did so quickly and noiselessly. Then she unbound her hair, brushed it and braided it for the night.

When she went to the bed and pulled back the covers, about to get in, she became aware again of her inexperience as a hostess. She went to the little fireplace and added a log. Then, although her feet were cold, she crossed the room to where Morgan was standing and whispered to his back, "I have only one spare blanket, and that I gave to Lieutenant Richards. I have no extra covers for you. Maybe we can share the bedcover."

He shook his head, indicating that she need not worry about it, but he did not turn around.

Only when she was in bed and had the covers pulled up around her did he turn around, without looking at her, and sit down in the armchair. He took off his boots, softly. Then she heard him shift several times, as if trying to get comfortable. She lay awake for some time, staring into the darkness, listening to the sounds of the now-quiet house. From the sitting room came the buzz of regular snoring. From the other side of the wall that separated her room from Lieutenant Richards's, she heard nothing, not even the creak of the bed when he tossed, for the wall was very thick. She lay there, aware that Morgan was wide-awake, too.

After a while, she sat up. She let her flannel-covered arms and shoulders absorb the temperature of the room for a moment before deciding what must be done. Finally she crawled across the top of the bed, reluctant to expose her feet to the bite of the cold floorboards, and angled toward the armchair where Morgan was sitting. She leaned over the side of the bed. When she was close enough to him to see the gleam of his open eyes, she whispered, "You can't stay in the chair the whole night. You'll be stiff and tired and cold in the morning, and you'll not be able to hide it."

He peered at her in the darkness, not immediately responding. "What do you suggest?" he returned slowly.

She took a deep breath. "That you come to my bed. It's warm and comfortable," she said, her tongue tangling a little over the words, "and I can give you one of Jonas's nightshirts that I've saved." She paused. "I think you know what I mean...that what I mean is only...that..." She let her words trail off, unable to complete her thought.

"I do," he said, continuing to regard her, his face impassive, and impossible to read, given the dark shadows in the room. He did not jump to accept her offer. He saw that it would improve his physical condition in one way, but distinctly worsen it in another.

When he did not immediately respond, Barbara felt herself flushing in the darkness. "I didn't mean to suggest that you would even think...that is, that you were the kind who..." She broke off, then tried again, this time with dignity. "I did not mean to insult you, Mr. Harris."

He shook his head, raised his hand as if to cover her mouth, but without touching her, then shaped his lips as if to say, "Shh...." She was right, of course. To sit in the chair all night would bring a disaster of protesting bones and cold flesh come morning. He nodded and rose from the chair. She withdrew to her side of the bed, then got up to retrieve one of her husband's nightshirts from the back of a drawer. She crawled to the other side of the bed and moved across it slightly to give the item to him. Their hands collided in the darkness, and the electric spark of the touch surprised and disconcerted them both, albeit in different ways.

Barbara moved back quickly to her side and kept her eyes trained on a dark corner of the room while she heard the whisper-soft sounds of him divesting himself of coat, vest, shirt, breeches. She knew when he slipped the nightshirt over his head. Then she felt his weight when he sat on the edge. A man's weight on her bed, and it was both familiar and foreign, both repellent and exciting. When he moved in under the covers, she felt her heart pounding and her hands sweating from the fear that she had made a stupid mistake by inviting him in. With enemies occupying her sitting room and her spare room, she did not need a strange man invading her bed.

After a minute or two, as he lay there a few feet from her, breathing normally and not moving, her heart regained its usual tempo and her fear resolved itself into the knowledge that she had done the right thing by not letting him sit in the chair the night long, prey to the cold.

But he was awake, and she knew it. And she was awake, and he knew it.

He had found a pillow on his side, and his head was comfortable upon it. His body was warm under the covers, but he was a long way from being entirely comfortable in Mrs. Barbara Johnson's bed. He had foreseen the particular discomfort that would be his when she had asked him in, although he had also seen the wisdom of accepting the invitation. He needed the night's sleep, for he was tired after the past few days of hard riding. Tired, but not dead, he acknowledged—and death was the only condition that would have prevented him being mightily disturbed to find himself stretched out next to a beautiful, desirable woman without having license to touch her. The desire he felt for her was of his body, not of his heart. That much he knew. It was a paradoxical paradise.

As he stared up at the nothingness of the ceiling, he thought with a turn of wry humor that a beautiful woman's bed was near the last place he would have expected to find himself this night. A jail cell, perhaps. A pinewood coffin, just as likely. But here he was, improbably and damnably, lying next to this woman, not far from her baby, just able to catch her faint, milky scent on the bedclothes and the whiff of an unmasculine lavender on the nightshirt he wore. It had belonged to Jonas, she had said. Her dead husband, but not the father of her child.

He found a measure of pleasure in the fact that he had been able to take a bath that morning, and wash his hair. At least he was clean in her clean bed, and he felt he was entitled by right of cleanliness to settle into his position, being careful to keep his body to himself and on his side. He felt poised at several edges—the edge of death, the edge of sleep, the edge of hunger—and yet he felt himself being drawn back from those perilous edges. He could not have said just then whether he was oddly contented or deeply disturbed, satisfied or hungry, drowsy or aroused. He could have remained the night through, suspended in this complex state between waking and dreaming, between sharp awareness and relaxation, but the delicate tension of his balance was undone by the sleepy, cranky whine of a hungry baby.

Almost before the sound had penetrated his consciousness, he was aware that mother had already gone to child. She brought the baby back to bed with her and settled the covers around her in her half-seated position. He shifted his head, minimally, shamelessly, and saw her unbutton the bodice of her night shift. Through half-closed lashes, he saw exposed the tantalizing blue-white outline of a full breast and the baby's eager searching profile. He watched, himself eager, and awed, too, by the intimate beauty of the scene, feeling equal parts honor as a witness, envy of the infant and desire for the mother. For the life of him, he could not have looked away.

When the baby was sated, Barbara changed her and placed her back in the cradle. When she got back in bed, Morgan was facing away from her, breathing evenly. She knew he was not asleep. She stretched out and looked at the shape of his body beneath the covers and felt that his physical strength was both fearsome and reassuring. The night and the darkness were deep, and she felt a need to speak.

"I'm afraid," she whispered to his back.

She was not sure that he had heard her, for he did not signal that he had for a long time. But he had heard her, all right. He could remember only dimly the fear that she must be fearing now, for he had lost everything dear to him so long ago. After a while, he shifted slightly and said, partially over his shoulder, "You do not have to be afraid of me."

His words lifted a weight from her heart. He was right. For all her fears and worries, she did not have to fear him. He had supported her wild story of their marriage and his fatherhood; he had not taken the money from Lieutenant Richards and run when he had had the chance while chopping wood; he was not taking advantage of her vulnerability now, when she was not in a position to deny him a demand for the exercise of his "marital rights," while her enemies lay all around her, waiting to see or hear something amiss.

"Did you understand the lieutenant's implications?" she asked softly.

He turned onto his back, but did not shift his head to look at her. His eyes were open and on the ceiling. "Well enough, I think," he replied.

She felt he was owed some kind of explanation. "It was last year, during the British invasion of Baltimore," she whispered. "Mrs. Ross's husband was the commanding general of the British army." Her voice betrayed her anguish, shame and defiance. "There was nothing I could do. I had no defenses."

This pillow talk, and her confession, were more disturbing to him than silence, but a response was clearly called for. "I'm not judging you," he said softly.

"But others have, and others will," she whispered back, her voice wavering pitifully. "I'm afraid that Sarah may be taken from me."

He did not know how things went for an unwed mother when her child's custody was contested. He did not know the laws governing bastard children, American or otherwise, or what the effects of a hefty British bank balance would be in helping to interpret those laws. He had had his fill of lost causes, however, and this cause just might be one of those.

He asked, "Can the lieutenant easily disprove your story?"

"I'll be up before dawn to spread it in the neighborhood," she said, her low voice rich in resonance. Then, with less confidence: "I... I want to say... That is, Mr. Harris..."

His patience and his gallantry were being sorely tried. He cut her off with a quick "Consider my help part of the job, ma'am."

She said, just as quickly, "Half the money the lieutenant gave you is yours, you know."

He acknowledged this with a barely audible grunt.

Vastly relieved by this conversation, Barbara felt a pleasant tiredness seep through her body. As she drifted into the lovely, luxurious lap of sleep, it occured to her, for the third time this night, that she was wholly out of practice when it came to the fine points of social interaction.

With the laziest of lips, she murmured, "I must thank you, Morgan Harris, for all your kind help."

Morgan stared at the ceiling another good long while. Then he shifted his head and looked down, to see her eyelids droop shut and hear her breathing drift off into rhythms of sleep. He could not have comfortably choked out a "You're welcome, ma'am," and he was thankful that the effort was not necessary.

He sought and found that teetering edge between his drowsiness and his arousal, and he embraced it for the night. He hoped that, in the abandon of sleep, he would not do something unforgivable—which was to say husbandly.

Chapter Four

Sleep tasted delicious. Like a clover field in the afternoon with the sun scorching. That sweet buzzing of summer was in his ears, too, as if he were basking in that field, with no cares heavier than the sunshine on his shoulders. He cracked open his eyes and closed them again, blinded by a momentary flash of gold. He was lying beside an enchanted creek.... Yes, that was where he was. He must have been looking down at the sand in the creek bottom, for it was gold, bright-streaked by a high sun that glinted through the rippling water on this hot, lazy day.

But someone was missing. He could not remember who. The loss, and the lapse, disturbed him. Clouds came, covering the sun. He felt sad. No, more than sad. He felt that life had ceased to be worth living.

His eyes shot open because of this dream turned bad. He lay perfectly still, momentarily disoriented to find himself in a strange room, in a strange bed. The room was dim, and although the drapes had not yet been opened, he surmised that it was well past sunrise. He had overslept and would have to get on his way, fast.

He rolled his eyes about and caught sight of a woman who was standing at the end of the bed. She had thick, golden hair, bound in a heavy knot at her nape. Could it be the flash of her golden hair that he had seen in his dream?

Then he saw what she was doing and remembered where he was and mentally registered a mild *damn* for having opened his eyes a few minutes too late. She was standing over the cradle at the foot of the bed, and she was refastening the buttons of her blouse, which meant that he had just missed seeing her nurse her baby. He had enjoyed that rare moment of beauty the night before, and wished for it again. And yet it struck him as cruelly unfair that he should have to yearn for such a sight of beauty and intimacy and security, now that life held nothing further for him.

He sat up, and the slight creaking of the bed brought the woman's head around. In the dimness he saw the color rise in her cheeks as she fastened the last button of her blouse. Or else he imagined her blush, because of the way her eyes fluttered down, as if she were embarrassed by some look she read in his face.

He swung his legs over the side of the bed and sat there a moment, with his back to her. He listened for sounds coming from the other side of the bedroom door, but heard nothing. He placed his hands on his knees and let the fog of mingled sleep and sadness drift from his brain. Then he raked his hands through his hair and stroked his stubbled chin. He was wondering what he would do about finding a razor when a wholly unrelated and far more important thought occurred to him.

He turned his head and asked, softly, over his shoulder, "What do we do to alert your neighbors of the part I'm now playing in your household?"

She had picked up little Sarah and was holding her to her breast. She looked over at him. He guessed that the flush he perceived on her cheeks was due, this time, to her feelings for her child, strength of which had driven her to take a strange man into her bedroom and into her bed.

With one hand, she tugged her shawl into place across her shoulders. "I've taken care of it," she whispered back.

He frowned. "How?"

"I've already been to Ben Skinner's farm," she said, "and told him to spread the news about us this morning at the meetinghouse."

He must have overslept, and it must be much later in the morning than he had thought. He stood up and took the few steps from his side of the bed to the window. He pulled the heavy curtain back from the window and gazed outside. He thought the window faced west. There was only the faintest glow of daybreak red on the horizon. A distant cock began to crow. It was not late at all; it was, in fact, the very early morning.

His frown deepened. "What time is it?"

"Not much past five-thirty," she answered.

He looked back again, over his shoulder, at her. The grogginess was leaving his befuddled brain. "How far is Ben Skinner's farm?" he inquired.

"About three miles. Through the fields, that is. Not by the road."

His eyes had not left her face. He let the curtain fall. He glanced at the baby in her arms. "It's a good thing she didn't waken. I confess I would have been somewhat at a loss to know what to do to comfort her if she began to cry."

"I took her with me."

His brows raised, half in surprise, half in inquiry.

"Oh, she was bundled warm," Barbara assured him hastily. "I debated the risk of exposing her to the cold, but I've had her out with me before. She was in a sling under my coat, next to my heart the whole time." She nodded at the coat cast across the armchair by the window. She added, almost humorously, "I think she liked the little outing."

With fully adult sensibilities, he asked, "But did she like the hour?"

Her lips curved up into a sketch of the unselfconscious smile that had dazzled him the evening before. "She's hardly old enough to know what time of day it is, or to care," she answered, "as long as I'm there to take care of her."

"Wasn't she a bit of a hindrance, given the, what—six-mile ride?"

"No, and I walked," she replied. She registered his continuing surprise, and felt compelled to explain. "A horse might have made noise and awakened the men."

"True," he nodded. He looked at the cast-off coat, then at the door of the bedroom. "How did you get out of the room and back into it without making noise?"

With her head, she gestured toward the window. She shrugged.

So she had gone in and out the window. She must have left the room somewhere around four-thirty and returned just recently. He was impressed. He also recalled wisps of several dreams he had had this night, when the cold hand of death had grazed him, not once but twice. He considered, for a moment, that the dream might have been caused by little more than the drafts from the window passing over him; he acknowledged, on the other hand, that the dreams might have been a double portent of his fate.

"A six-mile trek with a baby, on a raw November morning?" he commented at last. "I'm not that inept—or that untrustworthy. I might have held her, if she had wakened."

Barbara's face softened a little. She shook her head. "It wasn't you," she assured him, "but the situation. I considered leaving her behind. In truth, I doubt she would have wakened during my absence. But...but I just couldn't imagine leaving her here, knowing they were in the next room." She glanced at the bedroom door. "I wouldn't have had a moment's peace, if I had left her behind, not knowing..." She shook off the thought and summoned up a shaky smile. "It was far, far better for me to take her with me."

He realized that she had a fierce love for her daughter. He admired her for it. He even understood it, but it left him cold, the thought of this fierce, living love. He felt as if a knife had sliced through him, or at least through the room, separating him from her. The phrase *Lost causes!* flashed through his brain. Then he nodded, as if satisfied with the information she had given him, and turned back to the window. He lifted the curtain again and squinted into the barely perceptible light of day.

"I'll have to get dressed," he said to the windowpane. He looked down at the sleeve of the nightshirt, which did not quite reach his wrist. His feet would soon be chilled if he did not get his stockings on.

She made an inarticulate noise of agreement. When he heard her busy herself at the little fireplace in the corner, thereby providing him his privacy, he went to the chair, where she had dropped her coat next to his clothing. He stepped into his buckskin breeches, then put on his stockings and pulled on his boots. He shrugged out of the nightshirt and into his relatively clean day shirt, which had come into his possession by less-than-honest means. He was not a bit sorry about having it to put on his back today.

He was poised to button the shirt when he heard sounds of movement in the sitting room, followed, almost immediately, by a peremptory knock on the bedroom door.

Barbara and Morgan exchanged a quick glance. Morgan silently motioned to Barbara to put the baby down as he took several strides toward her. When her arms were free, he clasped her hands in his, drew their arms between them so that they were standing close together. He called out, "Come in!" His voice was muffled, for he had bent his lips to her hair.

Lieutenant Richards opened the door, not waiting to be asked twice, and saw an affecting scene of the sweetest intimacy.

Morgan looked up over Barbara's head at the lieutenant. He lifted his brows in lazy inquiry, seemingly indifferent to the man's presence.

For Barbara, the moment was startling. Morgan had not yet buttoned his shirt or hitched his breeches, and he was holding her so that she was pressed against his bare chest and her forearms were flush against his skin. He was still warm from sleep and the bed, and he smelled good—musky and masculine, with the faintest trace of her lavender still clinging to him. His shirt was clean. Part of her cheek was against the cloth, and part was against his bare chest. Her heart beat uncomfortably beneath her ribs, and she did not quite know whether Morgan's nearness or the lieutenant's appearance had caused its quickening.

"You're still here," the lieutenant remarked.

"We live here," Morgan replied tranquilly. "How were your accommodations?"

"Satisfactory, thank you. The bed was comfortable, the room warm, and the house very quiet. Very quiet indeed."

"Of course. It's the country." Morgan said, resting his chin lightly on the top of Barbara's head. "We like the quiet, and we like our country hours for work. It's time I was getting to my chores." He looked down at Barbara, and she raised her eyes to him. "After I eat, that is. Do we have what we need, my love, to offer our guests a fine American breakfast?" At her nod, he smiled with his eyes and looked over her head again. Lifting one of Barbara's hands idly and raising it to his cheek, he said to the lieutenant, "We'll be out in a moment." He nuzzled Barbara's fingers with his lips. "We are still saying good morning to one another, and I'm not yet decent."

It was a dismissal, politely done, but with a hint of indifference and insolent laziness. He was, indeed, personally indifferent to the lieutenant. However, he had determined that an insolent laziness would be the most effective way to deal with a man like Lieutenant Richards. Morgan knew only two things about him, but those two things were significant: that Richards had attained only the rank of lieutenant, and that he had accompanied a woman across the Atlantic on the strength of one of her dreams.

Upon seeing Morgan Harris return his attentions to the lovely woman in his arms, the lieutenant felt a flash of annoyance. Knowing that he would look awkward simply standing there, watching the loving couple, the lieutenant shut the door, just as Morgan had wanted him to do.

When the door was closed and they were alone again, Barbara broke the embrace, and she felt Morgan release her willingly. In truth, she did not know whether she stepped away from him before he stepped away from her. She took a deep, steadying breath that she worried might betray her somehow. In some confusion, she stared down at her hand, which he had placed next to his cheek.

Before turning away from her to button his shirt, he noted the direction of her glance. "Sorry about the beard," he said, imagining that he had scratched her hand with his bristles. "I'll have to shave again one of these days."

"I was going to bring in your bedroll from your horse, when I came back in through the window," Barbara said, "so that you could have your things with you when you woke up. But then I realized that it might look odd, if you suddenly had your things in the morning when you did not have them the evening before."

He paused a moment before he said, "I don't have a razor with me."

"Oh," she said. She opened her mouth to speak again, but decided against it.

After a moment, he said levelly, "What I have in my bedroll is a bedroll."

She had wanted to ask him how it was that he had, apparently, come so far with so little, but knew it was none of her business. Instead, she said, "Well, you might wish to be growing a beard just now."

"I might," he agreed. He finished buttoning his shirt, stuffed his shirttails into his breeches, and finally hitched the breeches. Then he raised the suspenders hanging down from the breeches and placed them over his shoulders. He retrieved the leather vest from the arm of the chair, buttoned it, as well, then worked himself into his worn-out navy blue jacket.

Seeing him dressing himself, Barbara was suddenly more aware of the intimacy of the situation than she had been the night before, imagining him undressing. It was a curious reversal, and it underscored the enormity of what she had done in claiming him as her husband and sharing her bed with him. She debated the effect of his scruffy appearance on her guests and came to a decision.

"I've never disposed of my husband's shaving tackle," she said as she knelt and pulled a trunk out from under her bed. She unbuckled the leather straps and fished around for a long-unused razor and strop and brush. She even found a cracked shaving mirror wrapped in a towel placed in a shallow bowl. She put these articles on the dresser, next to a coral cameo brooch she kept on a doily. "You're welcome to use them, if you wish," she said, and knelt again to push the trunk back under the bed.

When she raised up again, her color was heightened, but that might have been due to her exertions with the trunk. She turned to the door, spurred by the sudden idea that she would feel, strangely, more comfortable in company with Lieutenant Richards and his two thugs than in company with Morgan Harris in the intense privacy of her bedroom.

"Wait," Morgan said softly as he came toward Barbara again. He rubbed his chin in a reference to the much-needed shave and said, "Thanks for the offer of the shaving kit, and we'll see how the day develops. But whatever else we do, we had better leave the bedroom together."

With that, he encircled her shoulder with one arm, gave her a significant look, and bolstered her morale by whispering in her ear, "We'll get rid of Lieutenant Richards, the two brutes and Mrs. Ross today. You'll see. Now, calm and confidence!"

Barbara looked back, anxiously, over her shoulder at the cradle. "And Sarah?"

"I'll bring the cradle out to the sitting room while you begin preparations for breakfast. Let me know what I need to do."

Barbara nodded, and together they left the bedroom. Leaning slightly into Morgan, she felt a certain calmness, and the feeling carried her through breakfast. Morgan helped her, in the ways that he could. At one point Barbara saw him leave the house by the front door. A few minutes later, he returned, bedroll in hand, and disappeared with it into the bedroom.

By the time day had broken and breakfast was finished, the plans for the day had been decided. The lieutenant and one of his men were going to fetch Mrs. Ross in Baltimore and bring her out to the farm, while the other man would stay behind to keep an eye on things. Lieutenant Richards had not described this brute's purpose in Barbara's house explicitly as guard duty, but that was the effect of his presence when the other two had left. As she went about her morning chores, Barbara could not rid herself of the awareness of the brute standing silently by the front door, watching her with unblinking eyes. It was unsettling to be watched so closely, and it only heightened the anxiety she already felt at her imminent meeting with Mrs. Ross.

Little Sarah chose this day to be fussy, as well. It seemed to Barbara that every task took twice as long to accomplish, be it the sweeping or the baking or the washing, because Sarah needed attention.

At least she could be glad that Morgan chose to stay near the house. After he took his horse to the barn, where he pitched some hay, he chopped more wood out back, tended to the well and fed the chickens. He found a variety of things to do, without having to be told, and whatever he did he made sure to come in and out of the house with some regularity. Barbara was always reassured to hear his boots on the back steps.

Once Morgan came during the interval when the brute had stepped outside to relieve himself. The baby woke from a fitful doze and started to whine pitifully. Barbara was at the kitchen area, trying to make some muffins, and at the sound of her cranky baby's cry, she sighed and crossed to the cradle at the hearth. She lifted Sarah and coddled her, hoping to ease whatever discomfort was causing her fussiness.

She looked over at Morgan, who was hanging his overcoat on the peg by the front door, and said, "I think she might be teething."

Morgan took a couple of steps toward mother and daughter and critically surveyed the red, wrinkly baby face.

"A three-month-old would not be teething," he observed thoughtfully.

Barbara's heart skipped a beat. She might have made a serious blunder with Mrs. Ross if she had offered teething as an explanation for little Sarah's mood today. "You're right," she breathed, and reinforced the idea for herself. "She's just three months old."

"And she's big for her age, I think," Morgan continued. He reached out and placed his hands over the little shape in the blanket, examining its size. "She was big at birth and takes after my side of the family. I was a monster."

Barbara looked up and into his eyes and suddenly felt that the topic was too personal to pursue. She asked, "Do you want to hold her so that she gets used to you?"

At that moment, the brute returned to the house by way of the front door and took up his standing position there, next to the settee.

Morgan shook his head, nearly glad for the interruption, for he had had enough of holding the baby in that brief moment the night before when he had taken Sarah from Barbara's arms and claimed her as his own.

The rest of the morning and early afternoon passed placidly enough. Morgan found inside chores to occupy him, such as sharpening knives. The midday meal was taken without ceremony, and afterward Morgan decided to make an effort to shave. Barbara studiously avoided watching him perform this personal task, and she did not look at him afterward to judge the results. After duly noting that he stored the bowl with the shaving implements by the sink, she continued readying her house for the unwanted guest. When it was time for Sarah's feeding, she went into her bedroom and closed the door and nursed her in privacy.

During the nursing, she heard the sounds of a guitar. She assumed that Morgan must have taken it down to prepare for the concert he had so cavalierly promised for Mrs. Ross. What she heard were the warped sounds of a guitar lamentably out of tune. The last time the guitar had been played must have been well over twenty years before, a good year before her father's death. The unpromising pluckings and plunkings coming from the sitting room gave her a sinking feeling that the afternoon was doomed to disaster.

When she was done nursing, she rearranged her bodice, cleaned up her baby and reentered the sitting room. At her entrance, Morgan looked up from the guitar he held on his knee, and Barbara felt a quick spasm inside her at sight of his clean-shaven face. He was still not a handsome man in any classical sense, but he was mightily attractive when he raised his midnight-blue eyes to her and smiled at her in a way that seemed to acknowledge her response to him.

She put Sarah back in her cradle, smoothed her skirts and went to the table, where she busied herself with the teapot and teacups and spoons. Morgan continued to twang and hum and sing softly, but no real music emerged.

When the knock came at the door, Barbara's heart leapt to her throat. Morgan stood and hung the guitar on the wall in its place. The brute turned and opened the door.

To Barbara's surprise, it was not the lieutenant who walked through the door, but rather her closest neighbor, who greeted her with a brisk, "Mrs. Harris, I've brought you a present! Well, actually, it's for your husband." The man looked past the unsmiling, unpleasant oaf who had opened the door and extended his hand to Morgan.

"Ben Skinner," Morgan said quickly, coming forward, and taking his hand. "I give you Good Day!"

"Morgan Harris." Ben Skinner opened his overcoat and drew out a scrawny excuse for a pup, with a white-and-liver coat, glossy brown eyes and a shiny black button nose. "You said you were wanting a house dog," Ben Skinner explained. "My bitch had whelped, and so when I heard you was wanting a dog, I couldn't resist bringing the prize of the lot over to you!"

Morgan sized up the neighboring farmer as he took the "prize" from Ben Skinner's outstretched hands. He saw an aging farmer with a gaunt frame and wizened features. He also saw sharp old eyes returning his scrutiny.

Barbara thanked her neighbor and exchanged a few conventional nothings with him. Privately she was at a loss to understand Ben Skinner's offer of the pup. Then she remembered having told him earlier this morning of Morgan Harris's rather whimsical recommendation that she get a dog to announce the arrival of visitors.

The pup was not yet trained for the task, for it seemed more interested in gazing quizzically into Morgan Harris's face than in yipping and yapping at the jangle of the carriage that drew up to the house just then.

Barbara's heart began to beat uncomfortably. She glanced at the cradle and resisted the impulse to go to it. She looked down at her work-roughened fingers and contemplated the wedding band on her finger, her magic circle of protection. When she raised her head again, her features were set and smooth.

Then came the dreaded knock at the door.

Chapter Five

Barbara nodded, first to Ben Skinner, then to Morgan Harris, signaling that she would open the door. She moved forward and gestured to the brute guarding the door to get out of the way. He obeyed.

She made a mental effort to control her expression when she lifted the latch and swung the door open. However, she was aware that her face must have registered some kind of shock to behold the woman who was leaning delicately on Lieutenant Richard's arm.

She was the most elegant woman Barbara had ever seen. She wore a hat with a stylish brim and a dainty crown encircled by a wide riband finished with a pretty bow. The hat framed blond curls that feathered her forehead and cheeks, setting off her delicate coloring to perfection, while her brown eyes were enhanced by her coat of golden brown silk. The coat was trimmed with applied piping arranged in flower shapes on the bust and at the wrists and in elongated curves on the skirt borders, and it fastened with loops. She carried a matching parasol and wore kid boots.

She was of a height with Barbara, but built on less generous lines. She was perhaps ten years Barbara's senior, and she was in the fullness of her mature beauty. She was, at once, everything Barbara had expected and nothing she could have imagined. She was not the ugly monster Barbara had half hoped for, half feared. Nor was she the pitiful, shrunken, grieving widow. She was beautiful and elegant. She seemed ladylike and refined. But Barbara knew her to be rich and powerful and determined. She had crossed the ocean on the strength of a dream, with the intention of taking away another woman's child. From the look in the older woman's eyes as she surveyed Barbara—a look that was at once warm and inviting and assessing and knowing—Barbara thought her wicked.

"Lieutenant Richards," Barbara said, calmly enough, stepping aside to allow the newcomers to enter her house, "you have returned and brought Mrs. Ross." Her voice ended on a faintly rising note, for although no question was involved, she was inviting an introduction.

"Yes, ma'am," the lieutenant replied, with his hand poised just behind Mrs. Ross's back, allowing her to precede him through the doorway. "This, as you must guess, is Mrs. Ross. Mrs. Ross, I present to you Mrs. . . . Harris."

Mrs. Ross crossed the threshold and was followed by the lieutenant, who told the brute to go outside and wait on the porch with the other man. When the door was closed behind the lieutenant's man, Mrs. Ross took a further step into the room and said, in a cultured voice, "How interesting it is to meet you, Mrs. Harris, after all this time. Nevertheless, I have the oddest feeling that I already know you, somehow." So saying, she sighed lightly, smiled sweetly, and looked expectantly at the other two men, awaiting the proper introduction.

Barbara indicated Ben Skinner, whom she announced as her most proximate neighbor, and then turned to Morgan Harris, who stepped forward. When Barbara introduced him to Mrs. Ross as her husband, he inclined his head. Barbara read the expression on his face as *I dare you, Mrs. Ross, to challenge our story!* From the chilling sweetness on Mrs. Ross's face when she curtsied so politely and yet so condescendingly in return, Barbara imagined that Mrs. Ross accepted the challenge.

Mrs. Ross did not look around her or survey her surroundings or betray any sign that she found herself any place other than the most fashionable drawing room in London.

"You are from Maryland, Mr. Harris?" she asked first.

"No, ma'am," he replied, offering nothing further.

"No?" She paused the proper amount of time, then asked directly, "Where are you from, sir?"

"The colony of Quebec," he answered, to Barbara's surprise.

"Ah, Lower Canada," Mrs. Ross corrected, insisting on the British division of the territory. "Were you born there?"

"In Massachusetts," he replied, surprising Barbara again, "the western part."

"I see," Mrs. Ross said, as if fascinated by the detail. She turned to Barbara. "And you, Mrs. Harris?" she inquired, and softened the question with the charming explanation that the young and mobile backgrounds of American citizens were endlessly interesting to Europeans. "You are from Maryland?"

"Born and bred," Barbara said.

"And married?"

"Of course," Barbara said without a blink and attempted to turn the tables. It was her house, after all, and she should not be subject to answering questions that set her at a disadvantage. "And you, ma'am? Where are you from?"

Mrs. Ross laughed, once, gaily. "I'm a Winthrop," she said easily, "and my long and tedious family history is to be found described in detail in *Debrett's*." After a moment, she added, *"Debrett's Peerage."*

Barbara felt the slap. It was a gentle one, but a slap all the same. She made a mental note not to follow through on any subsequent lines of inquiry that Mrs. Ross might initiate. She would not want to give her enemy another such opening.

"Let me help you with your coat," Barbara said. "That is, if you are still determined to stay."

"Determined?" Mrs. Ross echoed, considering the phrasing. "Compelled, more like," she said, with a wistful smile, implying that her will was subject to the dictates of some higher force.

"Fine, then," Barbara replied, extending her hands to help. "I'll be pleased to visit with you. Your coat, ma'am."

Barbara nearly sighed when she touched the fine material of the coat, and almost gasped when she saw the dress underneath. Although Barbara had no way of knowing the fashion that prevailed in foreign capitals, she guessed that Mrs. Ross's dress was an extraordinary garment.

Mrs. Ross's dress was fashioned of a golden brown silk that matched the coat. It had a high waistline to which was attached a slightly gored skirt with a gathered panel at the center of the back. The collar was high and stiffened and made Mrs. Ross's lovely face appear a very flower emerging from a splendid sheath. It was the sleeves, however, that drew Barbara's eye and admiration. They were long, with short puffed oversleeves of stepped bands, faced with satin, and with wristbands fastened with an exquisite little button. Barbara had never seen arms so curvaceously and cunningly covered.

"How kind," Mrs. Ross said as she relinquished her coat to Barbara's care. She proceeded to remove her bonnet.

Mrs. Ross handed this, too, to Barbara, who murmured that she would take care of Mrs. Ross's things. With the coat folded carefully over her arm, Barbara retreated to her bedchamber to lay the items across her bed. Standing beside the bed, she paused a moment, looking down at the line of fine golden brown silk curving against the coarse white cotton of her candlewick bedspread. In her mind's eye, the coat came alive and appeared to her as a silky, slithery queen snake sunning itself on white rock. She felt a tremor of fear pass through her.

The next moment, the bed itself came alive, and she remembered vividly what had transpired in that bed with General Robert Ross. Another tremor passed through her. Was it fear again? Or lust?

Barbara smiled. There *had* been lust in her on that late summer's afternoon, fourteen months ago, when she had entered her house to find the handsome British general waiting for her in this bedroom. He had been seated at his ease in the chair by the window, one leg crossed elegantly over the other, his hands resting comfortably on the arms of the chair, his gray eyes level and focused on her as she entered her bedroom. She remembered that the hateful blaze red of his army coat had offended her eyes. She remembered that he had forced her to undress at the point of his sword. And then he had forced her to undress him.

Yes, there had been lust in her that day. Blood lust. And she had lived to see him dead.

Her fear receded, and her resolve returned. Metaphorically she armed herself to do battle with the viperous Sarah in order to keep possession of her little one, and then she returned to the sitting room. There she found that Morgan Harris had, apparently, been asking the polite questions one asked of a traveler from abroad. Is this your first trip, ma'am, to the New World? Was your sea voyage pleasant? What sights have you seen in Baltimore? Do you appreciate the wild beauty of our country? Mrs. Ross was responding in kind. As Barbara crossed the room to her visitor, she noted that Mrs. Ross glanced, once, furtively, in the direction of the cradle.

Barbara came forward, saying, "I can offer you coffee and muffins, Mrs. Ross." She gestured toward the settee. "But first I must offer you a seat." She turned to Ben Skinner and inquired, "You came to give my husband some advice on the fences in the south fields, did you not?"

Ben Skinner was not a quick man to take a hint, and he was about to protest that he had come only to deliver the pup when Morgan followed Barbara's lead. He clapped the old farmer lightly on the back and informed the group that "Ben Skinner was never one to sit with a cup of coffee and plate of muffins in the middle of the day when there's work to be done, and neither am I." Morgan Harris pointedly regarded Lieutenant Richards and his two brutes. "Neither will I turn down an offer of help from three extra pairs of strong hands. What do you say, men?"

Morgan Harris had framed his question as a pleasant invitation, but something in his manner made it clear that he had no intention of abandoning Barbara to face an inquisition party of one woman and three men. It was also clear that Lieutenant Richards took his orders from Mrs. Ross.

Mrs. Ross glanced at her lieutenant and said lightly, "What a charming idea, Timothy, that you work for an afternoon on an American farm! Why, it will be an experience for you and your men, I am sure!"

The lieutenant hesitated minimally, then bowed obediently and snapped for his men to come to attention and follow him. The men proceeded to leave the house. Still holding the adoring pup, Morgan went to the peg to retrieve his coat, examined one of the capacious pockets and decided, on an impulse, to put the pup in it. "Should I call this poor excuse for a dog Pockets, do you think, Ben Skinner?"

"Oh, any name will do," the old farmer replied. Then he betrayed himself at last with the observation "We had not intended to name him at all."

Morgan laughed, once, mirthlessly. "You intended to drown him, then, this runt?"

The old farmer's brown, weather-beaten face reddened slightly. He coughed, bringing up phlegm, and said, "Well, now, he's a frisky pup, which is what I thought this morning when I had the idea to bring him over to you!"

"You're a good neighbor," Morgan said to that, holding the door so that Ben Skinner could precede him out to the porch, where the lieutenant and his two men were waiting. "As I've told my wife, time and again."

Ben Skinner's eyes crinkled, as if at a good joke, and he thanked Morgan Harris kindly. Before Morgan closed the door behind them, shutting Barbara in with Mrs. Ross, the older woman turned to Morgan. With a tiny frown between her lovely brown eyes, she said, "You'll not play the guitar for me, Mr. Harris? Lieutenant Richards promised me that you would."

Morgan Harris smiled a very winning smile, causing Mrs. Ross's brow to rise slightly, and said, "Upon my return from the south fields, ma'am, after you've had all your questions satsified by my wife." Then the door closed with a tug and a click.

Morgan's voice had sounded confident, but Barbara was hardly reassured that Morgan's guitar playing would convince Mrs. Ross that the guitars that hung on her walls were his. She would have to convince Mrs. Ross that he was her child's father on the strength of her own arguments. She needed authority. She offered again, with the edge of command in her voice, "You'll be seated, Mrs. Ross."

Mrs. Ross surveyed her hostess. "You'll not be needing help with the coffee and muffins?"

Barbara shook her head. "The tray is already prepared and awaiting only our appetites. Please," she said, and gestured toward the settee.

Mrs. Ross chose to sit. She arranged herself gracefully on the settee, spreading her skirts elegantly, enhancing the homely piece of furniture much as a valuable jewel would the plainest of settings.

Barbara walked the few steps to the table, where she had laid out a tray with the necessary china.

"You know why I have come, Mrs. Harris," Mrs. Ross said to her back.

"I do," Barbara said without turning around.

"Your husband," Mrs. Ross said, with a slight ironic intonation, "does not wear a wedding band."

Easy shot. Barbara's hands did not even tremble when she picked up the laden tray from the table. She turned around and walked steadily to the settee, next to which she had positioned a small table.

"He works with his hands," Barbara said with a brief, confident smile, "and finds the wearing of his ring, for many reasons, impractical."

Mrs. Ross shrugged artfully, but did not otherwise challenge the explanation.

Barbara poured Mrs. Ross a cup of coffee, and as she was handing it to her guest she asked, directly, "But why do you make the comment about my husband's wedding ring?"

Mrs. Ross accepted the cup and smiled, with no trace of self-consciousness. "Do I insult you, my dear?"

Barbara said, "That is not an answer to my question."

Mrs. Ross's smile faded, and was replaced by a look of dawning comprehension. "Why, yes, I almost see what my hus—" She broke off. "That is to say, I quite understand what it is between you and your—your husband. He is a handsome man. Well, not handsome, precisely! But we women do respond to that certain sort of something in a man that makes him irresistible, don't we? So we will agree that your Mr. Harris is not handsome, but rather more interesting for his lack of male beauty!" She smiled assessingly. "And you, my dear—! What he sees in you is entirely evident in every detail of your very appealing person."

Barbara had colored faintly at the casual acknowledgment of Morgan Harris's attractions. She suppressed her embarrassment in order to pursue her direct line of inquiry. "Given that, then, why do you doubt the reality of our marriage?"

Mrs. Ross's smile remained, and her voice was rather airy. "Perhaps because I do not know whether Americans have more…elastic, let us say…notions of relations between men and women than the English, whether Americans are freer in their habits, whether Americans—"

Barbara broke in. "You are in the land of the Puritans, Mrs. Ross, and more than one English traveler to this country has misjudged Americans by the standards that reign in European capitals."

It was Mrs. Ross's turn to color slightly, for she did not miss the barb, which might well have been aimed at her late husband. She took a strategic sip of coffee.

Barbara took advantage of Mrs. Ross's momentary silence to insist, "My husband and I have been married a year. Our daughter is three months old. How can you come to me, a woman you have never met and do not know, and doubt my story?"

Mrs. Ross looked straight over the rim of her cup. Then she lowered it and positioned it precisely in the saucer. She shook her head slowly. Something in her manner changed. She looked up, in abstraction, at the ceiling, and stated in a voice that might have been inspired by divine authority, "You see, Mrs. Johnson, I have never had such a dream. Timothy told you of it, did he not, this dream that my husband had had a child? I happened to recount the dream to Timothy the next morning. Indeed, I could hardly have done otherwise, for it was so vivid that I was still in the grip of it throughout the day. Throughout the week, in fact! So I told him the details, the precise details, down to the color of the hair of the mother of my husband's child, and he told me—" here her lustrous brown eyes lowered to focus on Barbara "—of you."

Barbara's heart was beating uncomfortably, but she felt in control of her facial features. She chose not to correct Mrs. Ross's use of her widow's name. Instead, she shrugged artfully, as Mrs. Ross had before, her careless shoulder giving her opinion of the predictive reliability of dreams. She knew that this was the moment to ask, "Would you like to see my baby, Mrs. Ross?"

"Oh, yes," Mrs. Ross said, a little breathless. She was unable, for all her elegant refinement, to keep the catch from her voice. She was unable to swallow the spasm of emotion that closed her throat ever so slightly. This catch, this tiny constriction of air, told Barbara all she needed to know of the desperate drive that had led this woman to cross an ocean.

Barbara placed her cup on the tray perched atop the little table and walked over to the cradle, where the baby was awake and beginning to fuss. She drew her precious love into her arms, wisely keeping her back to Mrs. Ross, so that her own desperate love for Mrs. Ross's dead husband's child could not be seen on her face. By the time she turned and walked back to the chair, she felt she had composed herself.

"This is Sarah," Barbara said, sitting back down, "who was named after my mother."

It was physically painful for Barbara to see Mrs. Ross's face as she gazed at the baby. It was the most naked face Barbara had ever seen. Gone was the aristocratic countenance of the elegant Englishwoman whose family had been among the nobility for God only knew how many generations. Gone was the mature beauty of a most fashionable woman. Barbara saw instead the face of a woman who grieved for her dead husband, a woman who craved a child, a woman who had known great loss and the continuing emptiness of the unfulfilled desire for new life.

"It is a remarkable coincidence, is it not, the fact that your baby bears the same name as myself?" Mrs. Ross asked, somewhat mechanically, as she gazed, at once critically, lovingly, covetously, piteously, and viciously, at the helpless baby, the flesh of her dead and beloved husband.

Barbara had the answer to that. "No more a coincidence than the fact that we both have blond hair," she said.

The naked moment had passed. The elegant beauty, rich and refined, had returned. Mrs. Ross looked away from the baby and smiled at Barbara with steely purpose. "Not entirely a coincidence, perhaps! After all, one might argue that what attracted my husband to me might also have attracted him to you."

Barbara maintained a dignified silence.

Mrs. Ross's face became warm and conspiratorial. "Let us speak woman to woman, Mrs. Harris!" she said, mistress of herself and the moment. "You surely do not mean to deny that my husband and you were intimate, do you?"

"Mrs. Ross—" Barbara began, but was cut off.

"Do not deny it, my dear, and undermine your credibility!" Mrs. Ross advised her. "I know from Lieutenant Richards exactly how it was between you and my husband. How, when, and under what circumstances."

"I do not recall seeing Lieutenant Richards..." Barbara began.

"And Robert's last letters to me were different. I think I knew, even then, upon reading them, that he had found someone..."

"On the various occasions I might have met with your husband," Barbara finished.

This last phrase caught Mrs. Ross's attention. *"Met?"* she echoed lightly, her mouth twisting. "When you *met* with him?"

"What would you have me say?"

"When you made love with him," Mrs. Ross said, an edge piercing the round contours of her cultured voice.

It would be pointless for Barbara to deny that General Robert Ross had invaded her body, just as it would be pointless to deny that his troops had invaded Maryland and occupied the North Point during August and September of the previous year. It seemed all the more ironic to deny it when she held against her shoulder the beautiful product of the masculine invasion of her body.

Barbara could, however, contest the phrasing. "It did not seem like love to me," she said.

Mrs. Ross's gaze was sharp. "My husband was a handsome and powerful man. I had many years of marriage with him to observe his effect on women and how they responded to him."

And Barbara had had the privilege of alerting American sharpshooters to General Ross's maneuvers on the day he was ambushed and killed. "It was war in this country, Mrs. Ross," Barbara reminded her, "and your husband was the commander of the enemy."

Mrs. Ross's voice was sharp. She rapped out, "Do you deny that this child, Sarah, was sired by my husband?"

Barbara hated to lie. She hated the necessity of it, for it violated her habit of stark honesty. Last year she had experienced the kind of violation that a woman could know only from the body of a man. Now she was experiencing a new kind of violation, that of a woman by a woman. It went just as deep, the outrage of this womanly violation, and it felt as sharp and humiliating as a rape.

"I do deny it, Mrs. Ross," Barbara said, her words low but unmistakable, her voice unwavering.

Mrs. Ross was checked. She had no way to prove otherwise; she had nothing but her strong intuitions. She had been initially elated and vindicated when Lieutenant Richards had recounted to her this morning that the American woman indeed had a baby. However, she and Lieutenant Richards had agreed that the presence of Morgan Harris in Barbara Johnson's house presented an unexpected difficulty. However, there must be ways of investigating legal marriage lines, Mrs. Ross imagined, even in this savage country.

"And you persist in denying it, even knowing that I can give this child all that you cannot?" Mrs. Ross said, with a fine blend of condescension and reprimand. "Education, clothing, entrée into the best society, a grand name recognized and respected everywhere?"

Barbara had never before seen in such sharp focus the material shabbiness of her life. She had never felt so poor. She had never felt so vulnerable. The violation was complete. She felt that a stake had been thrust deep in her love-softened heart, so that her tender mother's heart, with no defenses, was bleeding inside her. She felt a hemorrhage of mother love inside her. She felt blood drip down to soak her guts. She felt blood bathing her tongue.

She felt her baby's shuddery breathing against her breast and shoulder. She smelled her butter-biscuit skin and scalp. She felt the milk flowing in her breasts for her daughter and did not care if it seeped through her common, workaday blouse, staining it for this elegant witch to see. She was a pool of spilled blood inside, but she nonetheless knew how to resist Mrs. Ross, just as she had known how to resist Mrs. Ross's husband.

She shook her head and said, with a calculated pity, "You have come on a useless errand, Mrs. Ross."

Chapter Six

Half an hour or more later, the men returned from the south fields. By that time, the women had tacitly decided to continue their visit in correct conversation. Mrs. Ross might have drawn first blood in the encounter, but Barbara had effectively turned back Mrs. Ross's offensive by maintaining a firm position. Barbara knew that Mrs. Ross was not entirely vanquished, and so did not let down her guard, but she thought that the worst of the trial was over—for now.

They were discussing polite nothings when Morgan Harris walked through the front door, followed only by Lieutenant Richards. The two brutes were commanded to remain on the porch, and Ben Skinner was on his way home. Neither woman was sorry that their tête-à-tête was at an end.

Morgan took the little dog out of his coat pocket, then shrugged out of his coat and hung it, as if from long habit, on the peg next to Barbara's. He offered to take the lieutenant's greatcoat, as well, all the while informing the ladies that "The fences are mended, and it's a satisfaction to have them repaired, since I had left the chore undone for so long." He knelt down and, with hands cupped to let the dog down on the floor, said, "Go, Pockets, and find yourself a place on the hearth." Pockets scurried obediently across the floor to the fire.

Without taking further apparent interest in the outcome of the ladies' discussion, Morgan walked to the sink stone where sat a basin of tepid water. He dipped his hands in it, scrubbed them, and wiped them on a towel. Carrying the towel back across the room, he handed it to the lieutenant, silently inviting him to do the same. He came to perch on the arm of the chair where sat Barbara, so that he could face Mrs. Ross. He did not lean the whole of his weight on the chair, but counterbalanced it by levering his two arms against the arm of the chair, whose sides he gripped with both hands.

"All in all," Morgan continued easily, seemingly heedless of his leg resting casually against Barbara's side, "I cannot complain about having had the extra hands to help me today. Thank you, Mrs. Ross, for having encouraged them."

From the kitchen area, the lieutenant called out, "Does that mean that I no longer owe you the other half of the expenses for last night's lodging?"

Morgan looked over at the lieutenant critically. "Yes, then, let's call the account quits. It was an honest afternoon's work you did for me." He looked down at Barbara before he reached out for one of the muffins on the still-full plate. He smiled and asked, "Everything satisfactory here?"

Barbara felt suddenly susceptible to the effect of his smile, and she blinked in surprise. "Why, yes," she said, almost blankly, and nodded behind her to the cradle, where she had replaced Sarah when she had quieted down. "The baby's had a crankier day than usual, I am afraid, but other than that—" she turned back to Mrs. Ross "—we are agreed to understand one another."

Mrs. Ross's social smile was anything but agreeable or understanding. "Why, yes," she said, but refused to linger on the subject. She glanced at the instruments on the wall. "I believe that you had agreed to entertain us with some music."

Barbara's heart quailed at the thought that her staunch story might well collapse at the touch of a guitar string. She kept her face perfectly impassive, though need not have bothered, for Mrs. Ross was watching Morgan Harris intently.

He got up from the arm of the chair, walked over to the wall, took down the most valuable guitar—the one with the ivory-inlaid frets—and looked over at his expectant audience, his brows lifted in inquiry.

"Any requests?" he asked.

By that time, the lieutenant had done with his washing-up and returned to the settee. Mrs. Ross had generously made a place for him next to her, and Barbara was offering him coffee and muffins from the tray. Her heart was sinking.

"I am hardly one to ask to choose from an American repertoire," Mrs. Ross said, holding her hands up, palms out. "You must, of course, make it something quite indigenous and typical."

"Barbara, my love?" Morgan inquired. "A suggestion?"

What was the man's mood? Barbara wondered at the impudent question. He did not look at all uncomfortable with the guitar in his hands. "Oh, no, my dear," she returned, puzzled and a little bemused. "You must choose the song you think will please our guests most."

"Well, then," he said, "it's up to me." He began to stroll across the room, bending over the guitar, and with a few plucks and turns of the tuning pegs, the notes warped into tune. He began to strum randomly, picking notes and chords here and there, frowning in concentration. Then his face cleared abruptly, and he stopped at the trestle table. He leaned over, pulled out the bench, propped one booted foot upon it, and smiled up and over at his audience.

The opening flourish of his fingers across the strings caused Barbara's ears to prick up. Her heart beat now, not in fear, but in expectation.

He announced, "I'll play 'The Indian's over the Border.'" Without looking down again at his hands, Morgan struck his fingers and voice on perfect key, and he did not once falter after that. He sang,

"Come, frontier men, awake now,
By mountain and by lake now,

And make the mountain shake now
With rifle's wild alarms,
For the red men come in swarms,
So frontier men, to arms.
The Indian's over the border,
The Indian's over the border,
Prepared for pillage and slaughter.
Come, frontier men, to arms."

His fingers went on into the second verse, but not his rich, gravelly voice. He hummed a snatch, added the words "To sounds of the horn and the drum now," but then trailed off and finally stopped playing altogether. His last note twanged sour. He smiled, apologetically.

"Did you forget the words, Mr. Harris?" Mrs. Ross prompted—flirtatiously, it seemed to Barbara.

He shook his head, his remarkable midnight-blue eyes grave, but lit by a twinkle in their depths. "No, ma'am," he said solemnly, "the words are too fearsome for company."

Mrs. Ross shrugged off the comment. She had a pretty shrug. "Trying to scare me quickly back to England, Mr. Harris, with the choice of such a song?"

Morgan smiled, charmingly now. "No, ma'am," he said again. "I was trying not to insult you. You see, the most of our indigenous and typical American songs are overtly political." Here he played a spirited rendition of the opening sequence to "Yankee Doodle," then whistled a scrap of it. He did not go farther than the signature opening, and he closed it off with a series of fancy figures. "You see what I mean."

Barbara nearly laughed out loud in relief that Morgan Harris was so obviously an accomplished musician.

His fingers were warmed up, and they began to roam idly, aimlessly, melodiously, over the strings. His expression was distant, as if his mind were detached inside him and roaming just as aimlessly as his hands.

When no new melodies or songs emerged, Mrs. Ross said, "But surely, sir, not all of your songs are either too violent or too political?"

Morgan looked over at Mrs. Ross, as if from a long way away, and appeared to give her question consideration. "A love song, then," he said.

As if from nowhere, the notes he was strumming converged into a melody. Although the song was sad and mournful, it seemed to Barbara that the lovelorn minstrel was thoroughly enjoying himself as he sang the heart-rending words.

> "Of all the birds that wing the air,
> Or warble in the grove,
> None with their notes to me appear
> So soothing as the dove;
> She's built her nest by Laura's grave
> Upon the willow tree,
> And whilst I sit beneath the shade,
> She gently mourns with me."

From the last note of that familiar song, he moved into a deeper, more complex melody, unknown to Barbara, with words that spoke of another place, a place to the north, a landscape of blue mountains and streams, of cold winters and brave inhabitants. He sang as if he knew the map of the place in his heart, and his voice was as wistful as such a deep, masculine voice could be.

When he was done, a little silence fell, which Mrs. Ross broke by saying, perceptively, "Ah, now there was a *real* love song, Mr. Harris."

His brows rose.

"A love song for the place of your youth," she clarified. "Canada, was it? Do you love it?"

The expression on his face was devoid of anything more than the pleasure of a performer who has reached his audience. "Only when I'm away from it," he replied. "I love elsewhere now, of course."

"Of course," she agreed.

He put the guitar down, positioning its rounded butt on the floorboards, casually holding the neck with long, loose fingers. It was a definitive gesture.

Mrs. Ross knew the niceties. She would not overstay her welcome. She rose. The lieutenant rose with her. However, she could not suppress a little huff before she said, "Well, then. We will be off now."

Barbara rose, a little slowly, the movement of rising causing the blood to flow from her tired brain, which had been overanxious the day long. She asked, cautiously, "Off?"

"Back to Baltimore," Mrs. Ross said.

"And surely back to England," Barbara said, slipping up for the first time during this trying encounter. Her voice betrayed her devout hope that she and the lieutenant would be leaving the country.

"Not so quickly as that," Mrs. Ross said dismissively. "I'm in no hurry, and I just got here."

"I see," Barbara said. To cover her embarrassment, she turned to go to her bedroom to retrieve Mrs. Ross's things.

As she entered the bedroom, she heard Morgan follow up politely on her question, "Mrs. Ross, do you plan to grace the thriving port of Baltimore with your presence for a while, then?"

Barbara heard Mrs. Ross's hesitation and felt immediately better. When she emerged from her bedroom, carrying Mrs. Ross's coat and accessories, she heard Mrs. Ross answer, "Well, I do have friends in the area."

After that, the leave-taking passed in something of a blur in Barbara's mind. She was aware that Morgan took her hand in his when they stood at the door to wave goodbye to Mrs. Ross and the lieutenant. She was aware that the gray day was dying and that the gloom of the November twilight was stealing up from the earth to wrap the sky in its veil. She was aware that the goodbye she called out to her guests, to her enemies, was merely temporary.

When Barbara and Morgan were alone in the sitting room, with the door closed behind them, he still did not let go of her fingers. After a moment, she tugged at them and looked up at him. He gave his head a quick shake and put his finger up to his lips, silencing anything she might say, wishing to hear the departure of Mrs. Ross's carriage. As the receding sounds of the carriage carried into the house, he let go of her hand, paused another long moment with his ears cocked, then said, "I'll go in a few minutes and ride behind them, just to make sure they are headed back to Baltimore, with no intention of returning to us tonight."

"Good idea," Barbara said with a nod. She imagined that the first thing she would do when he left was to collapse in the chair from exhaustion and relief.

When the jingle of bridle and the click of carriage wheels were no longer perceptible, Morgan heaved an exaggerated sigh and turned to Barbara, a question on his lips.

He was never allowed to ask it, however, for just then Barbara's wits returned, and she was blinded by an idea. She held up her hand for him to hold his thought and left the sitting room with the renewed energy of inspiration. She went straight to her bedroom, to her dresser, pulled out the top drawer, found a little leather box, opened it, and stirred around in it a moment in the half-light of the room. When she found what she was looking for, she returned to the sitting room.

Without a word, she went straight to Morgan, took his left hand in hers and held up in her other hand a circle of gold whose braided design matched the circle of gold on her left hand. She said, "I think you had better have this for now."

Morgan frowned down at the wedding ring. "Mr. Johnson's?"

"Yes, Jonas's," Barbara said. "He was not as tall a man as you, but he was thicker, and his hands were large, so it's possible that this just might do."

Morgan hesitated. "Do you think I need it?"

Barbara looked up then, bravely, coloring slightly, and said, taking a breath, "Mrs. Ross noticed first off that you wore no wedding ring. It's not a significant detail, and I easily explained it away, but over the next day or two, if inquiries are made, I was thinking..."

Morgan took the band from her hand and tried the ring. Barbara let go of his hand and watched him slip the circle over the tip of his finger and push it over his knuckle. He twisted it experimentally. "It's snug." He tried to remove it. It would not cross back over his knuckle. "A little too snug."

"Does it hurt you?"

Morgan shook his head. "No. Tight is all, but not uncomfortably so." He tried to remove it again, and again it would not budge over his knuckle. He tried the same maneuver again, without success, until his finger became a little swollen with the effort, making any further efforts all the more counterproductive.

Barbara picked up his hand again and experimented, gingerly, with the ring on his finger. She sighed and gave him back his hand. "It'll come off, eventually," she said, "for it's only a shade too tight. We'll have to leave it alone for a minute or two. Or else," she said, putting her fingers to the bridge of her nose, trying to solve this latest, quite trivial problem, "we could try some butter to smooth the passage." Suddenly, however, Barbara was too tired to walk to the trap at the back door to scoop some butter from the mound. "But we can wait on that, too," she said, a little wearily. "And, right now, all I want to do is sit down."

Morgan tried the ring again, and when it did not come off, he dropped his hand, and the topic, for the time being. Seeing that she was dead on her feet, he guided Barbara to her rocking chair and, when she was seated, took a place opposite her on the settee. He stretched out in the place Mrs. Ross had lately occupied, hardly the perfect jewel the Englishwoman had been, much more a very rough nugget of ore. He laid an arm across the back of the settee.

"Tell me," he invited simply.

Barbara blinked and focused on him. Suddenly a wave of pure amazement passed over her, and the hairs on the back of her neck stood up. Awestruck with wonder, she said the first words that came to mind, "What would I have done if you had not turned up on my doorstep an hour before the lieutenant?"

Morgan made a wry mouth. "Invented a second dead husband?" he suggested.

"I suppose," Barbara conceded. "Nevertheless, a live one is so much more . . . convincing."

Morgan glanced at the ring on his finger as his hand lay over the top of the settee. He felt the constraint of that circle as if it were a noose around his neck. He worked his shoulders to free himself of the constraint, and the slight but perceptible weight of sadness that accompanied it. He glanced back at Barbara and put the ring out of his mind. He saw that she was smiling that illuminating smile that had dazzled him the evening before. He had opened his mouth to speak, but the response he had been about to make to her comment had flown right out of his head. He closed his mouth again.

"And a dead man cannot sing nearly as well as you," she pronounced, as if that clinched her argument.

"Thank you kindly," he said, and vowed he could not remember a time when he had been so nicely complimented.

Chuckling at the absurdity of both her compliment and his response, and at the absurdity of the excruciating hour she had spent with Mrs. Ross, almost hysterical now with relief and exhaustion, Barbara laughed, and had a hard time stopping. She held her stomach to regain control of herself and said, "Oh, my Lord! Oh, my dearest Lord, what a time I have had!" Her recent experience was too fresh to make comment upon, and when she sobered, she asked instead an entirely wifely question: "And the fences, sir, they are mended?"

It was his turn to laugh at the absurd normalcy of the question, but he answered it straight. "Ben Skinner, bless his wizened heart, showed me the way through the pasture and got us to where we needed to go without exposing my ignorance. The lieutenant is not one for hard work—except, perhaps, on the battlefield, and that I do not know—but he was a true officer in getting his two standing slabs of beef to help me with the heavier rails. How long were those fences down?''

"Not more than a year," Barbara said dreamily. She was working her tight neck muscles by rolling her head back and forth. She laughed again, this time less merrily. "To say so calmly, 'Not more than a year'! What must you think of me?''

"That you've had a lot of work to do."

"Oh, I have. I have. So very much. And to think that some woman thought she could come and take it all away from me—just like that! By asking! It is beyond comprehension!''

"That it is. And then again," he said meditatively, "it is understandable."

"Perhaps," she agreed. Then she cocked her head to one side and asked, "You were born in the colony of Quebec?''

He nodded.

The corners of her mouth pulled down. "With a name like Morgan Harris?''

"Would you prefer Jack Carter—or Jacques Cartier?''

Her mouth curved upward. "Yes, I suppose." She repeated, experimentally, "Jacques Cartier." Then, more easily, "Jack Carter." She paused. "If you were born in Quebec, you must have some French in you, after all."

"I do" was all he said to that.

She did not probe. However, the topic of his identity altered the atmosphere of companionable camaraderie between two people who had succeeded in achieving a goal against a common enemy. She asked a nonthreatening question. "You sing Canadian songs, as well?''

"Only in French."

"Which I don't understand," she answered, by way of dropping the topic of his background, which she felt was, somehow, too personal at the moment. "Well, then..." she said. She placed her hands on the arms of the chair, preparing to rise. "You must be starving after working the fences and having eaten only a muffin since the midday meal." She got to her feet, feeling very tired. She put her hands against the small of her back and stretched. "Do you want some supper?"

He did not answer. Instead, he rose with her and said, "Ben Skinner showed me the tenant's house at the end of the drive behind the barn. It's in shape for the next inhabitant, I noted, and so I'll be putting my bedroll there for the night."

She straightened and looked him in the eye. "Is that wise?" she asked, without elaboration.

He went to get his hat and coat down off the peg. "I'll know as soon as I've ridden out and confirmed that our English friends are on their way to Baltimore."

Barbara saw him tug, yet again, at the ring on his finger, but it still would not come off. She said, "All right, then. You need go no farther than the meetinghouse. Surely someone there will have seen them drive by—or not. And the ring will probably come off easily once you've been out in the cold for a while."

Morgan grunted his agreement and was gone before Barbara knew it.

She was about to sit back down when Sarah awoke with a frightful cry. Under other circumstances, Barbara would have felt her ears flinch at the high-pitched whine. At the moment, however, it was the sweetest sound in the world. Barbara knew just what Sarah wanted most, and what Barbara wanted most was to give it to her.

A minute later, Barbara was cuddling Sarah to her breast and the baby was sucking sloppily and noisily. It was the most wonderful draining imaginable, the flow of her milk to her daughter. The pleasure that Barbara derived from the nursing was almost obscene in its wanton depths, in its fierce satisfaction, in its sheer physicality. As Sarah took from her body, Barbara did not feel violated, as she had with Mrs.

Ross and, more especially, with General Ross. Now she felt fulfilled and at peace.

The moment could not last. Sarah was quickly satisfied and then made a fine mess of herself, requiring that Barbara leave the chair and put her own clothing to rights. It was just as well that all this was accomplished before Morgan returned, for she had planned to try to persuade him to take his supper with her, and he had seemed reluctant to accept.

Sure enough, Morgan's boots sounded on the porch before Barbara had missed him. He knocked, poked his head around the door, and responded to her gesture bidding him enter. Upon perceiving his master's entry, Pockets lifted his little head, sneezed, and rose from his warm place at the hearth. He pranced over to Morgan, who was determined to ignore him. Abashed, the puppy retired again to the hearth.

Morgan did not take off his coat. He said, "The carriage was sighted passing the meetinghouse well before I got there. There is no returning to your farm any other way, is there?"

"Only by the Patapsco," she said. "The river, that is. The lieutenant would have to find a boat and figure out how to dock at Old Roads Bay."

"Old Roads Bay, is it?" Morgan repeated, then considered. "The lieutenant is surely resourceful enough to hire a boat in Baltimore and travel the river tonight to the bay, wouldn't you say?"

"Ah, but our ferryman is partial only to locals, and I doubt he'd let a stranger pass at night. No," Barbara said, shaking her head, "they won't be returning by that route tonight—or any other time, by my reckoning."

"Good enough, then," Morgan said. "The man I spoke to at the meetinghouse—his name is Gorsuch, I think—said he would alert you if any carriage returned this night. He knew who I was, too, because Ben Skinner had told him about me after he left me this afternoon."

"I see," Barbara said. She was about to invite him, again, for supper, when he walked into the bedroom and emerged a few moments later, his bedroll in his hands.

"I'll be bedding at the tenant's house, as we've decided," he said, "and I have to finish eating what I brought with me before it spoils. If you hear me out back later chopping wood, it's because there isn't any in the house, at least as far as I could see through the windows."

He walked past her then, without giving her a chance to protest, and was at the back door when bootsteps sounded on the porch and a loud knocking rattled the front door.

Morgan frowned and swore softly at Pockets, who was warming himself blissfully by the fire, oblivious of the newcomer's arrival.

Barbara turned to Morgan with wide eyes and gasped, "Could it be them again?" She urged him quietly, "Now, wait."

Morgan had half opened the back door, and he kept his hand on the latch. He watched Barbara cross the room.

She opened the door and looked into the face of a man she had never seen before. In the shadowed light cast by the fire, she could see that he was of medium height, medium build, neither elegant nor slovenly, mostly nondescript.

"Good evening to you, ma'am. I am speaking with Mrs. Harris?" the man asked.

Barbara was surprised. He did not have a British accent. He sounded, American, in fact. She was confused. Why would an American address her as Mrs. Harris? That name existed only to fool the British.

"Yes," she answered cautiously.

"Pardon my intrusion, ma'am," the man said, lifting his hat, "but I'm looking for a man named Jack Carter, and I have reason to think he's headed through this part of the country."

Behind her, Barbara heard the back door close with a soft click.

Chapter Seven

Barbara did not dare turn to see whether Morgan Harris had left the house. Keeping her eyes on the man on the porch, she repeated, "Jack Carter?" The name made her heart pound painfully. "Is there some reason I should know this man?"

The stranger's manner was polite. "No, ma'am. He's not from around here. He's from the north. I've been following him for four days now."

Barbara regarded the man closely. "Are you with the police?"

The stranger shook his head. "No, ma'am."

Although her mind was somewhat relieved, her heart continued to pound irregularly. She smiled, briefly. "I'm sorry I can't help you, but I've encountered no one named Jack Carter recently—or ever, for that matter."

"You've seen no man foreign to these parts in the past day or two?" the stranger persisted.

She felt her stomach flip-flop. Not trusting her voice to remain steady, she merely shook her head. To signal that the exchange was over, she inched the door shut and repeated, "I'm sorry I'm not able to help you."

The stranger asked quickly. "Is there anything thataway down the lane?" He was pointing toward the route at the end of the drive, indicating the opposite direction to that from which he had come.

Barbara saw the stranger look up and over her shoulder, and then she felt Morgan Harris at her back. So, he had not left the house upon hearing of someone at the door asking for a man named—disturbing coincidence!—Jack Carter. Morgan's shadow blocked the firelight that had illuminated the porch. He had shed his coat, and was dressed as would be a man in his own home.

Before Barbara could answer the stranger's question, Morgan said, displaying his newly acquired knowledge, "At the end of the lane is the river, the Patapsco. The ferryman there at Old Roads Bay is very partial to us locals. So if you're thinking to cross there—" he nodded in the general direction of the river "—you'll be sent right back. Why do you want to know?"

Morgan was regarding the stranger calmly, and Barbara noted that neither man evidenced any sign of recognition.

Barbara looked up at him and answered for the stranger, "This man is looking for someone named Jack Carter."

Morgan did not bat an eye. He put his arm around Barbara and pulled her slightly to him. It was a protective gesture, one natural to a husband in such a situation. His voice was matter-of-fact. "Never heard of him." He infused his voice with a measure of challenge, which was also natural in the situation. "Nor do I know what you are doing at my doorstep."

The stranger's manner was unfailingly polite. "I'm begging your pardon, sir," he said, "but I've been following a man—Jack Carter—for four days now. I had a lead that brought me yesterday to Baltimore and then here today, to North Point. Just now, I was traveling on Long Log Lane, I think it is called—" he jerked a thumb behind him "—and chanced to see a rider a half hour ago that vaguely answered to Jack Carter's description. I followed him here." He paused, looked down at his boots, then raised his eyes again and said, apologetically. "I think I've made a mistake."

Morgan nodded. "It must have been me who you saw just now," he said, "for I was on Long Log Lane, making sure our afternoon guests got safely on the road to Baltimore. I returned home not above ten minutes ago. In any case, you will relieve my mind if you can tell me whether you passed a carriage on your way out here from Baltimore."

"A fancy carriage," the stranger affirmed, "bowling along at a spanking clip down the lane."

"That's the one," Morgan said, as if satisfied that the afternoon guests were well on their way. He nodded. "It's a trouble you've had these past four days, and it's a pity your journey has been for naught."

"And you saw no one else, sir, while you were out?" the stranger asked, hopeful still.

Morgan shook his head. "I think you had the bad luck to be following only me."

"So it seems," the stranger agreed, clearly disappointed and slightly puzzled by his mistake.

Morgan asked, as if on an apprehensive afterthought, "Is there some reason we should be wary of this man?"

The stranger lifted his shoulders, once. "I doubt it. It was a personal matter Jack Carter was involved in, and there are those who want to bring him to justice for his actions. But he's not a criminal, and he won't harm those he comes in contact with, I'm thinking."

Morgan demanded pointedly, "And did I hear you tell my wife that you're not a policeman?"

"No, sir, Mr. Harris, I'm not," the stranger said, "but I can see what you're thinking. Why's a man who's not a criminal being pursued by a man who's not a policeman?"

Morgan replied, "Something like that."

"Well, sir, Mr. Harris," the stranger said, looking him in the eyes, "there's some things that are above the law."

A tiny, taut pause fell. Morgan let it stretch. "That's right," he agreed. To round off the encounter, he said, his deep voice definitive, "Well, then, it's a trouble you've had, as I've said, but we've nothing for you here."

The stranger looked anxiously from Morgan to Barbara. He said, respectfully, "You've been kind enough to answer my questions, and since it's late and I'm far from the nearest inn, I'm wondering if you could extend your hospitality...."

Barbara looked up at Morgan for guidance in answering this man's unspoken question. Morgan's midnight-blue eyes were steady on her and held another question in answer to her own. It was her house, he seemed to be saying, and he was as much a chance traveler as the man standing on the porch.

Barbara weighed the matter rapidly. Although she thought it wise to send the man on his way, her curiosity got the better of her. She reopened the door a fraction and said, "We've not got much for dinner, but you're welcome to share it with us."

The stranger was visibly relieved. His brow lightened, and he said, "You've shown me a continuing kindness, Mrs. Harris, for which I can only thank you." He bowed his head respectfully. To Morgan, he extended his hand and said, "And I thank you, too, Mr. Harris. I'm pleased to share your supper. I'm Evan Rollins. From Boston."

Morgan shook the man's hand and expressed conventional interest in the detail. "From Boston, is it?" he repeated noncommittally as he allowed Mr. Rollins to cross the threshold. He closed the door behind the newcomer and indicated the peg where the man could hang his overcoat next to Morgan's and Barbara's.

Barbara withdrew from Morgan's light embrace and walked toward the table, saying over her shoulder, "Let me offer you something to drink while I fix our supper. Would you prefer cider or coffee, Mr. Rollins?"

"Coffee, if you please, Mrs. Harris," the stranger said.

"Can I help you, my love?" Morgan asked her. "You're tired, I'm thinking, from our afternoon guests."

She met his eyes and quickly looked away. She wanted distance from him, from her questions about him, from the unsettling emotions that had been stirred up within her during the day, emotions that refused now, in the face of this new twist, to simmer down. Her earlier exhaustion had fled. She felt wide-awake now, and on the alert.

"No, no, not tired, Morgan. I'm fine," she said, but just then Sarah began to fuss, and Barbara sighed with a hint of fatigue.

"I'll tend to her," Morgan said. "That is, if she's not hungry."

"She had better not be!" Barbara said in exasperation. "I fed her while you were out." She watched Morgan lift her daughter out of her cradle and hold her up, wiggling her and admonishing her to mind her manners for Mr. Rollins. "She's freshly diapered, too," Barbara added, "so you're in luck."

Barbara saw that Morgan's face had softened when he had taken the baby in his arms. His blue regard crossed the room, and he said, "I am."

Barbara did not respond to that, or examine too closely the implicit thanks she perceived in his comment. She went straight to the tasks of preparing for supper, and was content to listen, without having to participate, while Morgan made conversation with their guest. While she busied herself, she heard Morgan invite Mr. Rollins to sit, while he took the rocking chair. He did not look the least bit uncomfortable holding the small bundle. Nor did he have difficulty making conversation with a man Barbara imagined might well be dangerous to him.

At the same time, Barbara realized, Morgan Harris would have every reason to be confident when facing Mr. Rollins. Here he was, apparently in his own home, holding his own child, visiting with a guest while his wife prepared their supper. As Barbara brought Mr. Rollins his cup of coffee, she glanced at Morgan. He was holding Sarah against his right shoulder, rocking gently back and forth. He had brought his left hand up to her little back. The wedding ring that had been stuck on his finger earlier was prominently displayed.

Morgan acted very much at home, but his look of profound hunger, Barbara decided, might rouse Mr. Rollins's suspicions, if Mr. Rollins was of a suspicious nature. Barbara wondered how Morgan Harris would look with ten more pounds filling out his frame, but then she realized that his look of hunger came not from the lack of fat on his bones, but from his soul, through his eyes. From the friendly talk, it was apparent, as well, that Morgan was a farmer, or at least had been one at one time in his life. No, Mr. Rollins would have no reason to suspect that the man sitting in the rocking chair was anyone other than the legal man of the house.

However, at one moment, Mr. Rollins called into question Morgan's presence in the house. They were discussing, in a general way, Mr. Rollins's movements of the day, which had brought him to this farm and to this house. Mr. Rollins said, conversationally, "I was surprised just now, sir, when you came to the door, as well. The men at the meetinghouse over yonder did not mention a Mr. Harris when they told me to go to Mrs. Harris's farm."

Morgan had no difficulty with that. He glanced over at Barbara and let his eyes linger on her when he said, "The men at the meetinghouse tend to like to forget my existence."

"Oh?" Mr. Rollins prompted, interested.

"My wife was the widowed Mrs. Johnson," Morgan explained, "and I have not quite been forgiven for having come in and wed the most beautiful woman in North Point."

Mr. Rollins's face lightened with comprehension. "So that explains why one man first called her Mrs. Johnson, then the other man poked him in the ribs and said, flustered, that she was Mrs. Harris now!"

Morgan commented dryly, "I'll have to get over there more often, so the boys'll remember I'm alive."

"Been married long?" Mr. Rollins inquired.

"A year."

"Yes, we celebrate our first anniversary this week," Barbara interjected from the kitchen area.

While Mr. Rollins congratulated them, Morgan rose to replace a contented Sarah in her cradle. He looked over at

Barbara, quirked his brows responsively to her remark, and smiled, which brought a very attractive twinkle to his eyes.

"And Sarah is three months old," Morgan informed him, seating himself again.

"Big girl," was Mr. Rollins's observation. "I have seven children myself, ranging in age from five to twenty-five, and only one or two of my boys were as big as your daughter is at three months, if I'm remembering correctly. But then, they grow so fast that one forgets!"

Morgan acknowledged the truth of that and turned the topic by trying to draw the stranger out on the subject of his children. However, Mr. Rollins was far less interested in speaking about himself than in getting to know more about the Harris family.

"Do I gather that when you came and snatched up the beautiful widow Johnson you were not from around here?"

"That's right."

"Where are you from, Mr. Harris?"

"Quebec."

"How did you end up here?"

Barbara did not look up when Morgan responded, but she heard the lazy, comfortable, at-home tone in his voice when he said, "By great good luck."

Mr. Rollins seemed satisfied by that. If any further detail was needed to set the seal on his absolute belief in the domestic picture presented by Mr. and Mrs. Morgan Harris, it was provided by the stringed instruments on the wall.

Mr. Rollins pointed at the instruments and asked, "Are those yours or Mrs. Harris's?"

Morgan identified them as his own, and when Mr. Rollins requested a ditty, Morgan carefully placed the now-sleeping Sarah in her crib and said, "I was hoping you would ask. I play with great pleasure and at the drop of a hat, as my wife knows to her cost. I warn you, I think myself an excellent strummer, and love the sound of my own voice."

Barbara, who was at the stage of setting three places at the table, said, "He is, indeed, *very* good, as you will discover."

Morgan nodded and said gravely, "My wife is loyal." Then he began to play. He had warmed his fingers up earlier during his little concert for Mrs. Ross and Lieutenant Richards, and now the guitar was in tune and he was relaxed. His fingers were nimble, his voice was rich in depth and melody, and the songs he chose were familiar and comforting.

The tired Mr. Rollins was lulled and charmed, and drawn so deeply into the illusion of the Harris household's contented domesticity that even if another bountyman had turned up on Mrs. Johnson's doorstep to expose Morgan Harris as the womanizing, cheating son of a bitch Jack Carter, Mr. Rollins would have told him he was on a false trail and sent him back to Baltimore.

Morgan was in the midst of "To the Troops in Boston," meant as a compliment to Mr. Rollins's home, when Barbara called them over to supper. She had seated herself next to Morgan, with Mr. Rollins across the table. The moment they all sat down, Barbara realized her mistake. Morgan did not look at her or otherwise signal that he was aware of her next to him, but she felt the difference. It was subtle, but discernible, the change between them, the extra charge in the air, now that this new stranger had come to them, to raise questions in her mind about Morgan Harris's identity.

She had no wish, of course, to expose their charade, for that might expose her to danger, as well. Yet, suddenly, she saw that the story that had worked to her benefit the night before—and for the acceptance of which she had been so grateful to Morgan Harris had taken a strange turn whose consequences she could not foresee. Now that they were seated next to one another, their touching was inevitable, though minimal, and each successive touch became infinitely electric. She felt awakened by the danger of the situation. She felt aware of the length of his leg next to the length of hers under the table. She felt alive to the way he shifted his arms on the table, sometimes with his forearms resting across the tabletop, sometimes with his elbows planted down, his interlaced hands supporting his chin.

She felt frankly curious. It was not curiosity, pure and simple, that roused her now. It was curiosity, tainted and complex. It was not innocent, this curiosity. It was tinged with an unfamiliar shame. She was shamefully curious to know who he was, this man who had shared her lie and her bed last night. She was burningly curious to know where he came from and why he was here. She was achingly curious to know why Evan Rollins was looking for a man named Jack Carter.

Morgan, too, felt the change, the charge, in their relationship. He could hardly have ignored it. He had a pretty good idea of where the evening would end, with the weary and unfailingly polite Mr. Rollins as a guest in the spare bedroom. Under other circumstances, he would have thought the evening's end an intriguing, appetizing one. Under these circumstances, he thought it might be hell. He thought of his bedroll, which he had stashed outside the back door when he heard the stranger ask for Jack Carter. He wished he could take it to the tenant's house to spend the night there, but he did not think that was going to be possible.

For the duration of the meal, he kept himself contained and out of Barbara's way as much as possible, but he could not keep himself from perceiving her scent and the shape of her body as it affected the shape of the air around him. The rare moments when their eyes met, she shied away from his gaze. Not an encouraging sign.

Still, she was moving through the meal cool and composed. He wondered, idly, if some aspect of Jack Carter's past, some lurid detail, might be exposed to cause her to lose her cool composure.

However, since he had nothing to lose that was of any value to him, he would let her take the conversation with Mr. Rollins anywhere she wanted. She had betrayed no hint of recognition when Mr. Rollins uttered the name Jack

Carter. Nevertheless, he did not think she was totally disinterested in discovering what she could of a drifter who had landed on her doorstep and who had just associated himself with the name Jack Carter.

He did not underestimate her. Halfway through the meal, she asked, with the correct amount of polite interest, "And exactly who is this Jack Carter that you've been following for the past four days?"

"Who, ma'am?" Mr. Rollins asked, evidently temporizing.

"Well, maybe not 'who,' since I wouldn't know him anyway. I should, rather ask *what*—what he did to put you on his trail," she amended.

"Cheated at a card game," Mr. Rollins answered, surprising her, "is where it all started."

"It must have been quite a card game, with unusually high stakes," Barbara remarked, "to have made it worth your while to follow a man for four days—and more, since you have not caught up with him yet."

Mr. Rollins had had himself a good meal. Furthermore, he had been relaxed by the entertainment before supper, and he was in an expansive mood. "It only started with the card game," he said. "That was the precipitating event, you might say."

Barbara lifted her brows and said, lightly, "My, how you interest me, Mr. Rollins!"

Morgan interjected, "My wife always loves a good story, so oblige her, by all means!"

Barbara exchanged a wordless glance with Morgan, whose expression, she decided, was cool, and calmly challenging.

"By all means," she said, softly, encouragingly.

Mr. Rollins was happy to give something in return to this couple who had treated him so kindly. "Well, it began four days ago—really five nights ago, now," he said, with a relish that suggested he fancied himself something of a storyteller. "And this Jack Carter was in a pub, going about his business."

"Which was—?" Barbara prompted.

"Gambling. The man is a gambler by profession, if you want to call such activity a profession," Mr. Rollins informed her. "So he was, as I say, gambling and winning. Jack Carter won a lot."

"By cheating?" Barbara inquired, naturally enough.

"No, ma'am," Mr. Rollins said judiciously, shaking his head. "He was not *known* for cheating."

Here Morgan entered the conversation. "A man known for cheating," he said, "would not be able to make his living at the tables. No one would be willing to play with him."

Mr. Rollins nodded at the truth of that remark. "That's right, Mr. Harris. A man who earns his bread from cards had better not only be skilled, but also have a reputation for honesty."

"So, until five nights ago, this Jack Carter had a reputation for honesty?" Barbara pursued.

"Spotless," Mr. Rollins emphasized, "in gambling circles." Then, with a wink, he added, "But not in other circles."

Barbara looked down at her hands, which she had placed on the tabletop. She was aware of Morgan shifting slightly on the bench. "Are you referring to the ladies, perhaps?" she said, as lightly as she was able.

Mr. Rollins winked again. "I'll come to that!" he assured her. "But it was the strangest set of circumstances— so I was told when I took the job of finding Jack Carter— that started the whole thing, as I was saying, and it was not a night like any other at Kelly's. That's the pub! So, here was Jack Carter, losing large pots and winning them back, cool as you please, and he and his table were playing for high stakes, when a young fellow comes into the pub."

Mr. Rollins paused there, significantly, causing Barbara to prompt him: "A young fellow?"

"Not just any young fellow, but an Injun. He was big, even for an Injun. Black-haired and black-eyed, like an Injun, but he didn't look completely like one of them, nor quite like one of us. But he was dressed like an Injun—no mistaking that!—with his war paint and beaded britches and jacket. Onondaga, he was said to be. Rode into Boston from the north! Alone, too, and young. Not yet bearded—but that's not odd for an Injun. Couldn't have been much more than fifteen, so I was told.''

"He was never seen there before?" Barbara asked.

"No, ma'am."

"And he challenged Jack Carter to a game of cards?"

"No, ma'am. He never got as far as Jack Carter's table. You see, he was all fired up, this young'n. Some said he was drunk. Others said he was looking for somebody, or just for a fight, and he was determined to get it! Well, we don't get many Injuns in the city, as you must be knowing, but the farmers in the west of Massachusetts still remember the problems they had with the redskins! Anyway, this young Injun caused quite a fuss that night!"

Barbara was puzzled. "I am not quite sure what the appearance of this rather interesting young man in the pub has to do with allegations of Jack Carter's cheating."

"Nothing directly!" Mr. Rollins told her. "But just when it looks like this young'n was going to get himself thrashed, or even killed, Jack Carter is accused of cheating, and even caught red-handed! Well, I can tell you that attention was riveted on the table where Jack Carter was playing!"

"Jack Carter was caught red-handed?" Barbara repeated.

Mr. Rollins nodded sagely. "He practically admitted it, too!"

"But why would someone with such skill need to be familiar with cheating?" Barbara asked.

Morgan chose to enter the conversation again. "A man who makes his living from gambling would have to be very familiar with various forms of cheating in order to recognize it when it happened to him."

Mr Rollins favored Morgan with an approving look. "That's right, Mr. Harris, and that was the strange part of Jack Carter's bad business. His cheating was clumsily done, almost as if he wanted to get caught!"

"Which he was," Barbara observed. "And then?"

Mr. Rollins, polite, mild-mannered man that he was, smiled with relish. "Then there was a brawl such as Kelly's has never seen, and Jack Carter got away!"

"And the Indian boy?" Morgan asked noncommittally.

"Got away, too—almost thrown out!" Mr. Rollins said. "Anyway, if he had wanted to pick a fight, his desires were not obliged once Jack Carter, of all people, became the center of attention! It was almost as if Jack Carter started it all to save the boy. Strange rumors began to fly, then, about how Jack Carter had been an Injun-lover years ago."

"So Jack Carter got away, and you have come after him now to retrieve the money he cheated to get?" Barbara asked. It was a logical enough question.

"No, the money stayed on the table—or rather it scattered across the floor when the table was overturned," Mr. Rollins replied. "Although I will say that the man Jack Carter cheated was his biggest rival, and he swore up and down he was going to go after him!"

"And is he after him?"

"Don't know," Mr. Rollins admitted with an unconcerned shrug.

"And you're pursuing Jack Carter to make good on the cost of damages at Kelly's?" she tried again.

He shook his head. "No, ma'am, although Jack Carter better not show his face again in Boston anytime soon. If Jim Kelly doesn't kill him first, the police will arrest him for having disturbed the peace. Never seen nor heard the like in Boston since the First War of Independence!"

Barbara knew that some essential element of this story was missing. "Then why *are* you after him?"

Mr. Rollins smiled broadly. "I told you'd we'd come to the part about the ladies." He thrust his chest out proudly. "Me, I'm in the employ of Mrs. Layton, and according to her, Jack Carter's cheating wasn't just at the gaming tables."

Chapter Eight

Barbara was aware again of Morgan's leg next to hers under the table. She was aware that he had shifted slightly at the mention of Mrs. Layton. She did not look at him. Instead, she merely smiled and said, "Ah . . . It would have to involve a woman, of course."

"More than one, as it turned out," Mr. Rollins added, for the sake of accuracy. He wiggled his eyebrows suggestively.

"You mean that Mr. Carter was cheating on Mrs. Carter with this Mrs. Layton?"

"As far as anyone knows, there is no Mrs. Carter," Mr. Rollins said. His voice betrayed a hint of disappointment that the scandal was not juicier. But then he rallied. "But his unmarried state is not necessarily to Jack Carter's credit!"

"No?" Barbara queried.

"Well, ma'am, what do you think of a man who can't settle down? And him no longer a young man! Unsteady, I call it! Me, I've been married for as long as I can remember—to the same woman! Faithful all these years, too, and with seven children to my credit, aged five to twenty-five! But I hardly need be convincing you of the virtues of married life, since you've been a respectable married woman not once, Mrs. Harris, but twice!"

Barbara thought back over her marriage to Jonas Johnson, an aging widower with nothing to offer her, no love, no affection, no children. If that was respectability, she wanted no further part of it.

"But we were talking about Jack Carter," Mr. Rollins continued cheerfully in the face of Barbara's small silence, "and it seems that at the same time he was paying Mrs. Layton court, he was getting sugar from another woman across town." He paused dramatically. "A woman down at the wharves—if you catch my meaning."

"A woman of no good reputation?" Barbara ventured.

"That's right, Mrs. Harris," Mr. Rollins said approving. "He was careless about it, too, and Mrs. Layton found out!"

Barbara was torn between a proper desire to end the trend of this conversation and a shameful desire to hear more. Unable to decide how she wanted to proceed, she sneaked a peek at Morgan to judge how he was taking this recital of the unsteady Jack Carter's amorous adventuring. She saw that his disconcerting midnight-blue eyes were focused on her. In their depths she read a dare to continue this line of questioning.

She dared. She turned to look at Morgan straight on and said to him, by way of responding to Mr. Rollins, "It sounds as if Jack Carter wanted to get caught cheating on Mrs. Layton, just as he wanted to get caught cheating at cards. What do you think, Morgan?"

"That depends on his relationship to Mrs. Layton, I would guess," he replied easily, holding her level gaze. He turned to Mr. Rollins. "What was Mrs. Layton's claim on Jack Carter?"

"She was fixing to marry him," Mr. Rollins answered.

"Mrs. Layton is a widow, then," Barbara concluded.

Mr. Rollins shook his head. "Not quite—or, I should say, not yet! Her husband is a sick man, a very sick man. On his deathbed, you might say."

"And Mrs. Layton was carrying on with another man while her husband lay dying?" This from Morgan, who sounded quite shocked at Mrs. Layton's infidelity. He turned back to Barbara. "I hope, dear wife, that you would not subject me to such an ignominious cuckolding if I were on my deathbed!"

Barbara met his eye. She smiled sweetly. "That would depend on the faith you had earned from me during the years of our marriage, and on the strength of the temptation presented to me during your illness."

Mr. Rollins watched this byplay with a benevolent eye. "Such was Mrs. Layton's reasoning, Mrs. Harris! Her husband was—is!—one of the richest and most influential men in Boston, and it was rumored that he drove his first wife to her grave with his philandering. Now, the second and present Mrs. Layton is a good sight younger than he is—could have been his daughter. But not for all that did he stop his wandering ways! So, when this Jack Carter come along, she...well, she fell hard for him...."

"With his unsteady character?" Barbara interjected. "And after her experience with her equally unsteady husband?"

Mr. Rollins explained. "I'm not in Mrs. Layton's confidence, but my wife has been with her since she was a baby—come from a good family and married into an even better one—which means that I've been with her since she was ten years old, when I married my wife, over twenty-five years ago! So I know from my wife that Mrs. Layton developed a tendresse as the ladies say, for Jack Carter, and although I never set eyes on him myself—he only came around at night, and to her bedroom, I'm thinking, where *I* never went, of course—he was said to be tall and lean, with black hair and blue eyes, why, like Mr. Harris here, and attractive to women—though I am no judge of such things!"

Barbara stole another glance at Morgan Harris, who seemed to be listening to this exposition without embarrassment. He shook his head and said, conversationally, "I am no judge of such things, either, Mr. Rollins, but what I am wondering was whether Jack Carter had promised Mrs. Layton anything beyond his companionship in her bedroom."

"I don't know," Mr. Rollins admitted, "but he being poor and she being rich, it seemed likely that he would want to take advantage. She certainly wants to marry him!"

"Eventually, you mean," Morgan said. "After her husband has died."

"Of course they could not get married before her husband dies. That would be illegal," Mr. Rollins acknowledged.

Morgan studied his empty plate for a moment before repeating, "Illegal." He raised his eyes to Mr. Rollins. "And, yet, what I still do not understand is why you're after him."

"To bring him back to Boston, to Mrs. Layton," Mr. Rollins said, as if surprised to have to state the obvious.

"But why should Jack Carter return with you, if you were to find him?" Morgan wanted to know. "If he left, it was because he did not want to be with her, I suppose."

"He's left her high and dry, you might say, with the whole town knowing about the affair.... Well, it's a question of pride and commitment!"

"Jack Carter's commitment?" Morgan inquired, but he did not expect a response. He followed that query immediately with a more pertinent question: "And what—if anything—are you going to do when you do catch up with him?"

Mr. Rollins smiled. "Have him arrested!"

"For disturbing the peace in Boston?" Morgan's voice had not lost its easy cadences, but it did contain an inflection of dubious surprise now. "What if you catch up with him here in Maryland? Is the arm of Massachusetts law so long?"

Mr. Rollins shook his head. "No, but I have a list of men to contact in each state who will find the appropriate charges that would take him back to Massachusetts—in proper custody!" He smiled, as if at his own cleverness.

Barbara was, by turns, shocked at Jack Carter's callousness and outraged by Mrs. Layton's unscrupulousness. She also was finding Morgan Harris a pretty cool customer.

"Trumping up charges? Isn't that illegal?" Morgan asked, with a smile of his own. Barbara noted that it did not reach his remarkable blue eyes.

Mr. Rollins's eyes slid away from Morgan's. "Mr. Layton is a lawyer," he said, "and I'm thinking that Mrs. Layton has learned a deal about laws in the fifteen years she's been married to him. She'll find a way to make it legal, all right!"

"That relieves my mind, then," Morgan said evenly. "I'd sleep less well at night if I thought the laws of this country were being bent out of shape by its most respected citizens."

Mr. Rollins had confidence in his employer. "She'd not do anything illegal, my Mrs. Layton! She's a smart woman. Beautiful, too! But she's had a rough time of it these past years, and isn't getting any younger, and now she wants a measure of her own happiness."

"And some things," Morgan said, "as you said earlier, are above the law." He reached out for the loaf of bread and absently broke off a corner of the crust. Barbara ventured a look at his profile; it was sharp and clean, with a deep line running from his nose to the corner of his mouth, which was turned down.

Mr. Rollins agreed, pleased to share this view with his host.

Morgan looked up and asked, "Who else besides you is after the man?" His smile was wry. "The Boston police? The gambling rival? The trollop's man?"

"Just the last two," Mr. Rollins replied cheerfully, "since, as you pointed out, Massachusetts law does not extend outside the state. It's a pity I've not had better luck. I was hoping to get him first!"

"Yes, it is a pity, Mr. Rollins," Barbara said, "after all your efforts."

"That it is, Mrs. Harris, that it is." He stretched and yawned and complimented Barbara on the fine meal he had consumed.

Suddenly, Barbara was too tired from the day's exertions to get rid of Mr. Rollins in any other way than inviting him to spend the night. When she told Mr. Rollins of the spare bed in the spare room, she felt Morgan shift next to her again. She was aware of his leg next to hers. She looked up at him, but he did not meet her eyes. He was looking at Mr. Rollins and repeating the invitation—rather woodenly, she thought.

Mr. Rollins thanked them dutifully and accepted their continuing hospitality. He offered to help with the washing-up, and Barbara accepted. Morgan helped, too, and it seemed to Barbara that he was avoiding her eyes and the kind of casual touch that might occur when two people were working together in a relatively small space.

Before she knew it, the dishes were clean, Mr. Rollins's room was readied and he was installed, and she was alone again with Morgan Harris.

The moment he closed the bedroom door behind him, shutting them in together, she felt a change come over her, as if a wash of new colors had spread through her, all blues and dark reds. He walked straight up to her, but did not touch her. He said, low, moving his mouth toward her ear, "You did not have to invite him to spend the night."

The embered darkness wrapped them in intimacy. She felt none of the fear she had experienced the night before, when Lieutenant Richards and his men had been beyond her bedroom door and Morgan had covered her mouth with one hand and held her against him with the other, and yet her heart was beating as erratically as it had then. However, it was no longer due to the mystery of the man, but rather Mr. Rollins's inadvertent revelations about this man's life and loves.

Barbara realized that they could not risk moving farther away from one another or talking louder.

"It seemed easier, finally, to invite him to stay the night than to send him on his way," she said. She felt a flash of irritation with him, with herself, with the world. "Indeed, I was too tired to turn the conversation and convince him of how much he wished to be back out on the road, looking for Jack Carter."

"I'm tired, too," he said meaningfully, "but I could have found a way to send him packing."

"To find Jack Carter's trail?" she whispered in tones that matched his.

"Jack Carter's finished," he said. Without elaborating on that interesting point, he continued swiftly, "I'm sorry that you had to hear all of that."

She had no response. She simply looked up into his eyes, which were steady on her. She had seen him before as an attractive man, though not in the ordinary way. She pictured him now as a sexual man, as comfortable seducing a rich lawyer's wife in her own house as bedding a dockside harlot. She would have been surprised to discover that he preferred the latter's charms, and that he had avoided both women for the past several months.

"What?" he prodded, his beautiful eyes narrowing, his deep, gravelly voice low and warm, almost teasing. "No comment on Jack Carter's career?"

He had not moved a fraction closer to her, but Barbara was acutely conscious of his body, his stance, the slope of his shoulders, the distribution of his weight across his two feet. He had kept to himself since entering her house and her life, and he had not changed his manner. Nevertheless, Barbara began to understand the ease he might have had finding his way into a rich woman's bedroom.

Although she had not the least shred of sympathy for the jilted Mrs. Layton, she thought it all mightily unfair, the attractions of this man before her. She shook her head slowly. She was irritated. "No," she murmured. "No comment, beyond the observation that it seems ridiculously easy for a man to come and go and change his name, Morgan Harris."

"That is my name," he replied.

"And Jack Carter isn't?"

"Jack Carter's finished," he repeated. "And what makes you think it's so easy?"

"Why did you run?"

It was too dark for her to catch and interpret precisely the look that came into his eyes before he lowered his lashes and took a step away from her. Moving around her to cross the room in the direction of the windows, he said, "I'll take the chair."

Another flash of irritation flared. It shot through her body and made her back ache. *I'll take the chair,* he said, as if they were a married couple having a spat. *I'll take the chair,* he said, as if she would think him less of a threat to her in the chair by the bed than in the bed itself! *I'll take the chair,* he said, as if to protect himself from her—or from the woman, or the women, after him!

He could take it or leave it, as far as she was concerned. It was his choice, the bed or the chair. After a moment, she said, "You'll encounter the same problems in the chair this night that you would have had last night." She turned toward him and spoke to his back. "We're both tired from the day's activities, and we both need a good night's rest for tomorrow's work." Her voice sounded snippy, even to her own ears. "I'll be leaving the room now for a few minutes, and I'll leave the nightshirt for you at the end of the bed, if you want it. I'll ask you to draw the curtains, if you please."

She left the room then to perform her nightly duties, whereupon she discovered, to her complete disgust, that her woman's courses had chosen this day, of all days, to begin flowing again. Her period had not returned since Sarah's birth, and so liberated had she been from the monthly curse that she had forgotten all about it and was hardly prepared. It seemed a perverse trick of fate that her courses should return now, when a man was in her house and in her bedroom, posing as her husband. And in her general mood of tired irritation, she decided that, in some vague and mysterious way, Morgan Harris—or whatever he called himself—was to blame for the return of her womanly functions.

She returned to her room to find that Morgan had taken the wiser, and certainly more comfortable, choice of sleeping in her bed. She decided that he would have had better manners if he had turned down her invitation to sleep in the bed, and she thought him an intruder. She mentally cursed him for not knowing that she would want the bed all to herself this night.

However, when she had unbound her hair, brushed it hard and readied herself for bed, and was finally able to crawl between the sheets, which had been warmed by Morgan's body, she was almost—and all against her will—glad that he was there. She found comfort in his rhythmic breathing, in his masculine weight upon the mattress, in his filling of the space in the bed, a space meant for two. She lay on her side, hands clasped prayerfully under her right cheek, facing him, in her accustomed position. Before her lashes shuttered down, she noticed that his eyes were open and he was contemplating the ceiling. She let her tired bones sink into the supportive softness of the bed. He was so contained on his side that she knew he would not touch her, as he had not touched her the night before. Was that a twinge of disappointment she felt, at the thought that she was not attractive to this wild, womanizing man who was also known as Jack Carter? She was too exhausted to decide such a delicate issue, so she simply let her bruised soul be pillowed in the darkness and warmth and completeness of a bedroom in which slept—on the face of it—a husband and a wife and a child.

No sooner had she snuggled into repose than the child awoke fitfully, demanding attention pitifully. Barbara nearly groaned aloud. She lumbered out of bed, picked up the heavy lump of crying flesh and dragged herself back to bed. If she could just hold her fussy baby for a while, Barbara figured, they would both go back to sleep. It was only when she tried to lie back down with the baby in her arms that it became clear, from a gustier cry and Sarah's angry movements toward her mother's breast, that the little one was hungry.

Barbara pulled herself up with a sigh and tried to remember why it was that Sarah should be hungry. The day was such a fractured memory of information and emotions that she realized that Sarah did, indeed, have legitimate cause to be hungry. That allayed Barbara's irritation only slightly. Her feelings were further soothed when she put Sarah to her breast and the baby guzzled noisily. That sound—impolite, uncivilized, even indecent—was far better than the crying and whining, and Barbara was relieved, in turn, to be drained of at least some of the fluids filling her. As Sarah sucked and drank, Barbara's relief shaded into contentment to be holding her dear, dear daughter. That mood slid into happiness, then joy, then a kind of sisterly sadness for Mrs. Ross and her emptiness, then a moment of blessedness at the thought that Sarah's life had enriched hers—the widowed, barren Barbara Johnson's life—and that she would never let her baby go. More fluid came to prick at the corners of her eyes.

She felt like a wet mess of milk and blood and tears. As she fed the sloppy Sarah at her breast, she imagined that no woman could look more unappealing to a man than she must right now to Morgan Harris, for she knew his eyes were on her.

Barbara looked over at him and met his eyes in the darkness. He did not look away or apologize for his blatant regard. Their eyes held. They did not speak. Barbara felt an unaccountable desire wash through her, and more fluid filled her already bloated body. It was blue and delicious, the color and the feeling, and it was new. It was not the familiar white of milk, or the annoying red of blood, or the elusive clear of tears, but rather the blue of attraction, the mauve of apprehension, and the purple of mysterious desire. She caught her breath and looked away from him, suddenly conscious that the baby in her arms was a solid, obscene symbol of her sex and her body's desire. She was not embarrassed, but she did feel exposed.

When she spoke, it was with her head turned slightly away from him, so that she was talking into the darkness. Her voice held none of its former snippiness. It was husky. "No one, not even Mr. Rollins, would hold it against you if you wanted to make your bed in the sitting room in order to get some sleep." She let her words hang there a moment, then added softly, "Sarah's likely to be fussy the night long, and we're a noisy pair."

Morgan did not immediately reply. Nor did he take his eyes off Barbara, off the blue-white flesh of her full breasts. Barbara knew by his deep sigh that he had heard her. Then he said, his voice cutting between his own tiredness and a fugitive humor, "She might cry the night long, for all I care, but don't make me move. Just don't make me move."

Barbara looked back over and down at him. "I won't."

"Because I can't move. Not until morning."

"All right, then. I only wanted to warn you."

He grunted his thanks and sighed again. "It's too bad I can't take her off your hands, so that we could spell one another through the night." His voice was warm and gravelly, and it came from deep within a man on the edge of sleep or oblivion, neither happy nor sad, but rather simply, equilibrated. "Nevertheless, it can't be done, so it can't be done."

That was all they said. Sarah finished her meal. Barbara rearranged her gown and just sat there, holding Sarah, unable or merely unwilling to get up to return the baby to her cradle. She felt pleasantly drained just then, of milk, of emotion, of worry over the past and the future and the present.

Morgan turned his eyes away from mother and daughter and trained them again on the ceiling. It was a curious feeling of envy he had then. This time he was not envious of the baby and her claim on the mother's body, as he had been last night. This time he was envious of the mother and her motherhood. She had a child. She had a new life. She had her farm. She had happiness. She had all that had been taken away from him.

He relaxed his head into the pillows and closed his eyes. He had a sudden, horrible, gut-wrenching vision of fire. Of flames. Of conflagration. Burning his home. Burning his fields. Burning his wife. Burning his child. Crackling. Cackling. Consuming. Denying him love and a life worth living.

He opened his eyes quickly and focused on a dark, imaginary spot in the ceiling. He brought into control his suddenly irregular heartbeat. He tried deep breathing to calm the light sweat that had broken out across his body. He was happy for the distraction of Barbara rising from the bed and returning Sarah to the cradle. He watched her, more dispassionately now, as she laid her little bundle down, as she fiddled with the baby-soft coverlet, as she crooned with motherly noises, soothing her already soothed and sated infant, as she returned, heavily, to bed.

Then there were, suddenly and predictably, further distractions. Her body stretching out next to his, her tired sigh, her light weight and textured scent floating next to him, her undeniable beauty, and the knowledge that she knew more about his other life now than he had intended for her to know. It struck him as a luxury, to be in bed with a woman and not make love to her. To be in bed with a wife, knowing that they had made love the night before and could do so again the next night, making this night's love making unnecessary. To imagine sleeping with a woman, really sleeping with a woman, to imagine past and future satisfactions, always available, always dependable, always there, making present urgencies deferrable.

Something stirred inside him. The ripple of an emotion. Interesting. After all these years of trying to negotiate a flat, unvaried emotional landscape with no vertical slopes. He avoided the valleys when he could, but that meant he had to avoid the mountains, as well. Flat landscape was the way he liked it. No valleys, thank God, but no mountains, either.

Something else stirred inside him. Sexual interest. Irritating. After all that he had just concluded about the subtle pleasure of pleasure deferred.

So now he had to deal with arousal. Just like last night. This was the hell he had anticipated at dinner, when it was clear that they would have another guest for the night and he would once again enter the paradoxical paradise of Barbara Johnson's bed. The night before, the arousal had been of his body, not his heart. And tonight? All body, and some heart? Could his desire have something to do with the emotional ripple he had just felt stir inside him? The thought caused his desire to cool and wither immediately.

He grimaced inwardly. Here was a twist, impotence in the presence of caring. But then why had he felt no further desire for Mrs. Mary Ann Layton these past months? Or for the hot and spicy Roxanne? It was not from too much caring about those two women, certainly, he thought, acknowledging that complete indifference was just as fatal to desire as too much caring. He brought the rich, slim, black-haired Mary Ann Layton to mind—and felt nothing. He summoned the sultry, red-headed Roxanne and felt a similar nothing. When he thought of another black-haired woman, he remembered deep caring, love and life. And his aroused desire died instantly.

He shifted and glanced over at Barbara, who was sunk in slumber. He felt neither too little nor too much for her. He felt just enough to want her, to feel his desire rise. So much for impotence! He had the curious satisfaction of knowing he was willing and able, and he felt the clear frustration of knowing that neither his willingness nor his ability would be called upon. This, then, was not hell, and it surely was not heaven.

Purgatory.

A new state for him.

Not an entirely satisfactory one, either, but that, of course, was in the nature of purgatory.

He gazed at the ceiling. He would have to chop some wood. Mentally. He had enjoyed chopping wood last night and today. He had forgotten how good it felt, to grasp an axe between his hands again, to lift the tool above his head, to work the muscles in his arms and back and shoulders. His rhythm had been off at first, since he had not chopped wood in well over a decade, but the movements had come back, easily.

Yes, it had felt good to raise the axe above his head, to bring it down, accurately, into the wedge at the center of a wide hip of wood, to see the wood split and separate, and to repeat the motion again and again and again, with body, axe and wood in rhythmic harmony.

He halted his train of thought. It was doing little good to dampen his desire. A man was supposed to *saw* wood to get to sleep, not chop it like some randy young farmer, full of energy.

Think about music, then. It had been equally wonderful to hold a guitar in his hands again and to raise his voice in song. He had sold his guitar ages ago. His fingers on the strings this afternoon had felt exquisite. It had been an honest pleasure to pluck and to strum and to tease and to arouse and to—

He realized that this train of thought would be equally unproductive, if his purpose was to quiet the blood in his body.

He glanced down at Barbara. Beautiful new mother in the world. Beautiful new woman in his life. Beautiful new emotion in his breast—neither too much nor too little emotion, but just enough for him to desire her.

It was going to be a long night.

Chapter Nine

Barbara awoke some time later, in the depths of the night. The first split second of her waking was given to pricking her ears for the sound that must have awakened her. She heard nothing. Or, more precisely, she did not hear Sarah. No baby's whine. No crying. No fussing.

In the next split second, still submerged in the confusion of a heavy, dissatisfied sleep, she was not a mother awakening to the demands of her baby. She was the widow she had been over a year ago, when the British army had invaded North Point and she had caught the fancy of General Robert Ross. She was in his arms, in her bed, waking to him the last night he had spent with her before being killed.

In the kaleidoscopic vision of half-waking dreams, she remembered the first time she had laid eyes on General Ross. It was the early morning of a hot August day. She was in her wagon, carrying eggs to the meetinghouse. He was in the company of two British officers. The first thing she noticed about him was his red coat. The second thing she noticed about him was his frank appraisal of her, the appreciation of her womanly self that shone from his gray eyes. She had seen that look in a man's eyes a hundred times before and wanted it no more now than at any other time. Only this time she knew that she would not be able to hold this man off, as she had all the others, with a firm, simple, dignified "No."

In the dream, he was astride his stallion, sitting tall, looking strong and fit. His dark hair was pulled back at the nape with a ribbon. His temples were touched with silver. His eyes were keen and fine, his nose was thin and aristocratic. His mouth was hard, his chin was firm. He was handsome and distinguished and the enemy officer in command of the region. She felt a wall of hatred grow up within her at sight of him.

In the dream, it was the early morning of the fine September day when she had sent him to his death, when she had awakened to find him next to her, when he had reminded her of their night's lovemaking. She had looked at him that morning and recalled how it was that, for the first time in the dove gray morning light, she had seen him up close, as only a lover or a mother sees another human's face. She saw his steady eyes, focused on her with the complex lights of passion remembered and passion anticipated. She saw his dark hair, graying with distinction at the temples. She saw his chest and shoulders above the sheets, muscled and disciplined, still strong, but tempered by the maturity of his years.

He had told her then, when he had forced her to bend to his body and receive it in a way no man had asked of her before, of the secret plans he had made that day for his attack on Baltimore.

And the moment he had left her house, his passion satisfied, she had gone to the meetinghouse and alerted Ben Skinner and Michael Gorsuch of the British army's advance that afternoon.

But— No. Her half-waking mind floundered in further confusion. General Ross was not dead. She was only wishing for his death. He was still alive. Next to her. Breathing regularly. His heartbeat was steady. She could feel his heart thumping lightly against her back. She could feel his thighs pressed to the back of her thighs. She could feel his arm lying heavily across her shoulder, his hand lying innocently, insolently, on her breast. She could feel his rhythmic breathing on her neck.

She had been confused, but in this dream she knew clearly that it was that infamous night in August when General Ross and the British army's Forty-fourth Foot had entered Washington, D.C., and set it aflame. He had come to the house in Riverdale where she was staying outside the capital, and he had forced her to bend to his will. He had undressed her in the glow of the burning of her country's capital, the fire for which he took credit, the burning of the American dream. Then she had undressed him—but only after a brief humiliation had convinced her of his purpose. He had taken her most masterfully. And more than once.

She awoke now, fully, with a start, to find herself in her own bed, hot and sticky and drenched with feelings she had never permitted herself to feel. She discovered then that she was not being held by General Robert Ross, who had departed this earth fourteen months before, but by a very live man who might—or might not—be named Morgan Harris.

Her shame and desire were replaced by an odd sense of amusement, even relief. It was Morgan Harris's body that had inspired her wild, lustful dream, not the memory of the brilliant and powerful General Ross. The dream had not been inspired solely by her memories of her enemy, General Ross. The dream had not been inspired by a married man, now dead, whose wife now threatened her happiness. The dream had not been inspired by the father of her child. She wondered why she had dreamed so vividly of the fiery destruction of Washington, which she had witnessed from afar in August the year before, but which had never yet entered the depths of her dreams.

Later she would have to examine these very strange emotions and come to understand why she had confused her memories of Robert Ross and the body of Morgan Harris. For now, she needed to effect a more immediate escape from Morgan Harris's sleepy embrace. She had, as well, that unclean, dreadful feeling that she would have to change her menstrual cloth.

When she returned to bed, some minutes later, she noticed that Morgan had shifted his position and had rolled back over to his side of the bed, away from her. Although nothing in his breathing had changed, she was sure that he was awake. It made her feel, at once, uncomfortable that the privacy of her night had been invaded and comfortable that she was less alone in the world.

She noted—it was a tired, absurd afterthought—that having another body in bed made the space very warm, and her feet, after being exposed to the cold, were rapidly warmed.

As she was sliding back into sleep, Sarah awoke, ending the pleasant lull. Barbara rose, held her baby, had a difficult time quieting her, lost her patience, tried the breast—to no avail—and settled into pacing with the squirming bundle, cajoling and crooning. It was a tiresome exercise, and her only consolation lay in the fact that she had apparently absorbed enough of Morgan's heat to keep her warm in the relative chill of the room.

So went the night. And it was a very, very long night for both Barbara and Morgan.

They awoke early and unrested. Barbara, in particular, was out of sorts. When she threw back the covers to get out of bed, she nearly groaned aloud to see a rust red spot of blood flecking her side of the sheets. Embarrassed, she covered the spot quickly with the bedclothes and glanced over her shoulder to discover whether Morgan had seen it. Fortunately, he had not, and was just then pulling on his breeches and was looking out the window since he had already opened the drapes.

At least today, Barbara mused irascibly, could not possibly be as trying as yesterday. She decided it would go much better if they got rid of Mr. Rollins as soon as possible.

This was not so easily done, for Mr. Rollins had conceived an affable liking for the young Harris couple. Breakfast went smoothly enough, but Barbara's mind was focused wholly on the spot on the sheet on her bed, and so she overcooked the eggs and burnt the muffins on the edges. Nevertheless, the meal was edible, and neither Morgan nor Mr. Rollins complained.

When it seemed, at last, that Mr. Rollins was on his way, Barbara jumped at the chance to go to her bedroom and strip the bed of its linens. When Morgan went outside to see Mr. Rollins off, Barbara rolled up the sheet, along with her stained night shift. She brought the bundle into the kitchen and laid it out on the sink stone. Surveying the stains, she decided to work at them with cold water from the well, so she bundled up the cloths again and went outside by way of the back door.

When Morgan came back in the house and saw that Barbara was not there, he decided to make good his escape to the tenant's house. He got his bedroll from the bedroom, and he was about to exit through the back door, carrying it, at the moment Barbara entered it.

They were face-to-face. Before Barbara had a chance to question him about what he was doing, he glanced down at the cloths in her hands, whose stains had been wetted in preparation for a salting. He was puzzled for a moment, but then comprehension dawned. He lifted his brows delicately, and Barbara's cheeks reddened. The next moment, Mr. Rollins knocked on the door and announced that he needed to check his room for forgotten items.

Morgan turned away from Barbara with the swift thought, *Now, if that isn't the epitome of marriage, sleeping with a woman during her courses!* He tried to remember the last time he had been in a woman's bed when she was in such a condition, and the memory of it cost him a dull pang.

He put his bedroll down. "Yes, Mr. Rollins, you forgot something?" he said pleasantly to the guest who would not leave.

"It's my penknife," Mr. Rollins explained as he crossed the room. "I think I left it on the table by the bed." He stuck his head through the door to the spare room. "Or at least I thought I had. Well! It's not there." His head came back out of the room. "Now, what could I have done with it?" He was patting his various pockets. "I always keep it in my breeches pocket, but now I don't— Oh! *Here* it is!"

He withdrew the misplaced knife from his vest pocket. "Now how did I come to put it there, I wonder?"

Since Morgan had no answer to that, he simply smiled and said sympathetically, "They're the devil to keep track of." He added helpfully, "Now, is there anything else you need before you set off?"

Mr. Rollins did not think so, and he thanked his host and hostess again at length.

Barbara had turned to face him with the linen bunched up behind her back. She smiled tightly and murmured another goodbye.

Morgan ushered Mr. Rollins back out the front door and onto the porch. "Where are you off to now, sir?" he asked conversationally.

"To the South, I suppose," Mr. Rollins replied. "Mrs. Layton said that Jack Carter always had a hankering for the South." He scratched his head before he put on his hat. "I don't know how I lost the trail so quickly yesterday, but I'll retrace my steps in Baltimore. Perhaps there'll be signs indicating that he's gone to Richmond." Mr. Rollins shrugged and smiled. "We'll see!"

"Perhaps the other two men who are on his trail will have a lead for you—that is, if they have made it to Baltimore," Morgan suggested.

"Perhaps, but if I meet up with them and they have nothing for me, I'll send them out to the Harris farm for an evening of entertainment and hospitality!" Mr. Rollins said cheerfully.

Morgan was less cheered. "I wish you wouldn't," he said.

"Oh?" Mr. Rollins was interested, perhaps even faintly suspicious.

Morgan smiled. "It's Mrs. Harris. She won't be in the mood to receive visitors in the next few days, I'm thinking."

"Oh?" Mr. Rollins said again, not quite catching on.

"It's that time of the month," Morgan clarified.

"Oh!" Mr. Rollins said, expressively. He nodded wisely. "That explains it, then." He was not an evasive man. "I thought you two had had a spat! Now I see what it was with Mrs. Harris this morning. The eggs and the muffins—if you know what I mean!'' He smiled benevolently and lowered his voice to a conspiratorial level. "I have experience with females," he said, unaware that he was speaking to a man of singularly wide experience. "Been married over a quarter century! I've learned a thing or two, and do you want to know what my advice is to you, as a newlywed, Mr. Harris?"

"Please," Morgan invited graciously.

"Humor 'em!" Mr. Rollins confided. He was in a helpful mood this morning. "For these few days each month, humor 'em! And never, *never* tell them you understand why they're acting as angry as a wet hen during that time of the month, for they'll like to kill you!" He shook his head sorrowfully. "My Gwendolyn—Mrs. Rollins—was nearly unlivable when she was going through her time of the month, although it didn't come all that often, since we had seven children, don't you know. So she was either pregnant or nursing most of the time before she went through the change of life!" Mr. Rollins shuddered. "Thank the Lord that *that* is over, too!"

"I'll remember," Morgan replied gravely, and offered, "Can I help you onto your horse?"

Mr. Rollins declined the offer. As he swung himself into the saddle, he said, thoughtfully, "Maybe Mrs. Harris needs another child. I've never seen a woman love a child the way your wife loves yours! It's a wonder to behold, mother love. But she needs another to spread it around! Maybe two or three more!"

"I'll see what I can do," Morgan said.

Evan Rollins gave Morgan Harris one last, long look. His smile held a trace of lingering puzzlement. For his final piece of wise advice, he said, "If you weren't already married and to a woman who's a good enough cook, I'd tell you to settle down and put some meat on those bones before you get any older. Take it from me, man, to be married all these years to the same woman is not the worst thing in the world.

So enjoy what comforts you have. Goodbye to you, Mr. Harris!''

Morgan bid his guest a cordial goodbye.

As Mr. Rollins turned his horse away, he said, ''And don't worry about me sending either of those other two fellows from Boston out to North Point! No sense wasting your time or creating more work for Mrs. Harris! I thank you again, sir!''

Morgan watched his pursuer ride away. Then he rubbed his palms across his thighs and returned to face his fate in the house.

When he closed the door behind him, Barbara turned away from her task at the sink and toward him. He saw from the look on her face that the inevitable conversation was not going to be easy.

''So,'' she said.

''So,'' he repeated, leaning against the door so that the latch clicked decisively.

She looked impatient and irritated. ''Mr. Rollins is gone? Truly gone?''

''Once and for all,'' Morgan said, ''I can only hope.''

''You can only hope!'' she echoed. ''It was an interesting visit Mr. Rollins provided.''

''Interesting enough,'' he agreed. He crossed the room and chose to occupy himself with tending to Pockets, who had perked up when he reentered the house and was wagging his tail excitedly. Morgan sternly explained to Pockets that he was supposed to react to strangers coming to the house, not to his master. Morgan knelt and scratched the pup's ears absently while he picked up the bowl of water from its place next to the pup's blanket. With the bowl in hand, Morgan approached the sink stone, where a bucket of water stood.

He brushed by Barbara, who did not move away to provide him space. Nor did she try to hide what she was doing there with her stained linens.

When he had filled the bowl and was going to return to the hearth, she stopped him by moving slightly to bar his easy passage. "And that's all you have to say about Mr. Rollins's visit?" she demanded. She looked straight into his blue eyes. "That it was interesting?"

Morgan paused and looked down at her. He was not now, nor was he ever, in the mood for confessions. "You heard everything he said and can come, easily enough, to your own conclusions."

"And you think it is as easy as that?" she said, her voice caught between surprise and impatience.

Morgan's lean features were impassive. "What don't you understand about the activities of a man named Jack Carter?"

Barbara put her hands on her hips. "Well, I know for one thing that he has turned up in North Point, Maryland, calling himself Morgan Harris."

Morgan Harris smiled perfunctorily and complimented her. "I did not think you lacked for understanding."

This remark was not calculated to improve Barbara's mood. "You either rate my intelligence too high," she snapped, "to think I have pieced together the whole, or you rate it too low, to think you can get away with explaining nothing!"

"You put me in an impossible position with respect to rating your intelligence," he replied.

"Fancy talking, Morgan Harris!" she shot back, a flash of fire in her voice. "Or am I addressing Jack Carter?"

"Jack Carter—or Jacques Cartier, if you're wanting accuracy," he said, cool and dispassionate, "is the name my mother gave me at birth as a legacy of my father's family. He was of French-Canadian stock, and his family was Breton." He walked around her then, taking the bowl of water to the waiting pup. "Some years ago, I renounced that name and took that of my mother's father, namely Morgan Harris. He was Welsh-English. That name served me well for a while," he continued as he set the bowl of water down. He turned to face Barbara again. "However, the time came when it no longer served me so well, and I reverted to Jack Carter."

"And now you're Morgan Harris again."

"For obvious reasons."

"The only obvious reasons I can see are that you are escaping charges, both legal and financial, of cheating and of disturbing the peace. Oh, and of breach of promise."

"Breach of promise?"

"To Mrs. Layton."

Morgan shook his head. "Jack Carter never made her any promises."

Barbara regarded him unwaveringly. "I still say it's too easy for a man to simply change his name and disappear."

"Do I detect a note of jealousy?"

"Yes," she answered. In her frustration with him and her irritation with the world, she had admitted what she had never before admitted to a living soul. "You can't begin to imagine the scorn that has been heaped on me here—for all my neighbors' understanding and willingness to help me! I'm still a fallen woman. Or more of one now, with General Ross's child, for I was already a fallen woman years ago, before Jonas married me! How wonderful it would be to go somewhere and start over! No history! No past! A new name! What makes me maddest is the fact that night before last *I* told *you* about General Ross, while *you've* told *me* nothing! I don't ask for anything elaborate! A simple explanation will do! And I can tell you that I felt better—much better!—for having got my story out in the open!"

He was watching her with no change of expression. His voice remained cool when he said, "Then that's the difference between us." He had been hired to do a certain job on her farm. He had unquestioningly lent her his help with Lieutenant Richards and Mrs. Ross. He did not owe her an explanation of his life or his actions. He returned decisively to the kitchen area, got some food scraps for Pockets, and fed the miserable critter. He was about to pick up his bedroll again and retire to the tenant's house when a new thought occurred to him.

Without explanation, he sat down in the rocking chair, facing away from the fire and toward the front door.

Barbara was exasperated. She put her hands on her hips. "What are you doing?" she wanted to know.

"Sitting here," he informed her.

"With all the chores waiting to be done?" she asked, in the voice of a good housewife.

He rocked back and forth calmly. "I'm aware of them," he answered, glancing over at her. "I was a farmer before I was a gambler, as you've probably figured out." His gaze was trained on the front door. "However, the chores will have to wait until we have received our next visitor."

Barbara felt like shaking him. She took several steps toward him. "Our next visitor?"

"I'll lay you five to one that we have another visitor today."

"Any bets as to who it might be?" she inquired, with a touch of sarcasm.

He acknowledged her tone with a sly glance that explained his success at the gambling tables, and with the ladies. "There's John Finch, for one, who's after me," he said.

"The gambling rival?" she inquired.

He nodded. "Then, too, there's Bobby Dale."

"Who is—?"

"Roxanne's man. Roxanne—my wharf floozy," he explained. "Although why he would come after me, when he could only be happy that I had left town, I wouldn't know. However, Rollins said that two more men were on my tail, so..."

Just then, as if on schedule, the sounds of an approaching horse's hooves could be heard galloping down the farm lane toward the house. Morgan's expression did not change, but he did look expectantly over to the hearth, where the runt of a pup was eating, blissfully unaware. Morgan frowned his disapproval of the useless animal.

Barbara was openmouthed with surprise. "Are you a psychic, as well?"

He shook his head. "Not in the general way of things, no." He shrugged. "This morning, however, I simply knew that another man was coming. I don't know how I knew it, but I knew it, and I wasn't wrong." He paused. He listened for the sound of boots on the porch. He waited for the knock that came a few seconds later. "And here he is."

"It's for you, I think," Barbara said.

"It is," he agreed tranquilly.

As Morgan crossed the few paces to the door, Barbara was far less tranquil. If it was one of two men who knew Morgan Harris as Jack Carter, her own cover with Lieutenant Richards and Mrs. Ross might be ruined.

Morgan opened the door to a remarkable-looking man with a body the shape of a perfect pear supported by two sticks. Atop the man's small head sat a stiff black hat, from under which wisps of pale blond hair escaped. His small, pudgy face was set off by two dark button eyes and a bump of a chin, which receded into the several folds of his neck. His remarkably misshapen girth was swathed in the soberest black.

"You," the man intoned, poking a pudgy finger in Morgan's face, "should be ashamed of yourself!"

Chapter Ten

Morgan had never seen this man before. However, from the details of the man's dress, he was able to make an educated guess as to who the man might be.

"No doubt," Morgan replied, and opened the door wider. "Would you like to come in?"

The man seemed satisfied with Morgan's admission, and he accepted the invitation to enter. As he crossed the threshold, he proceeded to soften his dark accusation. "At least I *think* you should be ashamed," he said, in less dramatic tones, "assuming that I have correctly understood, point one, the story of who you are, and point two, the explanation of what you are doing here!"

Morgan addressed point one. "I am sometimes known as Morgan Harris," he replied, extending his hand.

The man took Morgan's hand automatically and pumped it vigorously. "Sometimes known. Heh, heh!" he chuckled, as if at some private joke, then repeated, "Sometimes known! Quite right! Quite right!"

Barbara had come forward at the entrance of this man, the most prominent inhabitant of North Point. "Reverend Austin," she said, "I give you good morning."

"Good morning to you, Mrs. Johnson," the good reverend replied, tipping his hat. "Or should it be Mrs. Harris, as the talk in the neighborhood has it?" He frowned, scrunching up his already small features so that they virtually disappeared. Then his face cleared, causing them to resurface.

"But that, of course, is why I am come." He smiled with satisfaction. "Which brings us to point two." He regarded Morgan and explained seriously, "I am most emphatically against the kind of conversation which announces itself as having two parts, but which never gets beyond the first point. But I digress," the reverend pronounced, pouncing upon his own lapse as a cat upon a mouse. "We have clarified, one, that you are called, upon occasion, Morgan Harris, and we are attempting to arrive, by degrees, at point two—the question of what you are doing here."

"I have hired Mr. Harris to oversee the farm throughout the winter," Barbara offered.

"Ah, but that does not explain how you came to be married," the reverend pointed out.

Barbara had known this man her entire life and was quite accustomed to his quirks. "But, of course, we are *not* married, we are only *saying* we are married."

The reverend's relief was evident. "I am glad to hear you acknowledge that *saying* you are married is not at all the same thing as *being* married." He shook his head wisely. "A marriage has to be done properly, according to the rules, by the correct person saying the correct words."

"Yes," Barbara said, "and we did not have the marriage done properly, so we are, I repeat, not married."

"In that case," the reverend said, turning to go, "I don't need to trouble you any longer." He stopped, turned back around, pulled himself up straight and said sternly, "But I am afraid that your awareness that you are not, in fact, married does not improve the situation at all!"

"It doesn't?" Barbara managed, exchanging a helpless glance with Morgan.

"In fact, it might make it a good deal worse, given your history, Mrs. Johnson," Reverend Austin said.

"Perhaps we would benefit from discussing the matter more thoroughly," Morgan said reasonably.

Barbara took Morgan's cue and gestured toward the settee. "Would you like to sit down, Reverend? May I take your coat?"

The reverend shed his cloak and sat down heavily on the settee, settling the book he was holding across his knees.

"It makes no difference that you had a child out of wedlock, Mrs. Johnson. But the fact remains that having deviated once from the rules does not sanction you to *continue* to deviate from the rules. It is unacceptable that you are not married to this man, with whom you are engaged in marital congress!"

Barbara had taken her seat in the rocking chair, while Morgan had pulled up the bench from the table and was sitting next to her. She did not dare look at him.

"But we are not so engaged," she managed to say with a perfectly straight face and even voice.

Reverend John Austin considered this information. "Well, now, that is sufficient grounds for an annulment."

"We are not married," Barbara reminded him.

The reverend perked up, as if he had suddenly remembered the purpose of his visit. "However, you should be!" He held up the book in his hand, waving it emphatically. "That is why I am come! To marry you! Properly! In the eyes of God!"

"You misunderstand, Reverend," Barbara pursued patiently. "We have done nothing to warrant a marriage."

"Nothing?" the reverend repeated.

"Nothing," Barbara affirmed.

"But this man has lived under your roof for the past two nights, has he not?"

"Yes," Barbara stated cautiously.

"So, I have come to make legally binding what you have already established in practice."

"You intend to *marry* us?" Barbara asked, aghast and amazed.

"Yes."

Morgan spoke up. His voice was wary. "Is that a Bible you have with you?"

The reverend looked at the book he was shaking for emphasis, as if he were surprised to see it there. He frowned. "Ah, no! This is Trapping Reeve's *The Law of Baron and Femme; of parent and child; of guardian and ward; of master and servant.* Appeared just this year, and I ordered it straight from the publisher in New Haven."

"Shouldn't you be carrying a Bible, rather than a legal text, if you are intending to perform a marriage?" Morgan asked reasonably.

The reverend laughed jovially. "I have as much interest in interpreting the laws of man as I do the laws of God. You see I have the gift of interpretation, but I wasn't trying to rush you into anything. You should have time to think it over, taking such an important step in one's life as getting married!"

Morgan was glad to hear this. "So we—Mrs. Johnson and I—are allowed to think it over?"

"Why, yes, for I don't intend to perform the ceremony anywhere but at the meetinghouse. However, I should tell you not to tarry too long in making up your minds, for everyone is waiting for us over there."

Barbara arched a brow. "We have the twenty minutes it takes to get to the meetinghouse to think it over?"

Barbara was not pleased. This past year and more, she had survived the disapproval of her neighbors. They did not blame her openly, of course, for they knew the circumstances of General Ross's invasion of North Point and the general's interest in her. Nevertheless, she had experienced their horror when they had discovered that she was pregnant, and she had experienced her own horror of understanding their unspoken criticism when she had refused to "lose" an unwanted baby.

For her baby—her Sarah, her life—had not been unwanted, but had been devoutly desired, despite the circumstances of her conception. Barbara had endured her neighbors' subtle ostracism because of her daughter. And because of that ostracism, she had no intention of marrying to satisfy the propriety of those same neighbors.

"Do you need, say, an hour to decide?" the reverend asked hopefully, willing to accommodate them.

"Marriage between us," Barbara told the reverend, with a pointed glance at Morgan, "is out of the question."

"Are there impediments?" the reverend wanted to know.

"No, but—" Barbara began.

She was cut off by the reverend, who lived for discussions of this sort. "*You're* not married, Mrs. Johnson, so any obstruction would have to arise from Mr. Harris's side." He turned toward Morgan, who was wearing a look that was anything but inviting. The reverend was an amazingly insensitive man, and was hardly warned off his course. "Are you presently married, sir?" he asked.

"No."

"Never married?"

Morgan paused. "Yes. I was married. Once."

"But you're not married now."

"No."

The reverend's beady eyes lit up. "Now, don't tell me you were divorced," he said, hoping that Mr. Harris would tell him just that.

"No, I was not divorced."

The reverend's eyes dimmed. "Your wife died," he said mournfully. A widower provided no scope for his gifts of legal interpretation.

"Yes."

Barbara looked at Morgan. His face was impassive, but his voice was as cold as a Canadian winter.

"Insane?" the reverend asked next.

Morgan did not bother to answer that.

"Not even feebleminded?"

"Not that I am aware of."

"Well, now, a feebleminded person wouldn't be aware of it, would he?" the reverend observed. "But I won't belabor the point." He moved right along. "Any contagious diseases?"

"No."

"It's not a question I ask lightly," the reverend said. "There was a most interesting marital case where the wedding had taken place and afterwards it was discovered that the husband had a contagious disease, but the fact that they had never lived together was sufficient to make the marriage null and void. Ah, well." He did not miss a beat and asked, "Impotent?"

The look Morgan sent him would have slain a lesser man. The reverend perceived it and waved the question away with a negligent gesture. "Just asking."

Barbara was beyond embarrassment. She was on her feet, her hands on her hips. "Now, look here, Reverend! It's not that I do not appreciate what you are doing, but the fact of the matter is that Mr. Harris and I have only *claimed* that we were married so that I could tell the general's widow that my Sarah was Morgan's child!"

"General *Ross's* widow?" the reverend asked, obviously not having been brought completely up-to-date. "She is here, in North Point?"

"General Ross's widow is in Baltimore," Barbara confirmed, "and wishes to claim my Sarah as her husband's child in order to take custody of her."

The reverend was nodding, deep in thought. "In that case, then, you would not wish to call Mr. Harris impotent," he reasoned. "However, your daughter *is* the late general's illegitimate child, is she not?"

Barbara reined in her impatience. "Yes," she said, as calmly as she was able. "But if Mr. Harris is said to be the father, then the child could not be the general's illegitimate child, and Mrs. Ross can have no claim on her."

The reverend was shaking his head. "I am sorry to say that the appearance of Mr. Harris on the scene *now* will not save your child from the taint of illegitimacy, Mrs. Johnson!"

"You have forgotten that we are only *saying* that she is our child, and only to Mrs. Ross," Barbara explained yet again, "and we are under no illusion that she is legitimate, or that Mr. Harris is her father."

The reverend was momentarily confused. "Now, why are you saying such a thing to Mrs. Ross?"

"Because she is wanting to take *custody* of my daughter on the assumption that Sarah is her husband's child!"

The reverend was shaking his head. "She can't do it. The custody of an illegitimate child is automatically given to the mother until the child is sixteen years of age."

Barbara felt a glorious wave of relief.

It was premature.

The reverend began to run through the contingencies of which his legal mind was so fond. "Unless the mother does not wish for the child, and the father claims it as his own."

Barbara's relief remained. "Her father is dead, and her mother very much wants her."

"Ah, but the father might have written a will, claiming the child as his heir," the reverend was quick to point out, "in which case everything would be different."

"What do you mean, different?"

"When an inheritance is at stake, the illegitimate child can become of great importance to an otherwise childless man."

Her relief lingered. "General Ross could not have known of the child's existence at the time of his death," she countered.

"A will can be written generally, for any and all heirs, legitimate and illegitimate."

Barbara began to experience some doubts. "Is such a will likely to have been written in the general's case?"

The reverend mulled the question over. "For a man in his position, I would suppose that it's done all the time."

"But I should be able to retain custody of my child until she is sixteen," she argued.

"That is correct, and such a legal stipulation is right and good, since it is based on natural law, the child being a product of the mother's body," the reverend said. "However—" he exhaled heartily "—all that could be contested by man's law, if the general's widow is concerned about a question of inheritance."

"I wouldn't know anything about questions of inheritance, but it's my belief that she simply wants the child for her own," Barbara said, again feeling scared and threatened.

The reverend was a practical man, and he came straight to the heart of the forces affecting man's law. "Is Mrs. Ross rich?"

Barbara began to pace. "Yes."

The reverend rose from the settee. "Better to get married, then, and claim Mr. Harris as the child's father. It's irregular, of course, and such a strategy is not to be found in any law book, for your claims might be interpreted by some as *lying,*" the reverend admitted. "However, in matters such as these, God's law is above man's law. What is right is right, and a mother shall retain her child, if she so desires." He added, somewhat less piously, "By hook or by crook."

Barbara continued to pace. Far from finding the idea of marriage to Morgan Harris absurd, she now thought it convenient, even necessary. Her married status and Morgan Harris's claimed paternity would act as charms against the possibility that Mrs. Ross possessed a will that she was prepared to present in court, in which her husband recognized any and all heirs. Barbara had faith in her home country's system of justice, but she had the same practical streak as the reverend and fully understood the rights that could be bought with money. She had faith in the American legal system—but only just.

She ceased her pacing when she came to her decision, and she looked down at Morgan, a shameless plea in her eyes.

Chapter Eleven

"Would you consider discussing the reverend's suggestion?" she asked him.

Morgan rose slowly to his feet and faced her. "About us getting married?"

"It isn't such a bad idea," she said quickly.

Morgan felt something tighten around him, like a rope, like a noose. Was it his neck that felt squeezed? No. Was it his heart? He did not know. It was most likely his feet that felt bound, for he had not planned to stay in this place for more than a few months. And he had not planned on getting married again, now or ever.

"It was one thing to offer me up as your husband for the benefit of Mrs. Ross and Lieutenant Richards," he said, "but it is another thing to tie the knot, properly and legally."

Morgan saw an idea flash in Barbara's eyes. "That's it!" she said brightly. "That's it! It *is* another thing to tie the knot properly and legally—especially when, to hear the good reverend tell it, there are so many ways for the ceremony to go wrong!"

"Eh...what's that, Mrs. Johnson?" the reverend asked, looking up from his book upon hearing his name.

"That there are so many things that can go wrong, to prevent a marriage from being done right."

"Oh, my, yes," the reverend said, "just the least little irregularity! There are one hundred and one difficulties that can render the most normal-seeming marriage null and void."

Barbara nodded with approval at the reverend and asked him, sweetly, if he would mind if she and Mr. Harris removed themselves for a moment for some private conversation.

The reverend readily granted his permission, and Morgan followed Barbara into the kitchen area, whereupon she told him in a low voice, her blue eyes upon him in added appeal, "It would not have to be a *real* marriage, you know."

"What kind of marriage would it be, in your opinion?"

"One that would be null and void," she answered. "But the impediment would not be publicly revealed until after Mrs. Ross has left the country. That means that we would not even have to obtain a divorce. What could be simpler?"

Morgan did not know. However, Barbara smiled the smile he imagined she did not often smile, the one he had been lucky enough to see three times in as many days. The ties he had felt tightening around his feet suddenly untangled themselves, and he had the vague, pleasurable sensation of beginning to coast happily downhill.

He caught the spirit of the occasion, which was an extraordinary mixture of threat and whimsy. However, if he was going to accommodate Mrs. Johnson and her request that he play along as the father of her child for a few more weeks, he did have one demand to make. "While I am sure that securing a legal marriage cannot be as difficult as the Reverend Mr. Austin seems to think, I do see where a legal flaw could work in our favor. However, I refuse," he stated categorically, "to allow the publicly named impediment for the dissolution of our marriage to be that of impotence."

He was surprised and rather charmed to see Barbara blush, faintly and becomingly.

"We can certainly choose the flaw or hitch that suits our taste best, I suppose," she replied, with admirable composure. "Your name, for instance. If you were to marry under the name Morgan Harris, and Morgan Harris is not your real name, I imagine that the contract would be invalid."

"I imagine it would. However, a public declaration of any other name would possibly expose me to the kinds of investigations that I am expressly trying to avoid."

Barbara slanted him a glance. "Which is your real legal name—Jack Carter, or Morgan Harris?"

Morgan equivocated. "That depends on whose laws you are invoking."

"Well, we could invent any name you wanted to offer to the community as the legal impediment rendering our marriage void. It would not have to be Jack Carter."

"But we would still have to explain why I used a false one in the first place," Morgan observed.

Barbara frowned delicately. "I see your point. Well, then, we could say that you are—"

Morgan cut her off. "We do not invariably need to make *me* the cause of the invalidity of the contract. Surely there is some less personal approach we could take."

Barbara's frown deepened. "I am sure there must be one...."

"Although you cannot think of it."

"Not at the moment, but we still have time," she replied with spirit.

"Not more than half an hour, I believe," he answered.

Her blue eyes flashed with determination. "I refuse to argue over so insignificant a detail when my overall plan is such a perfect one!" The blue of her eyes softened again. "I also refuse to question how it was that you turned up so opportunely on my doorstep, giving me a chance to make everything right in my life when so much has always gone wrong! But here you are!"

Morgan perceived that events had taken on a momentum of their own. He looked down at the wedding ring on his finger, which he had not been able to remove the day before. He tugged at it, and to his relief he found that he could now ease the ring over his knuckle. He decided to settle back and enjoy the ride in the cart coasting downhill.

"All right, then," he said, replacing the ring on his finger as he took Barbara by the arm and led her from the kitchen area. "I suppose we should proceed to the meetinghouse, since everyone is waiting there for us anyway."

Morgan's words caught the reverend's attention. He looked up again, startled, from the fascinating legal convolutions in his book. "Eh? Oh! I almost forgot! Yes! The meetinghouse! Heavens, we're late, and everyone is waiting for us!" He glowered at the couple. "Now, come along, and be quick about it!"

Barbara said that she wanted to take a few moments to get ready. She excused herself, presumably to take care of bodily functions, and while she was gone Morgan took care of Pockets and banked the fire. When she returned, she prepared the baby, whom she changed and bundled warmly for the trip out-of-doors.

As Barbara lifted the baby up and into her arms, playfully, lovingly, she felt that all would soon be right with the world. She was still caught up in her wondering love for her daughter, and at this moment, when her relationship to her daughter seemed most threatened, she felt strong and whole and absolutely certain that, with Morgan Harris's help, everything would turn out all right.

She had no reason for thinking that everything would turn out all right, for so much in her life had gone wrong. Sometimes—and this was one such moment—when she would hold her baby up and gurgle and laugh and make funny faces at her, she would remember the day fourteen months before when she, Barbara, had been reborn. That was the day she had learned that General Ross was dead. That was the day she had permitted herself to cry for the first time in as long as she could remember.

But she had not cried for General Robert Ross. Nor had she cried over the love and passion that might have existed between them under other circumstances, in another time and place. He had been a handsome, elegant, refined man.

If he had not been her enemy, she might have loved him. However, he had been her enemy; and in any case, before his death, before the birth of Sarah, she had not been capable of love.

The general's death had avenged her hardened heart, and softened it. Her life had been a singularly loveless one. She had been the child born after her five brothers were killed by the British in the First War of Independence. She had been the poor little girl whose mother died in childbirth. She had been the orphan whose father died from the weight of the losses of his sons and his wife, and from his unbearable grief. She had been the young beauty who was raped by the rich merchant's son from Baltimore. She had been the fallen woman left in disgrace to marry the cold widower Jonas Johnson, who had not been able to give her children. She had been the mature beauty who caught General Ross's eye and was violated by him, though not violently.

The general had desired her, and had known how to bring her to desire, as well. She had never before experienced such desire, but she had not loved him, for she had not been capable of love. And when, that September morning the year before, he had aroused her and satisfied her and told her the precise time of his intended attack on Baltimore that would win the war for the British, she had known what she would have to do. She had alerted the beleaguered American forces to the details of Ross's military maneuvers, and an American sharpshooter had killed him on the road to Baltimore.

She had caused his death, and he had given her precious life.

With his death, she had absolved her deep hatred for the British, who had taken the lives of her brothers. On the evening of the general's death, she had cried in relief at having been released from the ancient iron bands around her heart. Her tears had begun to dissolve those bands. Her laughter had finished the job. The softening of her heart had made her vulnerable, but it had made her perceptive, too, aware of the possibilities of life, of the power of love, of the magic of laughter.

Then she had laughed some more, six weeks later, when she had allowed herself to believe in the miracle of her pregnancy.

Holding her daughter, thus, this one split second in the air, wiggling her nose and cooing and seeing Sarah scrunch her face and coo in response, Barbara felt happy and humorous. Even with the fluids filling her body with mother's milk and women's courses, which made her feel fat and cranky, she suddenly saw humor everywhere.

When Morgan saw Barbara turn toward him, ready to go, his breath caught in his throat. It was a revelation, this lighthearted and radiant woman who gazed over at him from across the room, holding her baby with a love that seemed less forbidding and alien to him now. So different she looked from the composed beauty who usually faced him.

"Your coat, ma'am?" he inquired, taking her wrap down from the peg next to his. He helped her with the logistics of putting on her coat while transferring the baby from arm to arm.

He donned his own overcoat and, holding his black hat, he addressed the reverend. "You have come on horseback, sir? Good, then we'll follow you in the buggy."

The small wedding party was leaving the front door when the puppy scurried over and began nipping at Morgan's heels. Morgan had thought he had done with Pockets earlier, and he tried to hush him and calm him down, but to no avail. Morgan had the idea that Pockets needed a quick run outside to relieve himself, but the quick run produced nothing in the way of wetting his spot. When Morgan tried to get him back inside the house, Pockets would have none of it. He simply yipped and yapped and jumped up on Morgan, aiming shamelessly for his master's overcoat pockets, until Morgan realized resignedly that they would not be going without the pup. He bent down and scooped him up and into his pocket.

"Are you satisfied, annoying creature?" Morgan asked his unwanted pet.

In high pitch, Pockets noisily answered the question.

"There's no harm that I can see," Barbara said, "if he comes along." Then her brows raised shrewdly. She turned to the reverend, who was approaching the most sway-backed beast to roam on four feet in tidewater Maryland. "Tell me, Reverend, would it be considered a flaw or a hitch or an impediment if we were to be married in the presence of a dog?"

The reverend stopped dead in his tracks to consider the weighty question. After a moment of great deliberation, he shook his head slowly and pronounced, "No, Mrs. Johnson. There is nothing irregular about being married in the presence of animals."

Morgan went to get the buggy, and the reverend spoke to Barbara about a variety of legal matters. Presently Morgan drove up next to the pair, pulled in the reins and hopped down to help his wife-to-be and her baby onto the perch next to him. He made sure that her skirts were tucked in around her ankles, for it was a clear November day, and cold. He walked back around the buggy, mounted, and picked up the reins. Pockets jumped out of Morgan's pocket to perch on the dashboard. Before moving forward, Morgan turned to Barbara and caught the look of amusement on her face.

"What's so funny?" he asked, then followed her gaze to focus on the reverend, who was lumbering ahead of them on his swaybacked animal.

Barbara chuckled and began to rock her baby. "I am afraid that I have never appreciated the reverend quite rightly until this moment—with all his talk of flaws and hitches and perfectly ordinary legal matters going wrong."

"Yes, perfectly ordinary legal matters going wrong," Morgan repeated.

Barbara glanced at him and said without a blush, "We have already discounted *one* impediment that could be invoked to render our marriage illegal, and since you are a widower and I am a widow, we cannot claim an existing marriage as the problem, either." She paused. "How long ago did your wife die?"

Morgan looked straight ahead, between the horse's ears. "Fifteen years."

She nodded, but asked no further questions on that topic. "Oh, and neither are we going to say that there is a legal problem with your name," she continued. "So what other problems could there be?"

"Do I suppose correctly that the Reverend Mr. Austin has all the necessary credentials to marry people?"

Barbara replied a little glumly, "Yes, I suppose he must, or he would have been found out by now. And if he does not, there are quite a few neighborhood couples living in sin! No, I don't think we'll find a flaw in the good reverend's credentials."

They fell silent while they considered other possibilities. At length Morgan suggested; "Perhaps it would be considered a flaw if the reverend were, somehow, to pronounce the wrong words."

Barbara brightened. "Why, yes, I am sure that we would not be legally married if he failed to say 'I now pronounce you man and wife.' Some official person has to say something of the sort for the marriage to take place, isn't that so?" She thought it over. "But how likely is it that he would not say the right words?"

"High unlikely," Morgan admitted. "What other aspects of the marriage ceremony are there to go wrong?" he asked. "You and I are marriageable, and the reverend is official. Well, what about the license? With such a precipitate marriage, there might not be time to get a license."

"The reverend has one," Barbara informed him, "for he told me just now, while you were getting the buggy."

"Isn't there some sort of certificate that must be signed and dated, as well —"

"That's it!" Barbara exclaimed. Her blue eyes were dancing. "The certificate! Our names will be correct, but the date will not! The whole point of our getting married is to convince Mrs. Ross that we have been married for one year. The date on the certificate should then, necessarily, read 1814 and not 1815. If we could contrive it so that the date reads 1814, the marriage will necessarily be void whenever we decide to take out the certificate and present it as public evidence that our marriage ceremony contained a flaw. And,'' she added on a breathless whisper, ''the actual month and day will not be a problem, since we are claiming our anniversary for...this week!''

Infected by the lighthearted spirit of the occasion and pleased with the excellence of her suggestion, Morgan felt the emotional cart inside him pick up its pace as it rolled down its pleasant slope. ''All right,'' he said, ''but how do we contrive for the local magistrate to write the wrong year on the marriage certificate?''

''Tickle him, perhaps, at the moment he comes to writing the number five? Or put a pinch of pepper under his nose?'' Barbara suggested.

Morgan smiled at her serious silliness, then offered a more practical idea. ''Why do you not simply ask him to write in the wrong date?''

He saw Barbara's quick frown.

''Well?'' he prodded.

''I dislike asking favors,'' she said, a little tersely.

''Do you know the magistrate?''

''Yes, it's Michael Gorsuch,'' she replied, ''and I have known him most of my life.''

''And is he such a bad fellow?''

''No. It is simply that is it difficult to ask favors of my neighbors,'' she replied, somewhat stiffly.

Morgan pressed. ''Yes, all those who heaped scorn on you, I think you told me. Well, Michael Gorsuch knows the circumstances of your baby's birth, does he not? And he knows of Mrs. Ross's visit. He was willing to uphold your story of being Mrs. Harris—which did not do me any harm, either—and so he seems the kind of fellow you might ask to write in the date 1814, by a slip of the pen, if he wishes it. Otherwise, there is no point in our being married today.''

Barbara thought over what Morgan had said, and agreed slowly, ''You are right. Michael will surely do that for me, but I do not think we should mention it to the reverend.''

"No, he would enjoy the circumstance so much it might kill him," Morgan said dryly.

Barbara's gravity vanished. "In that case, we *must* not tell him!"

The rest of the journey passed with Barbara pointing out to Morgan the landmarks he would have to get to know over the next few months, and describing to him life on the North Point of Chesapeake Bay. At the meetinghouse, they found assembled a few of the locals Barbara had expected to see, including Ben Skinner, who had brought his wife and Jacob Shaw. Mr. Shaw was the largest property owner in the vicinity, and he had courted Barbara, unsuccessfully, after Jonas Johnson had died. Mr. Shaw's daughter, Jane, had been a good friend to Barbara the year before, and Barbara was missing her, as she had married her dashing engineer and moved west with him. Several other men, who had just happened by the meetinghouse that morning, had lingered to participate in the unexpected event.

After Morgan had set the brake on the buggy and helped Barbara down, he renewed his acquaintance with Ben Skinner, who had given him a good report in the neighborhood and who seemed pleased that Pockets had taken such a liking to his new master. The pup was on the ground now, yipping excitedly. Morgan hushed his unruly pet, then shook hands with the other men, who were eyeing him with expressions compounded of curiosity, suspicion, envy and awe. The men were friendly enough, though, and showed him around the meetinghouse. There was little to see in a simple one-room structure, which served for a variety of official purposes. It had a low vaulted ceiling pitched above the rafters. The windows were long and tall, and the cold, blue winter daylight gleamed through.

Morgan looked over at Barbara and saw her in low, private conversation with an older man, presumably Michael Gorsuch. Then everyone assembled at one end of the large room, and Barbara handed her baby to Mrs. Skinner for the duration of the ceremony. It was a quick and tidy affair, the only odd part coming when they had to remove the wedding rings that were already on their fingers and put them on again. Before Morgan knew it, the reverend was intoning, "I now pronounce you man and wife. You may kiss the bride."

It was a moment that Morgan had not foreseen. He hesitated fractionally, but decided that failure to kiss the bride, while it would not be considered a flaw in the ceremony rendering the marriage invalid, would be considered a grave insult to the bride. So he grasped Barbara's shoulders lightly and drew her to him. As he bent his head toward hers, he saw surprise and something more interesting light her blue eyes before she closed them to receive his kiss.

Then he placed his lips on hers, and the moment she returned his kiss he felt the little cart inside him that had been rattling so pleasantly downhill speed downward. The sudden acceleration startled him. He lifted his head immediately and turned away from her. He did not remember much of the next few minutes, but he had the impression that he was beside a smiling bride and within an accepting community and receiving congratulations. He had a glass of something pressed into his hand and discovered that it contained fire liquid. The alcohol shot through him like a bullet. He absorbed the shock and made the requisite replies to the various comments directed his way.

Presently he and his wife and her baby and his shameless excuse for a dog were back in the buggy, returning to the farm. They rode in relative silence, for his interior cart was hurtling down, down, and there was nothing he could do to prevent its perilous downward progress.

They made it back to the house. Morgan did not initially respond to Barbara's invitation to share a cup of coffee with her inside. However, the moment he entered her sitting room and took one look at the orderly room, saw the pup frisking about and his happy and sweetly youthful wife holding a baby girl who was not his, he knew he could not endure the space, or her presence, another moment.

He did not even take off his coat, but said gruffly, "We've wasted the morning with this business, and now it's done."

He knew he was being ungracious, but he could not help himself. "The chores await," he announced curtly, and walked out the back door.

He did not look at Barbara. Even if he had, he would not have had enough of his senses about him to perceive the look of hurt and incomprehension on her face as he closed the door behind him.

Chapter Twelve

Morgan strode across the backyard to the shed. He went straight to his horse, mounted it and walked it out of the shed. Once on the pathway behind the house that led to the barn, he dug his heels into the animal's flanks. Horse and rider thundered down the path, past the barn and across an open field.

It was his intention to inspect the fences around the whole of the property, to make himself useful.

It was his desire to ride as far away from the house as he could get, away from the pup, away from the baby, away from the sweetly youthful mother.

He did not want them. He did not want a pup he would have to groom and train. He wanted a dog, in his middle years and faithful, a dog he could depend on. He did not want a five-month-old baby he would have to raise and provide for, a daughter he would have to love and lose. He wanted a son, his son, who should have been already a young man of sixteen, to plow and to plant with, to ride alongside of. He did not want a wife of one hour, or even two days, a woman he would have to learn to know and live with. He wanted a wife of sixteen years and more, comfortable and familiar, who knew what to demand and what to let pass. He did not want the life he had now as Morgan Harris, although it was an improvement over the previous one he had just lived as Jack Carter. He wanted the life of Morgan Harris, who had taken his mother's father's name so that he could marry an Iroquois maid, young and dark and beautiful.

He also wanted a world without prejudice, but he did not think he was going to get that, any more than he could turn back time, save his wife and baby son, or even prevent the men who torched his farm from setting the blaze.

For now, he simply wanted to stop careening down the pathless slope of hopelessness. He had been down that slope many times, and he had invariably relieved himself with long bouts of drinking and dicing. But he had no means of getting himself dead drunk now, and he had only a horse as a means of escape. He was surprised and angry with himself, for usually he could tell when such a black mood was coming upon him. He had apparently not been wary enough earlier in the day, when the enchantment of being in Barbara Johnson's company had so unexpectedly drawn him down the pleasant slope and he had let himself go happily.

He drew his horse to a halt when he reached the first fenced boundary. The animal was breathing heavily under him, and he was breathing hard, too, seeing his breath blow white on the November air, then vanish. It was cold, but not really cold, not by his standards. It was not winter cold, Canadian cold, Iroquois cold.

He looked around him and felt scornful. *This* was November weather, a November landscape? It couldn't pretend to be! Where was the frost? Where was the first snow, crisp and brilliant? Where was the wind that would rip the roar from his breast and shred it, slapping it back at him? Maryland November felt wet to him, wet and limp. No bite. No backbone. Flat landscape.

Flat landscape. That was good. His slide down that inner slope seemed to be halting. He was on flat land again. No ups. But no downs. That was good. He recognized where he was. It was the same place he had been yesterday with Ben Skinner and the lieutenant and his men.

Had it been only yesterday? Or last year?

It made no matter. The landscape was flat, and that was good. But today the fall had happened with little warning, with no black mood preceding it, and he did not think he could be completely safe quite yet.

He urged his horse forward, down the lengths of fence he and the others had mended. He began to feel a prejudice against wooden fences. He preferred stone fences. They were better. He breathed in the winter-wet Chesapeake air. He preferred crisper winter weather. It was better. He glanced at the earth beneath his horse's hooves. It was not black enough, and it smelled brackish. He traveled toward a copse of trees. Even the trees in Maryland were not as fine as those he had left behind, fifteen years before, on his farm in western Massachusetts. To be sure, when he had left them they had been blackened and scarred, little more than spent matchsticks. But before, sixteen years before, when he had lived that first year in peace with his Indian bride and his infant son...

Those had been trees. Birch. Maple. Ash. Not these skinny, piney things that grew here. Then he saw a tree, bent against a line of straighter, darker trees, and his heart stopped to see it bent so.

He imagined some boy swinging on that tree, bending it down, bowing it repeatedly, then permanently. But he did not think that a boy had been on this property in a long time, if ever. He remembered such swinging trees from his youth. How he had loved them. He remembered another little boy, his tiny toddler's legs as bowed as those birch limbs, a little boy for whom he would have wished a childhood's fill of such swinging trees. How he had loved him.

Before his eyes, the bent tree transformed itself into the image of a graceful Indian woman, dark and naked, on her hands and knees, throwing her hair before her over her head to dry it in the sun. That beautiful image slid into a terrifying one, of that same naked Indian woman on her hands and knees, hair thrown over her head, to cover the shame of her rape by a group of white men come to burn her farm.

Then flames. Bright and beautiful and terrifying and final.

The safe, flat, horizontal landscape of emotions tilted wildly and became vertical. Suddenly he was streaking again down the side of an infinite black mountain into hell.

Barbara had not liked the look on Morgan's face when he stalked out of the house. She had not appreciated it, either, for it was not as if *she* were going to demand some marital favors from *him,* after all. His look had been so accusatory, as if she had done something wrong. As if she were not in her own house. As if he were not the hired hand. As if she intended to take this marriage seriously!

She decided to waste no more time thinking about him. She had so many better things to do, all the tasks left undone these past few days of turmoil and visitors. And yet she devoted the better part of the next hour precisely to thinking about him. As she went about her chores, she pondered a series of questions that ranged far and wide. Where would he eat that evening? Where would he sleep that night? What would they do, the two of them, come tomorrow? When would they end their not-valid marriage? Would Michael Gorsuch be chastised for having written the wrong date on the marriage certificate? Would he accuse her of having persuaded him to do it? Would her reputation be in worse repair than before? *Could* her reputation be in worse repair than it had been ever since her disgrace at the age of seventeen?

When she had fed Sarah her late-morning meal and stood to put the baby in her cradle by the fire, she thrust all the unanswerable questions aside and thought, *No, we aren't going to begin this way!* She arranged her blouse and gathered her shawl over her shoulders. *No, I won't let him do this to me!* She felt a double pang in her stomach, one from her women's courses, one from hunger, and she went to tend to her sanitary needs. She knew what she had to do. *Yes, he will share the midday meal with me!*

Having arrived at that firm decision, she was faced with another problem: What to do with Sarah while she went out searching for Morgan? Now, she assumed that Morgan was somewhere on the property. But what if he had not gone into the fields, where he would be visible, but into the woods, where he would be hard to find? In the latter case, it would not be a good idea to bring Sarah with her and expose her at length to the cold, since she had been out for part of the morning.

Still, Barbara hated the thought of leaving Sarah unattended for any period of time, given that Mrs. Ross was in the neighborhood. But Mrs. Ross, she assumed, was in Baltimore today. But what if Mrs. Ross decided to return to North Point and to the Johnson farm? What if she found Sarah cooing happily in her cradle and Barbara absent from the house? What if temptation overcame her?

What if? *What if?*

This train of thought was patently ridiculous, and Barbara halted it. Ensuring her baby's safety was one thing, finding Morgan was another, and her baby was safer just now than was her strange relationship with Morgan. She peeked at Sarah, who was content and would not need her for the next little while, then threw her coat on and left by the back door. She planned to go first to the barn, then walk out toward the south fields to look for him. As luck would have it, just as she rounded the end of the drive that led to the barn and to the tenant's house, she saw that Morgan had ridden up at that same moment and was dismounting in front of the tenant's house. She presumed that he had the intention of settling into the house for the first time.

"There you are!" she called to him as one of his legs swung down to the ground, then the other.

He looked over at her across the horse's back, and she felt his gaze stab her with blue ice. She shuddered, but then she roused herself, feeling rather more angry and insulted by the look than fearful of it. She knew an impulse to leave him to his cold little house, but suppressed it. She had come with a purpose, and she would not let some foul mood of his throw her off course.

The black look she read on his face looked like nothing other than a rude *What do you want?* She answered the unspoken question before he had time to articulate it in a more acceptable form.

"I've come to ask you to share the midday meal with me," she said, raising her voice to carry across the ten feet separating them. Before he could decline, she continued, "You've had nothing since a fairly mediocre breakfast, hours ago already, and I know you've little to eat in the house." She nodded to indicate his accommodations.

He turned away to loop the reins of his horse around the nearest post, and when he looked back at her she saw that the bleak, soul-hungry look that characterized him was even more pronounced. She perceived it now as something beyond hunger. His soul seemed positively famished, like a wild, uncivilized thing. Although he had not yet spoken, she could tell from every line of his body and the set of every feature of his face that not only did he want to decline her invitation, he also wanted to get rid of her as quickly as possible.

It was a cold, frightening look, and she had to renew her resolve not to let him get away with treating her like this. She repeated, "I want you to come and sup with me."

He opened his mouth to protest, but she shook her head and cut him off by raising her hand authoritatively. She did not invite a third time, but simply said, in a commanding tone, "I'll expect you in fifteen minutes." She turned to go, and added over her shoulder, on an inspired afterthought, "You can play the guitar while I prepare the meal, and entertain Sarah at the same time."

Before she turned completely away, she thought she glimpsed a slight change in that soul-hungry expression, but decided it would not be wise to look at him twice and give him an opportunity to decline. She strode decisively back to the house, with the wind lifting the hem of her coat and whipping color into her cheeks.

When she was once again in her kitchen and preparing the vegetables for the stew she meant to serve, she wondered whether he would come. It seemed that the time had stretched out beyond fifteen minutes and was approaching half an hour when she finally heard the fall of his boots on the back steps. Then came his knock, followed by his entrance.

She nodded to him and favored him with a level glance. She noticed that he had lost none of his ravenous look.

"You were right," he said without preamble, his deep, resonant voice still bristling with rough edges. "There was nothing in my house to eat." He crossed the room and hung his coat and hat by the front door.

His tone, which bordered on the rude, hardly served as an apology for his earlier boorish behavior. She decided to let that pass. "No, of course not," she replied evenly, "which is why I insisted you eat with me, for this meal at least."

He headed straight for the guitar on the wall. His back was to her. When he grasped the neck of the guitar, she saw his shoulders rise and fall, as if he had taken a deep breath, or sighed.

"After all the unusual exertions of the morning and the chores that awaited you, I imagined that you would be particularly hungry," she added, hoping to get a response out of him. When he did not respond, she tried a direct question. "What chores did you choose to do during the rest of this morning?"

Half turning toward her and strumming a first resonant chord, he said, absently, "Cleared withered bracken, cobwebs, and heaps of shattered glass."

The answer made no sense to her. She did not know him in this mood, and she turned away, disgusted and out of sorts with him. If she was going to feed him, he could at least offer a civil reply to a perfectly unobjectionable question. She thought that she deserved—she was, in fact, paying him for—a straight answer to that question. She turned away and busied herself putting extra muffins in the breadbasket.

She heard him strum and thrum on the guitar, just splinters of melodies, fractures of verses that contained words like *bereft* and *forsaken* and *chill.* The effect was eerie, and strangely beautiful. It had a visual quality about it, something that brought to mind broken crystals, or the heaps of shattered glass he had referred to. As she listened, not with her ears but with her vulnerable, mother-softened heart, she was no longer vexed with him, or with his mood. She did not understand it, but she no longer felt out of tune with it.

As she was placing two crockery bowls on the table, the music stopped. She turned toward him suddenly, and found him staring into the flames, with one booted foot on an interior brick ledge of the fireplace, his raised thigh balancing the guitar, his fingers massaging the strings.

She asked, "Where is your guitar now?"

Without missing a beat, he said, still in the voice of abstraction, "Sold it."

"When you were Jack Carter in Boston, did you ever make a living by your guitar?"

He looked up, then, from his absorption in the fire, and stared at her. He focused his midnight-blue eyes on her, and the effect was startling. He looked as if he had seen all the bad that life had to offer, and had survived. She was used to thinking that the trials and travails of her own life had been rougher than any man's, but now she thought twice about that deep-rooted assumption. As his eyes rested on her in studied scrutiny, as if he were seeing her for the first time since they had been married, just a few hours before, she felt something move inside her, like a sifting among embers.

"I sang for my supper on occasion," he admitted, his harshly chiseled features lightening, taking on an expression that resembled one of fond remembrance, "but I never sold my singing."

"Only your guitar."

"Only my guitar," he said, glossing over that admission with a chord in a minor key, "for that is not an inalienable part of me." He illustrated by removing both hands from the instrument, so that for a moment it was poised solely on his raised knee. He immediately grasped the neck and the belly again to keep the guitar from falling.

She nodded. "I was dying to ask Evan Rollins about Jack Carter's singing career last night," she said.

"Dying?" he questioned.

She felt a flush creep up her neck. "Well, curious."

He raised a black brow slightly. It was a suggestive gesture, mildly flirtatious, and seemed to acknowledge that the difference between them was that of man and woman.

She decided that the guitar playing must have filed down some of his rougher edges and fed his ravenous soul. He was smoother now, and she liked him better now, but she was not sure she wanted to play *that* game with him. She said, matter-of-factly, "Aren't you curious about me, too, a chance-met human being for whom you are now working?"

He played a particularly lavish flourish, and the wedding band he wore flashed in the light of the fire. "You could tell me about General Ross."

She noted that he did not admit to being curious. She was moving about the kitchen, finishing her preparations for the meal. She selected the impersonal details. "He was killed on the day of the attack on Baltimore by American sharpshooters."

"That's right," he remembered suddenly. "September, last year. It was the talk of Boston." He asked, "And you were... happy with his death?"

She shrugged. It was a complicated matter, his death. Fortunately, she did not have to answer, for with the end of Morgan's playing Sarah had started to fuss noisily. Barbara sighed, and Morgan hung up the guitar and went to the cradle to distract the baby by making funny faces. Regarding him a moment, Barbara felt vaguely confused by his strange, distant, yet flirtatious mood this afternoon. She did not pursue the subject of General Ross and announced that the meal was ready. He asked what should be done with Sarah, who seemed reluctant to see the amusement end.

"You could pull the cradle next to the table for me, please, and I can rock her with my foot while we eat."

Morgan obliged her, and then man, woman and child were at the table. Fragrant steam rose from the two dishes. When the prayer had been said and the napkins shaken out,

Barbara said, "But we began talking about you and ended by talking about me."

"Curious again?" he asked.

"Curious still," she replied, "for you have yet to tell me anything about yourself."

"Although you know far more than I ever could have told you," he said.

She smiled. "Or ever wanted to tell me. But knowing a few things about the gambler Jack Carter hardly tells me about the farmer Morgan Harris."

She saw his spoon hesitate on its path from dish to mouth. He looked down, and then his lashes swept upward. He looked at her, straight. "What is it you want to know?" he asked. His voice was pleasant, but not inviting.

"To begin, where was your farm?"

"Berkshire County," he said. "Massachusetts." He resumed eating.

She had assumed he would say that he had only worked on the farm. What she inferred was that he had owned the farm. He had not been ignominiously fired from his job as a farm laborer and taken up a life of gambling. Rather, he seemed to have lost his land. She passed him the breadbasket, which he accepted.

"What did you grow?"

He said offhandedly, "Same as here," he said, "but no tobacco. We had more livestock than you have here."

"It's not profitable," she said.

"But the lack of livestock, along with the continued cropping of wheat, corn and tobacco that Ben Skinner described to me, will reduce the fertility of the soil over time."

"That may be," she said, "but I do rotate the crops."

"When the soil is exhausted, I suppose. How much corn and wheat do you yield per acre?"

"Not above twenty bushels of corn," she admitted, "and twelve of wheat."

"And the percent return on your investment?"

She pulled a face. "Three."

"Leading, no doubt, to a widespread belief that there's no longer any profit in farming," he commented astutely. He smiled; it was a rather attractive smile. "You did well to hire me. In more ways than one."

"That may be," she said again, recognizing that she was being led down a false trail, "but I am not trying to defend my own farming practices, but to learn about yours."

"Not so very different from your own," he said, "but maybe a different utilization of the land. We had more meadow, but that is to be expected. You have wedge drains, I notice, which are different from our open drains, but again, that is to be expected. Otherwise, when I checked the tools in the barn a while ago, everything looked familiar and in very good order."

"Thank you."

"You have done a remarkable job alone."

"Thank you again, but you can't think I'll be diverted yet again from the topic at hand."

"What, your curiosity is not yet satisfied?"

She persisted. "How many people did you employ?"

His face suddenly closed. "Did I say that I had employed anyone?"

"No," she said, "but you seem to know more about farming than the typical field hand. So I imagine you owned a farm and had hired help." He did not agree, disagree, or otherwise react. She continued, "And I don't think Negro slaves have been much used lately up north."

He shook his head. "No, no Negro slaves."

"Indian slaves, then?"

She felt a sudden tension spring to life across the table, then die just as quickly. "No, no Indian slaves," he said. Then, with an intriguing mixture of the cool and the seductive, he said, "Now it's your turn, and you've told me little more about your life than I've told you about mine. I'm curious to hear something I don't already know about the famous General Ross."

She saw that she had inadvertently hit a raw nerve with her question, so she asked, "Truly curious, or just changing the subject?"

His brows quirked appreciatively. "Truly curious," he said.

Barbara looked skeptical.

"I swear," he added, summoning up that flirtatious tone again. Then he added, "With my right hand on the Bible."

Barbara's mouth fell open. The horrible realization of a grievous oversight gripped her. "Oh, no—the Bible," she whispered. "I cannot think how I came to forget it! Or how everyone else came to forget it, as well! This could ruin everything!"

Morgan had begun eating again, but paused momentarily with a half-raised hand. "Ma'am?"

She looked back at him, anxiety darting about inside her, as it had two evenings ago, the moment before he had first shown up on her doorstep. "The Bible," she said. "The family Bible. I neglected to take it with me this morning so that Michael Gorsuch could write in the date of our marriage to match that on the certificate. Mrs. Ross would only have to ask to see the marriage lines in my Bible to prove that I had no case!"

Morgan exchanged a long look with Barbara. "You'd risk desecrating your Bible with a falsehood?" he asked.

She caught the note of awe in his voice, and squirmed a little at the question. She bit her lip, thought it over, then folded her hands decisively in her lap. "Yes. I've falsified one legal document today, and have no reason to stop at the next step on this trail of lies."

She rose and gestured for him to stay seated. She moved across the room to the small set of shelves that stood in the corner next to her spinning wheel. The grip of anxiety on her heart grew tighter. She was having difficulty breathing, and she made an effort to calm herself.

"Go ahead and finish your meal," she said. "I'm sorry to be such a bad hostess when I'm the one who's invited you in for the meal, but," she explained as she picked up the Bible and pressed it to her breast, "I've got to get back to the meetinghouse, and I have a very sick feeling that I might already be too late!"

Chapter Thirteen

Morgan rose with her, placing his napkin on the table by his bowl. "There's no need for you to trouble yourself. I'll go to the meetinghouse and do it for you."

She closed her eyes and tried to compose a response to his logical suggestion. She opened her eyes, then blinked, unable to think of anything to say. It was as if all the years of fending for herself had caught up with her and rendered her unable to think or act upon the simplest thing. She felt depleted, like a deep well gone suddenly dry.

"Yes, that *sounds* like a perfectly reasonable suggestion," she said at last, "but I don't know. Let me see ... if you go to the meetinghouse and find Michael Gorsuch, then I'll stay here with the baby, and that will be good. On the other hand ..." She stopped. She pinched the bridge of her nose with two fingers, trying to concentrate. Uncustomary tears of fear and frustration and exhaustion welled up inside her. "On the other hand," she continued, "I don't want to stay here. I want to go and do it myself. Maybe *you* should stay here with Sarah while *I* go and take care of the Bible. Or maybe I should take Sarah and you go back to the fields and tend to the chores. Or maybe ..." She let her words trail off again.

She looked over at him, and a craze of humor appeared in the fear. "I sound like the good reverend!—unable to move from point One to point Two! Maybe he is right, and everything is far more complicated than I ever imagined!

And I know I am breaking the law—man's law *and* God's law—but I want that false date in my Bible, and I don't care!'' Her face was ashen. ''Why don't I know what to do?'' she asked. ''Why is this so difficult?''

Morgan perceived that Barbara was on the verge of panic. She was obviously used to dealing capably with problems on a grand scale. It seemed to him oddly appropriate that the smallest of small details should stymie her now, after she had handled so much so well.

As he crossed the room toward her, he answered her purely rhetorical question. ''It is so difficult because it is entirely inconsequential,'' he said, straight and matter-of-fact. ''It does not matter one way or another how the Bible gets into Gorsuch's hands. I suggest that we return together to the meetinghouse.'' He stood before her and looked down at her. ''We'll go in the buggy. I'll drive. You can carry Sarah. Does that suit?''

His tone braced her, and his suggestion spanned the great abyss that had suddenly yawned within her, separating her thoughts from her ability to act on them. She looked at him gratefully and nodded.

He told her to bundle up Sarah and overrode her protests against leaving the dirty dishes on the table. He assured her that they would still be there when they returned. Then he fetched her coat and put it around her shoulders. He donned his own, fit his hat on his head and left the house to prepare the buggy. When he had done that, he returned to lead Barbara and Sarah out of the house. The pup, excited by all the sudden activity and rightly inferring the prospect of another trip, was making a nuisance of himself. This time Morgan would have none of it. In the sternest of stern tones, he harshly recommended that Pockets mind his manners. Pockets whimpered sadly at being left behind, but obeyed his master with no further comment.

For the second time that day, Morgan helped Barbara, who was balancing baby and Bible, into the buggy, and he arranged her skirts, as well as the blanket over her knees. Barbara let him do whatever he wanted, for she felt helpless. She had made the jaunt to the meetinghouse a thousand times alone, in blistering heat, in freezing cold, when she was married, when she was a widow, when she was pregnant and unmarried, when she had Sarah with her. Today it would have been too much to have done it alone. She was glad to have another human being at her side, an adult, someone who could take responsibility, someone who could take control, someone who could make decisions, someone who could act on them.

When Morgan had mounted the buggy and moved it forward, she began to speak. "I don't have the faintest idea why I feel so awful, but I do! Strangely enough, I felt this way the other night just before you—and Lieutenant Richards—showed up at my door! Only this odd, anxious feeling wasn't as strong as it is now. Isn't that strange?"

Morgan replied noncommittally, but his grunt encouraged her to talk more.

"I *never* have such odd feelings," she continued randomly. "I'm not one of those women of extremely fine sensiblities who seems to know when something is going to happen. Why, I've always been exceptionally dull, I would say, when it comes to such things. I've just minded my business and kept to it. I've had no other choice, really! What else could I do?"

Morgan was nodding here, grunting agreement there, and generally providing an ear for her to talk to, for this was his notion of gratitude. She did not know it, but when she had demanded that he join her for the midday meal, she had unceremoniously yanked him off the steep, sickening slope of blackness and despair. He felt on level ground again. The feeling was fragile and might only be temporary, but his inner landscape was flat, and that was good enough for now.

"But then I had Sarah," she was saying, still thinking aloud, "and everything seems to have changed! Why, the morning I woke up on the day I gave birth to her, I decided—out of the blue, never having given it a previous though!—to name her *Sarah!* Why, Sarah isn't a family name. My mother's name was Abigail. But there it was in my mind—Sarah. That name, and no other. And I'm thinking that Mrs. Ross must have had her strange and strangely accurate dream on that same day. There seems to be a force surrounding Sarah's birth that I don't understand. For I knew, I just *knew*, two nights ago, that something was wrong. And I know now, too, that something is wrong. Am I crazy?"

"No, you're careful, and you're right to attend to the matter of the family Bible."

Barbara brightened. "I *am* right to attend to this, aren't I?" she said, rather pleased. "Yes. I'm right. I'm not crazy. It's an important detail, and I'm glad I thought of it before it was too late. I just *know* Mrs. Ross will think of coming back and asking to see the family Bible. Or maybe she could even summon it in a court case! That is what *I* would do, in all events, if I were her! And I have the oddest sense of connectedness with her, as if I seem to know what she is thinking and feeling."

She turned toward Morgan and said, wonderingly, "I never had a mother. I never had sisters. I've had very few women friends, except Eleanor Shaw—Jacob's late wife— and then her daughter, Jane. I've never thought about it before. Isn't that odd?"

"You've never had to," Morgan pointed out.

"True," she replied, on a deep sigh. She looked down at her beautiful baby and felt a rush of feminine understanding for which no words had ever been invented. "But now I have a daughter, my very own daughter. And I am her mother. She is all I have, and I am all she has." She considered that statement. "And yet, I suppose Mrs. Ross might have some kind of claim to a relationship with Sarah, but I would be hard-pressed to know what to call it!"

After that, Barbara lapsed into silence, wrapped in her musings. By the time they had turned onto Long Log Lane and reached the meetinghouse, her will and her decisiveness had returned, for these few minutes during which Morgan had taken control had been enough to bring water back into her well of strength.

As he had done only hours earlier, Morgan set the brake on the buggy and helped Barbara and the baby down from the perch. "I feel so much better!" she exclaimed lightly as she alit. He released her hand, and she smiled up at him, looking straight into his midnight-blue eyes. She said, simply and forthrightly, "Thank you."

She did not bestow on him her dazzling smile, but there was something steadying in her expression and in the fact that she had needed him and had acknowledged it. It made him feel effective. "Do you need my help inside?" he asked, nodding toward the building.

She shook her head and said, "I'll only be a minute."

"I'll wait here for you." He looped the reins of the horse around the hitching post.

She lifted her skirts to take the few steps to the porch and entered the door of the meetinghouse after a swift knock. Inside, she found Michael Gorsuch swapping stories with the old men circled about his desk by the fire. She greeted the men by name, motioned them to sit back down, received their congratulations on her marriage yet a second time that day, and asked to see the magistrate in private. He quickly refilled his pipe, excused himself from his cronies and came toward her, whereupon she presented him with the Bible and her blasphemous request.

When he hesitated fractionally, Barbara lifted the baby higher on her hip and smiled. She said, pleasantly and confidently, "It's my soul, Michael."

This man of law, who had known Barbara Johnson, née Smith, for most of her life, was not proof against her smile or her quiet determination; and like others in the region who knew the truth about the events of the year before, he felt he owed her a favor. He withdrew his pipe from his mouth and held his hand out for the Bible. "I'll only be a minute."

She handed it to him, and while Michael Gorsuch went to the lectern where stood his ink pot and quill, Barbara drifted over to the windows, away from where the old men were seated, gabbing and jawing and laughing at old jokes. She held Sarah in the sun to warm her and gazed out, in abstraction, into the bushes and trees beyond the clearing surrounding the meetinghouse. Her feeling of anxiety had dissolved, and she was thinking, *It will all turn out all right!*

Hardly had the comforting thought been formulated when she caught sight of movement in the woods about thirty feet away. It was just a slight movement, a rustling of low branches, as if some large animal, like a deer, had wandered too close to human territory and would turn to go deeper back into the forest.

However, that retreating movement did not occur. Again Barbara saw the winter-naked branches of brush rustle, and then she was almost sure she glimpsed the side of the face of a young man, rising a fraction above a tangle of branches, then crouching down again, out of sight. He was dressed so that he blended into the leaf-barren colors surrounding him. His actions seemed to indicate that he was spying on the meetinghouse. There was something striking about the cut of the jaw and the cheek of the face that she had caught that made her heart beat a little faster. She moved away from the window, so that she could not be seen watching him, and moved thoughtfully toward the back door of the meetinghouse.

She decided to investigate and determined that if she stayed in the clearing, within sight of the windows, and did not venture into the woods looking for the man, she would run no risk of danger to herself or her baby.

When she got outside and began to stroll, leisurely, down the side of the meetinghouse toward the front porch, glancing regularly into the woods, she wondered if she had been mistaken. She detected nothing more of the young man she thought she had seen. Feeling curiosity but no anxiety, she came to the front of the meetinghouse and spared only one more backward glance to scan the woods, which were now motionless.

When she rounded the front corner, she had the vague idea of walking back to where she had left Morgan. However, as she looked by chance down the road leading to Baltimore, she saw a fancy carriage racing toward her, and then she *knew*.

She knew she had been right in her feelings of anxiety; she knew she had been right to bring the Bible to Michael Gorsuch; she knew she had been right to go ahead and marry Morgan Harris. She shifted the baby in her arms and smiled righteously. And she knew, further, that she was equal to the encounter. She walked forward to confront the carriage upon its arrival.

And, sure enough, a few moments later, out came Lieutenant Richards, who offered Mrs. Ross a hand to help her descend from the interior of the coach. A third man alit after her.

Barbara greeted the older woman with confidence. "Mrs. Ross."

"What a surprise, Mrs. Harris," the lovely English-woman replied, coming forward with equal confidence, "and so unexpected."

"The very nature of surprises," Barbara answered.

Mrs. Ross's brows drew together in a quick frown. "Well, yes, but then I suppose the surprise works boths ways. You could not have been expecting me, either."

Barbara shrugged, not about to tip her hand and say that nothing could have surprised her less just then than to see Mrs. Ross here, at the meetinghouse, this afternoon. She could even have told the older woman what her business was here and that, no doubt, Michael Gorsuch was free now to help her search the local legal records. Barbara did pause to wonder whether ink that was only a few hours old would look discernibly different from ink that was a year old. However, she was not worried that Michael Gorsuch would do anything so foolish as to present her family Bible to her in front of Mrs. Ross.

He did not. It had taken Michael Gorsuch only the predicted moments, pipe clamped between his teeth, to write the marriage lines into the Bible and to dry them with sand. When he was done with the simple, sinful task, Barbara was no longer in the room, so he naturally went to look for her out the front door. At the moment when he stepped out onto the front porch, he saw Mrs. Ross's carriage drive up and Barbara move toward the carriage.

Morgan Harris was leaning against the hitching post, his head turned to watch the arrival of the carriage. His face was impassive, and beyond a slight narrowing of the eyes he did not look the least troubled to see his almost-legal wife take on the Englishwoman.

Michael Gorsuch came up to Morgan Harris and passed him the Bible, saying low—although they were well out of earshot of the carriage, "The deed is done."

Morgan straightened up and accepted the thick, black leather-bound book. He smiled, a little, at the magistrate's phrasing, and queried directly, "The evil deed?"

Michael Gorsuch took a long puff on his pipe. The smoke was as white as hoarfrost, and it hung for an endless moment in the cold, wet air. "It's not my soul, as—" here the magistrate struggled with the correct name for her "—your wife pointed out to me."

Morgan's smile broadened. "She did?"

"She did."

Morgan stashed the Bible under the blanket on the seat of the perch of the buggy and looked at the interesting scene over yonder, the two strong-willed women speaking to one another, all gentleness, all civility, all determination. He admired the way Barbara had gone to meet the carriage. He admired the straightness of her back and her unhesitating step. He felt something ripple inside of him. It was a horizontal rippling. Nothing tipping. Nothing dangerously vertical. Nothing threatening. Rather reassuring. The flat landscape was settling down, solidifying its steadiness. It felt good. It felt like pride in a fellow human being's actions. It felt like caring.

He looked at Michael Gorsuch, straight, and said, "She has a nerve."

"And then some," Michael Gorsuch agreed.

Still with his eyes on the distant tête-à-tête between the two women, he asked, "Will it work, this ruse of ours?"

Michael Gorsuch puffed again thoughtfully and said, "It might, yes." He, too, had his eyes on the two women. "She just might outmaneuver the general's widow by sheer strength of will."

"What if strength of will is not enough?" Morgan wanted to know. "Does Mrs. Ross have a legitimate case?"

"Legitimate? Surely not" was the magistrate's reply. "But legal? Possibly. I'm inclined to think that your wife cannot be too careful where Mrs. Ross is concerned."

Morgan glanced at the magistrate, who met his eye. "Well, she has nerve, as I've said—and a steady determination, I would add."

Michael Gorsuch nodded wisely. "You don't know the half of it." He clamped down on his pipe, then removed it from his mouth, holding the hot bowl cupped in his hand. "She might not be wanting me to tell you this, but—" he tipped his head minimally in the direction of Mrs. Ross "—Barbara was responsible for the general's death."

Morgan's eyes widened slightly. "She killed him?" he asked, in a tone of mingled awe and disbelief.

"Had him killed," the magistrate explained. "General Ross was picked off by American sharpshooters, not far from here, down Long Log Lane, on the afternoon of the British attack on Baltimore."

"September, last year," he said. "Nine months before the baby was born."

"Yes, and how do you think the Americans knew when and where the general would be that day?"

Morgan's brows rose. His eyes focused intently on Barbara, standing there, back straight and confident, protecting her baby from the light wind, talking to the woman whose husband was the father of her child, the woman whose husband she had had killed, the woman who wanted to take her baby away. An awesome pride in her rippled again inside him.

Michael Gorsuch explained. "But Barbara Johnson never said a word to anyone about what she had done! Why, we didn't even know she had been—" the magistrate coughed into his fist "—noticed by the general until she was five months pregnant! That is, we knew that he had noticed her, but she assured us that he had not done anything improper, which was kind of her, since we could not have protected her. Well," he continued bracingly, glossing over the embarrassment. "Jane Shaw had set up a chain of communication originating from the Shaw house, where the British had established their headquarters, and she was passing along information of the British military plans through a chain of which Barbara was an early link. So, on the morning of the general's planned attack on Baltimore, Barbara passed word to the link at the meetinghouse of the exact time the general would be traveling down Long Log Lane, with his army behind him. A couple of days later, Miss Shaw let it slip that the knowledge of the general's movements that day had not originated at the Shaw house."

"Meaning?"

"That after Barbara's pregnancy was apparent we figured it had to have come directly to her by way of the general."

"And she betrayed him."

"Her five older brothers died back in the First War of Independence," Michael Gorsuch said quickly, "and the British have never been much loved in these parts, particularly after their haughty occupation last year, so it was not held against her that she—"

Morgan broke into this with an easy smile, "Don't get me wrong. I'm not accusing her. She has all my admiration."

He looked over at her again and saw a woman of strength and resolve, unafraid and independent. He thought of pretty, shallow Roxanne, and of how blindly she had adored him. He thought of the rich and alluring Mary Ann Layton, and of how desperately she had needed him. Blind adoration had fed the little cock that strutted around inside him, and their desperate need had kept his own need at bay. But both women had left him with a hunger, a hunger that could never be sated and became greater the more he saw them, until a few months ago, in the first life-affirming act he had performed in fifteen years, he had chosen to see them no more.

Then the young half-breed, painted and drunk, had barged into Kelly's, and the pain of remembered loss had nearly cost him his life and left him with little of his will to live. Now, just a few days later, he was here, involved with a different woman, a beautiful woman, a beautifully different woman who needed him, but not desperately, and who liked him well enough to have invited him into her bed.

The flat landscape spread out inside him and became as strong and as spacious as the earth beneath his feet.

Michael Gorsuch said, "Only your admiration?"

Other emotions came in then to occupy the wide, hospitable territory, emotions he had not felt in a long time, rich emotions, strong emotions, very masculine emotions. He had been a farmer for some years of his adult life, but a gambler for many more, and the face he showed the local magistrate gave away nothing of the cards he held in his hand or the way he intended to play them. He said gravely, "My respect, as well."

Morgan saw that the magistrate was slightly consternated, and Morgan began to enjoy himself.

"You're not quite legally married, you know," Michael Gorsuch reminded him.

"Then, again..." Morgan offered by way of counterpoint.

Michael Gorsuch tried an indirect approach. "A man rode through here yesterday and spent the night with you out at the Johnson farm."

Morgan nodded. "Evan Rollins," he affirmed. "From Boston."

"He was looking for a man named Jack Carter, it seems."

Morgan had mastered the poker face. "But Mr. Rollins failed to find him."

"You wouldn't be knowing anything about a man named Jack Carter, would you, Morgan Harris?" the magistrate asked.

Morgan was shaking his head. "Not a man I know."

"You said a moment ago that you were from up north," Michael Gorsuch went on. "Where in the north are you from?"

"Quebec," Morgan informed him.

"Ever been to Boston, Morgan Harris?"

Morgan was spared the necessity of a reply. Barbara had ended her conversation with Mrs. Ross and was walking toward them. She was close enough to say, sweetly, "Morgan, it's time to go. Did you get what you needed here at the meetinghouse?"

Morgan exchanged a regard with Michael Gorsuch before turning to Barbara. He said, "Yes, I've got what I came for. I'm ready to go, if you are."

"Well, then, good," she said, walking to the side of the buggy so that she could mount.

Morgan came forward to give her a hand. Barbara put her gloved hand in his ungloved one and looked up at him, her blue eyes sparkling with fire and determination and satisfaction. It was an electrifying moment for Morgan. He felt the newest, most remarkable sensation come to life inside of him.

The flat landscape was gone. The little cart that had carried him so often and so terrifyingly down the black slope of despair now seemed to be headed uphill.

It was going slowly, very slowly. But it was definitely going up.

Chapter Fourteen

Barbara thanked Morgan for his ministrations and sat straight in the buggy, happy and satisfied. Although she managed to suppress a broad smile, she was unable to keep a look of smug satisfaction off her face. She looked down at the little sleeping face of Sarah in her arms and felt triumphant.

As Morgan walked around the buggy, she leaned over to exchange a word with the magistrate. She confined herself to a restrained "Thank you, Michael, for all your help." Nodding in the direction of Lieutenant Richards and Mrs. Ross, who were making their way toward the meetinghouse in the company of the other man who had come in the coach with them, she added, "I predict that you are going to have company. You can guess who is Mrs. Ross, and to her left is Lieutenant Richards. And they have brought a lawyer."

The magistrate was unimpressed. "A lawyer now," he commented. He ran his eye over the threesome coming toward them. "The legal documents and certificates of the vicinity are a matter of public record. I'm glad I've kept mine in good enough order to withstand the scrutiny of any man of law who cared to review them." He added, on a quick whisper, "Your Bible's on the seat next to you, under the blanket."

Without taking her eyes from the magistrate, Barbara placed her hand down on the seat next to her and felt the thick book under the wool of the blanket. She tipped her head slightly to acknowledge having located the Bible, saying only, "Until the next time, then, Michael. I'm not sure when Morgan and I will be returning, for we have so much to catch up on now at the farm."

By then, Morgan had walked around the buggy and climbed up onto the seat. Taking the reins in his hands, he glanced at her and said quietly, "Am I to gather from the look on your face that your encounter with Mrs. Ross went well?"

Barbara attempted to pull the corners of her mouth down, but without success. "Is it so obvious?"

Morgan snapped the leather bands, urging the horse forward. "Does the phrase 'the cat who swallowed the canary' mean anything to you?"

In her relief and happiness, she felt a self-conscious smile blossom on her lips. "I make no apologies for being unsubtle."

Morgan glanced over at her again, but did not respond. He called a goodbye over his shoulder to Michael Gorsuch, and it was returned. He snapped the reins again, and the buggy moved forward.

Barbara was surprised when he did not lead the buggy away from the meetinghouse, but instead drew up alongside Lieutenant Richards. Morgan lowered the reins and rested one elbow on his knee so that he could bend over toward Barbara and speak with the lieutenant, who was standing on her side of the buggy.

"Richards," he said good-naturedly, as if greeting an old friend. "You've returned to North Point, I see." He tipped his hat, minimally, and murmured, "Mrs. Ross, ma'am."

"We've returned," the lieutenant replied crisply, "at the urging of our lawyer." Here the lieutenant gestured to the third member of their party, a tall, gaunt man who nodded his head gravely and distantly.

Unconsciously Barbara stretched out her hand again and laid it on the Bible hidden under the blanket next to her. It made her feel immeasurably better.

"Well, now," Morgan was saying easily, "I suppose you've got things to attend to here, so I won't keep you." He looked up at the sky and squinted at the westering sun. "If the business takes you longer than expected, and it gets too late to return to Baltimore for your supper, I'll ask you to drop by our house and share our meal with us."

Barbara quickly lowered her lashes. Had she heard correctly? Was Morgan actually *inviting* them to sup at her house?

"My love?" Morgan inquired smoothly, looking at Barbara.

Barbara recovered. She returned his regard, then looked back at the three hated persons. "Why, of course," she said, seconding the invitation. "You must come and sup with us."

"I always like an audience for my music," Morgan added.

"Thank you, Mr. Harris," Mrs. Ross said politely. "We shall have to see how the afternoon progresses."

"And if you're stuck for a place to stay tonight," Morgan continued, to Barbara's further surprise, "you know that we have a spare bedroom for you, Mrs. Ross, as well as the sitting room that can serve for guests, when the occasion demands. Lieutenant Richards knows the conditions of our hospitality."

"That we should pay, perhaps?" the lieutenant inquired, with a pronounced tone of condescension.

"No," Morgan said congenially, taking no offense. "That account is settled, as far as I'm concerned. Just a neighborly invitation this time."

The lieutenant looked skeptical, and it was left to Mrs. Ross to thank him kindly.

"We'll be off," Morgan said, "and good luck to you this afternoon. You'll find Michael Gorsuch a very able magistrate."

Civil goodbyes were exchanged all around. Morgan drove the buggy away down Long Log Lane, toward the farm.

When they were out of earshot, and before Barbara had a chance to comment on his extraordinary invitations, he said, as if eager to hear the news, "Now tell me all about your exchange with Mrs. Ross."

Barbara could not help but relive her satisfaction. "Not a thing!" she sang out musically, crowing a little. "Mrs. Ross couldn't catch me on a thing, try as she might—and she'd been well-coached, no doubt, by her lawyer on what to ask me! And she will only have all my information on record-keeping in North Point confirmed by Michael Gorsuch." She smiled her cat-with-canary smile, then turned her attention to more immediate matters. "But what I want to know is—"

"Michael Gorsuch has done us an invaluable service," he said.

"Assuredly, but—"

"And very determined he is to protect you and Sarah."

"Well, yes, that he is, but—"

"He told me that he has already filed our certificate in the records for last year, so that when he pulls them out for Mrs. Ross's lawyer they'll be in perfect order—and he told me all this without a word about compromising his integrity, which, I have gathered, is a quality he guards and prizes. You know," he continued meditatively, "I think you underestimate how well you are thought of locally, despite what you said to me earlier about the scorn heaped upon you as a result of your pregnancy. Michael Gorsuch is not the only one who is looking out for your welfare and standing ready to protect and defend you to the end."

"I never said that my neighbors did not stand by me when I have had difficulties," she said, her back straightening.

Morgan's tone was light. "Ah, but you've been so stiff-necked about accepting their help..."

Barbara turned on him, her mouth open. "Michael Gorsuch said *that*?"

Morgan smiled at her offended astonishment. "No, he said that you were a woman of independent character, and I inferred the possibility that you would accept many things—bad luck, disease, poverty—before you would accept help." He glanced at her. "You are more reasonable when it comes to accepting help in matters that concern Sarah, of course.''

If his intention was to get a rise out of her, it had certainly worked. She did not know what his further purpose might be, but it took all of her willpower not to pursue the subject, for she had one of her own to discuss. ''Sometime I will ask you to tell me exactly what you and Michael Gorsuch were discussing just now, but at the moment, what I really want to know is—''

He broke in yet again. ''I'll come to that!'' he assured her. ''Nevertheless, let me stress what a good idea it was that we got married, after all.'' His tone was serious. ''Although I was not in favor of it this morning, when the reverend came calling, I can now see your wisdom in having persuaded me to go ahead with the marriage, and without delay.''

He looked over at her and smiled. Barbara found it a very charming smile, but rather hard to read. It seemed straightforward enough on the surface, as if he were merely acknowledging a good idea well executed. Yet the smile also seemed to carry something more below the surface. A hidden current. An attractive current. It was definitely a man-to-woman smile. Or maybe it was one that a man would wear when anteing up in a poker game.

She said dryly, ''And I suppose you mean to compliment me on having taken care of the detail of the Bible, for which I thank you in advance, but what,'' she was finally able to demand, ''was *that* all about just now?''

''What was what all about?''

She met his bland expression with a curious one of her own. ''About inviting the lieutenant, Mrs. Ross, *and their lawyer,* to supper—and then to spend the night?'' Before she thought through the implications of her question, she asked, incredulously, ''Did you *want* them to spend the night with us?''

Morgan was looking at her with no change of expression. When he did not immediately answer, she had the odd notion that she recognized that deeper something in his smile. She felt the atmosphere take on some new spark.

They were in an open buggy—hardly an intimate setting—but she was aware that it was just the two of them now, alone. Alone for the first time, it seemed, with no new visitor at the door, no new development to absorb, no new oversight to fix. It did not fail to occur to her that if Mrs. Ross and Lieutenant Richards were to spend the night with them, she would have to share her bed with Morgan again. And maybe Morgan wanted it that way.

The idea awakened something in her that had been dormant for a long, long time. She thought of the evening ahead, of sharing her bed with him for the third night in a row. It was not an unpleasant projection; rather, it was intriguing. Even desirable. She looked quickly away from him and let her eyes roam across the barren November landscape. With thoughts of his warmth beside her in her bed, the chill of the afternoon air fanning her cheeks did not penetrate.

She looked down at the sleeping baby in her arms and realized that it was not just the two of them, alone, returning home. They were a threesome: man, woman and child. With a doubling of awareness, it occurred to her that this was the first time in months that she had thought of another human being before thinking of Sarah.

However, the next moment she wondered if she had imagined his delicate pause, for he was answering her question, in a perfectly offhand way: "Of course I don't want them with us tonight."

"Of course not," she agreed. "But then why did you invite them?"

"To make it look as if we have nothing to hide," he explained. "It was good strategy, don't you think?"

"Was it?" she asked, doubtful still.

"I thought you'd think so," he said, "since I was merely continuing the good offensive that you so wisely began."

That comment wrenched her thoughts from the intriguing, desirable possibilities of the night ahead. "What offensive?" she wanted to know.

"It was a fine act," he complimented her, "to go right up and meet Mrs. Ross when her carriage arrived. I was speaking with Michael Gorsuch at the time, and—among other things—we discussed how much we admired your courage."

She glanced back at him, and although his eyes were on the road, he managed to meet her gaze a moment. She did, indeed, see a gleam of admiration in his. Or was it a gleam of something else? She did not have enough experience to know if he was flirting with her, and she had no idea how to respond in kind.

She said, bluntly and unromantically, "However, if they took us up on the offer, the sleeping arrangements would be awkward."

"They won't," he said confidently.

Her suspicions about his motives were partially allayed. She was even momentarily embarrassed that she had imagined he would try to maneuver into her bed. "How can you be so sure they won't accept your invitation?"

His eyes were fixed on the rutted lane, for he was negotiating a mucky spot. "I made my living from gambling for more than a decade, and did so successfully," he explained seriously. "I know how to lay my bets."

Despite the gravity of his tone, she had the oddest sensation that the intense and melancholy farmer she knew as Morgan Harris had been replaced by the womanizing gambler known as Jack Carter. With the rush of events since yesterday, she had not followed through on even a fraction of the questions about Jack Carter that had come to mind since Evan Rollins's visit. She wondered, in particular, about that strange incident at Kelly's bar in Boston.

"Your bets were good until a few nights ago, when you got caught cheating at cards," she said. "Or rather—" she slanted him a sly glance "—until you allowed yourself to get caught."

Morgan turned toward her, and the gleam in his remarkable blue eyes was pronounced. "What would make you think I allowed myself to get caught cheating?"

"Because I think you're a pretty cool customer," she said directly, "and wouldn't cheat unless you wanted to get caught for some reason."

"Speaking of cool customers," he replied, playing his cards well, "Michael Gorsuch told me that you were responsible for General Ross's death."

Barbara was taken aback. "He told you that?"

Morgan nodded.

Barbara was vexed, and she lost her original train of thought. She bit her lip. It was hideous to admit to having, even indirectly, killed the father of her child, but she refused to compromise on this particular subject. To evade the truth of her actions would compound the violations she had suffered from General Ross last year, and was now suffering from his wife. To tell the truth could help cleanse the grubby smudges she felt clinging to her as a result of the web of lies in which she was now, necessarily, enmeshed.

"Yes," she said at last, "I was the one who gave to the American sharpshooters the precise time of the general's maneuvers on the morning of his death."

"Does Mrs. Ross suspect your hand in her husband's death?"

Barbara shook her head.

"The lieutenant?"

Barbara shrugged. "I doubt it."

Morgan gave the subject a practical turn. "At least they cannot have come to you with revenge in mind, then."

"Only theft."

Morgan glanced down at the baby in Barbara's arms to acknowledge the truth of her comment. "In any case, your part in the general's death would hardly be held against you in an American court of law, if Mrs. Ross wished to use that as a further point in her favor of gaining custody."

Barbara laughed, once, mirthlessly. "The irony is that Mrs. Ross no doubt imagines that my relationship with her husband was a love match."

"Which it was not."

From his inflection, Barbara did not know whether he was making a statement or asking a question. She looked down at Sarah. General Ross had given her her beloved baby on the day he died. She looked up again and had no ready response to his statement, for the subject of her love, or hate, for the father of her child could not be adequately addressed with a simple yes or no.

Morgan did not press. "It took some fortitude, nevertheless," he commented, "to follow through on what you saw as your duty."

"Resolve," Barbara answered with resolution, clear on this point, at least. Then, to turn the conversation, she said, as lightly as she was able, "But what a sorry subject! And one that we have already rehashed more than once!"

"On the contrary, we had not fully discussed it at the table earlier today when you suddenly remembered, in such timely fashion, the family Bible."

She reconstructed the context of that conversation and said, "That's right! I was doing my best to find out about your varied life, and you were doing your best to divert me."

"But I answered all your questions in the end."

"Almost all," she replied.

He shook his head. "It's your turn now, nevertheless."

She tossed back, "Curious?"

He quoted back what she had said to him earlier. "As one human being to another." He negotiated a rut. "Besides," he added, "you told me yesterday, I think it was, that it made you feel so much better to unburden yourself. You had your resolution, yes, but it still cannot have been easy for you."

He looked at her then, focusing his full attention on her, in sympathy. She was new to this kind of interaction with a man, and it was startling, the effect of his attention on her and the way it aroused memories of her anguished desire for General Ross. It was also comforting, for no one had ever asked her about General Ross or acknowledged that it must not have been easy for her. The men were embarrassed that they had been unable to defend one of their women against the British invaders; the women were embarrassed that Barbara had had to carry her shame so evidently in her swollen belly.

"No, it was not easy," she said, "and it was not very pleasant."

But then she realized that she had permitted no one to ask her any questions about General Ross. Only her friend Jane Shaw had ventured sympathy and support, and Barbara remembered having taken them only grudgingly.

Had she really been as stiff-necked as Morgan said? She considered the question, and did not like the vision of herself that resulted.

"Then again . . ." she began, then stopped.

She suppressed her impulse to explain that it had not been entirely unpleasant to be desired so thoroughly. She could not tell Morgan Harris that, of course, without sounding provocative; and she did not know how much of the episode with General Ross and her feelings for him had been softened in retrospect by the loving brush of her pregnancy.

"Then again?" Morgan prompted.

"He gave me my daughter," Barbara answered, thinking this answer was safe enough.

"And you had no other children?"

Barbara shook her head. "My husband was somewhat older than I, and a grieving widower with no children, when I married him ten years ago," she said. "He gave me no children, either, but he did leave me the farm."

"And a wedding band," Morgan said, holding up his left hand to display it, "and a shaving kit, and a variety of nightshirts. I know that he died four years ago, and his name was Jonas, I think."

Barbara laughed. "Yes, and it is amazing how much you know about him."

"Except how he died."

"It was winter," she recounted matter-of-factly. "He went out without his coat once—just one time—to chop wood, and died two weeks later of a very severe cold." Since she felt that there was absolutely nothing left to tell about her life, she asked, naturally enough, "And how did your wife die?"

"Not by the cold," he answered her evenly, not evading the subject, "but by fire."

She looked at him quickly, but his eyes were on the lane, and his attention was fully occupied by the ruts. She was shamed by the realization that she had been used to thinking her life more difficult than any man's, when she might only have had her share of the usual hardships a woman faced in this world. It occurred to her that her assumption of her life's difficulties might be, instead, a measure of her inability to accept help from others. She had always prided herself on her noble independence, but she wondered now whether she was not just banally and cussedly stiff-necked. And for all the indignities she had suffered at the hands of men, one man had left her a farm, and another had given her a daughter.

As she contemplated the man next to her in the buggy, highly aware of the open intimacy of the ride, he turned and met her eye. He did not say another word; neither did he have to. With the same newfound intuitions that allowed her to guess at Mrs. Ross's thoughts and movements, she felt his profound losses and his unhealed pain. She knew that she could never take them away or relieve him completely of what he had experienced. Yet nothing prevented her from extending herself, reaching into his eyes and sharing the burden with him, if only for a brief space, for these moments of human intimacy were too rare and unpredictable to sustain themselves indefinitely. If it was possible to share in another's grief only for a moment, then a moment would have to do, and that moment would be all the more precious for its brevity and for the realization that such moments could not be manufactured at will.

Their bones were jarred when the buggy hit a particularly bad rut, and Morgan turned his eyes back to the road. The moment was gone. But it had been enough, and Barbara was satisfied. However, she still felt a taste of interest in the details of Morgan Harris's life.

Hardly before she realized it, they had turned to drive down the trail to the farm. The rest of the afternoon and evening loomed ahead, and although some of Barbara's questions had been answered, not all of them were settled.

"Back to work," she said as Morgan drew in the reins in front of the house.

"Back to work," Morgan agreed. He pulled the brake, jumped down from the perch, walked around the buggy and held up his hand to help Barbara and the baby down.

Barbara accepted his hand and returned his reassuring grasp. When she was on the ground, she looked up at him.

He glanced to the west, then back at her. "I'm going again to the south fields. I'll be back in about—" he calculated rapidly "—two or three hours for supper."

Barbara's eyes widened.

"I still don't have any food in my house," he said quietly.

"That's right, you don't," she said quickly. "I should have invited you myself." She frowned a little. "And you really do not think that Mrs. Ross and the lieutenant will take advantage of your invitation?"

He smiled slowly, warmth lighting the depths of his eyes. She was aware that he was still holding her hand. "Not a chance," he said. He released her fingers, leaving them tingling through the wool of her gloves. He nodded and climbed back into the buggy so that he could drive it around to the barn.

"Should I count on your return more toward the two hours, or more toward the three hours, then?" Barbara asked, calling out to him as he moved the buggy forward.

He glanced down at her over his shoulder, and the look in his eyes nearly melted her on the spot. "I'll try and make it two, but it will probably be more like three."

Chapter Fifteen

As Barbara walked to the house, she was strongly aware that if Morgan had wanted to maneuver himself into her bed this night he would not have employed so ignoble a stratagem as inviting the lieutenant and Mrs. Ross to dinner. He would probably not want an audience, either, if he was bent on seduction.

But was he bent on seduction?

She did not know, and the not knowing was somehow desirable and seductive in and of itself. She had no experience with flirtation—and she was not even sure if Morgan's interaction with her in the buggy qualified as flirtation. She thought back on the men she had known in her life and could come up with no man similar in style or approach to Morgan Harris. No man as interesting or as empathetic. No man as intense or as secretive. No man as attractive, in his own particular way.

It was not that she lacked experience, as such, with men. Or was it? Barbara could not even decide the point, for her experience with men to date had been so flat, so one-dimensional, having no contours, no rounded corners, no hidden folds in which desire could lurk and grow and spread its tendrils like ivy. No, it was not that she lacked experience with men; it was, rather, that she lacked a certain kind of experience with men.

With a shudder, she remembered the first horrible, hurtful time she had been with a man. She had just turned seventeen, and she was living in Baltimore with her strict aunt, her father's maiden sister. The man—she remembered his name hazily as Jonathan Harlan—had met her at church and badgered her, for months, it had seemed, for a look, for a touch, for a kiss. Because she had found him obvious and uninteresting, she had not been the least attracted to him, although he was not a bad-looking young man; and her lack of attraction to him had been just as well, for she had been smart enough to know that the intentions of a Baltimore Harlan toward a poor North Point Smith could not be honest.

And she was right, completely, humiliatingly right. Her disgrace happened at a public event, at a Sunday-evening church social, no less. Her aunt forced her to attend, although Barbara pleaded to be allowed not to go. She knew that Jonathan would be there and that he had crossed the fine line between badgering and bullying. So she went, and she danced with a handsome young man who fancied her, and they went out on the porch for some fresh air and moonlight. The night was warm and velvety, and she had dared to think about kissing her fine young man under the sky, that black canopy scattered with sequins.

Then Jonathan appeared, and since that handsome, kissable young man had the misfortune to work for old man Harlan, he retired from the lists when Jonathan dismissed him. Jonathan grasped Barbara roughly by the arm and dragged her into the bushes before she had a chance to resist. He threw her on the ground, threw himself on top of her, and, with all the finesse of a spoiled rich boy who always got want he wanted when he wanted it, ripped into her body in what she could not remotely have labeled an act of love.

His personal, sweating satisfaction and her private, raging humiliation were not, in the end, the worst she had to endure that night. Jonathan returned to the social and bragged widely of his conquest, and when Barbara put herself together enough to reenter the church in order to find her aunt, she knew from the speculative looks on the faces of the men and the refined disgust on the faces of the ladies that she was finished in Baltimore. The look on the face of the fine, kissable young man was hurt and distant—a look, above all, of rejection.

She knew she was supposed to thank her extraordinary good luck when, less than two years later, so upstanding a man as Jonas Johnson of North Point needed a woman to help him on his farm. In the ten years of her marriage to him, she and her husband had what she guessed was a normal marriage, but she still would not have said that their physical relationship had been—strange to say—sexual. Their physical joining had been commercial, a business proposition, but it had yielded no profit in children. It had added up to nothing: no hurt, but no pleasure, either. She did not think that in all the years of their marriage her husband had ever "made love" to her.

After his death, she was surprised by her popularity. It seemed that every man in North Point wanted her, or her farm, or both. Her youthful disgrace was widely known, but her previous unmarriageability had apparently been canceled by her age and her respectable marriage. She derived some belated satisfaction from her popularity, but mostly she was completely indifferent to it. She had no intention of marrying again, for she did not know what would compel a woman to put herself within a man's legal dominion, if she did not need him financially. Nor did she know why any woman would ever want a man in her life at all. She rejected her suitors firmly, unmistakably, unequivocally.

Then General Robert Ross of the British army came to North Point. He saw her, he wanted her, and she had only to look into his eyes to read there what she had read in many another man's eyes. Only this time, she knew that he would get what he wanted. But he was not crass or hurtful or boastful, like Jonathan Harlan. He was handsome and masterful, experienced and refined, and he knew the art of desire. He was the first man with whom she could say that she had made love.

But she did not love him, because she was not capable of loving anyone, truly, until he died and her score with the British was settled.

When she crossed the threshold to her sitting room, she suddenly felt extremely dirty and in need of a bath. The impulse to bathe was seconded by an impulse to act on the impulse, and the secondary impulse was so delicious that it filled her with a kind of joy that she did not dare deny. Although her previous bath was well within the past week, she rationalized that she could make an exception and advance her bathing because of the return of her woman's courses. Indeed, it was a rationalization, because this first bleeding since the birth of the baby was spotty, and the bleeding was more or less finished. She rationalized further—since the return of her woman's courses was not sufficient to allow her to bathe early without feelings of guilt—that a nursing mother could not be too clean for her child. She hurried through a number of her chores, which included tidying the hastily abandoned midday dishes and putting a fresh bowl of water out for Pockets, who was prancing around, overjoyed at her return, and making the usual nuisance of himself. After that, she reckoned that she still had almost two hours in which to wash her hair and bathe before Morgan would return. If she was quick about it, she imagined, she would even have more than enough time to begin preparations for dinner.

She dragged the copper tub from the shed and began filling it with the water she had heated over the fire. She spread the oilcloth to protect the floor and fetched the washstand, all the while relishing again that sense of illicit pleasure. She was breaking from routine and performing a task merely because she wanted to. Somewhere in the luxuriant tangle of her thoughts and reflections and memories she wondered whether she was cleaning herself, making her body sweet and soft, for Morgan.

She did not have long to wonder. She had washed her hair and was lying, half stretched out in the tub, with her clean, wet hair cascading down the outside, hanging to dry in front of the fire. She was musing in an idle way on the enigma of Morgan Harris, imagining him behaving toward her in ways appropriate to her condition of lying naked in a tub of deliciously warm water. However, she was having difficulty finding the path to pleasure in the various scenes she was drawing for herself, imagining herself in Morgan's arms, with Morgan's lips on hers, surrounded by his strength and his intensity, ready to satisfy his hunger. Even though she was mistress of her mental images, there always came the moment when he would go beyond what she knew how to give him, when he would demand, when he would bruise.

Then she heard bootsteps at the back door and a quick knock, followed by the opening of the door.

She swirled around in the water to see with her eyes if her ears had deceived her. With equal parts interest and fear, she saw that Morgan had advanced several paces into the room. He had stopped and was looking at her. Whatever was in his gaze the moment he met hers was quickly hidden in the depths of midnight blue, and she could not accurately read it.

"I didn't expect you for another long while yet," she said quickly, a little breathlessly, over her shoulder. She could not have him thinking that she had planned to provoke him.

He smiled briefly, in reassurance. "No, you could not have expected me for a while yet." He paused and took another step into the room, toward her. "I came to ask you where the tools for cleaning the drains are stored."

"Where the tools for cleaning the drains are stored," she repeated, absently. She could not quite concentrate on the question. "The barn," she answered, more or less at random.

"I couldn't find them there," he replied, "which was the first place I looked, and that is why I came to ask you directly, in order to spare me time wasted in searching needlessly."

"They're not in the barn, then."

"No, not in the barn."

He took another step forward, and she turned around in her bath so that she was facing the wall opposite him. The pup had perked up at his master's entrance and left his warm place at the hearth, so Morgan was momentarily occupied in settling the eager dog down.

After he had ordered Pockets back to his bed, she asked, "Aren't you going back out?" Her throat felt dry. Her voice sounded wooden.

"No," he answered.

She heard his step behind her. He was crossing to the peg by the front door, apparently to hang his coat and hat. Then she heard his steps approach her. She kept her eyes fixed on the wall where were hung the instruments. For all her idle, illicit imaginings concerning Morgan Harris, she had not found one that was pleasurable enough for her to wish to pursue it in reality. She was furthermore angry that she should be caught naked when he was fully dressed, for it was not in her nature to play the seductress. His step approached. Her anger shaded into embarrassment, then took flight into panic.

"Why not?" she demanded roughly. "Why aren't you going back out?"

"Because I don't want to expose you to another draft if I open the back door," he said.

Was that a note of humor in his voice? He was behind her. Next to her. And then—

And then he walked past her and went straight to the wall with the instruments. He was in front of her now, where she could see him, and his back was toward her. "Besides which," he said, without turning around to look at her, "you had the excellent idea to relax a moment this afternoon, and I am persuaded by your example to do the same."

He kept his back to her, apparently contemplating the instruments. He raised his hand to the banjo, took it down and attempted to tune it. He tried a few notes and a chord, then shook his head definitively. "Not my type," he said, and replaced the banjo on its hooks. He passed his hand over one of the two guitars, then reached for the other one, which he had played the day before. Turning back around toward her, he said, "This one pleases me."

Barbara had done what she could to cover her breasts from his view with her arms. She was looking up at him as he walked past her again, back to the kitchen area. He did not look down at her. Instead, his eyes were on the ceiling, and his hands were fingering the strings, fiddling with the tuning pegs, finding the fit between his body and the instrument. She heard him slide the bench out from under the kitchen table, prop his boot thereupon, and then begin to play.

Barbara hardly knew how to react. Her panic had passed through her, leaving in its wake a relieved desire to laugh. However, the desire to laugh was not strong enough to come to the surface, but remained a bubble of unbroken merriment inside her. Mostly, she was confused, by Morgan, by her relief, by her inexplicable pique at his seeming indifference to her nakedness, which she was sure he had seen well enough through the transparency of the water.

Not knowing what else to do, she eased her tensed muscles back into the liquid warmth and allowed herself to be soothed by the sounds of his playing. The music was undemanding. He was playing for himself, and possibly for her. The atmosphere in the room settled into a kind of heightened intimacy.

At one moment, he stopped singing and asked, "Do you think the tools for the drains are in the shed?"

The little bubble of merriment slid up in her throat. She swallowed it. "I don't know," she answered, choking slightly. "Possibly."

"I'll look there tomorrow," he said, his tone matching the lack of urgency he felt for the task. He began to sing again.

At another moment, he stopped singing, and she heard him place the guitar on the table. He walked over toward her, and her heart started beating faster. His goal, however, was the hearth, where he placed another log on the diminishing fire and teased the flames into brightness. She wondered if he was teasing her as well, but she could not be sure.

Her heart slowed to a steadier but still expectant pace, and she wondered what would happen if he came to the tub, reached down and lifted her out.

But he did not. He crossed back by her and returned to his guitar and to his singing.

Finally, at the end of one song, she said, "The water is getting cold."

He plucked a string and answered, "Then you'll have to get out and dry off or risk a chill."

Behind her, she heard him walk over to the settee and sit down, still strumming the guitar. She felt momentarily paralyzed, because he had positioned himself to see her full nakedness when she rose from the tub. She remained in the water. She heard the quiet crackling of the fire and the sketchy melodies that left his fingers. She felt the seeping chill of the water forcing her to leave it. She felt the renewed warmth of the fire, encouraging her to rise from the tub. She felt Morgan's eyes on her. She felt him urge her to leave her watery protection, to expose herself to him, to give him a chance to show her she had nothing to fear, to give him a chance to admire her naked beauty.

"I'd get your towel for you," he said, his deep, gravelly voice drifting over to her lazily, "but I notice that it's at your side, which means that you need no help from me."

He was reassuring her in part, daring her in part, and it was clear from the way she heard him settle on the settee that he was not going to move from his advantageous spot. He plucked and strummed, it seemed to her ears, without further interest in the music, while he waited for her to come to terms with her position and his.

She would not demean herself with a request that he look away. She would not undermine her own authority by giving him an opportunity to refuse her request, as she guessed he surely would. She felt an old fear of humiliating exposure to masculine eyes that, at first, overwhelmed a very tender, hardly perceived desire to have his eyes touch her maternal body and luxuriate in the curves that had flowered since the birth of Sarah. Finally, she knew she had no choice but to leave the water.

Keeping her eyes modestly downcast, she reached out for the towel hanging from the washstand. She rose up and out of the water at the same time she wrapped herself in the large and absorbent linen, tucking it in place above her breasts. She stepped out of the tub and toward the fire, where she dried herself, her back toward him. Unwrapping the towel but holding it up as a screen behind her, she dabbed here and there with the free ends of the linen. With the pricking of the hairs at the nape of her neck, she was aware of the same kind of focused attention from Morgan that he had shown her in the buggy. Once again, it was extraordinary, the effect of his attention, which held so little threat and so much promise and expectation.

She stared into the flames dancing on the hearth, unsure what to do next, until she knew that what she should do was what she would do if he were not there. She lowered the towel so that she could wrap it at her waist. Now only the thick masses of her unbound hair shielded her. She refused to hurry. She turned slightly to pick up her chemise and blouse from the stool across which she had placed them, and put them on. Then she slipped on her drawers—which contained her menstrual cloth—under the towel, which she simultaneously abandoned. She donned her petticoat, then her skirt. She wondered if he would be as intrigued by watching her dress as she had been watching him dress the other morning, aware of the paradoxical intimacy implied by the covering, rather than the uncovering. When she turned to brave his regard at last, she had her answer.

He had settled into his seated position. One arm was resting across the top of the settee, and his legs were stretched out in front of him and crossed at the ankles. The guitar was leaning against one arm of the settee, its butt on the floor.

He did not move a muscle, but he looked as if he had touched her everywhere with his eyes. Their midnight blue was now a shadowed black, and something evasive and subtle in their depths was nevertheless able to reach out to her across the room and electrify her.

He said, "I'll take care of that for you."

He might as well have said, "I want you." His deep, gravelly voice reinforced the electric effect of his eyes, so much so that she was confused, at first, about what his remark referred to. She was on the verge of uttering the self-betraying comment "You presume too much" when she realized, from the nod of his head in the direction of the copper tub, that he meant that he would throw out the water. He evidently did not mean, at least not directly, that he would satisfy the desire she had supposed he was presuming of her.

Suddenly she felt the desire that he had not, in fact, presumed of her. It was just a spurt of feeling, a wash of blue in her stomach and her breasts. It felt as soft and layered inside her as the clothing covering her curves. It was textured, too, with the circumstances of the moment: the indulgent impulse of her luxurious bath, the surprise of his interruption, the effect of having been revealed naked to his eyes, the cozy cleanliness she now enjoyed, her brief misunderstanding of his remark, his evasion of the central issue, her knowledge that General Ross would have had her beneath him by now, would already have mastered her.

However, the strongest spur to her desire was the not knowing of his intentions once he had taken care of the water in the tub, and the not knowing was desirable and seductive, since all the other men in her life had been so obvious.

He stood up, then, and took off his well-worn jacket, tossing it on the settee, which left him in shirtsleeves and leather vest. He walked the few paces across the room, toward the tub, toward the fire, toward her. She looked on, eyes widening, as he unbuttoned his vest and dropped it on the floor, then unbuttoned his shirt, which he let hang open.

She held her breath and stepped away from the tub. She looked down, she looked away. Then she spied her brush on the mantel shelf and decided to arrange her hair, instead of protesting his behavior or asking him to cover himself. Brushing her hair turned out to be the right activity to engage in, for he explained his actions quite simply by saying, lightly, "Ah, to have something other than cold, cold water to wash in!" He shrugged out of his shirt and let it fall in a heap on the floor by the tub. He knelt down next to the tub and plunged his hands in the water. He began to splash himself and groaned in pleasure. "Although it had turned cold for you, it feels warm and delicious to me."

Barbara turned away to allow him to wash while she pinned up her now-dry hair.

"And soap!" he remarked, thoroughly pleased. She heard him scrub, dunk his head, and scrub some more.

"You might have asked me if you were wanting to wash in warm water," she chided him.

His voice was a happy, watery blur. "I didn't know I wanted to until I saw you in the tub. And I compliment you again on your idea to relax this afternoon."

She moved away toward the kitchen, to begin preparations for the evening meal, leaving him to do whatever he wanted to do with the water and the tub. His happy bathing was rapidly finished, and he was soon reaching for the towel she had replaced on the washstand. While his head was buried in the towel, she was able to observe his torso, which was lean and muscular. She saw a broad patch of skin under his right arm that seemed marred by a wide swath of scar tissue that could not have been produced by any sharp object, but more likely by burns. She did not have long to gaze at it, for he had rubbed his hair dry and slung the towel around his neck. His arms were now down at his sides, his hands holding on to the two ends of the towel, which were draped on either side of his shoulders.

He turned and smiled at her, very pleased with himself and the world just then. She could not help but smile in return.

Without another word, he dressed and dragged the heavy tub to the back door. With great efficiency, he maneuvered it out and dumped the water far enough away from the back step that it would not create an unavoidable puddle. Then he propped the tub against the outside of the door frame to dry and got back in the house before he had allowed too many drafts to circulate. He rolled up the oilcloth and stored it in the corner with the washstand.

No sooner was he finished with these tasks than Sarah awoke on a hungry cry. Barbara put down her knife and vegetables and crossed to her baby, lifting her out of the cradle and into her arms.

Barbara scolded her daughter lovingly. "We're hungry, too, little girl, and I see that you are determined to prevent me from feeding us any time soon."

"I'll help in the kitchen," Morgan offered, "so that you can tend to Sarah."

Barbara accepted his offer and told him what to do to get the evening meal prepared and cooking on the fire. She hesitated about where to feed Sarah, then decided, perfectly logically, that after bathing in front of Morgan it would hardly be indiscreet to nurse her baby in front of him. She preferred the rocking chair, anyway, as the most comfortable spot to sit, since the arms were just the right height on which to rest her elbows while holding the baby.

So she sat down in her rocker to satisfy Sarah at her breast. She was relaxed after her bath, yet at the same time expectantly aware of Morgan's presence in the room, with her for the evening. The nursing felt good, the draining and relieving of the pressure in her breasts.

At the moment she was changing Sarah from one breast to the other, Morgan came and sat down on the settee, facing her. Both her breasts were exposed. He regarded her openly, with interest, with desire, without moving, without saying a word. She still did not know his intentions, although she saw plainly his desire. Suddenly, the not knowing intensified the sensual experience in a way she had never known before, and she thought less of her baby and more of the man opposite her. She did not immediately cover herself. She wanted to push him into making a move, into declaring himself, into showing his cards, just like every other man she had known.

Into the thick, sensual silence, he said, "I can't help but wonder, you know, how it was that you found the resolve to have General Ross killed."

Sarah waved a little hand angrily at that point and nuzzled her face toward a nipple. Barbara shifted her baby and pressed the fresh breast into the seeking mouth. She slipped her other breast inside her chemise.

He was willing to toy with her a little longer yet. "That is, since he gave you your baby."

Barbara shrugged, minimally. The atmosphere was richly confessional. "He gave me Sarah only a few hours before he was killed, I think. Of course, I didn't know that at the time."

Morgan's brow lowered. His midnight-blue eyes were darker than ever. "Was he abusive to you?"

The question caught Barbara off guard. With the baby at her breast, with Morgan's attention focused on her, with her body alive with sensual awareness, the question brought to mind the intimate details of that last morning with the general, the last time she had lain with a man, so many months ago. General Ross had been many things to her that morning, but he had not been abusive. She could not help it: She blushed.

His eyes narrowed. "I see," he said quietly. "Do you regret having caused his death?"

Barbara knew the answer to this question. She shook her head. "No. He deserved to die, and I don't regret it."

Morgan's brows raised suggestively. "Should I take that as a warning?"

Barbara caught her breath. The exquisite not knowing was at an end.

Chapter Sixteen

She might have asked, "Is that a proposition?" but she thought better of it. She said, instead, "Do you need one?"

His blue eyes smiled at her. "Well, now, that depends on how the other men in your life died," he said. "You had the resolve to have General Ross killed...."

"To avenge my family's losses in the First War of Independence," she was quick to point out.

"Yes, Michael Gorsuch told me as much. You lost some brothers, I think."

"Five," she replied, "before I was born."

He nodded. "Fair enough. Let's agree, then, that the general deserved to die." He continued, "And I know that your Jonas was carried off by a head cold."

"That's right."

"And how long had you been married?"

"Ten years."

He nodded, considering the information. "If you had wanted to kill him, you would have had the resolve to do the deed long before ten years had passed. So I acquit you of any evildoing on his account."

He was teasing her, flirting with her, perhaps. If only she knew what flirting was. "Thank you," she said, with light irony. "It's a comfort that you believe in my good faith!"

His eyes, soft and sensual, held hers. "It's a comfort to me, too, that you did not kill your husband." His eyes dropped to roam the contours of the baby's form and face, traced the swell of her bared breast and followed the soft strength of the arms cradling the eager baby flesh. The topic of her part in the deaths of the men in her life was at strong variance with the sweet nurturing she was imparting. When he continued, his deep, gravelly voice was as soft and sensual as his eyes. "But we wander from the topic. You told me—when was it, yesterday, the day before?—that you had been a fallen woman before you married Jonas. What about the man—or men—who disgraced you?"

She was amazed by how much he had come to know about her in the little time they had been together. The mood of cozy, anticipatory intimacy did not allow her to take back what she had said about being disgraced.

"Man," she said firmly. "There was only one."

"Man, then. What happened to him?" He smiled seductively. "Is he still alive?"

"I don't know," Barbara admitted. "I didn't kill him, at any rate, and unless someone else has, he should still be living."

"Too bad. A local rogue?"

"Baltimore," she answered. "He was a rich merchant's son when I knew him, so he has doubtlessly become the rich merchant himself in the meantime."

Morgan ran his fingers, a rough comb, through his drying hair. "He'll have run to fat in the meantime, too," he said wisely.

Barbara laughed, once. She pictured the contrast between a well-fed Jonathan Harlan and the soul-hungry Morgan Harris. She felt a surge of desire for the soul-hungry one and was surprised to realize that such frivolous, serious, teasing talk as this could produce it. If this was flirtation, she was learning the art.

"No doubt," she said, "but he's rich, and since he was a handsome enough fellow in his younger, thinner days, it's likely that he still has a way with the ladies."

Morgan's brows rose delicately. "I had not imagined that you were susceptible to a pretty face."

"Not in his case." Barbara said it in no uncertain terms.

"Ah, then you did *not* succumb willingly to a pretty face in a moment of youthful indiscretion, or fall prey to the blandishments of a rich merchant's son?"

She found that she was rapidly succumbing to the scruffily attractive features of Morgan Harris's unhandsome face and falling prey to his unusual flirtation. Sarah's feeding was at an end, so Barbara raised the baby from her breast and laid her across her shoulder. Only then did she slip her breast inside her chemise, out of his immediate sight.

"No, it was far from a willing submission."

"He nevertheless escaped your exquisite sense of revenge."

She looked him in the eye and said, coolly, "If, as a young girl, I had had the resolution I have now as an older woman, I would have killed him with my bare hands and richly satisfied my sense of justice." She stood up and placed Sarah in her cradle.

Morgan followed her movements with his eyes. "Very far from a willing submission, I see," he commented. He was contemplative. "With his pretty face and his father's bank account, I must guess that he lacked finesse."

Barbara stood up straight. "The man was a pig." She began to walk toward the kitchen area. Then she looked back at him over her shoulder. "In addition, he was obvious," she said with a slight smile, "and entirely uninteresting."

Morgan stood, too. His eyes narrowed appreciatively. "I don't mind being obvious," he murmured, following her, "but uninteresting... Ah! that's fatal!" He pulled the ribbon out of his back pocket and tied his nearly dry hair at his nape. "I also have my reasons."

She glanced at him. "Do you?"

He nodded. "I'm hungry."

She ventured, "So am I."

"What can I do to help?"

She met his eye again and did not look away. "Put out the bowls," she said, pointing to the open shelves where the crockery was stored.

"Is that all?"

"For now."

"You'll let me know if there's anything else?"

Barbara paused. He was being obvious, but not uninteresting. "I'll let you know."

He went to the shelves and got down the bowls. In short order, the table was set and the hot food presented. Barbara lit the two candles on the table to resist the late-November gloom pressing in on the sitting room. The shadows skittered to the corners, where they lay down, tired and tamed.

They seated themselves across from one another. They shook out their napkins. They said the prayer. They began to eat. They spoke of noncommittal things and discussed the business of the farm. Barbara was aware that, with the gradual satisfaction of her physical hunger, her desire for the man across from her was increasing. She thought it amazing that a man would tease so much and wait so long. She was learning from Morgan new dimensions of this game of anticipation and desire.

Even their most ordinary negotiations over the pouring of the cider and the passing of the food seemed to increase the effect of his presence, her awareness of his obvious desire for her, which was so very, very interesting and so very, very restrained. She was wondering now, as her desire for him seemed to be increasing with every bite of food, with every flicker of the candlelight across the lean planes of his lightly stubbled face, with every moment of prolonged intimacy, if a violent ravishing produced by his unrestrained desire would be so horrible; and she decided, to her surprise and shame and surge of further desire, that it might be, rather, immensely enjoyable.

When they had settled into their meal, Barbara decided to show him what a good pupil she was. "Now tell me all about those events in Boston. The ones that chased Jack Carter down to North Point, Maryland."

He looked over at her and quirked his brows appreciatively. "Events?" he echoed. "Or women?"

For some reason, she did not need to know about the women he had left behind in Boston the way he had needed to know about the men in her life. She shook her head. "No women. Events," she repeated. "I am still puzzled about that card game at Kelly's—and the charge of cheating. That is the pivotal incident of the story, as far as I can tell. The one that sent you south."

Morgan had been enjoying himself since the moment after his conversation with Michael Gorsuch outside the meetinghouse, when he felt the flat landscape of his emotions spread out and steady about him in grand, rippling, reassuring waves. Barbara had come up to him, then, in the wake of her bold confrontation with Mrs. Ross. She had put her hand in his, and she had looked up at him with her brave blue eyes sparkling with determination and strength. It was at that moment that the little cart inside him had gripped the side of a slope and started to go uphill, slowly, slowly.

It had been an extraordinary afternoon, in fact. First, just before the midday meal, he had been rescued from his swift, slippery descent into hell. Upon their second return from the meetinghouse, he had been almost inappropriately happy when he had admitted that his wife had died by fire, and it had not hurt him bitterly to say it aloud. Then, when he had entered the house to find her in her bath, the slope had seemed solid and real.

The little cart had good traction, and it shot upward at an exhilarating rate. Still, he had been in no hurry for it to reach the top of the mountain; nor did he know how high this slope would be. But he imagined that the corresponding descent would be pleasurable and satisfying and entirely different from the usual blind fall into black terror he had experienced earlier in the afternoon.

However, with her question, he remembered the moment the half-breed boy had entered Kelly's, painted and drunk and looking for trouble. Of a sudden, the old, stabbing, fiery pain returned, and his sense of overwhelming loss, of the future denied him, was great. The steady ground that had been spreading out around him shifted and cracked. He felt between two worlds and between two lives. He was still on the edge of a slope, but he was no longer sure which direction he was traveling, or whether or not his little cart could hold on.

He fell back on his customary strategy for containing the mood. He fell with practiced ease into his role as Jack Carter, gambler and drifter and lover. He smiled secretively and said, "It was time to leave Boston."

She imagined he was still teasing her. "And you sought to leave dishonorably?"

He shook his head. "The dishonor was only on the surface. I didn't leave with anyone's money in my pocket that I had won dishonorably. In fact, I didn't leave with anyone's money in my pocket at all."

"But why taint yourself with even surface dishonor? I don't believe you had ever been involved in such an incident before."

Caught between two worlds and two lives, with the ground shifting beneath him, he heard the words slip out: "True, but I'd never had to protect a wild young half-breed before."

Surprised, she remembered what she had assumed was merely a colorful, insignificant detail in Evan Rollins's recital of the last, infamous evening in the career of Jack Carter.

Before she could question him further on the detail, he recaptured his persona of Jack Carter and continued, smoothly. "And I needed a dishonorable reason for leaving town that was sure to reach Mrs. Layton's ears."

"So she would consider herself well quit of you and not pursue you?"

The charming gambler, lover and leaver smiled seductively. "Something like that."

"It didn't work," Barbara said.

He shook his head slowly, undressing her with his eyes. "It didn't work."

He was teasing her still, drawing her in, pushing her away, teetering her on the peaks and slopes of anticipation and desire, and she was responding fully. He was not rushing her, for he was good at sensing what a woman needed in terms of space and time for seduction. He had refined his senses as an adaptive, life-preserving measure, for he had learned over the years that when his emotional pain became too great he could lose himself for infinite moments in a woman's body—any woman's body—and that those few moments of relief would be enough to keep him going for another minute, another hour, another day.

In the case of Barbara Johnson, he had guessed that she had never experienced the luxury of a flirtation or a slow, sensual seduction. Although she was not the type of woman whose path Jack Carter would have crossed—for she did not need him desperately enough or adore him blindly enough— she was present and available and exceedingly desirable in a new kind of way to him.

She had been raped once by a rich Baltimore merchant's son, and she had been mastered more than once by General Ross. In between those two men, he guessed, she had submitted to her wifely duties with neutral affect, but she had never had a man tease her and draw her into making the first move. He had been patient with her, and would continue to be patient. He was finding himself seduced and delighted, in turn, by her hesitancy, her dignity, her strength, and her girlish puzzlement.

At the unmistakable look in his eyes, Barbara got up abruptly, wondering and worrying and anticipating and desiring. She decided to clear the table. She picked up her bowl, then went around the table to take his. When she was behind him, she stretched out her arm to take away his empty bowl, and he surprised her by reaching out and catching her upper arm, drawing her down to him. He drew her against him so that her breasts were at his shoulder and her ear was at his mouth. He said, low, ''You'll have to tell me what you want me to do.''

She caught her breath at the firmness of his touch and at the definite intention that lay behind it. She did not quite know how to respond, and she was about to say something evasive and silly when he nuzzled her neck slightly with his nose and said, "And I do not mean that I wish to help you with the kitchen chores."

She shivered at his touch and the rasp of his day-old beard on the soft skin of her neck. At his grasp of her upper arm, her anticipation rushed down her arm to her fingertips and back up and around her shoulders to her breasts. His lips were at her neck, at her nape, at her ear, and flames streaked down her spine, down the back of her legs.

Forming her lips around words gave her the foretaste of kissing him. "I know what you mean," she breathed, "but what I do not know is why."

He eased his hold, but did not completely release her. He whispered into her ear, tickling, teasing with his breath and his lips, "Because you've been misused by the men in your life."

"Have I?" she breathed, amazed and fascinated by this perception and knowing it to be absolutely true.

"Yes," he said calmly, "and I mean to change that."

"Do you?" she asked.

He murmured, "Mm-hmm..." Then he said, into her neck, "I'd like you to experience something far, far different with me."

She was already experiencing something very different with him. What she still wanted to know was, "Why?"

He would satisfy her desire for the explicit. "Because I desire you and want you to desire me."

"And—?"

"Nothing more."

She repeated, "Nothing more?"

He shook his head. "I think you know what I mean, but I can be clearer still."

She shook her head quickly, denying the need for him to spell out just how much of the body—and not of the heart—the experience was to be. "And what do you propose?"

He looked up at her, his blue eyes stained so dark with his bodily desire for her that she already imagined him part of her. "I propose nothing," he said.

She was torn between exquisite disappointment and exquisite desire. He was very good at this. "Nothing?" she managed.

His black lashes lowered to focus on the expanse of her breasts, a mother's breasts. He shook his head. "Nothing," he repeated, "but what you want." He looked up at her again. "I propose nothing." He paused. "You are to propose. I am to obey."

It was a wholly novel idea to her, that she should be the one to desire, to initiate, to press, to consummate, and the very newness of it made it hard for her to know what to do. She moved away from him, and at her slight movement he released her. Again, she was disappointed, but she was also reassured. He had meant what he said, but she had no knowledge of how to proceed, of what to propose.

"I need help," she said.

"That's a start," he replied. He stood up and faced her. He bent toward her, as if to kiss her, but did not touch her. She swayed away from him. He immediately moved back so that he was half seated on the table.

"Not a very good start," she acknowledged shakily, perplexed by the contradictory forces filling her, fear warring with desire warring with that part of herself that she had given to no man. But she knew that he was not asking for that part of herself that she kept protected. He was asking only for her desire, so that he could satisfy it, the way he would satisfy himself with her. Nothing more.

She liked that "nothing more." It was their wedding night, it was true, but theirs was a falsely intentioned marriage. There was nothing more between them than their momentary desire. She judged it all the more exciting that it was of the moment and nothing more. She even judged it all the more exciting that she was not the first woman to respond to a charming, lazy drifter who played his cards so well.

He chose to help further. "Would you like to kiss me?" he asked, but he did not get off the table or make any hint to move toward her.

Her eyes dropped to his lips, which were smiling slightly and inviting hers. Critically she surveyed his lean jaw, which was darkened by a day-old beard. "Kiss you?" She shook her head, playing her own waiting game. "It might be rough going for me."

"Would you like to shave me?" he asked promptly.

The idea appealed to her. She raised a brow. "Do you trust me to hold a razor to your throat?"

He liked her suggestion of feminine rage and revenge. It released something strong and deep and masculine in him, something he had not felt in a long time. "One false move from you," he warned, his tone congenial but commanding, "and I withdraw my offer of obedience." He moved off the table then to come within a breath of her, but still did not touch her. "It will be you who obey me."

She was going to say, mockingly, "What? You would risk the same fate as General Ross?" However, some flicker deep in his eyes prompted her to ask instead, "Meaning that I should shave you while I have the chance?"

He nodded slowly. "While it's still up to you."

But not for long, she reckoned from the note of hot steel in his voice, a note that glazed over the light, teasing tones he had been using up till now. Since she would rather have his smooth cheek against hers rather than his rough one, she took the few steps to retrieve the shaving bowl, filled with razor, strop, brush, mirror and cloth, which he had stored the day before under the sink. She placed the bowl on the table, then came back to him. She put her hands on his shoulders and commanded him to sit on the bench so that he was facing away from the table.

He obeyed with pleasure and relaxed back against the table, his elbows propped across its top, while she went to fill the bowl with hot water from the kettle on the fire. While the water cooled a bit, she stropped the razor. Then she wet the cloth, dipping it with her fingertips so that it absorbed the hot water thirstily and thoroughly.

When she put the steaming cloth on his cheeks, his deep "Ahhh" produced an extraordinary reaction inside her body, making her wonder whether she would get through the shaving without demanding that he make violent love to her here on the bench.

She removed the cloth and rubbed the badger-bristle brush on a sliver of soap. When she began to soap his face, he opened his eyes and looked straight into hers as she concentrated on her task. She nearly quit right then to make her demand. Only the thought of his smooth cheek against hers kept her focused on her task. She picked up the razor and put the blade to his skin. He closed his eyes again and yielded the muscles of his neck and face to her touch. She maneuvered awkwardly around his knees and feet, which were stretched out before him, as she sought the best angles to catch the growth of his beard and shave the whiskers off.

With his eyes still closed, he reached out and grasped her lightly at the waist. Pulling her down to his lap, he murmured an explanation: "So that you don't have to move around my legs."

She turned as he pulled her down so that she was sitting across his lap, his legs turned out one way, hers the other.

"Much better," she agreed.

"But not good enough," he said, opening his eyes again and focusing on her. He lifted her skirts above her knees and shifted her dexterously. He placed one of her legs on either side of him, so that she was straddling him. Then, with his hands pressing heavily at her waist, he settled her down onto him.

She gasped, and he smiled. He closed his eyes and tilted his head back. "Proceed," he invited huskily.

She did not know if she could. With her legs spread so intimately around him, she could feel the heat spring up between them. She felt liquid desire within her, everywhere, including her wrists and elbows, making it difficult for her to hold the razor steady.

"I'm not sure I can proceed without killing you," she admitted.

"You won't kill me with that razor," he said confidently. "Not a chance of it." He opened one eye a crack, and she saw it burning with blue light. "Here, I'll help you." His hands slipped up from her waist, across the breasts, up her shoulders, back down to her breasts, then down both her arms. He drew her closer to him, so close that her breasts were against his chest and the crux of her femininity was located against his manhood.

He closed his fingers around the wrist of the hand that held the razor and whispered, "Steady now. Easy now. Long broad strokes. Yes, like that. Across my chin. Now, under my neck. Yes." He slid his other hand over her shoulder and down her back so that it cupped her buttock on his knee. He caressed her, moving her against him, teasing her unbearably, causing waves of delight and anticipation. "Long broad strokes. Easy now. Steady now. You've got it. Up one side. Down the other. You're almost there. Yes."

She could never have imagined such a sensual awakening. Her arousal was complete, and their skin had not even touched, nor had they begun to kiss. She wished to finish this lovely, luxurious shaving so that she could have him fully. She ran her hand across his cheek and neck, seeking with her fingertips the patches of whiskers she might have missed. At last she put the razor down and reached out for the cloth, plucking it steaming from its bowl of water. She placed it over his fresh-shaven skin. She dampened and wiped. She savored and soothed. She blotted and caressed.

She returned the cloth to the bowl and sat back to survey her work. He opened his eyes and held her regard for an infinite moment of mutual delight and satisfaction.

Since he had given her permission to set the pace, she took his clean face in her hands and held him, as dearly and as closely as she would her baby. She put her cheek to his and savored its fresh scent and its new smoothness. She drew her head back again so that she could regard him with desire and inquiry.

He nodded. He moved her hips away from him so that she could disentangle herself from him. Both of them regretted this momentary separation, but both of them knew it was necessary if they were proceed to satisfaction. They rose together to their feet, slowly, somewhat awkwardly, keeping their eyes locked, keeping the flames fanned, not caring if they were clumsy about it. They did not immediately move away from the bench and the table. They stood, besotted with one another, almost entranced, surprised, happy, desiring, tender, hesitant, eager.

She said, in wonderment, "And we have not even kissed yet."

He replied, "We did once today."

She looked a little blank until she remembered the end of the wedding ceremony and the strange, strong kiss he had given her then.

His hands went out to her shoulders. His head came down toward hers, blotting out the world. Then his lips touched hers with flames and the promise of passion.

Chapter Seventeen

Morgan put his lips to hers and tasted her strength and her desire and her uncomplicated need for him, at this moment, in this circumstance. He kissed her, and she returned his kiss, lingering. It was a remarkable kiss, this kiss. It was strong in its bountiful lack of reserve, in its giving, in its fulfillment of its promise. It was new in its freshness; it was ancient in its evocation of a past long dead, but not buried.

Somewhere along the way, this had ceased to be the usual seduction for him. He knew that Barbara wanted him. He had wanted her wanting him. He had done everything so that he would have her wanting him. But somehow her mere physical desire for him was not enough. It was not enough, this easy, lazy seduction, with its predictable satisfactions and its ever-hungry oblivion. It was not enough, to bring a woman panting to her need and then to satisfy her body with his. It was not enough to satisfy his body with hers, but not to satisfy his heart or his soul or any other organ that was so much more important than the one between his legs.

What counted now were his lips, the ones he had not given to a woman, not really, not in generous giving, not in fifteen years. He would not dishonor his wife by giving his lips promiscuously to another woman. Any other part of him, yes, and with abandon. But his lips, no. With his lips, then, to her, his beloved wife, long dead but not buried, he had been faithful.

This kiss, with its passion and desire and need, was much more than he had expected or even wanted, for it was too much. Or not enough. He did not know. He was between two lives and two worlds. The little cart inside him was careering wildly, well out of his control, well out of his experience. It traveled no recognizable geographical landscape now, not even the terrifying face of sheer descent. It obeyed no known law of physics. It threatened to explode. It threatened to vanish. Its loss was desperately to be desired. For the loss of the little cart carrying the unburied bundle of his emotions would leave him free and without anguish.

Its loss was desperately to be resisted. For the little cart, streaking downhill in terror, was the only part of him that seemed truly, terribly alive, and its loss would leave him with—nothing. He would have prayed for that nothing as recently as last month, last week, last night. But not now. The nothing was no longer enough.

Why was there suddenly a desire for something instead of nothing?

The ground had cracked and was rumbling beneath him. Two worlds and two lives were colliding. There was not just one vertical slope that threatened his equilibrium. There were hundreds of cracks and crevices, hundreds of vertical faces. It produced a complex geography, this shock of two worlds and two lives. The land around him, in her arms, surrounded by her scent, her curves, her desire, had become a prism of color and shape whose bright, sharp facets trapped him, blinded him, confused him. The land around him, with his lips locked with hers in an extraordinary giving, had become kaleidoscopic and terrifying and desirable.

He did not know how it had happened, exactly, only that it had happened. The two worlds had collided, and the surfaces of both had been broken. He had spoken with more truth than he knew when he had said, the night before, that Jack Carter was finished. Jack Carter was the son of another Jacques Cartier, French Canadian by birth and Breton by lineage, a charming, brutal man who had made an erratic living as a fur trapper.

From his father, Jack Carter had learned to mine Canadian silver: the silver fox, the silver wolf, the silver beaver. He had learned to tease and trap these beautiful silver animals with teeth of silver steel. He had learned to watch with pleasure as these creatures lay maimed and immobile, near death but still suffering, soon to be skinned of their silver fur. He had learned to appreciate the frozen, shivery beauty of the red rimming the voracious steel mouth closed tight, the drops of blood tracing a lace of red against the pure white of the snow.

From his father, he had learned to tease and trap women, too, to collect them like so many pelts of fur. From his father, he had learned to gamble, to drink, to smile, to charm, to roam, to hunt, to live life from the stomach down.

But it had never been enough, the life he learned from his father. Or it had been too much. Too brutal. Too violent. Too visceral.

Too aimless. Too unthinking.

Too unlawful.

From his mother, whom his father had never married, he had learned to sing. From his mother, Morgana Harris, daughter of Morgan Harris, he had learned to love. From his gentle, nurturing mother, he had learned to farm.

His mother had migrated from Canada to western Massachusetts when she discovered that she was pregnant and the charming, brutal father of the child laughed in her face. She had named her son Jack Carter after his father. She had kept her son with her for the first ten years of his life, but she had not been able to keep him when Jacques Cartier decided to claim the son he had previously rejected.

She had pleaded to keep her son. She had wept to keep her son. She had argued that the father had no legal right. Some things, the father had countered, were above the law. Any son strong enough to survive boyhood belonged to the father, and that was that. If the gentle, peaceable, nurturing

Morgana Harris wanted a child so badly, Jacques Carter would give her another, brutally and with pleasure.

And that was the last the young Jack Carter saw of his mother who died nine months later, giving birth to a stillborn daughter.

The loving, gentle son of Morgana Harris grew into the charming, brutal Jack Carter, who could trap and kill, tease and kiss. He had lived two separate lives, and he never gave a thought to integrating them until the *coup de foudre* struck him—the "bolt of lightning," as the French called it—love. He was trapping deep in Iroquois territory the winter of his twentieth year, and had been tracking a canny silver fox for days when he came upon an Iroquois maid who had strayed too far from her camp searching for winter berries.

He carried her off, made her his that night, and returned with her to her camp the next morning, ready to surrender to the force of Iroquois law. Nothing could have been easier for him than to shed his father's name and take that of his mother's father to marry the maiden. Nothing could have been easier than to abandon the world of Jack Carter and embrace that of Morgan Harris.

However, nothing could have been harder than to return to his peaceable life in western Massachusetts with a redskinned wife and a half-breed child on the way.

After his farm was torched and the flesh on his back forever scarred by the flames of prejudice, he reassumed the ways of Jack Carter. With a difference, this time. The brutal young man would no longer trap. The charming young man would no longer rape. The young Jack Carter did not have to, of course, because he knew how to smile, he knew how to talk, he knew how to play his cards, and the women came to him. He did not look at a woman who did not look at him first. He did not want a woman who did not want him more. He did not join with a woman who needed his care or his protection or who roused in him the slightest touch of his aggressive passion.

It was not that the two worlds of Jack Carter and Morgan Harris were at war inside him. It was rather that they were separate, untouching, unable to communicate. The victimized farmer Morgan Harris knew that the hunter and trapper Jack Carter needed to tame his aggressive passions, but that was all he knew.

Jack Carter's passive passion won him access to many a woman's bed. It roused in many a weak and beautiful woman's ample breast her own protective passions. During the past fifteen years, there had always been one woman who wanted to trap him and lame him between her legs while another woman wished to tie him to her with the bonds of marriage. He had slipped all traps and bonds, passively, dishonorably, successfully.

But now he was kissing, really kissing, a strong woman who brought the two worlds inside him together, so that they crashed into one another. One man inside him wished to take her here, on the bench, on the floor, now. Although the rudeness of the thought appealed to him, the actual execution did not, and this man's power got them, kissing, touching, desiring, to the threshold of the bedroom door. He had her with her back against the door jamb. He leaned himself against her and into her softness. The bed was a few steps away. Their clothes would soon be off. Satisfaction was at hand.

Another man inside him wished to find a way to make her want him more powerfully than he wanted her. He thought it might be too late for that, and something inside him shrank back from her. It was still his intention to master her, but there was desperation in the desire now.

He did not know which man was which, who was surging forward, who was shrinking back. And the landscape continued to reform itself around him in violent shifts.

A third man emerged, a man who was familiar in all his parts but not his composition. This man knew that he loved the woman in his arms. He knew that she did not love him equally in return, that she had no reason to love him in a way that he yearned to be loved. He knew that the way to her love was not through the entering of her body, although their joining would satisfy the thickness between them.

His ancient aggression flared out. His passionate passivity retaliated. The two impulses canceled one another, and he was left with a body alive in all its parts, all organs awake and saturated—his lips, his heart, his stomach, his liver, his brain—all except the one between his legs. The least important. The most important. The least governable. The most ungoverned.

Impuissant! one man inside him realized with magnificent horror. *Impotent!* the other identified with a curious relief.

He eased up on her. He lifted his lips from hers. He moved back just enough to lift his head and look at her. Her eyes slowly opened at his movement away. His heart seemed to twist inside out and drip black, putrid blood as he sank his gaze into the beautiful blue of her eyes, the pools of an enchanted lake where he could cleanse himself of old, un-cleansed wounds. Where he could submerge himself without drowning. Where he could surround himself without suffocating. Where he could drink his fill.

He had lost none of his desire for her—in fact, it had only increased—but his body was not yet reattached to his soul, and his manhood would not obey any of his animal appetites for her. His eyes must have shown some of his body's difficulties, for she looked at first puzzled, then slightly comprehending. He was not embarrassed by his condition, but he was apologetic and off-balance. He was about to say something to her, something he had never before said to a woman. Before he could speak, several things happened at once, although he could not have said afterward in what order they had come.

The baby awoke and began to cry. Barbara turned her head toward the cradle. She frowned and groaned, all the while trying to grope through her emotions and to come to terms with what would happen next between them.

Morgan quickly put his finger to her lips in a warning, silencing gesture, for at the very same moment Pockets had lifted his head and started to whimper miserably.

It was then that the front door to the house was kicked open in one violent blast, and a loud, piercing whoop rent the air. It could very well have been the whoop that had caused the baby to waken and Pockets to react in the first place, so simultaneous were the events.

Without thinking, Barbara shot to the cradle and scooped Sarah into her arms, to silence her, to protect her from the intruder, to save what was most precious in her life or to die trying. She was holding Sarah hardly before the intruder had finished kicking in the door, so that when she looked over in terror she was witnessing it at the moment the door was still being half ripped from its hinges. She saw it swing, drunkenly, on twisted bits of metal.

The creature that entered on blood-boiling whoops and yelps was like none Barbara had ever seen before. She dismissed the idea—though not in any conscious way, for she was not thinking now, only reacting—that it was a messenger from either Lieutenant Richards or Mrs. Ross. It was certainly human, with its two arms, two legs and a head, but it was covered in skins, and its face was a nightmare vision of fantastic colors. Its head was spiked with feathers.

Morgan's veins still flowed with his unspent energies. He was instantly on the alert and surprisingly prepared for this shock. He whirled, ready to defend against attack with only his bare hands. He needed but a flash to take in the garish and fearsome details of this extraordinary creature's appearance and less than another flash to notice that it brandished a very long knife whose blade was glinting malevolently in the firelight.

"Jacques Cartier!" the creature intoned.

The very name electrified Morgan's already alert senses. Images shifted rapidly before his mind's eye, and suddenly the vision of a wild young half-breed, walking drunk and belligerent into Kelly's tavern less than a week ago, blazed bright before him. That wild young half-breed had been looking for something that night—most likely a fight, he had thought at the time. Now a different, stranger thought flitted through his brain, but he did not have a chance to assimilate it.

The next instant, the creature called out scornfully, "Morgan Harris!"

In that moment Morgan remembered that Evan Rollins had said that two men were on his trail. One man—his gambling rival, most likely—would likely have been thrown off the track by Evan Rollins's solemn testimony that Jack Carter was not to be found on North Point. The other man—this one?—would not have been similarly thrown off, since he knew both of Morgan's names.

Morgan would not deny the truth of those names. He stepped forward, his veins alive, flowing, with male strength, bare-handed and unafraid in the face of this hideous creature. He crouched down and raised his hands for combat, circling slowly toward the kitchen, remembering without looking at the table the exact location of both the bread knife and the shaving razor. His trapper's instincts rose to help him calculate the weakness of this creature, to locate the exact spot in his neck where he intended to slit his throat.

Then the creature began to speak. The initial cries and yelps and whoops has resolved themselves into language, beyond the pronouncement of his two names. Morgan remembered that language, but it was not French, no. It was some other language. One he had not learned as a child. It was of his young adulthood. It was—

"I have come to kill you, Morgan Harris," the creature said in the recognizable tongue, the language of an ancient, proud, beautiful, dying people.

The meaning registered, but the individual words did not, and Morgan could not respond in that language. "My ancestors will protect me from your ancestors," Morgan replied in French, recalling the ritual prelude to combat. He might have forgotten the words, but he had not forgotten the formalities.

"I have no ancestors," the warrior replied unexpectedly, wholly breaking with tradition. He, too, was crouching down, circling in turn and raising his arms in combat.

"Then you have come on a dishonorable errand," Morgan answered at last in Iroquois, rather pleased with himself for having found the formula. "You will have no way to right the wrong."

He remembered those phrases from the morning when he had returned to the Iroquois camp, the night after he had defiled the Iroquois maid. Her father had initially denied Morgan permission to marry her, for Morgan had taken what was not his to take. Morgan had acted in defiance and dishonor, and years later, when his farm was torched and his wife humiliated and dead, he had remembered his father-in-law's words. Death had been the brutal outcome of his defiant and dishonorable deed. His father-in-law had been right: There had been no way to right the wrong, and he had been left with a life that was not worth living.

Now, however, he wanted life, and he was prepared to fight for it.

"I have come to kill you, Morgan Harris," the warrior repeated, circling closer, "and there will be no dishonor to me."

"It is not for you to judge where your honor lies," Morgan said. He felt contemptuous of the young warrior's defiance of the old ways. He felt old and wise and ready now to live.

"For now, yes, it is for me to judge where my honor lies," the warrior replied, with relish and blood lust. "I do not wish it that way, however. I want to reclaim my ancestors, for they were denied me shortly after I was born."

Morgan wished to repeat that the warrior had come on a dishonorable errand, but the words did not seem right. He did not know the next formula to say, for it was lost to him. Or perhaps he had never known it.

The warrior continued. He articulated carefully, as if he had practiced the formula a thousand times awake and a thousand times asleep. "I will reclaim my ancestors when I have killed you who have abandoned me."

"I who have abandoned you—?" Morgan repeated, wholly taken aback, unmindful of the grave error he committed in repeating the words of his opponent.

"Yes, you are the father who is no father," the warrior said, merrily and mercilessly, "whose ancesters I may claim when you are slain by my hand."

"Father," Morgan repeated haltingly in Iroquois, like a baby pronouncing the word for the first time. "Father?"

The hideously painted warrior closed in, and Morgan's eyes dilated in astonishment and a kind of stunned recognition. But there was no fear. Not a trace of it. He suddenly saw in the young warrior's face, beneath the paint, a vision of his own, the same planes of the cheeks, the same pinch at the bridge of the nose, the same carriage of the head on that neck whose vulnerable point Morgan had already identified and targeted with murderous intent. It was his face the young warrior wore beneath the paint, but with a just noticeable, half-breed difference. His eyes had the sloe and the slant of a beautiful Iroquois maiden's.

"The father who is no father," the warrior repeated, with hideous glee. "Whose soul will burn."

Morgan stopped moving, frozen cold in his crouch with his hands raised. He completed the essential formula, "So that the ancestors will be free to protect the son who had no father."

Still with hot male strength flowing in his veins, more alive than he had been since tracking a canny silver fox deep in Iroquois territory years and years ago, Morgan was having surprisingly little difficulty comprehending the impossible. It was as if scalding water had poured through his brain, and his perceptions of the world were irrevocably altered. Without a tremor of doubt, Morgan saw the boy, his son, hardly more than sixteen years old, defiant in the face of the dishonor he had lived with his entire life, and ready to kill to restore his honor.

Morgan traced the lines of his son's face and followed a swirl of red paint from the young warrior's nose, across his cheek, to his ear, down his neck. Somewhere in that swirl, the color red ceased to be that of paint and began to be that of scarred burns. The line of scar, like the crab that Morgan wore on his back, must continue on down the boy's chest under the skins he wore. The pain of that night of fury and futility raced through him.

Morgan felt the flames on his back again. That was one pain. Then he heard a baby crying. It was his baby, crying in helpless pain. His pain burned doubly for the infant son he had thought dead in that fire, but who had lived and bore the scars to prove it. He did not question how his son had survived, and the unasked question made the fire inside him burn triply. The pain of the threefold fire burned but did not consume itself. It became anguish. Almost unbearable. And in that unconsumable fire of anguish, the clear, calm thought composed itself: *I would have given my life a thousand times over so that he could have lived. Now I need only give it once.*

Morgan rose from his frozen crouch to his full height and dropped his arms. He spread his hands out and palms out. His head was up and proud, his chin a little raised to expose the jugular vein. He was pulsing with life. He was proud now that he had saved the boy—his *son*—with his dishonorable actions at Kelly's tavern. It was something he could die being proud of. He now understood that his son had tracked him down at Kelly's with the intention of killing him. If the boy had accomplished his goal then and there, in a room full of white men, his young life would have been forfeit.

Morgan felt like crying with happiness, but he would not disgrace himself or dishonor the occasion. He smiled with appropriate goodwill and understanding. This wrong, at least, could be righted. He found the correct formula.

"Do what you must."

He wished he could have added "My son," but he knew that fine appellation was not due him. He added, instead, "Laurence Harris."

Further words were not necessary. The warrior boy did not have the age or the experience to accept the invitation with the proper decorum, but it did not matter to Morgan. The warrior raised his blade high above his head. Then he bent down, so that he could spring forward and bring the blade down, once, into his most dishonorable enemy's neck.

Barbara had not the vaguest idea of what had been said between the two men. Even if she had known the translation of the words, she would not have been able to understand them. She was able to guess, correctly, that the young and hideous warrior was the same half-breed boy who had wandered into the Boston tavern and set off the chain of events that had brought Morgan Harris to her front porch. She was also able to guess the import of the fantastic choreography that she was witnessing. She could see clearly enough that the young man was going to kill Morgan and that Morgan was going to let the young man do it.

Never before had she seen such an act of bravery as Morgan's. It was pure and beautiful and transcendent. She had been breathless with wonder when Morgan had lowered his arms, straightened his head and spoken with such absolute serenity and confidence. It was a moment of transformation for her. If she never performed another worthy act in her life, she would act to save his life.

Before she had consciously formed her plan of action, she had moved next to the table and grasped the razor with her free hand. She was hardly aware that she was carrying the frightened and crying Sarah on her hip. At the moment the hideous creature sprang forward, his blade hungry and trenchant and ready to bite deep into Morgan's throat, she flourished the razor vigorously. She moved forward into the fray and called out, in angry, threatening accents, "Don't you dare harm my husband!"

Chapter Eighteen

The flash of her razor, her quick movement and her words were enough to distract the young warrior. He glanced away to judge this lateral attack, then back at his main target, and lost the precision of his aim. When the boy's blade came down on Morgan's undefended skin, the sharp steel did not slice into his neck, but penetrated near his shoulder blade, above his heart, and gashed down raggedly above his armpit and into his upper arm.

Morgan fell backward upon impact, with his son on top of him. The boy having at first lost his balance, regained his agility and rolled away immediately. He had also lost his grip on his knife. It clattered to the floor.

Barbara ran to the fallen blade and kicked it far out of reach. It skiddered across the floor, scratching a thin trace of bright red. She blazed like a Fury above the painted creature who had come to kill Morgan. She wielded her razor, unafraid, saying almost anything that came to mind, hectoring him, harrying him, kicking him while he was down on the ground. She was hardly able to think or hear herself above her baby's wailing and the frightened pup's piteous yipping.

Blood of anger throbbed at her temples. She cried, "Get out! Get out of my house, you murderer! You think I'm afraid of you? Do you? Get out! I could kill you, you know! I'm capable of it! Get out while you can!"

The tip of her shoe connected with one of his ribs with enough force to cause him to groan. He rolled over deftly and sprang to his feet to face her. He whooped and yelped, as if he would attack her.

She stared him down with magnificent rage. "You take one step toward me and you'll have to kill me and my baby!" A violence she had never before experienced coursed through her, and she knew with icy certainty that she would be able to slash the creature to the bone if he attacked.

"Try it," she taunted. "Come and get me."

She looked straight into the painted creature's black, black eyes. He glanced at the baby on her hip, then back to her, and she saw his eyes widen slightly. He hesitated infinitesimally, and she gestured again with her razor, threatening.

Without further sound, the painted creature turned and bounded out of the house with the speed he had entered it. Hardly two moments passed before Barbara heard a horse's whinny. She imagined that the creature must have leapt onto the animal. Then there was the thunder of hooves receding into the depths of the night and the blackness.

Barbara rushed to Morgan's side. On her way, she unceremoniously plopped Sarah, uncomforted and still whimpering in hiccuping gasps, into the cradle. Morgan was her greatest concern at the moment. She knelt down and took his head and shoulders into her lap, murmuring over and over, "My God! My God, Morgan!"

His eyes were closed, his breathing was labored, blood was flowing from his wound, and he was moaning in pain. She bent to examine his wound, not caring that his blood was staining her skirts. He flinched at her touch. She saw that the gash was long and deep at the point of entry, but clean and fresh, and she did not think he would have to die from it. Not if she acted fast. Not if she knew the right things to do for him.

What she wanted to do was hold him forever and comfort him and murmur soothing words and smooth the hair from his forehead with her hands. What she needed to do was far different. He was losing blood at an alarming rate, and his body had begun to shiver lightly. With great effort, she put his head and shoulders back down on the ground very gently, then ran to get some clean diapers. With them, she stanched the wound, changing the diaper when soaked, applying as much firm pressure as she dared, for as long as she could stand it.

The door was open, and drafts swirled throughout the sitting room. The fire on the hearth had burned down and was flickering uncertainly. The baby was whimpering. The dog was skittering nervously. Morgan's blood was still flowing. Barbara's head was pounding.

Think! she admonished herself. *Don't give up!* she encouraged herself. *First things first!* she repeated under her breath over and over until she could determine what that first thing was.

Then Morgan shivered, once, strongly, and she knew what to do. With single-minded intensity, she rose to her feet. She retrieved a hammer from an old workbox by the sink and hammered flat what she could of the twisted hinges so that the door could be put back in place. The fit was far from perfect now, but she battered the door and the hinges and jamb until it was flat enough. She jimmied the bar across the slots to hold the whole mess in place. She got rags and cloths to stuff into the many gaping cracks. She barred the back door, as well, then hastily tended the fire.

Instead of wringing Pockets's neck to keep him from driving her to distraction with his erratic movements and nerve-jangling cries, she decided to put him to use rocking the baby's cradle. Frazzled herself, she had little patience to train him to the exercise, but once she placed him in the end of the cradle Pockets was quick enough. After a frustrating minute, he seemed to get the hang of the motion and find the sport amusing. Little by little, Sarah quieted, rocked into gentleness by Pockets and exhausted from the extreme emotions of the past few minutes. Barbara's mind had calmed, and she could focus on the task of tending to Morgan's grave wound.

She took his head in her lap again and replaced a blood-soaked cloth with a clean one. She sat there until her back ached and the bones in her legs ached from the unsoftened contact with the hard floor and her arms ached with pressing the wound. She would have preferred to drag him to her bed so that he would be warm and pillowed in softness, but she knew that she should not move him in his present condition. She wondered if she should stay, thus, the night through, without moving him. She wondered if she *could* stay, thus, the night through. She debated going to get the doctor, but any number of reasons occurred to her that made it seem highly unwise to leave the house for an extended period.

Although his breathing was steady, it was labored, and she knew that he was in a great deal of pain. He was semiconscious and muttering incoherently. She was most concerned about the waves of heat alternating with the chills that had begun to wrack his body. She was feeling increasingly tired and desperate and helpless when her eye fell on the instruments hanging on the wall opposite and she was energized by a brilliant idea.

She put Morgan down again, smoothed his damp hair from his forehead and knelt down to whisper into his ear, "It will be all right now. I'm going to fix you up."

She hastened to the wall, surveyed the instruments with their lengths of catgut stretching in ample lines from neck to belly. She reached for the banjo. "I've known you a long time, old boy, but you're not his style," she muttered, addressing the instrument. "My father will soon be turning in his grave, but your sacrifice will be worth it."

She prepared hot water. She fetched her sewing basket. She rummaged in a kitchen cabinet for an old, half-full bottle of moonshine. She unstoppered the bottle, took a whiff of the stuff that made her eyes roll, then examined the cork, which had been partially corroded over the years by the fumes trapped in the bottle. She took a deep breath and tried to convince herself that she could do what she so evidently had to do.

She returned to Morgan, knelt down beside him and began to speak to him, to reassure him, to reassure herself. "I have to sew you up, you know," she said. She took her scissors and clipped the banjo strings without a qualm. "It's only the banjo, you know, so you needn't worry," she informed him calmly. "I know it's a pity to destroy so valuable an instrument, but it can't be helped."

She wiped a needle with a cloth she had soaked in moonshine, then threaded it intently. "I am a much more proficient weaver than I am a seamstress, but I should be able to pretty up that ragged line in your shoulder in a few minutes. It won't ever be beautiful, but it will be closed, and you'll thank me for it."

She poured some moonshine down Morgan's throat. He coughed and sputtered and tried to reject the firewater, but she pressed it on him until he was no longer writhing and moaning and had reached a state—she hoped—beyond pain.

"Now, you will know when I have put the needle through your skin, but it will only be that first moment that it hurts. I need all my resolve now, you understand. What I need is resolution. Yes. There. The worst is over. Ah, yes. Now I've placed the first stitch, and I must say it is a very fine one."

Barbara's hand was trembling. She thrust out her tongue and wiped the beads of sweat from her upper lip. The room had become warm, then very hot. Morgan was sweating, too, profusely. She was making her stitches small and precise, moving slowly, alternately laughing and weeping each time the needle pierced his skin. She wanted him to have to suffer only this once, reckoning that if she did the most meticulous job possible this time, the stitches would hold and not have to be redone.

"If I do a very good job," she said, her voice wavering, but her hand steady, "a very, *very* good job with this repair, I will be able to get you from the floor to the bed without you losing any more blood. Isn't that an attractive idea?" She clucked. She murmured. She sewed. She sweated. "Ah, you see, Morgan, I'm more than half done."

She ran out of gut and had to rethread her needle. During the slight respite, Morgan's face blanched entirely. Then he lay very still.

Her heart quailed. She thought he had died. She quickly pressed her hand to his heart. The beat was faint. Not knowing what else to do, she massaged his chest, continuously and at length, until every bone and every joint in her fingers and wrists creaked.

"I worked you too hard just now, didn't I? It was too much. I see that now. Too many stitches at once. I was too eager. Yes. But not now. I'm calmer now, and the deepest part of the gash has been sewn. You're not bleeding anymore. Isn't that wonderful?"

The color seeped back into his face. Her own heartbeat slowed to its accustomed rhythm. It was true what she had said, his bleeding had all but stopped, and she had rejoined in a tiny seam of exquisite stitches more than half the gaping flesh. The deepest part of the gash was repaired, and the worst was truly over.

Her tone became severe. "So there is really no point in dying now, Morgan. No, there isn't. I am sure you hardly feel my touch, because the wound is so superficial. No more than a scratch! And when you are better, you will explain to me exactly what occurred here tonight! Of course, I will be patient about it! Tomorrow, at your leisure, you can tell me, after I have fed you some hot soup and you have played the guitar and you feel much, much better!"

When her hand started to wobble, she brought herself around with the bracing words "It's nearly over. Just a few more stitches. Tiny, fine ones in your arm so that it will be as good as new. Now, your shoulder, I am afraid, will never heal without a scar, but so it has to be! There!"

It was all she could do to keep her head out of her hands when she was done, but she resisted the wave of weakness and relief that washed over her. She surveyed her handiwork and was astounded by its precision. She had never sewed such an elegant seam in her life. She felt a hysterical laugh well up inside her. Not wanting to succumb to that emotion, either, she rose, lumbering, from the position she had been holding for the past eternity and moved through the next series of necessary motions.

She shoved Sarah's cradle into her bedroom and lit a low fire there. She asked Pockets with extreme firmness and politeness not to make any noise, demand anything of her or involve himself in any other foolishness before the dawn. She prepared her bed to receive its precious charge and then returned to the sitting room to bend herself to the laborious task—certainly the most difficult and delicate of the night—of getting Morgan's body into her bed.

She verged on failure a dozen times, thinking at each moment that her muscles could neither push nor pull him any more, that she would simply throw pillows and blankets down on the floor for him. But then she thought how kindly her bed would receive his body, how safe and warm he would be above the swirling drafts. She thought how well she could care for him, holding him to her the night long, in her bed. Somehow she found the strength to continue, moving, pushing, pulling, making sure she did not disturb the delicate embroidery that ran across his chest and to his arm.

So she pushed and pulled him from the sitting room to her bedroom, smearing the pool of blood he left in his wake. When he was at the side of her bed, she stripped him naked and used his ruined shirt to wipe him off. She maneuvered him awkwardly into the nightshirt he had been using. Then she said, very sadly and very lovingly, "Morgan, you will have to stand up. I cannot conceivably hoist you from the floor to the bed. I know it is outrageous for me to ask you such a thing, but, really, I have no other choice."

Either he heard her and was physically able to obey or else she received a last surge of energy, for when she slid her arms under his good arm to help him he seemed to lift from the floor and fall across the bed. His position was awkward, but he was up and on the mattress. Without too much further difficulty, she had him tucked in under the covers with his head and hands arranged comfortably.

When she went back into the sitting room to bank the fire for the night, she saw the full horror of the smear of blood on the floor and knew that if she did not clean it up immediately she would not be able to close her eyes this night without seeing the stain. Thus, it was fully an hour before she was able to put aside her soap and scrub brush and pail of water. In her haze of exhaustion, she nearly forgot to bank the fire, but she was able to dispatch this last task with efficiency.

During the washing of the floor, she had periodically checked on Morgan for sounds of distress. She had pressed her forehead to his once or twice, checking for fever, but there was none. So she was not worried about him when she was finally able to slip into her night shift and drop her wretched, bloodstained clothes on top of his in a heap next to the bed. As she was about to climb in, she became aware of one last, vexatious, womanly chore left undone, a chore that could decidedly not be left until the morning.

"We're babies all of us, with our cloths," she muttered to both the other occupants of the room. Then, to Morgan in particular: "We'll bleed together this night, I suppose."

Finally, when she had put a fresh menstrual cloth in place, she slipped into the softness of her bed, which was already warmed by Morgan's presence. She nearly groaned aloud in response to the beautiful shock of the comfort after the hours of bone-hard, emotion-draining work.

She gathered Morgan to her. He seemed to yield with abandon to her touch, to her shifting of his shoulders into her lap, to her settling of his head against her breast. He was breathing deeply and evenly, with no shudders. Her work-roughened fingers pressed his forehead, massaged his neck and delicately traced the line of stitches that had saved his life. The stitches had caused his skin to swell, but not ominously. Her fingers came to rest atop one of his hands. Her fingers sank into the spaces between his fingers, where they rested.

She was tired, but not sleepy, and she gazed for a long, long time at the ceiling, not moving, just breathing in tandem with Morgan. Her thoughts spread to fill the vast stretches of the dark and the night.

At one moment, her fingers were touching him, massaging him, soothing him. Hardly realizing that she was speaking aloud, she murmured, "Three strangers in three days. I can hardly believe it."

A weak, gravelly voice replied, "And the last one did not even knock first."

Her exhaustion fled from her tired bones and was replaced by elation. "Morgan?" she breathed, low and with happiness. "Good God, Morgan? Are you really with me again?"

He grunted his response to that.

She shifted slightly to look at his face, but she could tell from his stiffness that her movement had made him uncomfortable, so she reverted to her original position—or almost. She had not relaced her fingers in his, and his hand searched blindly for hers. His back arched upward. She understood what he wanted and, sure enough, when she smoothed the back of his hand with hers and slid her fingers between his, he sighed his satisfaction and relaxed into her.

After she had absorbed the fact that he was conscious, she could comprehend that he had actually made a joke. "No, no manners, this last one." She thought it over. "I'll have to replace the door, you know."

His head made a movement that was something like a nod.

"Who was it?" she asked simply, worried mostly about the unexpected attack, but curious, too.

He had spent all his energy with his first response. He had a blinding headache. The next words came with difficulty. "My son."

The response left her breathless. Was that what he had been running from in Boston? His son wanted to kill him? But that made no sense, given that he had seemed ready to sacrifice himself to his son's murderous impulse tonight. From what she had come to know of him in the past few days, she would have said that he was a man very much alone in the world, and the creature's visit had been as much a surprise to him as it had been to her.

"Did you know you had a son?"

His head made a shaking movement. "No."

"Can you be sure that he is your son, then?"

His head made a nodding movement. "Yes." Then he managed to say, "Had one. Once."

It seemed fantastic, this story. She remembered now having thought she saw a boy lurking outside the meeting-house this afternoon, but she had not seen his face clearly enough to know whether it was the painted creature—his son!—who had kicked in her door like a wild Indian.

Wild Indian. The half-breed boy who had come into Kelly's tavern? The one he had said he had to save.

It almost made sense.

"You had a son once, but then you lost him?" she asked.

He shook his head.

"You did *not* lose him?"

He shook his head again.

"He ran away?"

He shook his head a third time. His back arched again. He seemed frustrated.

Her heart went out to him and his evident pain and the network of sorry circumstance that must have led to his willingness to be murdered by his own son's hand. She had made him anxious with her questions. She could wait for the answers. All night. Longer. Forever, even, if he did not want to tell her. If it was too painful.

She tried again. "It's too complicated to explain now, isn't it?"

He relaxed again and nodded his head, "Yes."

"All right, then," she said softly. She stroked the back of his hand. She nuzzled him with her neck. "It's all right, Morgan. Just rest." She kissed his hair as she would her baby's. "You need rest. It's all right."

He shook his head, "No." He seemed agitated. He formed the words. "Have to know."

She wished he would not try to speak, but since he so evidently wanted to, she asked, "You have to know something?"

He nodded his head. He regrouped his forces. He drew a deep breath. He said, "Have to know what you thought of... that." He gestured vaguely with his head, indicating the sitting room.

Somehow she understood what he was trying to ask her. She smiled, slightly, in the darkness. She put her hand very delicately at his temple to smooth his hair. She remembered that moment when he had let his arms fall to his sides and he had lifted his chin with dignity to his attacker. Her vision of him had been not so much transformed as solidified. She said the words from her heart: "You were magnificent."

Magnificent, she had said. Morgan comprehended her words as if through a beautiful dream. She had not been horrified. Not disgusted. Not even confused. No. She had thought him magnificent.

Perhaps he *had* died and gone to heaven. He had certainly thought so when he had been reborn in her arms a few minutes ago. He had regained consciousness when he felt her hands on him, touching him lightly, here and there, with a mother's touch, making sure all parts were safe and sound.

He had been aware first of her fingers tracing a tight, rough, numb line running from his collarbone across his armpit to his upper arm. It had been so strange, the tightness and the numbness of her touch against his skin, which he could both feel and not feel. It had taken him another moment to realize, with awe and another dimension of feeling for her, what she must have done in the aftermath of the attack on him. The searing pain associated with her repair work had come back to him in a wave that crested another few moments, then receded. His temples pounded with a different kind of pain.

Earlier in the afternoon, he had thought her strong and brave. Even so, he had underestimated her.

But before that first moment, when the touch of her fingers had brought him back to the land of the living, there had been another moment. A moment when he had not been aware of anything except being surrounded by her as she held him, surrounded by the softness of her bed. The last thing he remembered of life on earth was the moment before he must have died. Thus, to have found himself stretched out in this particular bed with this particular woman holding him seemed nothing less than his celestial reward for his final, virtuous deed on earth. It had been a divinely fitting reward, he had thought, his ascension. The last time he had been in Barbara Johnson's bed, he had hovered in the unblessed state of purgatory.

Then she had touched him, and he had come back to life. The last, dense, potent minutes of his life swirled through his brain. He hardly knew which experience to resolve first, for they all seemed part of the same tight knot: the fact that he had escaped certain death; the fact that his son was alive; the fact that he had finally wanted something more from a woman than her body.

So he was alive and warm and safe and comforted. He had been prepared to die, and she had saved him. According to the Iroquois law that guided his son, he would now owe her his life. However, he did not think she would want him on those terms; nor did he wish to be her slave. He did not live by Iroquois law, anyway. As for his son . . .

It was as if he had sprouted wings just at the knowledge that his boy was alive, so light did he feel. He did not know whether or not he would ever see the boy again. He did not know whether or not he would ever learn how the baby Laurence Harris had been saved from the fire, but he assumed that the miracle of his son's life was due to nothing less than divine intervention.

In his soul-famished state, he deemed it indelicately greedy to wish for even a few crumbs of his son's life: to see the boy again and to learn what he was so unworthy of knowing. Yet he felt that hunger inscribed in his body, like words carved into stone. A message had been slashed across his collarbone to his upper arm, a message from his son. It had been answered by a woman, in little letters, stitch by stitch, a woman who had written over the gash an answering message of courage and devotion and that something he had yearned for but never dared hope to find.

You were magnificent, she had said. The forces that had caused his earlier impotence had been destroyed in a single stroke. Here he was in Barbara Johnson's bed, in her arms, the recipient of her extraordinary love, just where he had hoped to be earlier this evening. He remembered his hot desire for her, and he joined it now to his fantasy of what it would be to make love to her, true, mad, passionate love. He was not lacking male life force now, or emotional impetus, only blood and muscle and physical energy.

The irony of his situation appealed greatly to the new man who was Morgan Harris. A ball of laughter rolled around inside of him. It would hurt too much to release it. He repeated his earlier observation, "That son of mine has no manners."

Barbara responded to the incredible note of humor she heard in his voice. "None whatsoever. You'll have to teach him some when he comes back. And if you don't, I will."

"Will he come back?"

Barbara sighed, happy and exhausted, and he luxuriated wantonly in the softness of her moving breasts. "I don't know, Morgan," she said, "but if he does, I hope it is not tomorrow. I would like one day—just one—when no one comes knocking, or kicking, at my door."

She was to have her wish.

Chapter Nineteen

Because she had failed to draw the curtains the night before, Barbara cracked her eyes the next morning to see the windowpanes luminous with blue-white light. It was a fresh dawn and clear, like the first day of the world. However, it was far from springlike. A dusting of early snow frosted the crisp air, and she imagined it falling to kiss the wet November ground, where it was not destined to stick.

She opened her eyes fully. She felt refreshed after a deep sleep miraculously uninterrupted by Sarah. Now that first light had come, though, the baby was ravenous and making her wishes known lustily. Although Barbara's bones and muscles were still aching from her work of the night before, this morning she experienced a lightness that made the climbing out of bed a delight. Adding to her happiness was the fact that when she returned with Sarah in her arms, Morgan was there, too. It was a simple happiness, his presence, lying next to her, slumbering peacefully, his face relaxed, his battered body and soul sleeping the sleep of the just.

She opened her night shift and withdrew a heavy breast to place at Sarah's seeking lips. The slightest movement, no more than the flutter of his opening eyes, caused Barbara to look down at the man next to her. They exchanged a long, wordless regard, enjoying the miracle that had allowed them to live to see the dawn together.

When Sarah was done with one breast, Barbara shifted the baby to the other. Morgan's eyes dropped and rested on the infantile kiss and the milky motherly flower. His breathing became deep and rhythmic. His eyelids shut languorously, then opened, each time reassured to witness the baby still at the breast. Finally Sarah was done, and Barbara slipped her breasts back in her night shift.

She felt so happy and content that she bent down and kissed the top of Morgan's head. He looked up and invitingly, wanting another, more significant kiss. She obliged.

It was nearly too much for him, this kiss on his lips, soft and sweet, with her breasts pressing against his shoulder and chest, the baby between them.

When she drew away, he said, "You are cruel."

"Cruel?" she queried lazily, propping Sarah in her arms, and turning to get out of bed.

"To kiss me like that when I can do nothing about it," he answered.

Her feet were on the ground. She looked back over at him, with as sultry a look as he had ever seen cross her features. She smiled beguilingly. "You teased me cruelly last night, I think."

His eyes narrowed appreciatively. He felt a twinge of embarrassment, in retrospect, at the thought that he would have been unable to have carried through on the promise of his passion for her if they had not been interrupted. His crooked smile conveyed something of his awkwardness. "I can do better," he assured her.

"Oh, I'm not worried," she tossed over her shoulder, and crossed to put the baby down.

The flicker he felt inside, at the juncture of his thighs, was unmistakable and reassuring and glorious and frustrating, all at once. One part of him knew he could do a lot better *now;* another part of him knew that he would hurt himself in trying, and not necessarily pleasure her.

The variety of thoughts must have passed across his face, for she was regarding him sternly. She put her hands on her hips and said, "What you need this morning is a clear broth to put through your body. We'll see if you can eat food later in the day.''

She got dressed and arranged her hair, all under his watchful, benevolent eye. She picked up the heap of their ruined, bloodied clothing that had been dropped by the side of the bed the night before. She held up what was left of his shirt. "This is now a rag. I'll see what I can salvage of the rest of these things.'' Then she left the room.

Morgan lay, contented, his eyes touching the ceiling, the cradle, the blue-white light of dawn glowing at the window-panes, which were decorated now with blue-white scurries of snow. He was glad for the dawn's light, glad for the window onto the world, glad for all the events that had brought him to this spot, glad for the mutiple healings he felt within his body, glad for his life. He felt so glad and so strong that he imagined himself capable of rising to relieve himself.

The moment he stood up, a blinding headache seized him, sapping him of what little strength he had. He realized that he would not be able to walk to the back door, but he realized, as well, that his need to relieve himself was great. Instead of getting back into bed, he figured, he would open the window in order to piss outside, which he did. Now, however, he had spent so much of his strength that he was feeling dizzy, and he stumbled back to bed without being able to reclose the window. He wanted to call to Barbara, but found he could not make any sound come out of his mouth.

Fortunately, Barbara heard his stumblings and ran into the room to find the window wide open. She hastened to close it, then came to Morgan's side to determine if he had suddenly contracted a fever. When she felt his cool forehead, she asked, "Why did you open the window if you were not burning from fever?''

His face was ashen from the effort he had expended. He looked away. "Body functions,'' he said.

Scolding words sprang to her tongue, but she bit them back. She understood his desire to have control over at least one part of his body. Then she saw a slight stain of red on his nightshirt. His clumsy movements had apparently undone one of her stitches. She had to summon up patience and tact, which did not come naturally to her. She bent toward him, put her hands on either side of his face in a loving gesture and said, "It's all right, Morgan. But next time let me know, so that I can help you get out of bed and open the window. All right? Now, let me look at your stitches. I am afraid that you've done something foolish to hurt yourself!"

She lifted the neck of his nightshirt and saw that he had not broken any stitches. The seeping of blood was minimal, and she breathed a sigh of relief. She got a fresh diaper to dab the blood from his skin and shirt, and when she was done she hardly had to recommend to him that he sleep for his eyes were already shutting heavily.

A few hours later, Morgan awoke, conscious of the sounds of housework coming from the sitting room. He looked around for the cradle, but did not see it, and it gave him a comfortable feeling to think of mother and daughter together, in the next room, busy with the day's work. He bathed in the comfort, able for the first time in years to recognize it.

Later, Barbara poked her head around the bedroom door and saw Morgan, his eyes open, contemplating the ceiling. "Hungry?" she asked.

He shook his head.

She smiled. "Too bad, because I have made you some broth, and you have to eat it."

She fetched the steaming broth and fed it to him. Little spoonfuls at first, then increasing portions, accompanied by the homely encouragement "Appetite comes with the eating."

He sipped and said, "Let's hope."

When he was finished with what his system could absorb, he settled back wearily on the pillows. Barbara shoved Sarah's cradle back into the bedroom. Then she went to get her sewing box, and from the trunk under her bed she withdrew a neat pile of Jonas's old shirts and breeches. She spread the garments out over one end of the bed and sat down in the chair by the window, her sewing box at her side.

She explained, "You have no clothes to put on your back when you are finally able to rise. I'm going to let down the cuffs on these shirts and reset the buttons, which will make them wearable for you. For the trousers, however, I'm less certain of what I can do to make a respectable fit, but I'll try."

So she sat and sewed, and time passed in companionable silence. Every now and again, she would rise to tend to the fire. Every now and then, she would leave the room for a bit. Sarah was lively, and at one point Barbara put her on the bed next to Morgan, where she snuggled. The baby took a nap against Morgan's leg, then woke up fussily, and Barbara put her back in her cradle. Morgan moved in and out of various states of consciousness but never lost his awareness of Barbara for more than a light sleep. He awoke later in the afternoon, clearly restless, stretching his fingers and working his arms.

Barbara got up and went to the sitting room. When she returned, she was carrying the guitar that Morgan preferred. She handed it to him. "I promised you last night that you would play for me today."

His eyes lit up. He accepted the guitar. "Did you? I don't remember."

"You are excused for not having paid better attention to me at the time. It was a most fascinating conversation I had with myself while I was tending to your wound."

He put his hand absently to his stitches and traced the line of his scar. Then he put his fingers on the guitar. He strummed, liking the sound and the feel. Something about the contact of his fingers with the strings caused him to ask, suddenly curious, "What did you use to sew me up?"

She smiled, rather proud of herself. "The banjo strings."

His eyes widened. He had a musician's respect for instruments. He said with regret, "It was a fine piece of craftmanship."

"The sacrifice was worth it."

He paused to mull that one over, and said finally, "Thank you." He played a little ditty. "Whose banjo was it?"

"My father's."

"Jonas didn't play?"

She shook her head. "He never touched them. They were all I had to bring to the marriage, and he was unimpressed."

Morgan did not comment. He strummed idly, picking out melodies, quilting them together in a highly textured patchwork. His right arm had not been affected by his attack, so his fingers were nimble and traveled easily. Seated as he was in the bed, it was equally easy to settle the guitar's body and neck in such a way as to cause his mauled left side little discomfort. The melodies spun out, looped around and tied themselves off, before spinning out again, swooping and looping.

Morgan paused and shut his eyes. He noticed that his headache had thinned out and evaporated.

Barbara had judged her moment. She put the mending down in her lap. She looked straight at him and said, "So?"

Morgan opened his eyes and focused on her. He registered her meaning. He sighed deeply. "Where to begin?"

"At the beginning, of course."

He gazed at the ceiling. "She was Iroquois."

Unexpectedly Barbara felt a kind of jealousy for the exotic woman Morgan had chosen for his wife. In a previous lifetime—any of the ones she had lived before meeting him—she would have denied the unbecoming emotion. Now, however, she allowed herself to feel the jealousy and to understand it as an indication of her love for him. It was a dimension of her jealousy that she desired to know the woman's name. It was a dimension of her understanding that she decided against asking it. She imagined that there was a part of his wife that he would want to keep to himself.

"And she died," she prompted, remembering a detail. "By fire."

Morgan's eyes came down from the ceiling to focus on her. He wondered now about his own culpability in his wife's death. "I was foolish, I suppose, to bring an Iroquois wife to Massachusetts. The neighboring farmers didn't like it, an Indian woman in the area, especially one who was pregnant and bringing more Indians, half-breeds, into the world."

"Why was that foolish?"

"Because I knew of the prejudice, and I ignored it. For over a year I ignored the warning signs and the threats. Then the men came to burn down the farm."

It was as if she were hearing the end of a story which was both unexpected and inevitable. She was shocked and, equally, unsurprised. "Do you blame yourself for the tragedy?"

Morgan began to nod slowly. "I suppose, in a way, I have been blaming myself all these years. It was preventable."

"You did not start the fire," she pointed out.

"I did, by bringing her there."

Barbara shook her head. "You take too much on to yourself. You cannot be faulted for not having the prejudices of others or for not anticipating the violence those prejudices would produce."

He did not know if he had accepted too much of the burden. At the moment, the weight of grief seemed distinctly less. That relief might be due to his knowledge that his son was alive, and yet that knowledge had brought with it a very different burden of guilt.

Barbara had enough pieces to make the mosaic. "You thought your son had also died in the fire?"

Morgan's deep voice was gravelly with grief at the loss now, not of his son, but of his own fatherhood. "He was just a baby at the time, hardly more than a year old. He could crawl and toddle some, but I never once in all these years imagined that he had escaped death, for I thought he was with his mother in the bedroom. Once the fire had been started and the men had left, I went in after them, but it was already too late, for the bed was the first thing that was torched."

"And you were burned, as well."

"I was burned, as well, but I never experienced the hell that she endured."

A cold trickle ran down her spine. "How many men were there?"

"Five."

She could not meet his eye. She looked down at the sewing in her lap. "You sound very sure about the number."

"I am very sure," he said, with ice in his voice. "I was hauled out of bed in the middle of the night, and before I was taken outside, I was forced to witness the first man taking her. Then the other four men took their turns, while I was held outside the bedroom."

She felt her throat constrict with horror.

"And they did not even cover their faces, so unashamed were they of their actions," he added savagely. "I knew every one of them."

"May they roast in the eternal fires of hell," Barbara said devoutly.

"So I would hope, if I could believe in a just God."

She shared his despair. She began to sew. He strummed the guitar mournfully.

After a while, she asked, "And your son? What is his name?"

"We named him Laurence," Morgan replied, "but I do not know what he is called now." He paused, then stated, merely, "He thinks that I abandoned him."

She did not believe he had abandoned the boy. She let Morgan doze. He awoke some time later, saying that he needed "to go to the window." She helped him help himself by opening the window. Then she left the room and returned to help him back into bed and close the window. She fed him some more broth and added soaked bread to see if he could digest it.

It had been a peaceable enough day, Barbara knew, a rare oasis of comfort and companionship, a day when she could sit, contented, at Morgan's side and sew for him. It was a day when Sarah was dear and cooing, and not so much as a fussy frown crossed her cherub's face. The baby seemed to like the big man in the bed, too, and was happy to doze and cuddle against his thigh whenever her mother thought to put her there.

Yet Barbara felt some anxiety. Naturally. A painted creature had burst into her sitting room only the evening before with the intention of killing Morgan. It hardly altered anything that the boy was Morgan's son. In fact, their relationship only seemed to raise the stakes. She wished she knew whether the boy's murderous intention had been satisfied by his deed the night before, but she did not wish to ask Morgan about the fine points of Iroquois honor. Did a son bent on murdering his father get more than one chance?

Barbara was not taking any chances of her own. She had desperately wanted to ride out to Ben Skinner's and ask for his help, but she did not dare leave the property, not even for a minute. The front door was barred, as well as the back, but there were the windows, which could easily be smashed. She had placed her weapons in strategic places around the house, including Morgan's musket and Jonas's rusty old blunderbuss, and she kept her eyes on the windows, watching for signs of movement outside. She had even gone outside by the back door, once or twice, and looked around for a young face in the bushes.

There was nothing. Nothing but a cold white sky, naked branches, and a delicate lace of snow fringing the air and melting before it even touched the ground.

The sun sank lower and finally disappeared. Morgan was feeling stronger by the hour, and when evening came he was able to eat some solid food. He needed help "to go to the window" again, but instead of returning heavily to bed, he decided to walk around the bedroom. Emboldened by his steadiness, he ventured into the sitting room and surveyed the battered door and the splintered door frame. He examined the hinges for signs that he could somehow salvage them.

He discussed his plans for building a new door and door frame, and would have walked around some more, except that he decided, wisely, not to push himself beyond his limits on this first day, at least. He went back to bed and was glad when his head hit the pillow.

Barbara tucked him in, took care of Sarah, and prowled around the house, peeking out a window here, sticking her head out the back door there. She was tired, really tired, but she could not persuade herself to go to bed. She found prissy, tidying things to do. None of them were satisfying, and none of them were able to allay the growing anxiety she felt through the day, progressively weighting down the happy lightness with which she had risen from bed.

She finally went to bed, slipping in beside Morgan, who was breathing deeply. He was sleeping off fifteen years of unacknowledged self-blame, fifteen years of true grief for his wife, fifteen years of wasted grief for his son, fifteen years of unrealized fatherhood. He had a lifetime of loss to put behind him during this first night of real repose in fifteen years. In the work of healing sleep, he was continuing the restructuring of his inner geography begun the day before. He was finding the courage to go on, to live again.

Barbara was less rested. She liked being next to Morgan, for the fourth night in a row. It felt right and natural. She liked the fact that he had abandoned worry and let her share his burden. She had been happy to see him progress so beautifully during the day, to gain color and strength and a new light in his eyes. And yet, as he improved, the weight of dread pulled her down, as if they were attached to opposite ends of the same pulley. She was willing to accept part of his grief, if it would help him heal, but the sense of anxiety was so unsettling, so increasingly strong, and so unformed that she did not even know what the anxiety was about.

Would Morgan live through the next day?

She slept little and fitfully, but it was not because Sarah demanded anything of her, for again the baby slept through the night.

The next morning, it was as if a veil had lifted and Morgan had opened his eyes with a clear sight on the world, knowing exactly what he must do. Although his wound was not fully healed, he did not think lying in bed another day would improve his condition any faster. He tested his left arm for dexterity and quickly discovered its limits. He would be wise not to overdo. He rose and discovered that he was steady and strong on two feet. He liked the feeling. He dressed in Jonas Johnson's refashioned clothing, which fit well enough. He glanced at the wedding ring on his finger and discovered that it was not as tight as it had first been.

After pulling on his boots, he tiptoed around to Barbara's side of the bed. He looked down, in awe and wonder and love, at the woman lying there. She was warm and sleepy and desirable and strong. He had one overwhelming desire just then. He put out his hand and jostled her shoulder gently.

She snuffed and huffed. She opened her eyes to see Morgan standing next to her with the light of life in his deep blue eyes. Her foggy brain cast about for the reason he would waken her. "If you think we're going to do *that* now, you're—"

He put his finger to her lips. "Shh," he admonished. "*That* will have to wait. I woke you up just to see your eyes," he explained, rather pleased with himself and his whimsy. "And I wanted you to know that I'll be spending the day at the tenant's house."

That information cleared her sleep-webbed brain. "Why?"

"Because... Laurence..." He faltered, then continued with more confidence. "Because Laurence won't come to this house again. He'll find me there, though. I know it."

Barbara sat up quickly. She held out her hand, as if to grab his arm and keep him close to her.

He shook his head, smiling, and slipped out of her grasp. Then he left the bedroom.

Chapter Twenty

Barbara did not linger much longer in bed. While she dressed, she tried to convince herself that her anxiety was unfounded, merely the result of all the unsettling events of the past days. She forced herself not to worry, but had little success dispelling the unpleasant sense of waiting, just waiting, for something dreadful to happen.

When she entered the sitting room, she saw that Morgan's hat and coat were gone from the peg by the front door. While she went about her chores during the morning, she kept glancing at that peg, visualizing finding his hat and coat there again. However, that homely little exercise did not make her anxiety lie down like a good girl and go to sleep.

Instead, her anxiety grew and took command of her actions. It sent her constantly to the windows to look out in nervous anticipation—of what? It took her to the back door and sent her outside, where she was vaguely reassured when she saw a thin column of smoke rise from the chimney of the tenant house at the end of the drive. It made her drop things, silly things, like cloths and spoons. She dropped the kettle once, with a clatter, startling the baby into tears.

During one of her trips to the windows, she was sure she saw a bush moving, way off, to the east of the house, near the beginning of her drive. She imagined that she saw a face behind the bush, as well. This was it, then, what she had been waiting for.

Or so she thought.

She grabbed her coat from the peg by the front door and put it on hastily. Only then did she remember Sarah. She was torn between bringing Sarah with her out into the cold and leaving her inside where she would stay warm. She looked down in the cradle by the sitting room hearth and knew she must make a quick decision. The day before yesterday, when she had gone to get Morgan at the tenant's house, she had left Sarah by the fire, where she had been perfectly safe. Furthermore, Sarah was recently fed, freshly diapered, and content, and there were more dangers outside than inside. Besides, if Barbara caught up with Laurence, she had no assurance that the boy would spare her and her baby today as he had the night before.

Better to keep Sarah safe and warm inside.

At the last minute, Barbara armed herself with the kitchen knife, then left by the back door. She moved around to the front, staying close to the outside walls. Then she angled out across the drive to the place in the bushes where she thought she had seen the movement. She saw nothing. She penetrated the brush and moved around, despite the fact that the ground was getting sloppy because of the snow that was still falling lightly.

She tramped around back there, thinking to find the boy, until she realized that she was making so much noise with the cracking of branches underfoot that she was announcing herself to him with every step. She sought the drive again and walked down it, away from the main road, meandering somewhat aimlessly, looking in the shed, moving down to the barn, always keeping her eye on the tenant's house. After some minutes of this futility, she decided that she had been mistaken about having seen any movement in the bushes.

She went up to the tenant's house and walked around it, as if creating a magic circle of protection for Morgan inside. Again, however, she thought she saw some movement in the brush, off to the west now. The next moment, she was sure of it. She ran to the door of the little house, knocked once, and entered.

Morgan was standing in the middle of the sparsely furnished room, staring serenely with supreme vacancy, at nothing in particular. At her entrance, he lowered his eyes to focus on her. She noted, irrelevantly, that he had shaved. His expression did not change from its look of pleasant, but abstracted, welcome.

"Laurence is here," she said quickly. "I am sure of it."

"I know," he replied.

"You have to do something!"

"I am doing something," he replied calmly. "I am waiting for him."

"No, I mean you have to prepare yourself." She withdrew the knife from her coat. "Here."

Morgan looked at the knife, as if at a dish of repugnant food. "I will not use a knife against my son."

Barbara was exasperated. "I know you won't use it against him! I want you to have it, though, in case he threatens you again."

"He won't."

"You don't know that!"

"I do."

Barbara gave up. She left the knife on the table by the door and left the house. Her anxiety seemed to have steadily increased in proportion to his serenity. The configuration of circumstances was bad. Morgan was weak. He could not survive another attack. Neither would he defend himself against one.

Reason had fled. Her emotions were churning inside her and propelling her feet in all sorts of useless direction. She went to the edge of the south fields for no reason, looking for signs of Laurence. She went to the barn, looking for more signs of danger. Instead, she discovered, to her complete surprise, that Morgan had already accomplished most of the morning chores. How he had done it with only one good arm, she did not know.

She left the barn and looked again at the tenant's house, seeing the blue curl of smoke rising so calmly from the chimney. She could not help herself. She went back to the little house and looked through one of the windows to see Morgan still standing, motionless and serene, in the middle of the room, alone. Although his eyes were open, he looked deep in meditation.

She moved away, shaking her head at her own idiocy, and returned slowly to the back door of her house. She wished the pain in the region of her heart would go away. She wished she could breathe better. She wished the wild anxiety in her stomach would settle down. She walked with her head bent down as she guided her steps through the increasingly mushy ground. Then, when she came within a few yards of her back door, her head jerked up.

Was there more than one trail of footprints going from the back door around to the front of the house? Or were those squishy, blurry prints hers alone? Was the back door slightly ajar? Had she left it that way? How long had she been gone? A full and absurd half hour perhaps? More? However long she had been gone, she knew it was long enough for...

She ran the last few steps and bounded through the back door, denying her worst fear, thinking, *Foolish Barbara!* just as she had before opening the front door to Morgan Harris for the first time. The moment she set foot in the house, however, the unnamed anxiety she had been feeling so vividly during the last night and day took definite shape. Suddenly she *knew*. She knew what had been troubling her. Her emotions and her attention had been so focused on Morgan that she had not been able to correctly identify the cause. She knew her worst fear had been realized.

She knew the cradle was empty.

She hastened across the room. Her certainty did not save her from the physical wrench upon sight of the empty cradle. Every cell in her body winced in magnificent horror and loss and moaning, soul-deep pain when she found that her daughter was gone.

The flow of knowing continued. She knew that Lieutenant Richards must have come at just the right moment to find her away from the house. She knew that he must not have been able to resist taking the cooing, cuddling Sarah from her cradle. She knew that Mrs. Ross would pay him well. She had a vision of that wicked, beautiful witch holding Sarah, smiling at her, hugging her, kissing her, claiming her as a Ross.

Barbara panicked, and the world nearly went black. She was saved by the blessed thought that she was not alone, that she need not call forth any more of her dwindling inner resources to face this crisis, to surmount it, to rectify it. A word flashed into her frightened brain, and that was *Morgan!*

Morgan watched his son enter the room of the tenant's house. The boy's unpainted face was proud, and his manner was defiant, but his expression held some heart-softening hint of the chagrined child confronting the stern father. Morgan watched his son approach him, his face dark and determined and as familiar as his own.

After the night and day of extraordinary healing in Barbara's bed and in her arms, Morgan felt the ruined geography of his inner terrain become smooth and level, ready for excavation. He imagined the possibilities of a spacious, beautiful structure form inside his soul. He opened the conversation in French. "You have come, Laurence."

His son rejected the foreign name and claimed his Indian name.

Morgan shook his head. "I no longer speak Iroquois," he replied, again in French.

His son cursed him in Iroquois.

Morgan smiled, slightly. "I no longer speak Iroquois, but I still understand it." He unfolded his arms from over his chest and pulled away the shirt at the neck to expose the wound his son had inflicted. "And I cannot fight you again today."

"Then I have come for nothing," his son replied, in Iroquois.

"Not nothing," Morgan said. He felt deep foundations of his inner structure thrust downward. "You have come to tell me of the miracle of your life. I know nothing of it, you know." When his son did not immediately respond, he added, "From what I remember of your mother's tribe, the young braves spoke French."

At that, his son stepped forward, flourishing his chin and fist. "How is it that you know nothing of my life?" he demanded, grudgingly speaking French.

Morgan's eyes touched his son's throat. "Because I thought you died in the fire that stains your skin."

The boy's eyes widened. "You admit to the fire, then?"

Morgan was surprised by the question, but he was prepared to respond, honestly, to every question his son could ask. "'Admit?' Of course, I 'admit' to the fire. It lives daily in my heart, and I carry the burns on my back, just as you carry them on your throat and chest."

"You carry no burns," his son denied.

Morgan opened his jacket, unbuttoned his leather vest and lifted his old-new shirt from the waist of his breeches. It was strange how comfortable he felt wearing a dead man's shirt and breeches altered to fit him. He turned slightly so that the ugly red hand clamping his skin was exposed. He turned back and stuffed the ends of his shirt into the waist of his breeches. He rebuttoned his vest and let his jacket fall back into place.

Morgan said, "At the beginning, the men who torched the farm held me down. Only after the fire was blazing out of control and had done most of its damage was I let free. By the time I could go into the house, it was too late. Your mother had died." He paused. "I thought you had perished, too."

"*You* abandoned me to that woman," his son countered angrily, "after the fire had started."

Morgan frowned. "What woman?"

His son's face twisted with rage. "The white woman who sent me back to my people after the fire! After you abandoned me!"

Morgan was puzzled, but unshaken. "I know of no white woman involved in the fire. I know only of five white men."

He owed his son an avowal of the bald ugliness of the event. "Five men who, in their blind ignorance, destroyed all that I held dear. Or almost all, since you have lived. It is a miracle."

The boy was determined to contradict everything his father said. "It is no miracle. The story I've been told is that I was awakened by the shouts of the men who came to burn the farm. Just after the fire had started, I crawled outside and away from the house, away from the barn. You had already run away. A white woman—a Christian lady—had come to stop her husband from his deed. She was not able to stop him, but she did find me with part of my clothes burning. She tended to my burns and sent me back to my people."

A woman, a white woman, had saved his son? Such a simple explanation? Was it possible?

The phrase *Lost causes!* jangled in his brain. For fifteen years he had blamed himself for having lived a lost cause as a white farmer with an Indian wife, and had reckoned his losses as divine retribution for his sins. For fifteen years he had cloaked himself in a great cape of cosmic despair. Then, with his son's miraculous reappearance, he had experienced a blessed moment of redemption before he had offered himself to death.

However, it was not God, but a woman, who had saved his son. The wife of one of the men who had destroyed his life. A simple human act of kindness—no divine intervention—had saved his son's life; and as a simple human act of prejudice—no divine fury—had taken from him his wife and farm. He felt robbed of magnificence. Man's law, not God's law, ruled his life.

In his confusion, all he knew to say was "I could not have guessed that you lived, Laurence."

"You abandoned me! You knew I had escaped the fire, but you did not stay! You no longer wanted me! That is what my grandfather said!"

Morgan had not known that his son had escaped, but it was true that he had not stayed that fiery night to witness everything burn to cinders. It stunned him further to think that had he stayed a few more human-sized minutes at the scene, his life would have been very different.

"I did not know you were alive, Laurence," he repeated.

The accusations tumbled from the boy's lips. "You never came back! You never returned! You should have gone to my people and claimed me! You should have gone to my mother's father and begged his forgiveness! You did nothing! Nothing!"

It had never once, during fifteen years, crossed his mind to return to the Iroquois camp. The ruin of those fifteen years lay at his feet. He had thought he had lived a lost cause all these years, but he had erred, and his life seemed to him now to have been doubly wasted.

While he was attempting to formulate an appropriate reply to his son, Barbara burst into the room and ran to him. She grabbed him by the lapels of his jacket and tugged hard, stumbling into him.

"My God, Morgan! Oh, good God, Morgan!" She was sobbing. She could not get the words out.

Morgan looked down into her distressed face. He was at first vexed that she should intrude at just that moment, for he did not need or want her intervention. However, then he realized that she had not even noticed his son in the room, and he had a premonition of what she was going to say.

She was sobbing. "She's gone! It's the lieutenant's doing! She's with Mrs. Ross now, I'm sure of it! Oh, why was I so foolish to go walking around outside the house today of all days? As if I didn't know they would come for her! It is beyond everything! I can't think!"

Barbara was looking up and into Morgan's eyes, holding on to his steady gaze like a drowning woman clinging to a sturdy piece of driftwood. When he looked away from her, over her head, beyond her shoulder, she floundered. Suddenly, in her spine, she felt a dramatic storm of emotions swirling in the room. Yet Morgan was calm, like the eye at the center of the storm. Then she turned slowly, still clutching at Morgan, to see who stood behind her. With a frisson that traveled down her spine and spread to all her extremities, she realized she was looking straight into the face of a handsome young Morgan.

But he was Morgan with a difference. He had the same lean features, the same cut to his chin, but his cheekbones were higher, and his eyes were of an infinite black. Unpainted, his skin was the color of pale brick, and a serpent's tail of darker red stained his neck. He was almost as tall as Morgan, too, and seemed to have the same rangy strength. If Barbara had doubted that the painted creature of the night before was Morgan's son, she did not doubt it now.

In that second of recognition, her extreme emotional distress gave her a dimension of insight that she would not have had under other circumstances. After the first frisson of fear shuddered down her spine, she no longer saw the boy as a grave threat to Morgan's life, but as a extraordinary miracle. She turned from Morgan and walked to his son, not realizing that she was spanning a deep and perilous abyss between them. In the same way she had grasped Morgan, she put her hands on the lapels of the ordinary jacket the boy wore. Only this time she did not clutch, she held. She appealed.

"You can help me. I know you can." Her voice throbbed with emotion, but it did not waver with hysteria. "You found your father against all odds in Boston. You followed him here, never losing his trail. You did it over hundreds of miles and many days. It should not be difficult for you to track down Lieutenant Richards and Mrs. Ross, who have stolen my baby."

The boy did not immediately reply. His face seemed to register only astonishment to be looking down into eyes as clear and strong as an Iroquois river in spring.

She was not discouraged by his lack of response. She would focus every fiber of her being on persuading the young Iroquois to help her. She had only the haziest notion of Indians, none of them positive, and what she had witnessed the night before in her sitting room had done nothing to improve her notions. Yet she had seen his determination, his strength of purpose, and she desired to have them work for her.

"You have proven yourself by finding your father." She swallowed, once, hard. "Please. Help me. I know you can help me."

Morgan had walked around so that he was no longer standing in front of his son, but was behind him. Morgan exchanged some words with his son. They sounded very strange to Barbara's ears, as strange as the ones she had heard the night before. However, during the exchange, the boy's face lost its astonished and uncomprehending look, though none of his hardness.

Barbara looked at Morgan, her expression wearing a question now.

"He does not speak much English," Morgan explained.

"But some?"

"Yes. Some, I think."

"What does he speak?" she asked.

"Iroquois and French."

Barbara knew neither. However, the force of her emotions made her ignore the abyss between them, and thereby to bridge it. "Please help me," she repeated slowly. "I don't know how to say that in either Iroquois or French, but it doesn't matter. Just help me. Please."

Morgan said some more words to his son. At the explanation, the wild young half-breed—the unpainted Laurence Harris—regarded her with disdain, with hauteur, with contempt.

She faced him down and met the hard planes of his face with softness and appeal and a strength of purpose that matched his. "I know you can help me," she pleaded. "It's my baby. She's five months old. She's been stolen by a wicked woman who wants her." She looked over the boy's shoulder. "Morgan, translate that!"

Morgan said some words. The young man's face was hard as stone.

"I know many things," Barbara continued, "except how to find my daughter. Among the things I know is that you know how to do it, and that you are a godsend." She looked over at Morgan. "Translate that!" she commanded again.

Morgan did so. The boy's expression did not change.

Barbara felt panic again inside her, rising up to clutch her throat. "Morgan, tell him that he has to help me. Tell him. Tell him that you are wounded and in no condition to go after Lieutenant Richards alone. Tell him!"

Morgan's previous doubts about his life and his actions were suddenly dispelled. Barbara had saved him again—his body the night before, his soul just now. Her appearance, her distress, her need, gave his life meaning. He saw now, clearly, how the horrible and terrifying experiences he had lived until this moment had come together to serve a purpose beyond himself; how all his errors had brought him to her door; how all his errors had brought his son to her door, as well, so that his son could help her now in a way he, physically, could not.

He shed his black cloak of despair and felt his heart swell to embrace the two other people in the room. He tasted love, heart-twisting love for a son, thick love for a woman. He savored this many-layered emotion, this something beyond himself, this something worth living for. He found himself immersed in it and discovered that love had no slopes: no dizzying slopes up, no perilous slopes down, no edges to prick and hurt. It just was. Love. Glorious and blessed, but not divine. Love. Humble and human. Gloriously and blessedly human.

The foundations of his inner structure thrust down into the ground. The walls followed soaring into high vaults. They were windowed in gorgeous colors, drenching his interiors with patterns of stained-glass light, deep and brilliant.

What Morgan said to his son was "If you help the woman who needs your help, my life will be yours." Willingly, but not lightly, he offered his life in exchange for her daughter's. It was not a cheap or an easy trade, but it was a worthy one, now that his life was worth living.

Barbara saw the boy's eyes flicker with something she interpreted as interest. She pressed her advantage. "There's no time to lose," she said, pulling the boy, nodding at the door. "Don't think about it now, just *do* it," she said. "You have the rest of your life to work everything out with your father. But for now, help me find Sarah. Say it!" she commanded. "Sarah. Sarah! Say it!"

"Sa-ra-ha," the boy repeated.

Barbara dazzled him with her smile. "Yes, Sarah! And you can thank me later for having saved your father's life from your hand. Or, maybe, your help now *is* your repayment." She looked at Morgan. "Translate that!"

"Untranslatable," Morgan replied unhelpfully.

Barbara waved this irrelevance away. "It doesn't matter. Your son is helping me, and that's all that counts now! Explain to him who the lieutenant and Mrs. Ross are and what they look like, while we get ready to go!"

These details Morgan was apparently able to translate, for he began speaking rapidly while the three of them left the tenant's house. Barbara felt her spirits lift, until the boy ran off into the woods and she felt yet another wave of panic flow over her. "He's leaving! Go after him, Morgan!"

"He's gone to get his horse," Morgan explained calmly. "He'll meet us at the end of the drive."

Barbara closed her eyes and caught her breath. When she opened them, she said to him, "I don't know if I'm going to make it."

"You'll make it," he said, his eyes strong and steady on hers, his voice confident.

Chapter Twenty-one

Barbara and Morgan hastened to the shed. Once there, Barbara noticed that Morgan was having difficulty harnessing the horse to the buggy. Through the haze of her own panic and pain, she recognized that he was hardly physically able to sustain the pace of a chase if he had to do all the work. Since she wanted him with her at all costs, she brushed him aside and finished the job of preparing for their departure. She climbed up, holding the reins, and said, "I'll drive."

Morgan did not protest. He nodded and smiled serenely. "And I will tell you what to do."

They set off in the buggy and met up with Morgan's son at the end of the drive. Morgan exchanged quick words with the boy and pointed him in the direction of the road to Baltimore. The boy surveyed the ground around them, looking keenly, and shook his head. He pointed in the opposite direction, toward Old Roads Bay and the Patapsco River. He said something to his father, then dug his heels into his horse's flanks and took off toward the water.

Barbara's heart quailed. "My God, Morgan!" she breathed, inwardly writhing in agony. "They came by boat! They're probably already heading out to Chesapeake Bay by now. Then it'll be open sea, and I'll never see her again!" She sobbed, "My Sarah!"

Morgan paused a good long while before saying calmly, "We don't know yet which direction they're headed down the river, but at least now we know why Michael Gorsuch or someone else from the meetinghouse didn't warn us."

Barbara drew a deep breath, nearly swooned from fear and her acute sense of loss, and bent over with her head in her lap. She slowly raised her head back up and sat erect, as if determined to meet her doom with dignity. After a few minutes, she burst out, "Morgan, I'm scared. Really scared."

Morgan answered, "I know, but I'm here for you. My son is here for you."

Silence sat and settled between them. Swirling snow-flakes surrounded them. Suddenly Morgan's son reappeared on the near horizon, and as he approached, Barbara's spirits were insensibly lifted by the look of satisfaction the young Iroquois wore on his face.

The boy drew rein beside the buggy. "Not zat way," he said, shaking his head and pointing east, toward where the Patapsco opened into Chesapeake Bay. "Zat way," he affirmed, pointing toward Baltimore.

"They're headed back to the city?" Barbara interpreted, feeling relief spread through every pore of her body.

The boy nodded. Visibly frustrated by the effort required to speak English, he turned and spoke to his father. After several rapid exchanges in French, the boy turned to go. He said something else to his father, something that made Morgan frown, and then he flew back down the path to Old Roads Bay.

"Laurence spotted the boat with the lieutenant. It's small, hardly seaworthy. Mrs. Ross is not with them, only the two thugs. So, no doubt, the plan is to return to Baltimore to get her and to board a transatlantic vessel immediately. Laurence will be following their progress along the shore. He won't lose them."

"But there's no passageway at water's edge, not even a foot trail leading into Baltimore!" Barbara wailed.

Morgan smiled gently. "I do not think that will be a problem for my son."

Barbara was suddenly torn between shared confidence that the young Iroquois could do the job and hot outrage that three evil men had her precious baby in an open boat. Gazing at the boy's retreating back, she drew her thoughts momentarily away from Sarah. She looked at Morgan and asked curiously, "How did he survive the fire?"

Morgan met her eyes. "A woman saved him," he said simply. "She was the wife of one of the men who had torched the house."

"What was she doing there?"

"She had come to stop her husband. She wasn't able to stop him, but she did save my son."

"You didn't know she was there?"

Morgan shook his head. "Before the fire was finished, I was already beyond despair. I stole one of the men's horses and rode south that night, in the direction of Philadelphia, where I subsequently lived under the name Jack Carter. Only later did I wander back to Boston. No one would have known me to contact me. Perhaps no one tried. I don't know."

Barbara had no immediate response. She merely looked at him with sadness and understanding.

"A woman saved him," Morgan repeated. "Just an ordinary woman. One I do not know and cannot thank." He continued in bracing accents, "We're to meet my son at Baltimore harbor. He'll waste valuable time waiting for us if we don't get started."

Barbara moved the buggy forward. She was glad to have the reins in her hands, for the activity of driving gave a focus to her wild thoughts and emotions. Morgan settled back.

Barbara turned out from the farm drive into the lane, her thoughts engulfed now by worry for Sarah. She glanced at Morgan and blurted, "I think your son can help me."

"I know he can help you."

That was all they said for a while. When they had turned onto Long Log Lane and were about to drive by the meetinghouse, Morgan commanded, "Stop."

Barbara glared at him. "What? Stop now?"

"Yes, here at the meetinghouse."

"I don't want to stop! We've got to get to Baltimore!"

"Stop, Barbara," he repeated. His voice was gentle, but firm. "I have something to tell Michael Gorsuch, and we need to alert the neighbors of what has happened to Sarah. They can possibly help you. They can help us."

Barbara was about to say that this was *her* problem and no one else's. She was about to say that she could hardly ask her neighbor's help to retrieve the illegitimate baby they so disapproved of, this baby she loved beyond all reason.

Morgan did not allow her to utter any foolishness. He shook his head and said, "Don't be stiff-necked now. You need their help, one way or another, and they stand ready to help you. You underestimate them, and you overestimate yourself. You are not alone in this." Then he said, definitively, "Stop."

All her instincts strained to continue the chase without delay. Her pride, too, resisted stopping to ask the help of the neighbors she had known her entire life and from whom she had always stood aloof, while she had not hesitated a second to ask the help of a boy she did not know. Reluctantly, at Morgan's insistence, she stopped the buggy before the meetinghouse.

She sat, frozen, while Morgan got down from the perch. He approached Michael Gorsuch, who had come out of the meetinghouse at the sound of the arriving buggy. Barbara looked woodenly ahead and only half heard Morgan speaking with the local magistrate. The two men seemed quickly to come to an understanding. Then Michael Gorsuch said that he would take care of something, and before she knew it Morgan was back up beside her on the bench.

"It was worth the stop" was all Morgan said.

Barbara moved the buggy forward, increasing the pace as much as she could on the open road. Although Baltimore was only eight miles away, the distance seemed interminable, giving her ample opportunity to take in the full dimensions of the situation. She felt raw and defenseless, and she tried to imagine other moments of loss and pain in order to cope. She came up with nothing.

She remembered her father's death. And felt nothing. She remembered Jonas's death. And felt nothing. The nothing surprised her. Had she truly been so cold and devoid of emotions? She attempted to regain that state of cold emotionlessness, because she remembered it as safe and beyond pain, but she had lost that place within her and could not find it anymore.

Then she remembered the day she had learned of the death of General Ross. She had gone to her bedroom to absorb the news. She had stretched out on her bed in the warmth of the westering sun of a lovely September day, and she had cried for the first time in her memory. But she had not cried for General Ross. She had cried for all the previous losses that she had carried in her body, for all the times she had not cried, for all she had had to endure alone, for all the children she had never had.

And now she loved. She loved her daughter more than her life, and she no longer had any defenses to ward off the painful effects of that love. She considered trading that soft, liquid mother's love for the safe, cold place where she had lived most of her life. She considered climbing into that space forever, just to be away from the pain of loss she was now feeling.

Then she looked at Morgan, and he looked at her.

Feeling supported within his compelling gaze, she discovered some further cold space within her, behind her heart, a space of absolute independence and arrogance. She was surprised to find it within her; she was even dismayed. She was proud of her independence, but she had never linked it to arrogance. She had always desired to do everything herself, by herself, better than anyone else. She had been proud of her fierce independence all these years, and she had never realized that her pride had been cold and hard and veined with arrogance.

Bathing in the warm, loving light of Morgan's eyes, she felt the marble shrine of pride and arrogance behind her heart dissolve in the wash of her emotions. Its melting made that place as soft and impressionable as the rest of her baby-loving, Morgan-loving heart. It left her feeling humble and dependent and without inner protections.

These feelings were alien, and she did not wholly like them, for they were entirely unfamiliar, but she could do nothing to alter them now that she depended so desperately on Morgan and his son.

Morgan sat silent beside her, content to keep the silence, for nothing he could say to her would help her.

He knew that they would find her baby, but he could not tell her that, and his confidence would not comfort her.

He knew how she felt at the loss of her child, but he could not tell her that, and his sympathy would not comfort her.

He knew that her life was turning around, just as his had in the past several days, but he could not tell her that, and his understanding would not comfort her.

He knew that she would have more children—their children—but he could not tell her that, and thoughts of future children would not comfort her.

So he sat silent, allowing his silence to blend with hers, and although he knew his presence could not relieve her of the pain and terror she was feeling, he knew that his presence could comfort her.

As the sun was setting they arrived at the eastern edge of Baltimore, around Hampstead Hill, and discovered to their surprise that Morgan's son was waiting for them in a shadowy bosquet of trees. Morgan rapidly translated the news to Barbara: The lieutenant and his two men, upon disembarking from their small boat at Baltimore harbor, had joined up with an elegant woman who had been waiting for them. One of the men had handed to that woman a bundle that must have been a baby, judging from the way she was holding it and looking at it. Then came the intriguing part. Instead of boarding one of the large vessels docked in the harbor, the group had climbed into a waiting carriage and taken off to the north.

Morgan's son had waited, here, at the deserted cross-
roads of the turnpike the carriage had taken. He judged
them to be not too many miles ahead.

Morgan paused to assess the situation. He peered about,
seeing nothing but lonely road. Night had fallen swiftly, and
it was dark. The scurries of snow were still swirling around
them, and it was cold. His shoulder and arm were hurting
badly. Although there was a strange sense of goodness in the
hurt, he knew that he would not be able to forge on much
longer this night. He glanced at Barbara and saw that her
physical suffering had increased to rival her spiritual suffering.

He came to a decision and sent his son forward, to continue his surveillance of the progress of the carriage. They
agreed to meet again at the nearest inn along the road, when
Laurence would presumably have more information.

Barbara and Morgan forged ahead. She was having difficulty handling the buggy in the dark, given the condition
of the road. She was frozen to the bone, too, but unwilling
to admit it to herself. Fortunately, the intriguing new information gave them something to think and talk about. "But
why do you think that Mrs. Ross didn't board the first ship
bound to England from Baltimore?"

"I don't know," Morgan replied, turning the problem
over in his mind. "Too obvious, maybe. A seagoing ship in
Baltimore harbor would naturally have been the first place
we would have looked for them."

"So where are they headed now?"

"Wilmington, perhaps?" Morgan ventured. "They can
always sail away by the Delaware River, and why not? It's
very clever of them not to sail from Baltimore. They might
imagine that we are, even now, scouring the harbor for signs
of them."

"Yes, but I wonder how Lieutenant Richards and his men
got by old John the ferryman at Old Roads Bay?" she
wondered. When Morgan did not immediately respond, she
asked, aghast, "Is he all right?"

"He'll live," Morgan answered. "Back at the farm, when Laurence first returned from the river, he mentioned that an old man was in a bad way at the end of the lane. I guessed it was the ferryman, and I sent Michael Gorsuch to look into it."

Barbara had put her hand over her left breast, adding another worry to her careworn heart and another black mark against Lieutenant Richards's name. "Why didn't you tell me?" she asked accusingly.

"Well, now..." Morgan began.

"I suppose you thought I had enough to worry about," she finished.

"I suppose so."

Barbara did not pursue the topic, wrapped as she was in the dark, in the cold, and in her unspeakable fears for Sarah's well-being.

Presently Morgan spied an ordinary inn, little more than a grogshop, really, with no coach light burning to beckon the traveler, but through whose closed shutters squeezed skinny bars of light. Here they would find warmth and rest. He told Barbara to pull over into the yard, explaining that he had arranged for them to meet Laurence at the first inn.

Barbara did as she was told without protest, so tired was she that she knew she was unable to continue the chase. She set the brake, clambered down from the buggy and looked around the little coach yard. She said, on a tired sigh, "Wouldn't it have been nice if Mrs. Ross's carriage had decided to stop here for the night?"

Morgan answered, "Yes, but there's no sign of them here, since there's no sign of Laurence yet."

Barbara walked around to him. Together they approached the plain front door of the tavern, which suggested that the accommodations within were for travelers with not-too-fastidious tastes. Morgan knocked authoritatively.

She said, "Oh, I didn't expect to find them here at all. A woman of Mrs. Ross's class wouldn't patronize such an inn, or any inn, for that matter. My guess is that she established her route north according to the the great houses to which she carries introductions—which would probably be all of them. The planters in this part of the world never pay for a luxurious night's lodging."

Before a wave of exhaustion and despair could engulf her, the door to the ordinary was thrown open by a barrel-chested man who was wiping his hands on the apron swathing the girth at his middle. He let his apron drop, surveyed the somewhat bedraggled but unthreatening couple, and rumbled a "Welcome, travelers. How can I help you?"

"My wife and I need a place to rest awhile," Morgan said, handing Barbara across the threshold, "and shelter from the cold."

They entered a warm, low-beamed room that was humble in its furnishings, but cheerful enough, with a fire dancing on a wide hearth, winking coppers hanging on the walls, and a well-polished bar running along the far wall, behind which earthen mugs squatted peaceably on shelves. At their entrance, a few heads turned with mild interest to blink at the newcomers.

"A place to rest is all you need?" the host asked, his voice audibly disappointed that the couple would bring him no custom. Still, he could not turn them away on such a night.

Morgan acutely felt the lack of money in his pocket, and he had already cursed himself a dozen times for not having thought to tell Barbara to bring the money they had earned from the lieutenant's lodging. Morgan's gaze traveled to the long trestle table in the center of the room, where a half-dozen men, and one woman, were gambling over cards. Two more women of uncertain virtue were standing by the table, looking on, only partially absorbed by the turn of cards. Morgan calculated the possibility of joining the game and winning a meal, but decided against it. He had lost his taste for such shabby shiftings.

Then he spied a guitar propped against the outside corner of the hearth and came to a swift decision. He shook off his weariness. He greeted the room and received desultory greetings and nods in return. He raised Barbara's left hand to his lips, making sure that her wedding band flashed in the light so that he would retain the attention of his audience.

"My wife is tired and in need of rest," he announced pleasantly, "as I've told the taverner." He dropped her hand and crossed the room to the guitar. "We're poor farmers from North Point on our way to Hampton," he continued easily. He picked up the guitar and strummed a few melodious chords. "We have no money, so I'd like to sing for our supper."

The host grumbled that if he obliged every farmer who raised his voice in song he would soon be in the poorhouse. He was willing to offer them a place to rest awhile, but nothing more without payment.

Morgan smiled and said with bravado, "You have not heard me." He nodded to the cardplayers, winked at the two raddled beauties and, with a bit of showmanship, strolled over to a rather portly woman sitting at the end of one bench next to an even more portly, ruddy-faced man.

"A request, ma'am?"

The woman blushed and giggled and said that she had always liked "The Roving Gambler," and offered to hum a few bars to give him the melody, in case he did not know the song.

Morgan smiled at the woman in a way that caused her blush to deepen. He asked, "Is that the song that begins,

"I am a roving gambler, I've gambled all around,
Whenever I meet with a deck of cards, I lay my
    money down.
I've gambled down in Washington, I've gambled
    over in Spain,
I'm on my way to Georgia to knock down my last
    game."

"Is that the one you are referring to?"

The woman clapped her hands in delight. "Yes, that's the one! And what a beautiful voice you have, sir!"

He flirted with her with his eyes and said, "I know, ma'am, and I love to hear myself sing. Now, the song continues, does it not,

> "I had not been in Washington many more weeks
>   than three,
> When I fell in love with a pretty little girl, and she fell
>   in love with me,
> She took me in her parlor, she cooled me with her
>   fan,
> She whispered low in her mother's ears, 'I love this
>   gambling man."

"I think it goes like that."

"Oh, it does, sir, it does!"

Barbara watched, amazed, as Morgan shamelessly sang to the woman on the bench. She watched, as well, how he captured and held his audience, how he did not let their attention stray far from him, how he drew the host into his song and his showmanship. She knew that Morgan was tired and hurt, and yet he rose to the occasion to delight his audience. Even preoccupied as she was, she was able to smile as he warbled an interpretation of the next absurd verses:

> "Oh, daughter, oh, dear daughter, how could you
>   treat me so
> To leave your dear old mother and with a gambler
>   go?
> Oh, mother, oh, dear mother, you know I love you
>   well,
> But the love I hold for this gambling man no human
>   tongue can tell.
> I wouldn't marry a farmer, for he's always in the
>   rain,
> The man I want to marry is the gambling man who
>   wears the big gold chain.
> I wouldn't marry a doctor, he is always gone from
>   home.

All I want is the gambling man, for he won't leave me
    alone."

Everyone, including the host, joined in for the final re-
frain:

"Oh, mother, oh, dear mother, I'll tell you if I can
If you ever see me coming back, I'll be with the
    gambling man."

And that was just the beginning. Some time later, the host
personally escorted Mr. and Mrs. Morgan Harris to a little
table by the fire and generously offered them as fine a supper as was to be found on any Maryland table that night.

Barbara was acutely aware of the enormity of what Morgan had done in singing for his supper. When they were
seated and a hot vegetable soup was put before them, with
the promise of roast pork and sweet potatoes to follow, she
looked at Morgan mournfully and said, "You never do
this."

Morgan smiled. "This is different."

"No, it's not," Barbara protested, "and it's all the worse
because I'm not hungry."

"Eat," Morgan commanded.

Barbara shook her head.

"You'll offend our host."

"That's true," Barbara conceded, "but I can't."

Morgan picked up his spoon and began to eat, for he was
truly hungry. "If you don't eat, you'll make yourself sick."

"I already am sick," Barbara countered.

Morgan did not wish to be cruel in order to get her to eat,
but he had little choice. He said, gently, "If you don't eat,
you'll have no milk for Sarah when she is in your arms
again."

What little color was left in Barbara's face fled. The
mention of mother's milk raised horrific visions of her baby
squalling for food.

Morgan tried to soften his blow. "Eat, Barbara, in the confidence that you will find your daughter and that she will need you."

Barbara ate, choking through unshed tears and fear, her stomach resisting every bite.

At the very moment their host was setting a treacle pudding before them, the outside door to the taproom opened and in walked Morgan's son. Morgan's head turned to the door. Barbara stretched out her hand to cover his, and his fingers closed over hers automatically. Laurence made his way through the room to them, somehow making his presence unobtrusive to the other guests. Morgan's eyes left the boy only once, to glance up at his host and identify him as "My son."

The host beamed his welcome of Mr. Harris's son, but Morgan refused the offer of supper by saying that the boy had already eaten. The host withdrew. Barbara was at first aghast at Morgan's refusal until she realized, when Laurence had come within a foot of their table and stopped, that he would not sit with them. She could see from his face that he had news, and her heart leapt to discover what it was. By sheer effort of will, she remained seated, for she did not want to appear overanxious and create any suspicion.

Deliberately Morgan released her hand and rose. Barbara watched as he spoke, low, with his son. The boy gestured minimally. Morgan nodded, demanded further news, and received answers. Barbara watched father and son and felt that she was witnessing a miracle. The father was openly pleased and proud. The son seemed to lose the sullen, angry, defiant look, and to grow up before her very eyes. It was a revelatory moment for Barbara, to see reflected in Morgan's face the luminous feeling of love lost and love found. Her pain of the past few hours shifted and merged with his of the past fifteen years. Her own loss did not become less in intensity, but it became more universal, and strangely richer.

When Morgan turned away from his son and toward her, she said quietly, "I know exactly how you must have felt to lose him." She turned to the boy, speaking slowly, her eyes fixed on his, "I know how your father felt to lose you. I know how he felt."

The boy did not respond, but Barbara felt she saw a glimmer of understanding waver in the infinite black depths of his gaze.

Morgan nodded once, in acknowledgment, then said calmly, "Let us thank our host and be on our way."

Chapter Twenty-two

An hour later, Barbara and Morgan drove up the wide, tree-lined drive to the imposing Lloyd House. There were enough lights burning from the many graceful windows to allow them to see that the mansion was a stately brick structure. It was built around a main rectangular building that extended on either side into shallower wings, to whose extremities were attached rectangular buildings, larger than the wings, but not so big as the central building.

Barbara pulled the buggy to a halt at the front door, feeling a conflicting mixture of intimidation and righteous indignation. She took heart from the knowledge that a young Iroquois brave lurked in the shadows at the side of the front door.

Morgan lifted the knocker and let it echo authoritatively within. Not too many seconds later, the door swung open on well-oiled hinges to reveal the round black face of the butler.

Morgan stepped forward and said, "We're here to see Mrs. Ross and Lieutenant Richards, if you please."

The man's face registered surprise. He hesitated.

"To answer your questions," Morgan continued pleasantly, "no, they aren't expecting anyone, and yes, it's true that no one is supposed to know they're here."

The man's eyes widened. "May I ask who's calling, sir?"

Morgan smiled. "Mr. and Mrs. Morgan Harris."

The black man surveyed the extremely bedraggled couple. "I'll speak to the Missus Lloyd about this. I gots to ask the missus," he said before closing the door in their faces.

Barbara looked despairingly at Morgan in the dark. Morgan said, reassuringly, "We're not obliged to enter the house through the door, you know. It would merely be a convenience."

They waited.

And waited and waited.

Just as Morgan was picking up the knocker to try again, the door was opened, this time by a beautifully dressed elderly lady, obviously the mistress of the mansion.

She smiled at them, rather wistfully and dismissively. "I'm so sorry," she said in the cultivated accents of the upper crust of tidewater Maryland society, "but I know of no Mrs. Ross or Lieutenant . . . Lieutenant . . ."

"Richards," Morgan supplied.

"Well, there is no Mrs. Ross and no Lieutenant Richards here. You must be mistaken, or have taken the wrong turn somewhere."

"What you mean, of course, is that they are not receiving visitors this evening. Nor would they be expecting any," Morgan said, unimpressed. "But they *are* here, and you know it."

The woman paused, as if surprised by his effrontery in contradicting her. Then she collected herself, smiled again, and began to close the door on the gentle words, firmly spoken, "I'm terribly sorry. . . ."

Before the door was completely shut, Morgan motioned to the bush at the side of the door, and Barbara moved out of the way. To Mrs. Lloyd's astonishment—and everlasting horror—a wild Indian, complete with war paint, buckskins and blood-chilling whoops, pushed back the door and jumped over the threshold. He caught both of her hands neatly behind her back and had an enormous knife at her throat before she could utter a sound or command her equally dumbfounded butler to defend her.

Morgan took Barbara's hand, and together they entered the grand foyer. He turned to his piteously frightened hostess. His manner was courteous. "You'll show us to Mrs. Ross now, won't you, ma'am?"

Although the touch of the knife against her throat in no way impaired her from speaking, Mrs. Lloyd merely nodded at Morgan's question. Her bulging eyes referred him to her butler.

The nervous servant, his own eyes wide and white, began to mutter, "Well, I declare! I declare! Oh, Lordy! I declare!" and ushered them down the long central hall.

Morgan turned to the black man and said politely, "Please do not do anything foolish to jeopardize your mistress's health. Now, my wife and I, we are a peaceable pair, and we are here only to see Mrs. Ross and not to harm your mistress."

Neither the butler nor Mrs. Lloyd seemed measurably reassured. The butler was inclined to talk. "Not harm the missus. No, not harm the missus."

The progress of the ill-assorted party of five was slow. Barbara's heart was torn between elation at being close to Sarah and terror that something horrible had happened to her. Thus, she had turned a blind eye to the beauty of her surroundings which included carved moldings, chair rails and cornices, paneled walls, and a thick runner underfoot.

Morgan, still confidently holding Barbara's hand, did all the talking. "Mrs. Ross, you understand, took something from us today. Something that belongs to us. Something she mistakenly thinks belongs to her. We are here to retrieve it. We wish to harm no one."

"An' the Injun?" the butler wanted to know. "The Injun?"

Morgan's pleasant smile had an effectively chilling effect. "He's dangerous, I should warn you." He lowered his voice to a conspiratorial whisper. "Keep away from him is my advice! Tell the other occupants of the house to steer clear, as well. If he's left alone with Mrs. Lloyd, he'll do no harm to her or to anyone else. If he's threatened by the others, well, then..." Morgan make a slashing motion at his throat with one finger. With a casual nod toward the wild creature, he added, "When we've got what we want, we'll take him with us when we go."

The butler nodded and said, "Tha's good, tha's good," as if he were having difficulty finding anything good about it. He came to a stop before the door to the withdrawing room and motioned the group to enter.

The scene that greeted the entrance of Barbara and Morgan and the wild creature holding a knife at Mrs. Lloyd's throat was a tragicomic tableau of surprise. Lieutenant Richards sputtered inarticulately and half rose from his chair, his face transfigured by shock and flushed red with embarrassment, or perhaps guilt. Another gentleman, apparently Mr. Lloyd, sprang to his feet and cried, "What is the meaning of this! Release my wife at once!" Another elderly woman, composed gracefully upon an elegant settee, put the lace handkerchief in her hand at her breast, where it fluttered, and her head fell backward, as if in a swoon.

Morgan tipped his hat and said, "Lieutenant Richards, Mr. Lloyd, I am so happy to have found you at home." He looked about the room and said, calmly, "But I do not see Mrs. Ross."

This comment was met by consternated silence and an exchange of glances between Mr. Lloyd and Lieutenant Richards. Mr. Lloyd pointed a finger at the wild creature and said in hot, threatening tones, "You will have nothing to do with Mrs. Ross until you unhand my wife, you savage! This very instant!"

"Ah, you see, he doesn't speak much English," Morgan informed the master of the house. "His French, however, is excellent. If you would care to try—?"

Mr. Lloyd's brow lowered thunderously, and he focused on Morgan. He voice rose in pitch and volume. "You bring a wild Indian into my house, place my wife's life in jeopardy, and tell me that this, this *thing* speaks French?"

"Yes, French and—"

"This is an outrage!"

"No, I assure you, his French is excellent," Morgan said, "and so I would like to—"

Mr. Lloyd would have none of this. "You're breaking the law, you and this savage!"

Morgan's brow rose delicately. "Breaking the law?" he echoed, softly.

"Forced entry into a private home!" Mr. Lloyd shot back, gesturing angrily and helplessly at his wife. "As well as threatening the life of an innocent female!"

Morgan had not let go of Barbara's hand. He stepped farther into the room, drawing her with him. He dropped his pretense of civility and said, harshly, "Speaking of innocent females, we have come to retrieve our daughter. Richards here," Morgan continued, flicking a glance at the red-faced lieutenant, "had the misguided notion to steal—yes, *steal*—our daughter from her cradle in our home this afternoon. Now, I don't blame him directly for the theft, because he was only taking orders from Mrs. Ross...."

Morgan paused and allowed his contempt for the lieutenant to sink in. "However, I do blame him for the clumsiness of his methods, although I am sure that he thought himself quite clever to have come and gone from our home by way of the river. And now we have followed him here! As for breaking the law, I am afraid you might be charged, Mr. Lloyd, for aiding and abetting a thief and a murderer...."

Mr. Lloyd interrupted him. "As for theft, that remains to be proven, for Mrs. Ross has explained to us that she came to America to do right by her husband's child—living in illegitimate poverty as it was—and a more noble action I can hardly conceive!" Mr. Lloyd's face had turned quite as red as the lieutenant's. "But murder—! You cannot blame a field officer of the British army for American deaths that occurred in a war that was finished well over a year ago!"

"I wasn't referring to the late war, sir," Morgan said, "but to the life of the ferryman at Old Roads Bay, on the Patapsco River. I believe that Lieutenant Richards and his two thugs beat him within an inch of his life this afternoon."

Mr. Lloyd's eyes slid to the lieutenant, then back to Morgan. "But that doesn't give you the right to burst into my home unlawfully and threaten my wife's life and everyone else's!"

Morgan was rather enjoying the encounter. Nevertheless, it was time to cut line, and he could not afford to squander his advantage of surprise with discussion.

"Right now I have the right to do anything I want. What I want right now is to see Mrs. Ross," he said, "and the baby." He glanced over at his son, who was now holding most of Mrs. Lloyd's weight, given her partial swoon. He looked back at Mr. Lloyd. "Let's be quick about it. The boy gets bloodthirsty when he's made to wait."

Mr. Lloyd shook himself in fury, cast an angry, impotent glance at the wild creature holding his wife, then stalked out of the room.

Before following, Morgan said to the lieutenant, "Sit."

Not knowing what else to do, Richards sat.

Barbara and Morgan were led down the extravagantly lit hallway, up the graceful open stairway, and down another hall. Barbara's heart was beating less in fear and terror now, and more in happy expectation. Her ears were pricked for the sounds of Sarah's cooing—or, more likely, she mused, her cranky whining or lusty crying. Even those unpleasant sounds would be music to Barbara's ears, and she felt her breath catch and her lips curve upward in happy anticipation. Her arms itched to hold her.

They turned a corner and came to a closed door. It was silent within. Utterly, ominously silent. Barbara's heartbeat turned painful.

Mr. Lloyd knocked. After a swift, interminable moment, Mrs. Ross emerged. The discomposed, defiant, guilty look on her face, eerie in the shadows, caused Barbara's heart to stop short.

My baby has died! was Barbara's unmediated thought. Then came a succession of horrible possible causes: *She died of exposure to the cold in the open boat! She died of grief from being separated from her mother! She died by the*

*hand of Mrs. Ross, the witch who refuses my happiness be-
cause she can have none of her own!*

Mrs. Ross made as if to bar Barbara's entry, but Barbara
pushed easily past her, causing the older woman to crumple
against the door. Barbara ran to the large bed in the center
of which was lying her baby, motionless, on a blanket. Her
heart plummeted. She scooped her baby up in her arms, to
say goodbye to her love, to her life. All that remained was
to weep over her precious loss and to curse the wicked forces
that had made her life a misery and brought it to this bitter
end.

"My Sarah," Barbara gasped, wishing to die herself.

The baby moved, blinked her eyes open, and attempted
to whimper.

Barbara was so stunned and happy she hardly dared allowed herself to breathe. In question and accusation, she cut
her eyes to Mrs. Ross, who was huddled against the door,
wringing her hands, her face stricken.

Mrs. Ross, silent thus far, now began to speak. Her refined voice held a strain of hysteria. Her hands were nervous, flying out of control. "I couldn't feed her! She
wouldn't eat! Not a thing! I didn't know what to do! She
was crying! Crying! Until she could cry no more! That was
hours ago already! We've called in a wet nurse,
but...but..."

"How could you?" Barbara whispered harshly.

"It would have been all right, if I could have discovered
a way to feed her. I tried everything! She slept a little, and
her diaper has been changed. I know she must be hungry,
but there was nothing I could do! Nothing! And the crying—! Oh, my God! The crying!"

Barbara could look at the witch no more, and she turned
her back. Sarah was moving restlessly, listlessly, in her arms.
The baby turned her little head weakly and sought with her
cheek and lips. Barbara fairly ripped the buttons off her
coat and blouse to get at what her baby needed most. Her
eyes filling with relief and happiness, her breasts straining

with mother's milk and love, Barbara was at last able to satisfy the poor, hungry little Sarah.

Morgan took the cowering Mrs. Ross in a rough grip and pulled her out of the room. Then he closed the door behind them.

Barbara did not know how long she stood there nursing her baby, but at length she sighed, once, deeply, as if it were the first breath of her new life. She let her head fall back. Her arms were filled with her baby. Her ears were soothed by the sounds of slurping. Her cheeks were streaming. Then, through the tears, she smiled beatifically. She straightened and turned to thank the most wonderful man in the world.

But the room was empty. Sarah pulled away, fought more energetically now, and demanded the other breast.

Morgan propelled Mrs. Ross out into the upstairs hallway. He let her go so quickly that she stumbled backward against the opposing wall.

"So," he said, looking her up and down, "let me look at you."

Morgan looked at her then, keenly, critically. He felt anger burning within him, but he felt a burn-soothing sorrow for the woman in front of him, as well. She had aged ten years. Strands of hair were falling in disarray around her face. Her clothing was askew. Her eyes were dazed with the kind of anguish that both he and Barbara had lived.

"Do you like what you see?" she shot back.

He shook his head. "You made a drastic error."

"But I thought of the wet nurse," she told him, a little wildly. "I was not going to let her starve to death!"

Morgan continued to shake his head. "I mean that you came to take what was not yours, and we caught you."

She did not have control over her hands. They fluttered to her hair, to her breasts which had never produced milk for a beloved baby, to her skirts, without settling anywhere. "But *how?*" she demanded plaintively. "*How* did you catch us? It is not possible! Mrs. John— Your wife—" her tone was rough and transparently derisive, with no slick coating of civility to make the ugliness slide by "—was not at home when Lieutenant Richards took . . . *claimed* my Sarah as my own. The house was empty! No one saw him enter, and no one saw him leave."

"My son tracked you here," Morgan informed her.

"Your son?"

Morgan smiled.

"It is not possible!" she insisted.

"My son is downstairs," he said simply, on a note of pride.

She almost performed the unladylike gesture of stamping her foot. "Now you misinterpret me! It is not possible that anyone could have followed us here. Timothy went by boat from North Point to Baltimore. So no one from your charming meetinghouse could have spread the news of his passing."

"The lieutenant left signs of his trail everywhere, and my son is a very good tracker," Morgan replied. "Or call it God's will."

Mrs. Ross's eyes narrowed. "God's will?" she snapped. "God's will took my husband from me! God's will denied me children! Don't talk to *me* about God's will!"

"So you decided to take what was not yours?" Morgan asked.

Her self-possession was returning. The crazed look left her eyes, but there was nothing she could do to change her dishevelment. "I've always had everything I want," she said, a gloss of slick elegance returning to her voice. "Everything. And I've kept what is mine. I came for my husband's child, and since your wife was not listening to reason, I took my baby."

Morgan did not like the woman he was looking at, but he understood something of her desperation. "That's it," Morgan said. "You came. You demanded. You took." He understood her grief and her despair, for he had experienced such himself. Where he had turned his grief and despair inward, hurting only himself, she had lashed out and struck against others, not caring who she hurt, as long as it was not herself. He added, gently, "You took. You did not ask."

"Ask?" she mimicked derisively. "For what?"

Morgan felt his soul settling in to fully inhabit the spacious, luminous structure inside him. He still felt anger for the woman before him, but his anger had been overtaken by a wider, kinder pity. He thought of a woman he did not know, a woman he could not thank for having saved his infant son fifteen years before. He regarded the woman before him now, who grieved for her husband and desperately wanted his child. He did not think that showing mercy to one would repay his debt to the other, but he felt that now, with Mrs. Ross, some kind of higher justice could be served.

He recognized the passion that had driven Mrs. Ross. He knew it to be a dark, ungoverned passion, and he remembered well fifteen years of his own darkness, and what it had caused him to do. The darkness was gone now, and he let the light inside him guide his way.

"You could have asked to help," he said. "You could have asked to share in the care and the expense and the worries of bringing up a child." He nodded behind him. "You've been laboring under the willful hope that the beautiful baby beyond the bedroom door—the one you long to hold and love—is your husband's child. You do not know for certain that she is, but you have your intuitions. It seems that your willful hope and uncertain intuitions have allowed you to grasp out blindly."

Mrs. Ross opened her mouth to speak, then shut it again.

Morgan said, "What if the beautiful baby beyond the bedroom door *is* your husband's child. What then?"

Mrs. Ross's head ticked once. She straightened slightly. "Are you saying—?" she whispered. Her breath caught. A part of her understanding could not fully grasp the question, after her fears and emotions of the day. "Are you finally admitting—?"

"I'm not admitting anything. I've claimed to be Sarah's father, and I'm Barbara's husband. Let's talk instead about what if . . ."

Mrs. Ross's features lost their cast of devious craft and were transformed into a composition of wonderment. "If she is my husband's child, I'd do anything for her."

"Even leave her with the mother she so evidently needs?"

"Yes," Mrs. Ross said avidly, grasping again. "Until she's weaned. I'll take her then!"

"Take, Mrs. Ross?" Morgan chided.

"Help," she amended. "Share. Oh, I don't know! What do you want from me?" she cried helplessly. Then, pitifully: "*Is* she Robert's daughter?"

"You'll have to speak to my wife," Morgan said.

Mrs. Ross looked eagerly beyond his shoulder at the bedroom door, which was still closed.

"Not now," Morgan said, "because we had best be going—with Sarah."

Mrs. Ross came toward him, reached out to him. "No, don't take her! I'll help! I'll share! Let me talk to her, your wife! We can come to some agreement!"

Morgan unpried her fingers from his arm. He shook his head. "Not now. Later. Next week, maybe. After you've thought about what kind of help and sharing you want to do, what kind of arrangements you'd like to make."

"I'll have my lawyer contact you," she suggested eagerly.

Morgan shook his head again. "No. No lawyers. Some things are above the law, and this is between you and my wife and God."

Mrs. Ross's face crumpled. She looked confused. "What is it you want? Money? I have money."

Morgan had an acute sense of the material richness of her life, and of its spiritual poverty. "I do not want your money," he said slowly. "I want you to think how best to express your love and affection for Sarah. I want you to think about it before doing anything else."

"Have I done wrong?" Mrs. Ross asked, looking up at him with a hollow gaze, searching and hoping for absolution, as if she sensed the luminosity within him.

Morgan nodded. "You've done wrong, but you can put it to rights." He turned then, dismissing her, and headed for the bedroom door. "You have to think about it. In the meantime, go downstairs and comfort Mrs. Lloyd."

"But what do I do when I've thought about it?" Mrs. Ross wanted to know.

Morgan threw over his shoulder, "You know where we live." He added, on an afterthought, "And don't bring Lieutenant Richards. I don't like him."

Not too many minutes later, Morgan and Laurence and Barbara, holding Sarah, backed out the front door, leaving behind them Mr. and Mrs. Lloyd, their butler, Lieutenant Richards and Mrs. Ross, in various states of vociferous outrage, mute shock, muttering disbelief, guilty embarrassment and dazed hope.

Once outside, with the door closed behind them, feeling safe in the cold open air with her baby in her arms, Barbara looked up at Morgan with a smile that melted his insides. There was a moment of silence and happiness as they gazed at one another. Morgan broke the look by glancing at his son, who was moving away from them.

Unexpectedly Barbara thrust Sarah into Morgan's arms. She ran after Laurence, stopped him with her arm, then took his wildly painted face in her hands, lovingly. She could hardly see his features in the cloud-covered night, but it did not matter. She felt, for the first time in her life, part of a family. It gave her a surge of pleasure to think that the pieces of several families that had been ripped apart could be patched back together, albeit with many scars and seams, to make an odd mosaic of a family. It struck her as very American.

"Thank you, Laurence," she said, her voice warm and loving. "Thank you for my Sarah, my daughter. I could not have done this without you. I am indebted to you forever." She hugged and kissed him on both cheeks. She looked at him again. She had forgiven him for hurting his father. She wished to embrace him and envelop him in her love, acknowledging her need of others. She said, smiling, "Thank you, Laurence. Morgan's son. My son."

To her surprise, the boy pulled back from her. She was not sure, but she thought she saw a look of uncertainty, shading into horror, cross his features. Then, to her further surprise, he turned on his heel, ran to his horse, mounted it in a leap and rode off into the night.

Barbara walked back to Morgan and asked, "Good heavens! What did I do? What did I say to make him turn and run? Did I, possibly, offend him?"

Morgan gave Barbara a hand up to the perch of the buggy, then passed Sarah up to her. He mounted and took the reins, so that Barbara could hold her baby.

"I think," he replied, "that you have just saved me again."

Chapter Twenty-three

Barbara did not register Morgan's words. "But I don't understand it!" she mused as Morgan started the buggy forward. She was peering into the darkness, as if trying to see Laurence riding ahead. "I had thought everything was solved between you and Laurence, and so beautifully! I suddenly saw that what we were doing—together, all of us— was making a new family. Out of scraps of other families, you might say. Like a quilt. Scrappy, but strong and beautiful—"

Barbara broke off suddenly, eyed Morgan with surprise and suspicion, and demanded, "*What* did you say?"

"That I think you have just saved my life again."

"How can that be?"

"I traded my life for the baby's in order to get my son's help," Morgan explained, "and I think you put him in an awkward position by claiming him as your son."

Barbara was having difficulty assimilating this statement in one gulp, so she sorted through the last part of it first. "Why should that put him in an awkward position?"

"My guess is that no woman of the tribe where he was raised claimed him as hers, giving him no parent to answer to. His grandfather had more or less disinherited my wife when we left Canada for Massachusetts, so the old man would not have claimed parentage of Laurence, either. When the boy came of age—which must not have been much over a week ago, come to think of it—his grandfather must have sent him on a mission to find me and avenge himself in order to take his rightful place in the community."

"But how does my claim on him as my son put him in an awkward position with respect to you?"

"He would need your permission to take power over my life," Morgan said, "and he figures that you would deny it."

"He figures correctly!" Barbara exclaimed hotly. "But do you think he actually understood what I said to him?"

"He must have. It was not so difficult, after all, and he understands English much better than he can speak it."

Barbara sensed that this was true. She looked down at Sarah, who was in her arms, bundled within her coat, and adjusted the fold of the blanket around her little face, making sure that she could breathe properly and still be shielded from the cold November night. The mother in Barbara asserted herself. "If I have now claimed Laurence as my son, and he is responsible to me, why did he run away? Should he not have asked my permission?"

"Well, as I've said, you've put him in an awkward position."

"Good!" said the righteous mother. "It's an absurd notion he's had put into his head, that you abandoned him, and I'll be happy to disabuse him of it when next we meet. But what I can't quite understand is why you offered him your life in the first place!"

"It seemed a fair trade for Sarah's life, and I was frankly not in any physical condition to undertake the tracking of the lieutenant myself."

The latter part was true, but she refused to consider the value of Sarah's life against Morgan's. "What would Laurence have done with your life? Was he planning still to kill you?"

"I don't know," Morgan answered. "Perhaps simply return to the tribe, with me as his slave."

"And you would have submitted to that?"

"Yes."

They were silent a long while. The buggy slogged sloppily through the muddy, rutted road, heading back south. The snow flurries had stopped, leaving a damp undercurrent in the cold air. The clouds had parted to reveal an eyelash of a silver moon.

Finally she said, "I think it is all very stupid, and I do not approve. I would not have permitted him either to kill you or to make you his slave."

"You have already prevented or delayed either action on his part."

"And what does he plan to do now, your son?" she asked archly. "*Our* son?"

"I have no idea."

Silence fell again. Given this potentially dire news and the uncertainty of what Laurence would do next, Barbara tried to muster anger or indignation or one of the other dark emotions that had for so long been squeezing her from within, squeezing her from above. She failed. She felt, instead, a curiously light sensation. It was as if a large hand had been pressing down on her all these years, gripping her shoulders, keeping her down, keeping her at her work, and she had only noticed the effect of that large hand now that it had lifted from her shoulders. She glanced at Morgan, next to her, then down at the baby in her arms. She smiled.

She said, "I'd love to scold you for having placed yourself in further danger, but the words just won't come."

"Then you agree with my decision to have put my life in my son's hands in exchange for his help."

"Not at all!" she replied instantly. "I think it foolish in the extreme! Or noble—and maybe, in this case, it is both foolish and noble! No, if I don't feel like scolding you, it's because I am too happy. Despite all that could have gone wrong, I still have my daughter, *and* I have acquired a son. It seems almost a miracle that a little over a year ago I was a widow, alone in the world, with no one to depend on, no one to care for. Tonight I feel unusually enriched and blessed in my family."

Morgan said, "And you may just have acquired another family member tonight, as well."

"How is that?" she asked. "Or, rather, who is that?"

"A kind of mother, or an aunt, perhaps.

Barbara turned to look at Morgan, but his profile in the weak night light gave nothing away. Some indefinable note in the deep, gravelly voice caused her to shiver. "I never knew a mother," she said, "and I never liked my aunt."

"Why didn't you like your aunt?"

"She lived in Baltimore."

"And you hold that against her?" Morgan said. After a pause, he added, "Ah, this has something to do with the rich Baltimore merchant's son."

"No," Barbara replied with dignity, "I had to go live with my aunt when my father died, and she was strict and unpleasant and took no joy in life. But, more important, she did not love me."

Morgan nodded wisely. "She branded you as a fallen woman when the pretty boy disgraced you."

"That's true," Barbara said, "and you are determined to change the subject, I see."

"But it is such a delightful subject!"

"Oh, no, you don't! You said that I had acquired some strange new relation, and you have yet to explain yourself." Barbara frowned. "Does this have something to do with Mrs. Ross, by chance?"

"Yes."

"Namely what?"

"She and I had a talk while you were tending to Sarah."

"And—?"

"And I gave her some things to think over."

"Why am I apprehensive about what you are going to say next?"

"I don't know. Why?"

"Because you have been given to odd starts all day long. For one, you offered your life to your son in exchange for my daughter's."

"But it worked. You have your daughter."

"Yes, and you're still alive, but what is this about Mrs. Ross? And why," Barbara asked, "are you hedging?"

Morgan looked at her, and his face split into a wide grin. "Because when I had my little talk with her, I did not know what my fate would be, and I figured that I would be riding off now with my son. I had no idea that I would have to face the consequences of my conversation with her."

"What, exactly, did you say to her?"

"That she had come to you with the intention of taking, not asking. That she needed to rethink the kind of relationship she wanted with the baby."

"Did you admit that Sarah is the general's?" Barbara asked, aghast.

"No, I repeated to her my claim to be the baby's father," Morgan said, "and after today, I think that claim is a good one. Just as you acquired a son, I believe I acquired a daughter. However, it did occur to me that Mrs. Ross has some kind of relationship to the baby, but I was hard-pressed to define it. I like your idea of our family as a quilt, in which case Mrs. Ross would be another colorful scrap. What do you think?"

Barbara stomach tightened into a knot. Her heart beat painfully. Her emotions roiled. Every instinct protested. She did not want that woman in her life, or in her daughter's. She dearly wished to form the word "No," but just as her scolding words to Morgan would not come, neither would the negative.

She thought of Sarah Ross' strange dream about the baby and the strength of the elegant Englishwoman's emotions, which had caused her to cross a great ocean. She remembered her own strange thought on the day the baby was born when she had decided, out of the blue, to name the baby Sarah. She felt a bond with Mrs. Ross—an unwanted one, but an undeniable one, rival and mother—and knew that some relationships transcended water or blood.

She was willing to admit that Sarah Ross *did* have some relationship to her dead husband's baby, but, like Morgan, she was hard-pressed to define it. In addition, horrific visions of Mrs. Ross's grasping riches rose in her brain.

"Lawyers," she said ominously, her mouth pressed into a thin line.

"No lawyers," Morgan said. "That was one of my conditions."

"*What* conditions?" Barbara wanted to know.

"That she think about what she would like to give to Sarah, to share with her," Morgan said, "and that she talk it over with you. I left it up to you."

"Up to me?"

"Of course. You're the baby's mother."

"Let me think about it."

"That's all I ask."

Before she could think about it, she allowed a moment to give the little hot spurt of anger she felt toward Morgan grow into a bigger flame. However, the spark merely spit and fizzled out. She looked down at little Sarah and thought, *Sarah Ross can give you more than I can,* and she understood that her anger could not grow because her fear and jealousy were greater.

What would happen when little Sarah grew up and became a young woman? Did she, Barbara, have the right to deny her daughter a materially more secure life, or the other benefits of her lineage? Wasn't she, Barbara, jealous of all that Mrs. Ross had to offer her daughter? And had it not been so easy for her to adopt Laurence Harris into their quilt-worked family because he did not threaten her in the fearful way that Mrs. Ross did?

These were not particularly pretty thoughts, but Barbara was not ashamed of them, for she recognized them as part of her fierce love for her daughter. Having once recognized them, she thought she could overcome them, if need be.

"The woman is a witch," she said at last.

"A reformed one, perhaps," Morgan replied. "She had quite a scare tonight. She thought she could give the baby everything, and she realized that she could not even give her food."

"But the nursing does not last forever."

"Who knows what Mrs. Ross will be unable to give her at any later age that you can easily provide?"

"Humph," Barbara said noncommitally. "She doesn't deserve a moment of my daughter's life, or a shred of her affection."

"I'm no judge of that," Morgan told her. Then, after a well-timed moment, "Poor Mrs. Ross."

"Humph," Barbara grunted again. Yet she saw Morgan's point, and she felt herself extraordinarily rich by contrast with the general's widow.

They traveled further in the cold, in silence. Barbara thought long and hard about the patched-together family she suddenly belonged to. About the parts she accepted and the parts she did not accept. She thought about the baby Sarah, Laurence, Mrs. Ross, herself. Then she thought about the most important member of her almost-family, the one who had made it almost possible, her almost-husband. She looked over at him, and even in the weakest of pale moonlight she could see that his energies, at the end of this long and tiring day, were spent.

The ordinary where they had cadged their meal came into view. She imagined that Morgan intended to return to the farm tonight, but she did not think he could get there without killing himself. It was late, and the inn was completely dark, but she persuaded Morgan to pull the buggy into the yard. She handled the negotiations from there.

Although the host was a little grumpy at being roused from his warm bed, and confused to find that the Harris family had suddenly increased, Barbara and Morgan and Sarah were soon enough ushered into a spare little room at the back of one of the rambling wings. When a little fire had been set to blazing on the small hearth, Barbara saw that the room was sufficiently clean. Under the circumstances, she considered it a luxurious haven. Their host had even provided a cradle with blankets. Since Sarah had been fed the hour before at Lloyd House, Barbara's first worry was Morgan. His face was ashen from the physical strain of the past hours, and his shoulder and arm seemed unbearably painful. So tired was he that he allowed Barbara to help him to strip to nakedness and get him into bed.

Morgan stretched out, letting the bed take the weight of his exhaustion, and closed his eyes. He did not fall asleep, but listened instead to the quiet sounds of Barbara moving about the room. These sounds soothed him like a drug. His ear sought and heard her attentions to Sarah, the soft mother-baby kisses, the rustle of her clothing as she undressed, the silky slide of her body between the bed sheets.

Then she was next to him, her weight, her scent, his Barbara. He cracked his eyes and turned his head. She was looking at him. In the flickering firelight. His Barbara. With hair the color of fairy-tale gold and eyes the color of an enchanted lake. He looked at her and saw the face of love. He felt the spirit of love swell and the body of love lodge in his heart. He experienced an overwhelming desire...

To fall asleep.

A laugh rumbled up inside his chest, but did not quite escape his mouth. He felt like the butt of some extraordinary joke. This was the fifth night in a row he would sleep with his beautiful, desirable Barbara, and this was the fifth night in a row that he would not make love to her.

When he had been able, she had been unwilling. When she had been willing, he had been impotent. Now she was willing again—and he read that lovely, loving willingness in her eyes—and he was merely unable.

Morgan felt cursed. Or at least he *would* have felt cursed, if he had not felt so happy and comfortable and sleepy. The pain in his shoulder and arm had muted to an ache. He reached for Barbara's hand under the covers, and her fingers closed tightly around his. His arm touched her arm, and although they were not touching body to body, something about the feel of her next to him made him realize that she, too, had stripped to nakedness for the night.

It was not that he did not feel desire for her. He did. He had never felt such love for a woman. He was hungry for her, too, but he just had an overwhelming sense now of satisfaction such as he had never before experienced. And despite the strong male emotions flowing through him, his body felt battered from the work he had made it do today. The emotions would help him sleep a deep, restorative sleep more than they would help him make love.

"Barbara," he whispered. His head was still turned toward her, his eyes cracked open. "I can't."

"I know," she whispered back. "You're tired."

"More than tired," he said. "It's my arm."

And what does your *arm* have to do with it? she was tempted to ask. "I know," she said, transmitting her reassurance through her fingers to his. "Go to sleep, Morgan."

"I'm almost there," he replied, groggily.

It seemed like hardly a half second later that he was breathing deeply and evenly, and Barbara felt as if she had just been left alone with a burning torch thrust in her hand. She lay wide-awake and thought that when God had ordered her life so well this day He had overlooked one vital detail that would have set the seal on her utter satisfaction. She had never before experienced such a wanting for a man, and had not previously known that it was a hunger in the mouth, this wanting, so strong that she could taste it. The wanting seemed to be everywhere in her body. She considered waking Sarah up just to nurse her and relieve some of the wanting in her breasts, but she wisely recognized that Sarah was, in this instance, an extremely poor substitute for Morgan, his touch, his kiss, his feel.

So she lay there, desiring, until she thought she would expire from the unrelieved wanting. If she was to find any satisfaction in wallowing in this swamp of liquid love unspent, it was the realization that she had never experienced such for any man, and, in fact, had not guessed that this all-consuming desire was possible.

It hardly mattered now what she did, so she sidled up to Morgan's naked, sleeping form, glad that she was on the side of his good arm. She slipped in under that arm and pressed her naked length to his, settling her breasts against his side and chest, intertwining her legs with his. Since he was not awake, with her now, in her now, she could dream about him and his body and his love. So she nestled her head in the crook of his arm, settled her lips lightly against his neck and fell into a light, highly charged sleep.

Much later, Morgan opened his eyes, knowing without doubt that he had entered paradise. He recalled that this was what he had thought the last time he had awakened to find himself in Barbara's bed, in her arms, but on that previous occasion he had been in extreme pain; now his pain was gone. Relieved of pain, he imagined that he had been sainted for all his good deeds and that his naked body had ascended to receive his heavenly reward. He thought it highly fitting that the reward should be Barbara's naked body wrapped around his, with her breath at his neck. He mused that he had never really believed that the carnal and the spiritual existed in two separate realms, realms that could never touch. He was pleased to have this glorious proof.

It was really quite marvelous, he thought, to have died and achieved sainthood and still feel the burst of life between his legs. It was a blessed experience, to be sure, to turn his head ever so slightly and find that his lips could so easily touch hers. The kiss was sweet and beautiful and everything he would have expected of a sainted kiss, including a further burst of manly desire. How thankful he was that good deeds received their just rewards!

Then he turned to further the accomplishment of his heavenly reward, and in turning he jolted his shoulder and arm, causing a sharp pain to shoot through them. It was at that moment that he realized that he had not died and gone to heaven. Barbara awoke at his movement and his pained grunt. When she opened her eyes and looked into his with the purest of lusting earthbound love, he decided that he was happy he had not died, but he was sorry that pain was shooting through him.

However, this time, the desire by far overpowered the pain. He was wanting his just deserts and he would take them, with Barbara, on this earth.

The look he returned her caused her eyes to shoot open.

"Morgan?" she questioned, hesitantly.

"Mm-hmmm," he answered confidently.

"Are you all right?" she whispered, tickling his ear.

"Uh-Uh," he replied, sliding his hand down her full breasts, down her side to the swell of her hip, over her abdomen, where his fingers slid between the thighs she had wrapped around him. He shifted, causing pain and life to battle inside him, and found an opening. His fingers darted in and luxuriated in the feminine humidity they found. "But I'll be all right in a minute."

"In a minute?" she teased.

"At this rate, less," he said, "but I'll try my best."

"Morgan," she said, wanting to draw back, but unable to, given the exquisite feel of his fingers against her womanhood, stroking. "I don't want you to hurt yourself."

"I'll be in far worse pain if I'm not inside you within seconds."

This time she did not protest his measuring of time. The long fire that had been smoldering all night had been teased to life and was spreading through her at his touch.

A minute later, or perhaps it was only seconds, they were together at last, joined in their bodies, as they were in their hearts and souls.

"Heaven," Barbara murmured.

"Paradise," Morgan agreed.

Chapter Twenty-four

At a reasonable hour the next morning, they had been fed and were on their way. They were not rested—for the lovemaking, once begun, had continued throughout the night—but they were satisfied, and enormously pleased with the world and themselves and each other. They looked at one another and smiled. They looked away from one another and smiled. They smiled and smiled and could not stop smiling.

Barbara had melted everywhere, and she was wildly, girlishly in love. Morgan felt strong and tempered, his passion rich and abiding.

They traveled home, hardly counting the miles or noting the mud. Morgan held the reins and Barbara held the baby. When they came close to the meetinghouse, Barbara said, "Stop."

Morgan had already thought ahead to all the chores that awaited him at the farm, and he did not want to stop, but he was willing to pull the buggy over. When Michael Gorsuch came out onto the porch, Barbara hopped down nimbly with the baby, strode over to him and kissed him on both cheeks. With stars in her eyes, she said, quietly, "Thank you, Michael, for everything."

The magistrate, dazzled, nearly let his pipe fall from his mouth. He slid a sly glance at Morgan who had not left the perch of the buggy. Several of the magistrate's meetinghouse cronies had drifted out onto the porch, as well. While Barbara was absorbed in showing them the baby, telling them of their adventure and getting the good news of the health of the ferryman at Old Roads Bay, Michael Gorsuch wandered over to stand next to the buggy.

"Well, now, I see that you were successful in retrieving the baby," Michael said, with a pretty good imitation of a straight face.

"Yes, we were," Morgan replied. It would have cost him too much effort to descend from the buggy and climb up again. In order to speak to the man he hoped would become a friend, he leaned his good arm on his knee and let the other arm hang at rest. "It was a daring plan. We had to storm Lloyd House, where Mrs. Ross was staying."

Michael Gorsuch puffed on his pipe. "Lloyd House, was it?" He was suitably impressed. "When you stopped by here yesterday, you did not know where Mrs. Ross and the lieutenant were headed. Did they, perhaps, leave a signpost for you pointing to Lloyd House?"

Morgan shook his head. He said, pleasantly, "No, in fact, my son helped us track them down."

"Your son, then?"

"He's an excellent tracker," Morgan affirmed.

Michael Gorsuch puffed. "I see." When a tiny pause fell, Michael continued, "You'll be pleased to know that, because of your alert yesterday afternoon, we were able to get to the ferryman before he bled to death."

"I am pleased," Morgan said, "and you have my son to thank for that news, as well."

"Will I be thanking him in person, then?"

Morgan shrugged and smiled. He was smiling a lot. "I don't know. Maybe next week."

Michael Gorsuch would have had to be deaf and blind to miss the way things stood between Barbara and Morgan. Barbara was aglow, and Morgan was a man in love. Michael fell a little in love with Barbara, himself, with the idea of love. But he thought himself too old for such nonsense, and shrugged it off. He glanced at Morgan's bare hands on the reins and indicated with his head. "I have an extra pair of gloves inside. You'll be needing them?"

"When winter comes, I might," Morgan conceded.

"Winter's come."

"This is winter?" Morgan quipped, looking around skeptically.

Michael nodded and withdrew his pipe. "You told me once that you're from Quebec."

"That's right."

"Planning on returning?"

"Not anytime soon."

Michael puffed further and came to his point. He asked, offhandedly, "Do you think you'll be making your marriage legal one of these days?"

"The false date on the certificate, you mean?"

"And the family Bible," Michael added. "I'm just thinking of your immortal souls, you understand."

Morgan understood, for he had caught the twinkle in the magistrate's eyes. "My immortal soul seems in remarkably fine repair these days," Morgan answered. He glanced at Barbara, then back at the magistrate. "I can't speak for her. Maybe someday I'll ask her right and proper to be my wife, but for now, I'm not doing anything to upset the applecart, such as it is—if you see what I mean."

Michael did. He had been both shocked and reassured at the expression that came over Morgan Harris's face when he glanced that spare second at Barbara. He had felt privileged, as well, to see something so rare as this man's love for his woman. "Well, you two are living together legal on the surface of it, and that's good enough for me."

Morgan nodded his head and touched his hand to his hat at the magistrate's gracious acceptance of their irregular union. He saw Barbara approach the buggy, and was grateful that Gorsuch went around to hand Barbara up. When she was seated next to him, and he had lovingly arranged the blanket around her knees and helped her to settle the baby comfortably in her arms, he picked up the reins.

Michael Gorsuch raised his hand in parting and asked, with a provocative note in his voice, "Will we be seeing you, Mr. and Mrs. Harris, at the religious service tomorrow morning?"

Barbara was surprised and said, "Gracious! Tomorrow is Sunday?" She looked at Morgan to consider the question of what they would be doing tomorrow morning, and her expression was so transparent that Michael Gorsuch felt a stab of pure envy for Morgan Harris pierce his gut. She furrowed her brow and said to the magistrate, gravely, "I'm afraid we've left too many chores undone these past days to come tomorrow morning, but I'm thinking that next week . . ."

It was all the magistrate could do not to laugh at her seriousness. "And you, Morgan Harris? Do you have any particular religious convictions? Will a week more or less matter to you?"

Morgan replied with a smile, "Try twenty years more or less. As for my religious convictions, maybe I will have acquired some by next Sunday." With a final wave, he turned the buggy back out onto Long Log Lane.

Barbara could hardly believe that nearly a week had gone by since Morgan Harris had first knocked on her door. It was six days ago, last Sunday evening, that he had come looking for a job. She had gone to the meetinghouse that morning and prayed, cool and composed but with no heart for anything but her baby. All that was changed now, as a result of the unimaginably emotional six days since then, each one gaudy in its excesses, and all of them together so exhausting and exhilarating and preposterous that she felt she had lived a gorgeous year in those six days.

And tomorrow was a glorious day of rest.

She knew just how and where she wished to spend that day of rest.

She looked at Morgan.

He looked at her.

She caught her breath. She felt a swirl of pure desire. "Will we make it home?" she gasped.

He looked behind them, toward the meetinghouse, which was now out of sight for they had turned into another lane. He looked up at the clear gray sky above. He scanned the horizon and the fields around them. They were in an open buggy. They were heavily clothed. It was cold. The baby was with them. His arm ached.

These seemed trifling impediments. "I'm in no hurry to return," he answered, "and here is as good a place as any to stop."

"Morgan, no!" she protested as he came toward her.

"You started it," he teased, taking her chin in his hand and bringing her lips toward his.

"I did not!"

"You looked at me."

"And you call that 'starting it'?"

"I do," he said. "I call it deliberate provocation, as well, and I know of no reason not to respond in kind."

His hand was inside her coat, but not yet inside her blouse. His lips were on hers, but it was not yet a deep kiss. Still, they were both inflamed, and they were struggling to maneuver in the awkward circumstances of being in an open buggy with a baby, when they heard noises approaching somewhere behind them.

They hastily broke apart and attempted to put themselves to rights.

"Laurence," Barbara whispered.

"He wouldn't be so clumsy."

"Ben Skinner, then. He uses this road all the time."

"Or maybe some men from the meetinghouse going to check on the ferryman."

The mood was broken, but not their desire. Barbara cried, in distress, "Well, let's get home then, and out of sight." She urged, "Hurry!"

Morgan grinned at her urgency and felt the same. He hurried, but it was a painful, jolting hurrying, rendered interminable by the flush of love. The hot, quick desire that had sprung to life between them in the road and remained alive on their tongues acquired a sweet taste when their little farmhouse came into view. When they drew near enough to discern the wreckage of the front door, barred from the inside, Barbara sang out, happily, "We're home! I'm so glad we waited!"

Morgan paused long enough to kiss her tenderly at the delicacy of her thought.

They hastily took care of the buggy and horse and entered the house by the back door. It was all they could do to restrain the transports of delight that greeted them from Pockets; the poor, abandoned dog, who had whined continuously for twenty-four hours, had managed, nevertheless, to find enough to eat, although that effort had required that he destroy the kitchen in the process. Barbara did not immediately care, but merely surveyed the wreckage with a mild eye.

She and Morgan stumbled into the bedroom, quieted a fussy Sarah, shed their clothes and fell into a lustful heap on the bed, with the shameless Pockets, wagging his tail, for an audience.

When they were finished and rested and laughing and happy and floating above the surface of the bed, Barbara smoothed her hand over the top of the coarse white cotton of her candlewick bedspread. "I don't want this bedspread anymore," she said, out of the blue.

Morgan had no opinion of bedspreads, and had never objected to this one. "Any particular reason?" he asked, just out of curiosity.

"No," she said, "no particular reason. It's been here too long, though it's still in good condition. Perhaps I don't like it anymore because Mrs. Ross's coat was on it just a few days ago."

"Were you thinking of waiting until the spring to remove it, or do you have something to put in its place?"

Barbara turned her head and grinned at him. "I am feeling inspired—*very* inspired!—to continue with my weaving. I began a piece a couple of months ago, simply because I was given some of the most beautiful green-and-blue wool, but I didn't know what I was making, and I haven't had much time to work on it. But with winter here..."

"Ah, yes, I keep on forgetting this is winter," Morgan commented.

"*You* may not think it's much—"

"I don't."

"But it certainly suffices for *us* as winter. Now, it will get colder, and we do often have snow that sticks to the ground and ice storms in January," she explained. Then she dismissed the silly topic entirely. "But I am speaking about weaving, and what I can do to make myself useful indoors during the coming winter months."

Morgan smiled and thought how very usefully they would be spending the time indoors in the coming months. He did not speak, but laid his hand across her breast, where it rested.

"In any case," Barbara continued, "I know now that I want a new bedspread." She sent Morgan a sultry look, and the most minimal lift of her eyebrow caused him to feel hungry again. "It's symbolic, don't you think?"

Morgan still had no opinion of bedspreads, but he liked the symbolism. "What will you do with this one?" he wondered, humoring her, caressing her now. "It's still in good condition, as you say, so I'm thinking that you can find another use for it."

"I think I'll give it away," she said. "I am sure that there is some needy family that can put it to good use."

She had changed so much in the past few days that she did not even realize that she had never, ever, given anything away in an act of generosity. She had always thought she had too little to share with others. She had always thought her life too difficult to give to others, that the giving would diminish her already reduced life.

Now that the large hand in her life was no longer pressing down on her shoulders, she felt a new ease in living her life. It seemed to her now—without her noticing the change, so much a part of her new self was this sense of ease—that all the days stretching before her were smooth and light. Thinking of others, giving to others, was simply a natural part of the ease of her every day. She felt bountifully rich, as well, with Morgan next to her, Sarah in her cradle, a roof over her head and her fields surrounding her. She felt pleasure in the thought of sharing and giving. She mentally stripped the bed of the bedspread, washed it, dried it, and bundled it neatly for the use of some needful family.

But she had been so removed, emotionally, all these years from the community in which she lived that she could imagine no one family that would need it. The lapse surprised her, making her aware of her new self. She had sat in meetings every Sunday morning for years, and she knew that there were plenty of people in North Point and Baltimore who would benefit from any generous act, but she could not picture one.

Looking at Morgan, she said, seriously, "I'll have to ask Reverend Austin for the names of some of the people who need a helping hand."

At mention of the eccentric reverend, however, the gravity of her comment was lost, and over the next few minutes they gave themselves over to a merriment that they could never have adequately explained to another human being. When their laughter was resolved and their tears were dried, their appetites for each other were raised. They did not hesitate to make love again, this time slowly and languorously, without the soul-hungry intensity of previous joinings, but with much feeling.

Later, when Sarah's fussing could no longer be ignored, they rose and dressed to work during what was left of the day. Barbara was quicker, and pulled most of her clothes on before Morgan was fully dressed. While she was beginning to button her blouse, she walked over to Morgan's side of the bed, where he was seated, already with his breeches on, attempting awkwardly to pull on his stockings. She put her hands on his shoulders and lightly kissed the top of his head. His hands came up to reach inside her gaping blouse and caress her waist through the light fabric of her camisole. He pulled her toward him. The baby's cry became pitiful.

"Sarah," he said, with a nod toward the cradle.

"She can wait, troublesome child. I'm kissing you."

Sarah demanded attention more insistently.

"Tell me," Barbara continued, successfully ignoring the child, "what you want to do today."

"Chop wood" was his immediate reply.

Barbara bent to help him then with his stockings. He rose to his feet. She lovingly helped him get into the shirt and buttoned it for him, pausing at the top buttons to inspect the scar and her handiwork.

"Are you able to chop wood today?" she asked hesitantly, without looking up at him.

"No," he admitted, shaking his head.

She looked up at him and into his blue eyes. They were remarkable for the depth and luminosity of their color. "Good," she said, with a rush of relief. "I didn't want to tell you not to, you know, as if I were going to mother you. You'll have to set your own limits."

"I will," he assured her. "I don't want to do anything foolish now to jeopardize my recovery. I do want to be outside today, however. I can think of a few things to do that won't tax my energies."

"Good," she said again. Then she stepped away from him and rolled her eyes. "I'm coming, you naughty girl!" she said, scolding lovingly.

She picked Sarah up from her cradle, raised her high and kissed her. Morgan finished dressing and picked his overcoat up from the heap he had left it in on the floor, drawing it into a recognizable shape. He snapped his fingers for Pockets to follow him and left the room.

"Morgan!" Barbara called out after him. "What do you want for supper?"

He told her and left the house by the back door, with Pockets prancing behind him. While Barbara was putting the pots and pans in the kitchen to rights, Morgan walked to the well to survey the stack of unchopped wood next to it. He eyed the axe wedged forcefully into the chopping block. He imagined grasping the handle with both his hands. In his mind's eye, he lifted the tool above his head and felt the stretch of the muscles in his arms and back and shoulders. He bent into the rhythm of the movements and saw the wood split and separate.

He worked the muscles of his shoulders in a kind of yearning, and knew that he was yet some days—or even weeks—away from being able to perform the task. He calculated the amount of wood they still had left inside and made a mental note to ask Ben Skinner for the neighborly favor of chopping some wood for him.

He sighed heavily, looking away from the chopping block and the stack of wood, off into the south field. He began to tramp, aimlessly, around the edges of the field, with no more strenuous activity in mind than surveying the land. As he walked, he stuffed his hands in his coat pockets, although they were not cold.

Morgan breathed in and out, trying to catch a tasty bite of cold in the soggy air. He looked down at the brown dirt beneath his boots and inhaled the salty damp of it. He turned up his nose, not liking the smell. He looked back at Pockets, prancing behind him, the little runt, as if he had been born with no other purpose than to make a nuisance of himself. He looked over the fields, at a copse of trees, skinny, piney things without any beauty, and wondered if his son was hidden among them. It defied him to know what Laurence was going to do next, if anything.

Now it should come, he thought, *the end of my peace and happiness.* He was expecting that the rich pleasures of the past few hours were destined to fade and flatten. He was out in his fields now, the ones he might have for the rest of his life, and it came to him that he could never retrieve what he had had before on his farm in western Massachusetts. He would never again experience the sharp, exhilarating cold of northern winters, breathe in the deep, loamy scents of the soil, lean against the hardwood trees ablaze in autumnal splendor, hunt with a trusty hound dog, or raise his infant son from boyhood to manhood. He supposed that he had always held out the dream that the past would return, whole and unscarred. He supposed, as well, that that cherished dream, continually unrealized, had fueled his black depressions during a nighttime of fifteen years.

So this is what he had now, this life, this wet winter air, this brackish soil, this miserable pup. He found himself on flat landscape, solid and dependable, and that was good, but he wondered if that would be enough. There was only so much, after all, that one woman and one baby girl could do.

So now it should come, he thought again, *the end of my peace and happiness, along with the end of my perfect dream unrealized.*

At the thought, he felt a spiral of emotion. It stopped him short in his aimless tramping around the fields.

He waited, expectant and fearful, almost cocky in his knowledge of what would come next.

But the spiral did not have the downward course he knew so well. It felt not vicious, but delicious. It was not quite up, for he was already up. It was more like a spiraling out and away from himself, and suddenly he was not worried about losing himself in it, for he felt that the delicious spiral was tethered to the spires of the spacious, luminous structure inside him, which was strong and built on solid foundations.

He paused longer, absorbing the feeling, finding a soul-filling satisfaction and harmony in the moment and in the feeling. He felt surprise, as well, but then again, no surprise. It felt right and instantly recognizable, although he was sure that he had never before experienced it.

He looked back out to the far woods again and thought he saw the barest movement in the underbrush. He knew in his gut that Laurence was camped out in those woods. He imagined that the boy would circle and circle the house, coming ever closer, until he could approach it. Perhaps he would even be able to enter the house again. It would take the boy days, no doubt, for the circling to come close enough to the house for Morgan to reel him in further, but he would be patient, for he had his entire life ahead of him. Suddenly the waste of the years fell away, and Morgan saw his future roll out before him.

Then he heard a call behind him. He turned and saw Barbara, standing at the back door, waving to him from the distance, apparently wishing to ask him something. He saw, without being able to see, the smile on her face. He glanced back at the far woods and thought of his son. He thought, fleetingly, of Mrs. Ross. He waved back at Barbara and began to return to the house, to answer her question. As he walked toward her, the spiral kept spreading up and out. He no longer predicted the end of it, no longer worried about it taking a perilous, downward turn. He simply accepted it and slipped it on his shoulders, graciously, like the lightest of jackets.

He trotted the last few yards to the house, with Pockets—miserable dog—nipping at his heels. He felt a strong, paternal desire to enter the house in order to lift Sarah in his arms and hold her to his chest. He wished to kiss her.

As he crossed the threshold, Barbara spoke to him.

He responded.

However, the word that resounded in his head and filled his heart and soul was one he had never spoken before, nor an emotion he had never experienced, but he knew that it was *joy.*

* * * * *

Be sure to look for Laurence's story as he heads West to make a new life for himself in SWEET SURRENDER, *coming soon. But first, watch for Julie Tetel's next Harlequin Historical,* SIMON'S LADY, *a story rich in medieval pageantry, courtly intrigue and lasting love.* COMING SPRING, 1994

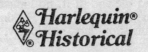

Harlequin® Historical

TEXAS

TEXAS HEART—A young woman is forced to journey west in search of her missing father.

TEXAS HEALER—A doctor returns home to rediscover a ghost from his past, the daughter of a Comanche chief.

And now, TEXAS HERO—A gunfighter teaches the local schoolteacher that not every fight can be won with a gun.
(HH #180, available in July.)

Follow the lives of Jessie Conway and her brothers in this series from popular Harlequin Historical author Ruth Langan.

Discover the glorious triumph of three
extraordinary couples fueled by a powerful
passion to defy the past in

Lingering Shadows

The dramatic story of six fascinating men and
women who find the strength to step out of the
shadows and into the light of a passionate future.

Linked by relentless ambition and by desire, each
must confront private demons in a riveting struggle
for power. Together they must find the strength to
emerge from the lingering shadows of the past, into
the dawning promise of the future.

Look for this powerful new blockbuster by *New
York Times* bestselling author

PENNY
JORDAN

Available in August at your favorite retail outlet.

PJLS93

COMING NEXT MONTH

#183   THE SEDUCTION OF DEANNA—Maura Seger
In the next book in the *Belle Haven* series, Deanna Marlowe is torn between family loyalty and her desire for independence when she discovers passion in the arms of Edward Nash.

#184   KNIGHT'S HONOR—Suzanne Barclay
Sir Alexander Sommerville was determined to restore his family's good name sullied by the treacherous Harcourt clan, yet Lady Jesselynn Harcourt was fast becoming an obstacle to his well-laid plans....

#185   SILENT HEART—Deborah Simmons
In a desperate attempt to survive her country's bloody revolution, Dominique Morineau had been forced to leave the past behind, until a silent stranger threatened to once more draw her into the fray.

#186   AURELIA—Andrea Parnell
Aurelia Kingsley knew Chane Bellamy was her last hope. Only he could help her find her grandfather's infamous treasure. And the handsome sea captain was determined to show her what other riches were within her reach.

AVAILABLE NOW: